TESSERACTS⁴

TESSERACTS^4

edited by
Lorna Toolis
and
Michael Skeet

A TESSERACT BOOK

Beach Holme Publishers
Victoria, B.C.

This edition is published by
Beach Holme Publishers Limited
4252 Commerce Circle, Victoria, B.C. V8Z 4M2
with financial assistance from The Canada Council
and the Cultural Services Branch of the B.C. Ministry of
Tourism and Culture.

Canadian Cataloguing in Publication Data

Main entry under title:

Tesseracts 4

"A Tesseract book"
ISBN 0-88878-322-1

1. Science fiction, Canadian (English). 2. Canadian
fiction (English) — 20th century. I. Toolis, Lorna, 1952-
II. Skeet, Michael, 1955-
PS8323.S3T48 1992 C813'.0876208   C92-091692-9
PR9197.35.S33T48 1992

•CONTENTS•

FOREWORD

Lorna Toolis

This is the fourth volume in the *Tesseracts* anthology series, the tesseracts' tesseract if you will. As with all the earlier *Tesseracts*, this anthology is a snapshot, freezing a moment in time for Canadians, showing who we think we are and what we are concerned about at this particular time.

Science fiction provides a fun-house mirror, making concepts malleable while not distorting them out of recognition. While the first rule of speculative fiction is that it must be entertaining, science fiction writers use their craft to ask questions and occasionally find answers that would not be accessible if they had not juggled with reality's rules. The question shapes the answer; it is always difficult to stand far enough away from our culture to ask meaningful questions.

Science fiction has many definitions; for me the most useful gives it as a literature concerned with humanity's attempts to define itself and its place in the universe. In pursuit of this we may change any elements of the space/time continuum that lends itself to the questions we want to ask. The elements common to Canadian SF continue: no easy answers, nor even any easy questions, present themselves. The traditional action/adventure SF story seems to

1

die at the border, lost in the Coastal mists, blown away by prairie winds.

At the Toronto Public Library's Merril Collection of Science Fiction, Speculation and Fantasy, where I work, patrons often ask if there is a distinctive voice of Canadian speculative fiction. After having read over 300 SF stories by Canadian writers, I find the Canadian voice as distinctive as a prairie wind in Winnipeg in February. Unmistakable, frequently uncomfortable, there is no one like us. From bizarre humour to fog-bound introspection this collection could only have come from Canada.

Kipling said there are only so many ways to tell a tale and all of them are right. Well, not quite all of them. Of the 300-plus tales submitted to *Tesseracts*[4] we felt that 21 of them (plus poetry) were most deserving of your attention. We wanted a variety of moods as well as stories in this *Tesseracts*; you will be the judge of how well we succeeded.

Some of the authors have familiar names; the newcomers are a welcome addition to the Canadian SF community. Many of the stories not included here were also well-written, but could not be included for the most practical of reasons. The physical impossibility of presenting an anthology with a density equal to that of small black hole, plus the anguished screams of our publisher, restrained us.

When I was asked to co-edit *Tesseracts*[4] I believed (erroneously) that I understood the workload entailed, reading manuscripts until the piles fell over and started backup stacks. I had not realized that an equally significant part of the task involved phoning the publishers and haggling, camel-trader-in-the-bazaar style for *just another 10,000 words*! Fortunately the Beach Holme staff are noted for their robust sense of humour.

So, here you have it. The happening world, Canada 1992.

WINTER WAS HARD

Charles de Lint

I pretty much try to stay in a constant state of confusion just because of the expression it leaves on
my face.

—Johnny Depp

It was the coldest December since they'd first started
keeping records at the turn of the century, though warmer,
Jilly thought, than it must have been in the ice ages of the
Pleistocene. The veracity of that extraneous bit of trivia
gave her small comfort, for it did nothing to lessen the
impact of the night's bitter weather. The wind shrieked
through the tunnel-like streets created by the abandoned
buildings of the Tombs, carrying with it a deep, arctic
chill. It spun the granular snow into dervishing whirligigs
that made it almost impossible to see at times and packed
drifts up against the sides of the building and derelict cars.

Jilly felt like a little kid, bundled up in her boots and
parka, with longjohns under her jeans, a woolen cap pushing down her unruly curls and a long scarf wrapped about
fifty times around her neck and face, cocooning her so
completely that only her eyes peered out through a narrow slit. Turtle-like, she hunched her shoulders, trying to
make her neck disappear into her parka, and stuffed her

3

mittened hands deep in its pockets.

It didn't help. The wind bit through it all as though unhindered, and she just grew colder with each step she took as she plodded on through the deepening drifts. The work crews were already out with their carnival of flashing blue and amber lights, removing the snow on Gracie Street and Williamson, but here in the Tombs it would just lie where it fell until the spring melt. The only signs of humanity were the odd little trails that the derelicts and other inhabitants of the Tombs made as they went about their business, but even those were being swallowed by the storm.

Only fools or those who had no choice were out tonight. Jilly thought she should be counted among the latter, though Geordie had called her the former when she'd left the loft earlier in the evening.

"This is just craziness, Jilly," he'd said. "Look at the bloody weather."

"I've got to go. It's important."

"To you and the penguins, but nobody else."

Still, she'd had to come. It was the eve of the solstice, one year exactly since the gemmin went away, and she didn't feel as though she had any choice in the matter. She was driven to walk the Tombs tonight, never mind the storm. What sent her out from the warm comfort of her loft was like what Professor Dapple said they used to call a geas in the old days—something you just had to do.

So she left Geordie sitting on her Murphy bed, playing his new Copeland whistle, surrounded by finished and unfinished canvases and the rest of the clutter that her motley collection of possessions had created in the loft, and went out into the storm.

She didn't pause until she reached the mouth of the alley that ran along the south side of the old Clark Building. There, under the suspicious gaze of the building's snow-swept gargoyles, she hunched her back against the storm and pulled her scarf down a little, widening the eye slit so that she could have a clearer look down the length of the alley. She could almost see Babe, leaning casually against the side of the old Buick that was still sitting there, dressed in her raggedy T-shirt, black body stocking and raincoat, Doc Martens dark against the snow that lay underfoot. She could almost hear the high husky voices of the other gemmin, chanting an eerie version of a rap song that had been popular at the time.

She could almost—

But no. She blinked as the wind shifted, blinding her with snow. She saw only snow, heard only the wind. But in her memory....

* * *

By night they nested in one of those abandoned cars that could be found on any street or alley of the Tombs—a handful of gangly teenagers burrowed under blankets, burlap sacks and tattered jackets, bodies snugly fit into holes that seemed to have been chewed from the ragged upholstery. This morning they had built a fire in the trunk of the Buick, scavenging fuel from the buildings, and one of them was cooking their breakfast on the heated metal of its hood.

Babe was the oldest. She looked about seventeen—it was something in the way she carried herself—but otherwise had the same thin androgynous body as her companions. The other gemmin all had dark complexions and feminine features, but none of them had Babe's short mauve hair, nor her luminous violet eyes. The hair colouring of the others ran more to various shades of henna red; their eyes were mostly the same electric blue that Jilly's were.

That December had been as unnaturally warm as this one was cold, but Babe's open raincoat with the thin T-

5

shirt and body stocking underneath still made Jilly pause with concern. There was such a thing as carrying fashion too far, she thought—had they never heard of pneumonia?—but then Babe lifted her head, her large violet eyes fixing their gaze as curiously on Jilly as Jilly's did on her. Concern fell by the wayside, shifting into a sense of frustration as Jilly realized that all she had in the pocket of her coat that day was a stub of charcoal and her sketchbook, instead of the oils and canvas which were all that could really do justice in capturing the startling picture Babe and her companions made.

For long moments none of them spoke. Babe watched her, a half-smile teasing one corner of her mouth. Behind her, the cook stood motionless, a makeshift spatula held negligently in a delicate hand. Eggs and bacon sizzled on the trunk hood in front of her, filling the air with their unmistakable aroma. The other gemmin peered up over the dash of the Buick, supporting their narrow chins on their folded arms.

All Jilly could do was look back. A kind of vertigo licked at the edges of her mind, making her feel as though she'd just stepped into one of her own paintings—the ones that made up her last show, an urban faerie series: twelve enormous canvases, all in oils, one for each month, each depicting a different kind of mythological being transposed from its traditional folkloric rural surroundings onto a cityscape.

Her vague dizziness wasn't caused by the promise of magic that seemed to decorate the moment with a sparkling sense of impossible possibilities as surely as the bacon filled the air with its come-hither smell. It was rather the unexpectedness of coming across a moment like this—in the Tombs, of all places, where winos and junkies were the norm.

It took her a while to collect her thoughts.

"Interesting stove you've got there," she said finally.

Babe's brow furrowed for a moment, then cleared as a radiant smile first lifted the corners of her mouth, then put an infectious humour into those amazing eyes of hers.

"Interesting, yes," she said. Her voice had an accent Jilly couldn't place and an odd tonality that was at once both husky and high-pitched. "But we—" she frowned prettily, searching for what she wanted to say "—make do."

It was obvious to Jilly that English wasn't her first language. It was also obvious, the more Jilly looked, that while the girl and her companions weren't at all properly dressed for the weather, it really didn't seem to bother them. Even with the fire in the trunk of the Buick, and mild winter or not, they should still have been shivering, but she couldn't spot one goosebump.

"And you're not cold?" she asked.

"Cold is...?" Babe began, frowning again, but before Jilly could elaborate, that dazzling smile returned. "No, we have comfort. Cold is no trouble for us. We like the winter; we like any weather."

Jilly could not help but laugh.

"I suppose you're all snow elves," she said, "so the cold doesn't bother you?"

"Not elves—but we are good neighbours. Would you like some breakfast?"

* * *

A year and three days later, the memory of that first meeting brought a touch of warmth to Jilly where she stood shivering in the mouth of the alleyway. Gemmin. She'd always liked the taste of words and that one had sounded just right for Babe and her companions. It reminded Jilly of gummy bears, thick cotton quilts and the sound that the bass strings of Geordie's fiddle made when he was playing a fast reel. It reminded her of tiny bunches

7

of fresh violets, touched with dew, that still couldn't hope to match the incandescent hue of Babe's eyes.

She had met the gemmin at a perfect time. She was in need of something warm and happy just then, being on the wrong end of a nine-month relationship with a guy who, during those many months of their being together, turned out to have been married all along. He wouldn't leave his wife, and Jilly had no taste to be someone's—anyone's—mistress, all of which had been discussed in increasingly raised voices in The Monkey Woman's Nest the last time she saw him. She'd been mortified when she realized that a whole restaurant full of people had been listening to their breaking up argument, but unrepentant.

She missed Jeff—missed him desperately—but refused to listen to any of the subsequent phonecalls or answer any of the letters that had deluged her loft over the next few weeks, explaining how they could "work things out". She wasn't interested in working things out. It wasn't just the fact that he had a wife, but that he'd kept it from her. The thing she kept asking her best friend Sue was: having been with him for all that time, how could she not have *known*?

So she wasn't a happy camper, traipsing aimlessly through the Tombs that day. Her normally high-spirited view of the world was overhung with gloominess and there was a sick feeling in the pit of her stomach that just wouldn't go away.

Until she met Babe and her friends.

Gemmin wasn't a name that they used; they had no name for themselves. It was Frank Hodgers who told Jilly what they were.

* * *

Breakfast with the gemmin on that long gone morning was... odd. Jilly sat behind the driver's wheel of the Buick, with the door propped open and her feet dangling outside.

8

Babe sat on a steel drum set a few feet from the car, facing her. Four of the other gemmin were crowded in the back seat; the fifth was beside Jilly in the front, her back against the passenger's door. The eggs were tasty, flavoured with herbs that Jilly couldn't recognize; the tea had a similarly odd tang about it. The bacon was fried to a perfect crisp. The toast was actually muffins, neatly sliced in two and toasted on coat hangers rebent into new shapes for that purpose.

The gemmin acted like they were having a picnic. When Jilly introduced herself, a chorus of odd names echoed back in reply: Nita, Emmie, Callio, Yoon, Purspie. And Babe.

"Babe?" Jilly repeated.

"It was a present—from Johnny Defalco."

Jilly had seen Defalco around and talked to him once or twice. He was a hash dealer who'd had himself a squat in the Clark Building up until the end of the summer when he'd made the mistake of selling to a narc and had to leave the city just one step ahead of a warrant. Somehow, she couldn't see him keeping company with this odd little gaggle of street girls. Defalco's taste seemed to run more to what her bouncer friend Percy called the three B's—bold, blonde and built—or at least it had whenever she'd seen him in the clubs.

"He gave all of you your names? Jilly asked.

Babe shook her head. "He only ever saw me, and whenever he did, he'd say, 'Hey Babe, how're ya doin'?'"

Babe's speech patterns seemed to change the longer they talked, Jilly remembered thinking later. She no longer sounded like a foreigner struggling with the language; instead, the words came easily, sentences peppered with conjunctions and slang.

"We miss him," Purspie—or perhaps it was Nita— said. Except for Babe, Jilly was still having trouble telling

9

them all apart.

"He talked in the dark." That was definitely Emmie— her voice was slightly higher than those of the others.

"He told stories to the walls," Babe explained, "and we'd creep close and listen to him."

"You've lived around here for awhile?" Jilly asked.

Yoon—or was it Callio?—nodded. "All our lives."

Jilly had to smile at the seriousness with which that line was delivered. As though, except for Babe, there was one of them older than thirteen.

She spent the rest of the morning with them, chatting, listening to their odd songs, sketching them whenever she could get them to sit still for longer than five seconds. Thank goodness, she thought more than once as she bent over her sketchbook, for life drawing classes and Albert Choira, her arts instructor at Butler U., who had instilled in her and every one of his students the ability to capture shape and form in just a few quick strokes of charcoal.

Her depression and the sick feeling in her stomach had gone away, and her heart didn't feel nearly so fragile any more, but all too soon it was noon and time for her to go. She had Christmas presents to deliver at St. Vincent's Home for the Aged where she did volunteer work twice a week. Some of her favourites were going to stay with family during the holidays and today would be her last chance to see them.

"We'll be going soon, too," Babe told her when Jilly explained she had to leave.

"Going?" Jilly repeated, feeling am odd tightness in her chest. It wasn't the same kind of a feeling that Jeff had left in her, but it was discomforting all the same.

Babe nodded. "When the moon's full, we'll sail away."

"Away, away, away," the others chorused.

There was something both sweet and sad in the way

10

they half spoke, half chanted the words. The tightness in Jilly's chest grew more pronounced. She wanted to ask, Away to where?, but found herself only saying, "But you'll be here tomorrow?"

Babe lifted a delicate hand to push back the unruly curls that were forever falling in Jilly's eyes. There was something so maternal in the motion that it made Jilly wish she could just rest her head on Babe's breast, to be protected from all that was fierce and mean and dangerous in the world beyond the enfolding comfort that motherly embrace would offer.

"We'll be here," Babe said.

Then, giggling like schoolgirls, the little band ran off through the ruins, leaving Jilly to stand alone on the deserted street. She felt giddy and lost, all at once. She wanted to run with them, imagining Babe as a kind of archetypal Peter Pan who could take her away to a place where she could be forever young. Then she shook her head, and headed back downtown to St. Vincent's.

She saved her visit with Frank for last, as she always did. He was sitting in a wheelchair by the small window in his room that overlooked the alley between St. Vincent's and the office building next door. It wasn't much of a view, but Frank never seemed to mind.

"I'd rather stare at a brick wall, any time, than watch that damn TV in the lounge," he'd told Jilly more than once. "That's when things started to go wrong—with the invention of television. Wasn't till then that he found out there was so much wrong in the world."

Jilly was one of those who'd rather know what was going on and try to do something about it, than those who preferred to pretend it wasn't happening and hoped that, by ignoring what was wrong, it would just go away. Truth was, Jilly had long ago learned, trouble never went away. It just got worse—unless you fixed it. But at eighty-seven, she felt that Frank was entitled to his opinions.

His face lit up when she came in the door. He was all lines and bones, as he liked to say. A skinny man, made almost cadaverous by age. His cheeks were hollowed, eyes sunken, torso collapsed in on itself. His skin was wrinkled and dry, his hair just a few white tufts around his ears. But whatever ruin the years had brought to his body, they hadn't managed to get even a fingerhold on his spirit. He could be cantankerous, but he was never bitter.

She'd first met him last spring. His son had died, and with nowhere else to go, he'd come to live at St. Vincent's. From the first afternoon that she met him in his room, he'd become one of her favourite people.

"You've got that look," he said after she'd kissed his cheek and sat down on the edge of his bed.

"What look?" Jilly asked, pretending ignorance.

She often gave the impression of being in a constant state of confusion—which was what gave her her charm, Sue had told her more than once—but she knew that Frank wasn't referring to that. It was that strange occurrences tended to gather around her; mystery clung to her like burrs to an old sweater.

At one time when she was younger, she just collected folktales and odd stories, magical rumours and mythologies—much like Geordie's brother Christy did, although she never published them. She couldn't have explained why she was drawn to that kind of story; she just liked the idea of what they had to say. But then one day she discovered that there *was* an alternate reality, and her view of the world was forever changed.

It had felt like a curse at first, knowing that magic was real, but that if she spoke of it, people would think her mad. But the wonder it woke in her could never be considered a curse and she merely learned to be careful with whom she spoke. It was in her art that she allowed herself total freedom to express what she saw from the corner of her eye. An endless stream of faerie folk paraded from her easel and sketchbook, making new homes for themselves in back alleys and city parks, on the wharves down by the waterfront or in the twisty lanes of Lower Crowsea.

In that way, she and Frank were much alike. He'd been a writer once, but, "I've told all the tales I have to tell by now," he explained to Jilly when she asked him why he'd stopped. She disagreed, but knew that his arthritis was so bad that he could neither hold a pencil nor work a keyboard for any length of time. "You've seen something magic," he said to her now.

"I have," she replied with a grin and told him of her morning.

"Show me your sketches," Frank said when she was done.

Jilly dutifully handed them over, apologizing for the rough state they were in until Frank told her to shush. He turned the pages of the sketchbook, studying each quick drawing carefully before going on to the next one.

"They're gemmin," he pronounced finally.

"I've never heard of them."

"Most people haven't. It was my grandmother who told me about them—she saw them one night, dancing in Fitzhenry Park—but I never did."

The wistfulness in his voice made Jilly want to stage a break-out from the old folk's home and carry him off to the Tombs to meet Babe, but she knew she couldn't. She couldn't even bring him home to her own loft for the holidays because he was too dependent on the care that he could only get here. She'd never even be able to carry him up the steep stairs to her loft.

"How do you know that they're gemmin and whatever *are* gemmin?" she asked.

Frank tapped the sketchbook. "I know they're

gemmin because they look just like the way my gran described them to me. And didn't you say they had violet eyes?"

"But only Babe's got them."

Frank smiled, enjoying himself. "Do you know what violet's made up of?"

"Sure. Blue and red."

"Which, symbolically, stand for devotion and passion; blended into violet, they're a symbol of memory."

"That still doesn't explain anything."

"Gemmin are the spirits of place, just like hobs are spirits of a house. They're what make a place feel good and safeguard its positive memories. When they leave, that's when a place gets a haunted feeling. And then only the bad feelings are left—or no feelings, which is just about the same difference."

"So what makes them go?" Jilly asked, remembering what Babe had said earlier.

"Nasty things happening. In the old days, it might be a murder or a battle. Nowadays we can add pollution and the like to that list."

"But—"

"They store memories, you see," Frank went on. "The one you call Babe is the oldest, so her eyes have turned violet."

"So," Jilly asked with a grin. "Does it make their hair go mauve, too?"

"Don't be impudent."

They talked some more about the gemmin, going back and forth between, "Were they really?" and "What else could they be?" until it was time for Frank's supper and Jilly had to go. But first she made him open his Christmas present. His eyes filmed when he saw the tiny painting of his old house that Jilly had done for him. Sitting on the stoop was a younger version of himself with a small faun

14

standing jauntily behind him, elbow resting on his shoulder.

"Got something in my eye," he muttered as he brought his sleeve up to his eyes.

"I just wanted you to have this today, because I brought everybody else their presents," Jilly said, "but I'm coming back on Christmas—we'll do something fun. I'd come Christmas eve, but I've got to work at the restaurant that night."

Frank nodded. His tears were gone, but his eyes were still shiny.

"The solstice is coming," he said. "In two days."

Jilly nodded, but didn't say anything.

"That's when they'll be going," Frank explained. "The gemmin. The moon'll be full, just like Babe said. Solstices are like May Eve and Halloween—the borders between this world and others are thinnest then." He gave Jilly a sad smile. "Wouldn't I love to see them before they go."

Jilly thought quickly, but she still couldn't think of any way she could manoeuvre him into the Tombs in his chair. She couldn't even borrow Sue's car, because the streets there were too choked with rubble and refuse. So she picked up her sketchbook and put it on his lap.

"Keep this," she said.

Then she wheeled him off to the dining room, refusing to listen to his protests that he couldn't.

* * *

A sad smile touched Jilly's lips as she stood in the storm, remembering. She walked down the alleyway and ran her mittened hand along the windshield of the Buick, dislodging the snow that had gathered there. She tried the door, but it was rusted shut. A back window was open, so she crawled in through it, then clambered into the front seat which was relatively free of snow.

It was warmer inside—probably because she was out

15

of the wind. She sat looking out the windshield until the snow covered it again. It was like being in a cocoon, she thought. Protected. A person could almost imagine that the gemmin were still around, not yet ready to leave. And when they did, maybe they'd take her with them....

A dreamy feeling stole over her and her eyes fluttered, grew heavy, then closed. Outside the wind continued to howl, driving the snow against the car; inside, Jilly slept, dreaming of the past.

* * *

The gemmin were waiting for her the day after she saw Frank, lounging around the abandoned Buick beside the old Clark Building. She wanted to talk to them about what they were and why they were going away and a hundred other things, but somehow she just never got around to any of it. She was too busy laughing at their antics and trying to capture their portraits with the pastels she'd brought that day. Once they all sang a long song that sounded like a cross between a traditional ballad and rap, but was in some foreign language that was both flutelike and gritty. Babe later explained that it was one of their traditional song cycles, a part of their oral tradition that kept alive the histories and genealogies of their people and the places where they lived.

Gemmin, Jilly thought. Storing memories. And then she was clear-headed long enough to ask if they would come with her to visit Frank.

Babe shook her head, honest regret in her luminous eyes.

"It's too far," she said.

"Too far, too far," the other gemmin chorused.

"From home," Babe explained.

"But," Jilly began, except she couldn't find the words for what she wanted to say.

There were people who just made other people feel

good. Just being around them, made you feel better, creative, uplifted, happy. Geordie said that she was like that herself, though Jilly wasn't so sure of that. She tried to be, but she was subject to the same bad moods as anybody else, the same impatience with stupidity and ignorance which, parenthetically speaking, were to her mind the prime causes of all the world's ills.

The gemmin didn't seem to have those flaws. Even better, beyond that, there was magic about them. It lay thick in the air, filling your eyes and ears and nose and heart with its wild tang. Jilly desperately wanted Frank to share this with her, but when she tried to explain it to Babe, she just couldn't seem to make herself understood.

And then she realized the time and knew she had to go to work. Art was well and fine to feed the heart and mind, and so was magic, but if she wanted to pay the rent on the loft and have anything to eat next month—never mind the endless drain that art supplies made on her meagre budget—she had to go.

As though sensing her imminent departure, the gemmin bounded around her in an abandoned display of wild monkeyshines, and then vanished like so many will-o'-the-wisps in amongst the snowy rubble of the Tombs, leaving her alone once again.

The next day was much the same, except that tonight was the night they were leaving. Babe never made mention of it, but the knowledge hung ever heavier on Jilly as the hours progressed, colouring her enjoyment of their company.

The gemmin had washed away most of the residue of her bad break up with Jeff, and for that Jilly was grateful. She could look on it now with that kind of wistful remembering one held for high school romances, long past and distanced. But in its place they had left a sense of abandonment. They were going, would soon be gone, and the

17

world would be that much the emptier for their departure.

Jilly tried to find words to express that, but as had happened yesterday when she'd tried to explain Frank's need, she couldn't get the first one past her tongue.

And then again, it was time to go. The gemmin started acting wilder again, dancing and singing around her like a pack of mad imps, but before they could all vanish once more, Jilly caught Babe's arm. Don't go, don't go she wanted to say, but all that came out was, "I... I don't... I want...."

Jilly, normally never at a loss for something to say, sighed with frustration.

"We won't be gone forever," Babe said, understanding Jilly's unspoken need. She touched a long delicate finger to her temple. "We'll always be with you in here, in your memories of us, and in here—" she tapped the pocket in Jilly's coat that held her sketchbook "—in your pictures. If you don't forget us, we'll never be gone."

"It... it won't be the same," Jilly said.

Babe smiled sadly. "Nothing is ever the same. That's why we must go now."

She ruffled Jilly's hair—again the motion was like one made by a mother, rather than someone who appeared to be a girl only half Jilly's age—then stepped back. The other gemmin approached, and touched her as well—featherlight fingers brushing against her arms, tousling her hair like a breeze—and then they all began their mad dancing and pirouetting like so many scruffy ballerinas.

Until they were gone.

Jilly thought she would just stay here, never mind going in to work, but somehow she couldn't face a second parting. Slowly, she headed south, towards Gracie Street and the subway that would take her to work. And oddly enough, though she was sad at their leaving, it wasn't the kind of sadness that hurt. It was the kind that was like a singing in the soul.

* * *

Frank died that night, on the winter solstice, but Jilly didn't find out until the next day. He died in his sleep, Jilly's painting propped up on the night table beside him, her sketchbook with her initial rough drawings: of the gemmin in it held against his thin chest. On the first blank page after her sketches of the gemmin, in an awkward script that must have taken him hours to write, he'd left her a short note:

"I have to tell you this, Jilly. I never saw any real magic—I just pretended that I did. I only knew it through the stories I got from my gram and from you. But I always believed. That's why I wrote all those stories when I was younger, because I wanted others to believe. I thought if enough of us did, if we learned to care again about the wild places from which we'd driven the magic away, then maybe it would return.

"I didn't think it ever would, but I'm going to open my window tonight and call to them. I'm going to ask them to take me with them when they go. I'm all used up—at least the man I am in this world is—but maybe in another world I'll have something to give. I hope they'll give me the chance.

"The faerie folk used to do that in the old days, you know. That was what a lot of the stories were about—people like us, going away, beyond the fields we know.

"If they take me, don't be sad, Jilly. I'll be waiting for you there."

The script was almost illegible by the time it got near the end, but Jilly managed to decipher it all. At the very end, he'd just signed the note with an "F" with a small flower drawn beside it. It looked an awful lot like a tiny violet, though maybe that was only because that was what Jilly wanted to see.

You saw real magic, she thought when she looked up from the sketchbook. You *were* real magic.

She gazed out the window of his room to where a soft snow was falling in the alley between St. Vincent's and the building next door. She hoped that on their way to wherever they'd gone, the gemmin had been able to include the tired and lonely spirit of one old man in their company.

Take care of him, Babe, she thought.

* * *

That Christmas was a quiet period in Jilly's life. She had gone to a church service for the first time since she was a child, to attend the memorial service that St. Vincent's held for Frank. She and Geordie and a few of the staff of the home were the only ones in attendance. She missed Frank and found herself putting him in crowd scenes in the paintings she did over the holidays—Frank in the crowds, and the thin ghostly shapes of gemmin peering out from behind cornices and rooflines and the corners of alleyways.

Often when she went out on her night walks—after the restaurant was closed, when the city was half-asleep—she'd hear a singing in the quiet snow-muffled streets; not an audible singing, something she could hear with her ears, but one that only her heart and spirit could feel. Then she'd wonder if it was the voices of Frank and Babe and the others she heard, singing to her from the faraway, or that of other gemmin, not yet gone.

She never thought of Jeff, except with distance.

Life was subdued. A hiatus between storms. Just thinking of that time, usually brought her a sense of peace, if not completion. So why... remembering now... this time...?

There was a ringing in her ears—sharp and loud, like thunderclaps erupting directly above her. She felt as though she was in an earthquake, her body being violently shaken. Everything felt topsy-turvy. There was no up and no down, just a sense of vertigo and endless spinning, a roar and whorl of shouting and shaking until—

She snapped her eyes open to find Geordie's worried features peering out at her from the circle that the fur of his parka hood made around his face. He was in the Buick with her, on the front seat beside her. It was his hands on her shoulders, shaking her; his voice that sounded like thunder in the confines of the Buick.

The Buick.

And then she remembered: walking in the Tombs, the storm, climbing into the car, falling asleep....

"Jesus, Jilly," Geordie was saying. He sat back from her, giving her a bit of space, but the worry hadn't left his features yet. "You really are nuts, aren't you? I mean, falling asleep out here. Didn't you ever hear of hypothermia?"

She could have died, Jilly realized. She could have just slept on here until she froze to death and nobody'd know until the spring thaw, or until some poor homeless bugger crawled in to get out of the wind and found himself sharing space with Jilly, the Amazing Dead Woman.

She shivered, as much from dread as the storm's chill.

"How... how did you find me?" she asked.

Geordie shrugged. "God only knows. I got worried, the longer you were gone, until finally I couldn't stand it and had to come looking for you. It was like there was a nagging in the back of my head—sort of a Lassie kind of a thought, you know?"

Jilly had to smile at the analogy.

"Maybe I'm getting psychic—what do you think?" he asked.

"Finding me the way you did, maybe you are," Jilly said.

She sat up a little straighter, then realized that some-

21

time during her sleep, she had unbuttoned her parka enough to stick a hand in under the coat. She pulled it out and both she and Geordie stared at what she held in her mittened hand.

It was a small violet flower, complete with roots.

"Jilly, where did you...?" Geordie began, but then he shook his head. "Never mind. I don't want to know."

But Jilly knew. Tonight was the anniversary, after all. Babe or Frank, or maybe both of them, had come by as well.

If you don't forget us, we'll never be gone.

She hadn't.

And it looked like they hadn't either, because who else had left her this flower, and maybe sent Geordie out into the storm to find her? How else could he have lucked upon her the way he had with all those blocks upon blocks of the Tombs that he would have to search?

"Are you going to be okay?" Geordie asked.

Jilly stuck the plant back under her parka and nodded. "Help me home, would you? I feel a little wobbly."

"You've got it."

"And Geordie?"

He looked at her, eyebrows raised.

"Thanks for coming out to look for me."

* * *

It was a long trek back to Jilly's loft, but this time the wind was helpful, rather than hindering. It rose up at their backs and hurried them along so that it seemed to only take them half the time it should have to return. While Jilly changed, Geordie made great steaming mugs of hot chocolate for both of them. They sat together on the old sofa by the window, Geordie in his usual rumpled sweater and old jeans, Jilly bundled up in two pairs of sweatpants, fingerless gloves and what seemed like a half-dozen shirts and socks.

Jilly told him her story of finding about the gemmin, and how they went away. When she was done, Geordie just said, "Wow. We should tell Christy about them—he'd put them in one of his books."

"Yes, we should," Jilly said. "Maybe if more people knew about them, they wouldn't be so ready to go away."

"What about Mr. Hodgers?" Geordie asked. "Do you really think they took him away with them?"

Jilly looked at the newly-potted flower on her windowsill. It stood jauntily in the dirt and looked an awful lot like a drawing in one of her sketchbooks that she hadn't drawn herself.

"I like to think so," she said. "I like to think that St. Vincent's was on the way to wherever they were going." She gave Geordie a smile, more sweet than bitter. "You couldn't see it to look at him," she added, "but Frank had violet eyes, too; he had all kinds of memories stored away in that old head of his—just like Babe did."

Her own eyes took on a distant look, as though she was looking into the faraway herself, through the gates of dream and beyond the fields we know.

"I like to think they're getting along just fine," she said.

GRYPHONS

M.W. Field

While carpooling kids to hockey
a voice on the radio revealed
agates are the eggs of gryphons.

In the bleachers oblivious
to the ice-clicking of laminate stick on puck,
I wrapped my dark
sweater around myself, swept away by a vision
of eagle-winged,
    sharp sighted lion-birds of prey arcing
        above the city/ the wind-emptied prairies/
        the poisoned seas;
        swooping down among the spires of the megalopoli
        raiding the jewels of modern commerce.

Within a week (semi-precious
stones being rare in our house)
I'd tricked my children into trading
all their banded marbles
for Transformers.
While the brats were at school,
I succeeded in hatching seven
of the ill-gotten agates

by microwaving gently under a paper towel.
The damp, downy cubs were so feeble I hurriedly
improvised an incubator—
the covered plastic tray
I sprout tomatoes in each spring—
nested them in torn Kleenex,
hid them in the furnace room.

That night, I told my children a horror story.
I located the gruesome events in *our*
furnace room...
and it worked:
they have not entered the basement since.
Now, when I secret myself there
the gryphon cubs circle my ankles
and pounce on one another; nibble my toenails
with their tough little beaks,
launch themselves into stubby flight
and sleep in a heap of tawny
uncalloused paws, translucent wings,
round baby bellies.
Yesterday, the boldest reached
my shoulder, settled and stretched
her wings for pride and balance, cawing.

Another season and they'll begin
brief nocturnal flights. Already,
they've thieved my husband's wedding band,
the little fiends...
The attic window will be their cliff.
One more year and tamed to my touch
they'll prowl the skies—
and I'll be clinging bejewelled
to their thick fur
in the cold, cold nights.

THE TOY MILL

David Nickle and Karl Schroeder

I
Emily Gets Her Wish

The Man in the Moon's smile began to slip. It turned into a leer. Then, breaking from the rim of the moon came a shape of crystalline hardness, led by eight bobbing points. Emily, perched straddling the peak of her auntie's home with the cold shivering through her spine, counted those points three times, and whispered aloud:

"Comet, Cupid, Donner, Vixen." She mouthed the rest of the verse, to hide that she didn't remember the other names.

The procession cut behind a black smear of cloud, and Emily scrambled higher on the roof, her back pressed against the frozen brick of the chimney. The winter air made a frost in her throat and she clutched her pink parka over her chest. The sleigh was gone. She'd missed it—if it had ever been there.

Emily turned away, filled with a deep and despairing sense of abandonment. The moon turned darker.

Iron runners hissed past inches above her head, and a breath of stratospheric cold made her shiver. For a moment all she could see was the swollen underbelly of the

26

sleigh, like the black bottom of a cauldron. Then the thing was landing, with unctuous delicacy, on the virgin snow of the roof.

The ski tracks began near enough to Emily that she could touch them, and that is what she did, even though they steamed with a black substance like the burnt drippings from an overcooked roast. The tracks were wider than her hand, and packed down so hard as to make the snow into a sheet of perfect, polished ice.

At the ends of those tracks, great iron skis whose ends spiralled four times glowed with tiny red embers from treetops brushed too closely, and creaked around the thick rivets that held the sleigh together.

She couldn't see the reindeer for the bulk of the sleigh. But Emily could clearly see her own tracks through the deep wet snow of the roof; they were the only disturbance in its blued perfection other than the tracks of the sleigh.

She forced herself to stand up, and cautiously sidled around the edge of the sleigh. The roof was steep here and she wanted to hold the sleigh for support, but she was afraid to touch it.

Her heart in her mouth, she peered up the steep side of the monstrous car and said, "Santa?"

For a moment nothing happened. Then, a creaking sound like frozen leather, and a hand whiter than the moon appeared, to clutch the rail of the sleigh.

It seemed as though the entire rooftop swayed, but it was only a shifting of runners on the sharp-peaked roof. The fingers, long and dextrous as only a toy-maker's can be, bent back at the third joint with the effort of movement. Santa Claus grew over the rail like a thunderhead over mountaintops.

His hair was whiter than his flesh. Thick whorls of ice embedded his beard in icicles like a January cataract. More

27

separated the thick hairs of his eyebrows into individual daggers, pushed back by the yuletide winds of the stratosphere so that they radiated from the bridge of his narrow, blue-tinged nose. Wisps of pale hair scattered from beneath his red cap, over his small pink ears. His eyes were tiny too, pink-rimmed and black at their iris; and looking, searching the eaves-troughs, the darkened windows, the empty playground three streets down, questing hungrily and never blinking once in an endless hunt for girls and boys.

"Ahem," said Emily in her politest voice.

Santa's little eyes narrowed even more, but still he didn't see her. He leaned out a long way from the sleigh, his breath coming in slow steady rasps like a dry bellows. Finally Emily screwed up her courage and reached up to pluck his sleeve.

He jerked back like a puppet, and his eyes widened impossibly as he saw her. For a second she thought he was angry, then maybe no, he was scared. But breaking past all those things came a kind of smile. It sent the icicles around his mouth into a macabre dance.

"Oooh," he said at last. "A *child*."

His voice was a high tenor, with breathy overtones. Emily could not see how such a vast and disordered bulk could produce a voice like that.

"Hello," she said.

"Well." He raised a trembling hand to clink the strands of his beard. "Well. Indeed. Yes, hello, hello, little thing. You are a little thing, aren't you?"

"Santa," she said with all of her eight years' determination, "I want to be an elf."

He didn't answer, just stared at her.

A wind curled up from the street below, sending a twist of cutting snow into Emily's eyes. A tiny part of her was crying, the same part that cried when she was six, when her parents went away and Auntie told her she could have the room with the grandfather clock that had stopped.

"I want to be an elf, Santa," she repeated, and stomped her foot on the frozen rooftop.

"Please!"

There was another shudder from inside the sleigh, and Santa gave a lurch and rose five more feet over the house of Emily's aunt. He gripped the sleigh's rim with a white knuckled fist.

In his other hand, he held a box, wrapped in blue shiny paper with a ribbon so red that it could only have been spun by elves. Santa Claus lifted that arm high, and suddenly bent at his waist so that his face was inches from Emily's.

Ice crumbled in crystalline avalanches as his smile widened and his narrow tongue darted across his blue, thin lips.

"A child," he breathed, sending a frosty wind at Emily that made her blink. "Yes, a good, good child, a child who is never naughty; never ever *bad*. Only one thing for this child."

Santa pulled away from Emily and his great head whipped towards the front of the sleigh, to the unseen reindeer.

"*Isn't that right, Rudolph!?*" he shrieked. Emily clapped her hands over her ears and nearly lost her balance.

And then, as fast as the echoes of Santa's cackling cheer died in the neighborhood, the shiny-wrapped box was trembling before Emily, Santa's right hand gripping it carefully so as not to damage the wrapping. His face hovered five inches behind it, and his tiny black eyes watched her with anticipation. The ice-bound eyebrows twinkled invitingly. The box, Emily saw, was doll-sized.

"No," she said firmly, and repeated her request slowly—in case Santa were hard of hearing:

"I! Want! To! Be! An! Elf! Please!"

He looked puzzled. Then he drew the present back, and with hurried, savage movements, tore the box up. He dangled a limp doll in front of her face, eyeing her with fixed concern over the back of his hand.

Emily shook her whole head, and her upper body too for good measure.

"Doesn't want the dolly," muttered Santa through an uncomprehending frown. "Don't want the dolly?" He tugged at his beard. Then with a quick decisive movement he stuffed the doll into a fold of his great red coat.

"Where's the, where—" He turned and scrabbled about in the back of the sleigh. "Aha. Here." He brought out an ornate snuff box and opened it. Taking out a pinch of powder, he tossed it at Emily.

Golden, shimmering dust settled about her with a sound like tinkling chimes.

"There. Saalaa, kaboom. You're an elf now." He turned away and grabbed the reins. Then he looked back.

Tears rolled down Emily's cheeks. She looked up at him resentfully.

"What?" he said, taken aback.

"I said, I want to be an *elf*. I want to go to the North Pole and make toys and sing with the other elves and see the reindeer and Rudolph and his nose and all the toys and be Christmas all year round!" she wailed. Then she was past words.

"You *want* be *my* elf?" Santa stroked his beard, and a thoughtful glint appeared in the outside corner of his left eye. Santa's uncertain lips twitched back into a smile. "Make toys? Go away"—he sniggered wetly through his nose—"go away... with Santa?"

Emily thought of her auntie and her room with the silent clock that loomed all night long, and about long division and detentions. "I want to be an elf," she repeated.

"All right then," he bellowed, and, reaching down with a long, branch-like arm, hoiked her over his lap into the seat beside him.

Emily fought to right herself as he drew up the reins and flipped them mightily. "*Gowan!*" he screamed.

She heard the sound of tiny hooves scrabbling in the deep snow. Emily righted herself in time to see eight impossibly tiny reindeer, hauling with all their might, fall in pairs off the edge of the roof.

With a crunch of iron against ice, the sleigh fell. Emily screamed as the ground rushed up—then they were plummeting, not down, but sideways between the tall houses. They continued to fall, higher and higher, into the sky.

II
A Night To Remember

The stars stood still above them, as Emily and Santa flew the world over. Emily had never been happier. It was a Christmas of frantic scrambling down chimneys behind Santa, whose great skeleton snapped and crunched to fit the tiniest aperture, some of which were too narrow for even Emily to pass. At the bottom of the larger chimneys, Emily watched Santa as his bones knitted and he painfully lurched to the base of a glittering tree and spewed gifts there from a great sack of green burlap that undulated with shifting boxes. Each box he would then arrange with a meticulous care, whispering, "A truck, Jimmy Thorne, see how you like *that*," or "You thought I'd finished with you after last year's dollhouse, Jacqueline Jones," and a terrific cackle over a pink-wrapped box bigger than Emily. And then it would be the next house.

Now the houses were all behind them. The runners

31

drew white contrails like cuts across the deep blue sky, and she dreamily traced those lines away and over the horizon, thinking of the vast web of such lines she and Santa had made over the entire globe.

The forests fell behind, replaced with glimmering ice. The sleigh careered over a range of saw-toothed mountains, then into a deep valley of black tundra patched with snow. At the centre of this bowl rose a vast building.

"The North Pole!" shrieked Santa, sending his whip twitching over the raw, foaming backs of his reindeer. The sleigh rocked as the reindeer scrambled madly against the frozen air, and for a moment they were all Emily could see, their wide and terror-struck eyes twisting in their emaciated sockets.

"No!" Santa bellowed, whipping again. "Down! To the Pole!

"Down to the Toy Mill!"

The reindeer disappeared as they arched downwards, and Emily felt a roller-coaster lurch as the massive sleigh descended into freefall. Emily clutched at Santa's deep red greatcoat and stared ahead, down at Santa's workshop.

The building filled Emily's vision. Seven great smokestacks, black as the tundra where the fumes had cooked the brickwork, grew like spikes from the structure, which itself sprawled under green metal roofing into long and labyrinthine additions. Tarmac lots surrounded the buildings. The sleigh levelled out, and one of the smokestacks suddenly loomed before them. Above, a plume of soot climbed high into the arctic night and a volcanic rumbling grew louder by the second.

"Damn you!" Santa screamed and his whip cracked like a thunderbolt. *"Up!"* Snap! *"Higher!"* Snap! *"Away!"*

The sleigh was enveloped in black smoke. It got into

Emily's eyes and made her cry, but when she breathed it for another sob it became impossible even to weep. The blackness passed, and she blinked away the filth.

The runners hit hard against tarmac with a butcher-shop crunch. They were in a space bounded by high walls, at the top of which ice-choked green metal eaves frowned over dark windows. Higher still, the aurora borealis sputtered and died.

The sleigh skidded to a halt in a shower of blue sparks, describing a twisting half-circle around the stationary reindeer and pulling three of them to the ground. There was a terrible shrieking and then silence, broken only by the distant hum of machinery.

Santa Claus leaned close to Emily and grinned a ghastly grin into her eyes.

"Welcome to the North Pole, little elf." He giggled in a small and girlish voice. "Merry Christmas, yes. Merry, merry Christmas."

* * *

With a frantic scrambling and pattering of small feet, a mob of elves surrounded the sleigh. Santa reared high in his seat, and glared at them.

The crowd parted and three of the elves approached. One held a shabby blue towel; Santa grabbed it and mopped his face, where the icicles were starting to droop. The second elf held out a fat brown cigar and the third a blue silk smoking jacket.

With a flourish Santa threw aside his great coat, blinding Emily. She pushed the smelly cloth away, and Santa reappeared, wrapped in blue. He bent and touched the end of his cigar to one of the smoking runners. Then, contentedly, he drew a deep breath and exuded a vast miasma of gritty grey smoke.

Santa Claus swatted his three helpers away with a broad arc of his palm, making even Emily duck involuntarily. But Santa's arm wheeled back and he snatched one of Emily's new ears between two fingers. He took a long, choking drag on his cigar and grinned down at her. Smoke rolled from his nostrils as he spoke.

"Well, little elf. Christmas year 'round, eh? Ha ha! Christmas year 'round is just what you'll get!"

Santa turned to the other elves, who were backing surreptitiously clear of his impressive reach. He snarled at them. "Yes, elves! Move off, back to work! One new elf doesn't mean long lunches for you lot! No, no, no! Back to the lines! Back to the shifts, by damn!"

The elves, who had been moving that way anyway now turned and ran, their thin, bent legs carrying them in terrified sprints. Santa clamped his teeth around his cigar and strode in the opposite direction, dragging Emily behind him.

They made a jog to the left between a pair of tall buildings, walked down a narrow alleyway choked with icicles as wide as Emily and finally emerged in a wide courtyard. This was lined with sheet-metal huts protruding from the brickwork. At the end was a wall with a single, gigantic doorway.

The roar of the mill was deafening.

Santa quickened his pace, pausing only once to drop his spent cigar, and soon they were at the door. *"Christmas all the time!"* Santa bellowed as the door swung open. His cackling was cut short by a tide of oily smoke. Emily held the greatcoat to her face, but it did little good. Through tears and acid coughs, she beheld the Toy Mill.

Dazzling light and knife-edged shadows cut through a vast space filled with huge machines in rows, like headstones. Coils of cable drooled down from catwalks festooned with pipes and valves. The catwalks crossed and recrossed, up and up in successive layers until they were hidden in darkness, a great iron spiderweb.

"This is it!" Santa waved proudly. "Your new home! What do you think of it, eh little elf?"

"It's dreadful."

"Yes!" The melting icicles in Santa's beard sparkled in the radiance of his glowing pride. "And it's just what you wanted!"

III.
A Matter of Correspondence

The letters had been separated into boxes, which were labelled by the age and nationality of their young authors. They rose in mountainous, teetering stacks beyond the rafters of Warehouse 12. Sometimes, one of those stacks would begin to wobble, and from the celestial gloom above a dozen or more boxes would plummet, bursting like ill-bound volumes on the cracked cement floor and spewing their multi-colored contents through the narrow canyons. Some of those canyons were all but impassable, blocked to twice the height of an elf with jaggedly torn envelopes and the crayoned, pencilled and—rarely—neatly typed lists.

"Put her to work!" Santa had screamed into the dark as he clutched the brass door handles and pulled the great metal-wrapped doors shut on the Correspondence Hall.

"Are all the letters from all the boys and girls in the world here?" Emily asked, wide-eyed, of the dark elf who led her deep into the maze.

"Yawm," drawled the elf. It darted a suspicious look at her. "Ah-whee, that's em innit."

"What?"

"Twirl yer gams, miss Hoitee toitee." The elf grabbed a long-handled broom up from the floor. "Sortenem's the way."

She clutched the broom, staring at the concrete labyrinth that stretched off into smog-hazed distance. "Please, mister elf, are my letters here? Did Santa read them?"

"Read?" The elf wrapped his wizened lips around the word as though he had never heard it before. "Who reads?" He made brisk shoving motions with his hands. "Sortem. Day, month, time, pla'. Sortem all." He made the shovelling motion again.

"You mean he didn't see my letters?" she asked tremulously. "He didn't read them?"

"Readem? Ach-eh, wot daftness be ye onit?"

Pouting, Emily dragged the broom along the floor, looking back every two or three steps at the elf. He tapped his foot impatiently, and after a while she stopped looking back.

Emily shovelled the fallen paper into heaps, which other elves picked over, tossing the correspondence into boxes that, paradoxically, were passed up to the tops of the stacks again. The operation seemed endless.

She gamely tried to keep up. After all, Emily was an Elf now, and that was a very special and important thing to be. And elves were industrious, and never ever tired. But she did tire, and the letters blurred together before her eyes. She tried to stop reading all the letters that she swept up. But even after the lists, the painstaking explanations of why Donnie or Sue or Millie had been good this year, all faded together into one big "Please!" in her mind, she kept seeing the words, over and over:

Dear Santa.

"Dear Santa," said the boys and girls of America. "Dear Santa," said England. "Dear Santa, Dear Santa, Dear Santa," said all the little children of the world. The words swirled around her; they were piled into quivering ziggurats above her, sprawled into a swelling maze in which, finally, she was lost.

Emily stopped pushing her broom, sat down, and began to cry.

Who *did* read these letters, anyway? The elves here didn't—Emily had begun to doubt they could speak properly, let alone read. And Santa? Emily tried to remember the last time Santa Claus had brought her something she'd asked for, and found that she couldn't. The only time he'd done anything she wanted was when she'd demanded it, face to face.

Emily wiped the tears from her eyes. "That's the problem," she said aloud. "Santa doesn't know!"

A heap of letters rustled beside her and the elongated soot-damaged face of an elf appeared. He glanced only briefly at Emily before hefting a watermarked carton to his shoulder and shuffling indifferently into the dark. Emily didn't care. "Santa doesn't know," she repeated. "He doesn't know what girls and boys really want! That's why it's so dreadful at the North Pole!"

Emily continued with similar exclamations for the remainder of her shift, but for all the gravity of her revelation, she did not sit idle. She scrabbled through the papers on the floor in search of an intact box, and although she could not find one entirely undamaged, she was able to repair one of the broken ones with the help of the tape gun that dangled from her tool belt. Then she set about filling her new box with letters.

The elves in the Correspondence Hall didn't try to stop her as she reached up and pulled down the brass handle on the great doors. Perhaps, thought Emily, they are secretly with me. As the doors opened and a whirl of wind-borne ice slipped inside, Emily turned to her co-workers as they huddled together in the gloom.

"Don't fear!" she shouted. "Santa will make things right!"

And then she turned with her box and stepped into the chill. Behind her, the great doors creaked shut.

* * *

Santa's quarters were on the roof of the Mill. There, amid an expanse of drifted snow, squatted a high peaked penthouse with gargoyled corners and tall, jaded glass windows. The arctic night cradled it and the whole Mill in icy greyness. Emily dragged the box up to the tall, bronze door to the building and tried to knock. Her tiny fist made no sound on the metal.

The door did respond to her push, though. She slipped gratefully into the dark warmth of Santa's Penthouse. She dusted the snow from her boots and said, timidly, "Santa?"

Firelight glowed through a wooden archway. Emily put the box down by the arch and looked through it.

Santa's vast living-room was lit solely from the fireplace. Silhouetted elves heaped logs bigger than themselves onto the fire, which was already spilling out onto the stone hearth. The heat was blistering.

A corpulent white bath tub had been wheeled to within a foot of the fire. Santa, wreathed in suds, reclined in the tub, shooting jets of smoke up from his cigar.

"More wood!" he bellowed, sweeping one arm over the high side of the tub. The elves avoided him adroitly, and ran for the wood box.

"Santa?" Emily asked timorously.

He frowned, glanced over, and said, "Zounds, elf! Aren't you working?" Sudsy bubbles rose from behind his head, to be withered into ash by the incandescent flames.

Emily bravely brought the box out. "Santa, there's something I think you should know."

"Nonsense." He sank slowly down, until only his cigar and eyes appeared above the rim of the tub. "I have no reason to know anything."

"These letters." She held them up. "Have you read

38

them?"

"Read them? What an idea." He crossed his eyes to look at the tip of his cigar. "What do they have to do with me?"

"They—it's because—" Emily wiped away a tear, and sniffled. He hadn't read them! "Because Santa, these are all the letters from all the boys and girls of the world, and they're all about what all the boys and girls want for Christmas!"

"Is that so?" His eyes slid half-closed. He dropped lower in the tub. "Never really thought about it, I guess." His eyes opened a bit. "What they want? What do you mean, what they want?"

"Santa!" Emily put her hands on her hips. She couldn't believe this. "Every girl and boy writes letters to Santa at Christmastime—"

"I know. It's *such* a nuisance."

"But they're telling you that they've been good all year, and they're asking you for presents!"

"Really?" His eyes opened wide, flicking suds away. He propped his chin on his hand, frowning and puffing madly. "Never would have thought...."

"But Santa! What did you think all these letters were?"

"Show me." One hand appeared, fingers snapping, above the mountain of suds. Emily moved closer to the blasting heat, and stretched out to hand him a letter. Santa held the paper up.

"'Dear Santa,'" he read aloud. "'From Billy.' Who in hell is Billy? Um um, `I have been very very good'—have you, Bill my boy?—um, um... `I wish I had a truck... I wish....'" Santa squinted and sloshed forward so that he loomed like a vulture over the letter. "By the Devil's flaming anus!" Santa sat up suddenly, splashing water everywhere. Blinding steam hissed up around him.

"'I wish my sister was dead!'"

Santa's red, bedraggled face emerged from an inferno of crackling flame and billowing steam. His gaze was beatifically calm. "Emily my good girl, I think you're on to something."

IV
Christmas Dinner

Emily did not see Santa Claus for some time after their fateful meeting, but that is not to say that his gratitude was unfelt.

"No more, my sweet pernicious little elf, will you crouch over your broom with no dreams to move you beyond your station," he had crooned, eyes half-closed and a towel concealing the bulk of his white, mottled skin. "Your sweeping-up days are behind you, now that you are at the helm of our mighty design, oh yes oh my oh yes. Your only task now, oh Emily mine, is to find me—" as he spoke, Claus bent and snatched from a steaming puddle the soaked and fast-streaking requests of angry young Billy "—find me more like him!"

Santa shook the letter over Emily's head, and she ducked back as Claus repeated: *"More like him!"* She was out the door and beyond the arch in no time. *"Do y' hear me, Emily! More! By Christmas, by Christ! More!"*

Starting back into work at the Correspondence Hall, Emily couldn't help but feel as important as Santa seemed to think she was. She started as Executive Elf In Charge of Correspondence at half past January, and by February she thought she was already beginning to see the light at the end of the tunnel. At least that is what she told the elves she had alphabetizing the stacks and repairing the scaffolding: "We are beginning to see the light at the end of the tunnel, people. Soon it will be Christmas the way it was meant to be."

By a quarter to March, Emily and her three assistants began compiling her first quarterly report for Santa. Emily had made her elves separate all of the gift requests into categories: *Animals*, which included such things as ponies, doggies, kitties and baby brothers and sisters, as well as more exotic pets such as boa constrictors and Nile crocodiles; *Machinery* was a broad category including automobiles, aircraft, munitions ranging from pellet guns to M-16s and AKMs, and chainsaws; and then there was the broader-still category that she had simply dubbed *Situations*. This last one often gave Emily an upset stomach. Billy's final Christmas wish fit the category, as did a plethora of others. One little boy named Albert wanted his whole town to catch incurable syphilis because he had been excluded from marching in the Santa Claus parade—"Let their noses rot off and see how they like that then," Albert had written in his awkward, boyish scrawl.

There were over fifty requests from little girls to be changed into mice or birds; a hundred and twelve little boys who wanted their driver's license; and thousands, tens of thousands it seemed, of requests from orphaned little girls and boys to have their dead parents returned to them.

But upset stomach or no, Emily pressed on. She worked through March, April, May, all the summer months and much of the autumn with scarcely a wink of sleep. Yet as far as she could tell, she didn't need sleep. Not when the true spirit of Christmas was at stake.

It wasn't until five to December that she was called away from her high, sloped desk. She did not get a very good look at the elf who brought the notice, nor did she recognize the script on the single milky-white card proffered to her so mysteriously. Though it was unsigned, the words on the card were unmistakable, and they buoyed her spirit every time she reread them.

41

A Christmas dinner would take place, the first of December, at the reindeer stables. And Emily, it appeared, had been invited.

* * *

On the appointed evening, Emily made her way to the stables. She knew in a general way where they were, but had never been to them because her responsibilities kept her so busy. To get to them, she had to pass through the darkest pulsing foundries of the Mill, past shrieking boilers and pounding triphammers, and up out into the vast, cold wasteland of the Pole.

Much of the land around the Mill consisted of tarmac runways periodically covered and unmasked again by twisting dunes of snow. At the end of the longest runway, a brave stand of spruce trees sprang from the tundra. Like sickly guards, they encircled a long low building of gingerbread construction. A thin coil of smoke came from the stout stone chimney above one end of the stable. Lights shone in the windows there.

Despite the cutting wind and the barrenness of the plain, Emily was warm with curiosity and anticipation as she approached the place. It was only as she neared the door itself that she realized hers were the only footprints leading here.

"Perhaps I'm the first guest," she said to herself, and knocked. No one opened the door, but she thought she heard a faint voice, bidding her enter. Emily hoisted the iron latch and let herself in.

"Hello?" She unwrapped herself from her scarf, and turned to close the door. Then she raised her head to look at the party scene.

After her months in the greyness of the Mill, Emily had hoped for brightness and warmth here, among the reindeer at Christmas. And, indeed, it was bright; candles glowed everywhere: on side-tables, in sconces in the walls, on wagon-wheel chandeliers and the long, long dinner table. They even flickered in unsteady ranks along the floor itself. And it was warm; a dry, pressing warmth that Emily felt in her sinuses.

The dinner table had been set for at least thirty. It was a great slab of wood, wide enough to sleep on. All along both sides were high chairs and low chairs, thrones and stools, with place-settings before each.

All were empty.

As Emily took her first steps into the room, a vapour of dust rose up around her. She sneezed, and along the table-top, a wave of dust rose, tingled in mid-air for a moment, then settled down again onto the still, pale plates and saucers.

"Come in, child," said a dry, listless voice. A figure at the far end of the table moved. Emily gasped.

It was a woman. A tall, stately creature, she sat in the lesser of two vast thrones at the head of the table. The lunar oval of her face held empty sadness. Dried mistletoe tangled her grey hair. Her green gown shimmered with highlights from the candle flames, except on her shoulders where it was dull with dust. On the table before her were a plate full of withered unidentifiable things, and a gold goblet overflowing with mold.

When she spoke, her eyes fell half-shut with a terrible weariness. "I have heard, child, of the work you have done for the Claus."

"Who are you?" Emily stepped carefully around the stalagmites of wax dotting the floor. "Am I early for the party?"

"You are... on time," said the ethereal woman. "I am Mrs. Claus."

Emily stopped, thunderstruck. She had approached to within a few feet of the woman. Now she could see that the throne next to Mrs. Claus' was as dusty and old as any

43

alongside the table. A fork had been jammed into the arm of the throne, and stood like a single mute protester on the silent lawn of the upholstery.

"I... I'm honoured to meet you, Ma'am." Emily remembered to curtsy. "Will... will Mr. Claus be joining us for dinner?"

"No...." A kind of animation entered the woman's eyes. "No. Sit down here." A delicate hand rose from her lap to point to a stool at her right. Emily sat.

"No one will be joining us, Emily," sighed Mrs. Claus. "No one will come." She seemed to withdraw into herself, gazing out over the silent place settings. Then, as if unbidden, words came from her lips.

"You have done an evil thing, dearest Emily. Long are the years that silence and peace have reigned here. Long has it been since the Claus has troubled us." She blinked slowly. "The Claus is not a messenger of good. Perhaps once... before the rot of years took their toll upon him, things were different. Although even I, I must confess, can barely recall." Mrs. Claus' hands trembled in the dust of her lap. "Now as his great sleigh takes to the sky, it flies not on the faerie-dust of good will, but is driven by the engines of his wrath. His gifts are wholly malicious, Emily. Or so... he has believed."

She turned her dull eyes towards Emily. "For many decades I have kept from the Claus the knowledge that his efforts have failed. He did not know that the children of the world welcomed his visits. I told him the letters contained complaint, that the children of the world begged him not to continue his cruel dispensation. Now you have told him the truth."

Emily thought about the letters Santa had told her to find. The ones whose young authors wished their parents dead, or for their schools to be swallowed up by cyclones.

Mrs. Claus bent forward, her sad, dark eyes

wide. "Do you understand," she whispered, almost inaudibly, "what Claus is going to do with the truth?"

Emily did not, but she was afraid of how she would feel if she did. She looked down and kicked her feet.

"Something must be done," Mrs. Claus continued in her whisper. "For the first time in centuries, more is at stake than even Christmas."

V
Best Of The Season

Emily wore a fuschia-dyed, ermine-lined greatcoat to the Christmas Inspection, and although it kept much of the arctic chill from her narrow elvish bones, she shivered as the doors to Claus' administration building opened and she filed along with the nineteen other supervisory elves outside, across the ice-strangled courtyard and into the Toy Mill proper.

As they arrived they were led to a raised podium, decorated with bright red velvet and green crepe-paper streamers. Emily was at once struck by the difference between the Toy Mill she had entered nearly a year ago and the one in which she now sat.

Where previously scaffolding, ductwork, deafening, sparking machinery had dominated every imaginable view, now every spot was hung with dark, impenetrable curtain. A year ago, the lighting was flickering and sporadic, but now fresh new fluorescents hummed brilliantly overhead, the new light not altogether flattering to the upturned faces of the assembled elves. The air smelled not of oil and ozone and rusty water, but something else that made Emily's nose wrinkle. It smelled like fresh pine, or soap.

A spotlight came on, and swept its luminous circle across the crowd and up the nearest wall. As it moved, a loudspeaker crackled deafeningly. The walls shook as a giant finger tapped thunderously on a microphone.

"Welcome!" Claus boomed through the Toy Mill. "Welcome all, welcome to the Twenty-first Century!"

A collective "Oooooh" rose up from the assembled elves.

Emily followed the spotlight to where it stopped, at a catwalk three storeys up. There it oscillated back and forth, until it finally speared a lone figure, made tiny by the distance.

Claus, wearing a neat white shirt and narrow blue tie underneath a freshly-pressed greatcoat, leaned forward and squinted through the light at the thing his Toy Mill had become. In one hand, he held his cigar, in the other a glittering cordless microphone.

"Wishes," thundered Claus into his microphone. "Who would have thought, eh elves? Who would have thought that the key to our recovery, yes, to our very salvation, could be based upon so simple a principle?"

At that, Claus snapped his fingers and Emily very nearly lost her hearing. The echoing had not yet died when a well-dressed elf handed Claus a clipboard with a wide sheaf of paper on top.

"I should have thought of it long ago," said Claus, his eyes scanning down the first of 152 pages on the clipboard—it had been 151, but Emily had seen that the 152nd was added this morning.

"Give the children what they want, and that shall be their undoing! What a principle! What a motto, eh? And we've put it to work for us, haven't we elves?" Santa snapped his fingers again, and this time the curtains that covered the Toy Mill began to part.

"Look now, upon the fruits of our labours," said Santa, as the needle-pointed, serrated-edged totality of the Toy Mill's GNP was revealed. "It has taken us a year, and

I would say we have worked harder and faster at it this year than in our entire three hundred years of production. By hell, I wouldn't even be able to remember where each of these were to go, even what they all are, I've seen so many requisitions cross my desk this year!"

The mass of toys was certainly daunting, and Emily wouldn't have believed Santa Claus could fit them all onto a hundred sleighs if she hadn't flown with him a year ago. The toys had been stacked in the same categories she had divided the wishes into. There were the *Animals*, horses and dogs and cats and babies, what seemed like a million babies, all drugged and stacked in cords like firewood; *Machinery*, filled with monster trucks and Sherman tanks and bazookas and chainsaws, guns and knives and hand grenades.

Situations contained objects that were harder to identify, but Emily knew their significance. There was a rack of glass ampoules, filled with a neurotoxin developed in July by the Toy Mill's R&D wing to leave no trace in an autopsy—Claus would deliver those personally, injecting brothers, sisters, former best friends and even parents depending on the specified wishes of the good little girls and boys. And Emily could make out the larger containers, in a portable refrigeration unit. In September, R&D had developed an incurable strain of syphilis, but there were strict rules as to the temperature of its storage. They had been about to develop an inoculant, but little Albert's wishes did not include immunity for himself, so the project had been filed away with the World Peace serum, abandoned in late November as too difficult for this year.

Claus went through them all, wish by wish. "Lot 543," he would call, and an elf would bring forward the weaponry or the twitching zombie of a recently-deceased parent or the working submarine with four torpedo tubes. Claus would inspect it carefully from his perch, sometimes ordering the elf to turn it upside down or around backwards so he could be certain the wish matched specifications. Then he would read off the next lot number.

Finally, he came to the bottom of the list.

"Lot 10761," said Claus. There was an uncomfortable silence. Claus repeated himself.

"Lot 10761, I said."

Still nothing. Claus tapped the microphone again. "Did you hear me?" he roared. "Where is my last wish?"

There was movement among the elves then. Emily saw it before Claus did, because the woman below stayed shrouded in relative darkness until she had risen. When the spotlight hit her, Mrs. Claus was at her full height, towering over the assembled elves like a twisted Hallow-een tree. She wore a fuschia greatcoat like Emily's, and she held a small black metal box in her hand.

"*By the thunder of hell's reindeer!*" Santa's eyes were wide red orbs. "*What brings the moribund back from perdition?*"

Mrs. Claus spoke, but she was drowned out by the shrieking feedback that followed Claus' shocked outburst. She repeated herself.

"The final lot," she said, her own voice filling the mill only by its own power, "is on its way. You need not fear, Claus. It will be here when it is needed."

Santa's elves began a worried muttering amongst themselves.

The loudspeaker hissed and crackled with Claus's sputtering rage.

"What do you mean with this, woman?" Claus sneered. "Do you think you can come *begging* to *me*, now in my moment of greatest triumph?" He gestured with his cigar, a trail of embers underlining his contempt. "Back to the stables, hag, with the other sows."

Mrs. Claus shook her head. "You were always too slow, Claus. Even when it's spelled out for you, you just can't keep up."

Claus was about to say something, but Mrs. Claus pressed a button on her box.

"Here's your final lot," she said. "It's for a little girl named Emily. You'll find her Christmas wish destructive enough, I'd wager."

The Toy Mill rocked with a distant explosion.

* * *

Claus went pale under the spotlight. "What is this?" he roared. "What Christmas wish is this?"

"The one you missed, Claus," said Mrs. Claus. "Once again, you were sloppy. And again, you stopped reading the wish lists that came across your desk, in your eagerness to fulfil them all. So it was easy to add one last wish...." Her voice was lost in a thunderous *whump* that shook the mill and brought a shower of dust down from the ceiling. Claus looked up with alarm.

Emily could contain herself no longer. She broke free from the crowd and ran to the open space below Santa's catwalk. "I wish your Christmas would never happen!" she yelled at him. "I wish it would all just stop! And I wish you would never, ever get to have Christmas your way again!"

The lights flickered and went out. Another explosion rocked the mill, and a tongue of blue flame licked through a sudden rent in the wall above Claus.

"By the blighted wastes 'neath Satan's sphincter!" Spittle trailed like broken scuds to the Toy Mill floor. *"Woman, you are my undoing!"*

The elves panicked as one. Eyes rolling, they broke into frenzied motion, racing for the giant rolling doors to the outside. Emily cowered in the darkness, listening to

49

the shrieking and continuing blasts, until a light hand descended on her shoulder.

Mrs. Claus led Emily out into the red-lit night. The mill collapsed, eaten from its heart by multi-coloured fires. The insensate machinery tore free of its moorings, smashing blindly through wall and pillar, window and cable. As the ceiling collapsed, great gouts of smoke poured out from ground level.

Emily and Mrs. Claus ran across the tarmac. Elves were scattering away in all directions.

A low ominous rumbling sound began. A weird flickering blue glow reflected across the frozen landscape. Emily stopped, pulling free of Mrs. Claus, and turned to look.

The core of the Mill turned into a pillar of electric fire, like the northern lights set loose. A fierce wind picked up, blowing into the heart of the fire. And silhouetted by the glare, his long crooked shadow darting across the snow at her, was Claus.

He battled against the hurricane, taking step after tortured step to follow Emily. His frozen eyes flashed with northern blue and his mouth opened in a noiseless scream. His greatcoat flapped out behind him like a raven's wings.

Over Emily's head, Mrs. Claus said, in tragic resignation, "Oh, Claus."

Claus slipped, and slid back ten feet. He grabbed a spire of ice, but it snapped in his hand. For just a moment, he stood poised, his icy hair flaring up around him like lightning.

"*Merry Christmas*," he bellowed, "*Merry Christmas, you ungrateful bastards!*"

And then the vortex had him, and he was swept into flailing snow, and burning blue light, and was gone.

Mrs. Claus turned away, a single gilded tear sliding

down her cheek.

But Emily could not look away from the sight. For the Toy Mill had been her home, terrible as it was, and now it was gone.

Mrs. Claus touched Emily's chin, and lifted it up so that their gazes met. Mrs. Claus' eyes held a measured kind of triumph, but their weariness was in no way diminished by that fact. The old woman's lips quivered like shreds of ribbon in a breeze.

"So young," she whispered. "So young."

Mrs. Claus held Emily's face in such a way for a long time. The explosions had finished, the wind was dead, and thick white flakes began to fill the polar air. But they were not snowflakes—Emily didn't even have to put her tongue out to know that. They were ashes; and if Emily and Mrs. Claus stood there for long, they might well be buried in them.

Wordlessly, Emily took Mrs. Claus' hand and led her back to the reindeer stables.

* * *

Emily was sick for Christmas, and had to stay in bed the whole day through. Her Auntie hadn't time to buy her presents. Emily had only arrived back from the North Pole Christmas Eve, and it was all Auntie could do to take her inside, call the doctor and tell the police that Emily had come back. The police had wanted to talk to Emily, but Auntie had put her foot down—"Not until after Christmas," she'd said, "and that's final." Then Auntie had given Emily a great big hug, and put her to bed, and made her hot soup that was the best soup Emily had ever tasted.

Auntie spent most of Christmas Day with Emily in the room with the grandfather clock that didn't work, and went to bed only after Emily had seemed to fall asleep.

But Emily was only pretending. When her Auntie had shut off the light and closed the door, Emily crept over to

51

her window and looked out.

The moon was in a quarter-phase, and cloud patterned the sky like wallpaper on a child's bedroom wall. If a sleigh ever crossed such a sky, it would do so empty of toys, and fly so quietly that Emily would never know it had passed.

POINTING NORTH
(after Christian Morgenstern)

Tom Henighan

McNulty's weird—he points his head
Northward when he lies in bed,

Avoiding south and east and west,
Just managing to get some rest.

A foolish trick, his shrink declares,
To catch the compass unawares.

Irrational, suggest the scholars,
As they recycle truth for dollars.

All this is manifest to seers
Who chart blue planets in arrears,

And poets, turning words on dimes
Drive nonsense home with backseat rhymes.

McNulty, not to be outdone,
Lies down beneath the midnight sun.

A stranger in a common dream,
He hears the polar foxes scream.

THE GREAT COMEDIANS
(for Robert Zend)

Tom Henighan

The great comedians fall, one by one,
        into a surprising cosmos.
    Galaxies roar out of sight;
somewhere near Vegas, through a desert of spaces,
        all jokes circle round.
        Heisenberg's agents are weeping
but gravity endures—the eternal gravity of humour—
    the pratfall, the banana peel, the pie in the face—
        and it's Chaplin, so nakedly manifold, one foot
        in a whirlpool,
            whose precarious spirals astound us
            before he disappears.

    O strange attractors, peering out of chaos,
        while Harpo holds time on a string,
forever, at the flip of a coin, Harold Lloyd will recover
        pure silence; Stan Laurel beside himself
            in the commotions of laughter,
            Lenny Bruce embracing death
                    with his spiral arms.

How artfully they bow and vanish!
      Mr. Fields will allow, sir,
      that the Great White Way dawdles
      at the edge of oblivion—
      queer quasars, real howlers,
      space expanding to shrink us.

And worse than Woody Allen's fears
      no universal dance, but dense
      fires winking into darkness,
      black holes in a tired script
      of stars.

      (Yet when Keaton is called back
      nothing human is laughable—
      and even the supernovas
      balance a moment in the love
      that urges a small man
      with sheer grace
      from one fall to another.)

ALSO STARRING

Cliff Burns

At precisely 11:00 a.m. (PST) a man who looked like Harry Dean Stanton entered a Savings and Loan on Wilshire, waved a pistol at a cashier and demanded money, as much as she could stuff in the brown paper bag he gave her. Once this was done he backed toward the door, saluted jauntily to the closed circuit cameras mounted overhead and made his escape.

The staff film buff immediately identified him. The cops who responded to the alarm were skeptical. Still, they did some checking and learned that the actor was on location, costarring in the new David Lynch film which was wrapping up six weeks of shooting in Gainesville, Florida. The plot of the movie was not immediately known but when pressed the publicist admitted that Stanton played the role of a depraved armed robber. All agreed that it was an interesting coincidence.

Less than a week later a Wilford Brimley look-a-like held up a jewellery store. It was strictly a smash and grab job but it was carried out with homespun perfection. Someone recognized him from his cereal commercials. The actor was briefly detained but his manager and a photographer provided convincing alibis.

It was clear that a pattern was developing. A man impersonating fine character actors was on a crime spree. A team of detectives was assigned to the case, which was given top priority by their superiors. A spokesperson promised quick results.

The police gained the complete cooperation of the Screen Actors' Guild and its counterparts. They investigated dozens of disgruntled actors, professional makeup people and wannabees. Acting on a tip, they staked out Paramount Pictures.

Two days later Maureen Stapleton knocked over a 7-Eleven.

The city was in an uproar. Edward Herrmann and Joe Pesci were accosted on the street. Both had to be hospitalized for their injuries. It was reported that Michael J. Pollard had gone into hiding for his own protection.

The major studios hired extra security personnel. New copyright laws were enacted which made the impersonation of famous figures punishable by hefty fines and jail terms. Several distraught drag queens committed suicide. Rich Little declared personal bankruptcy.

Then, a break.

A man reportedly a dead ringer for Ned Beatty was seen loitering outside an exclusive men's clothing store in Bel Air. A swarm of police officers converged on the scene, cordoned off several city blocks. The real Mr. Beatty was located in San Francisco.

The imposter somehow became alerted to the presence of police, dashed across the street and disappeared into a throng of curious onlookers. Unfortunately he emerged as Charlotte Rampling, accent and all. He was ordered to halt and was shot several times while attempting to remove something—later identified as a compact—from a small, stylish purse.

As the imposter lay dying, ringed by police and bystanders, there were no clever parting words, no glib one-liners like "top of the world, ma!" or even "the horror, the horror".

Many marvelled at how he stayed in character to the very end, batting those lovely lashes, pursing those thin, sensuous lips and expiring with grace and aplomb.

Like Charlotte would have.

EXTRAS

Robert Charles Wilson

1.

In the summer of 1983, an MGM/UA production unit arrived in Clapham and took over the local high school for five weeks of location filming, August and a week into September that hot year. I watched from the pumps at the Clapham Texaco as their astonishing trucks—three diesel trailers and ten Winnebagos—labored in from the blue North Dakota horizon like ships against the wind. Like ships, they carried cargo from distant places; like ships, they were bringing us—though we were not then aware of it—a new map of the world.

No one in Clapham knew what to expect from the movie people. They were Hollywood, with all the money and sophistication that name still implies. We were fascinated and even a little afraid of them—the Lutherans started up a movement to have them banned from the city limits, on the theory that they would import homosexuality and wholesale drug addiction. But that was never the issue. Oh, I do not doubt there were some or perhaps many lines of cocaine consumed out at the Travelodge, but most of us could deal with that. We are a long way out, but we get *Time* magazine. A small town, but I attended Robert A. Taft School for four years, and I can vouch that we do not have a crying need to import our vices.

The real threat they posed was very different. "Glamorous" is a word we used often those summer months, but here is a curious fact: when I looked up "glamour" in the dictionary, is said, "Magic, enchantment, beauty, ephemeral charm," and that is surprisingly near to the truth.

The project they had come to film was a musical remake of *High School Confidential*. The original—you may remember—featured Russ Tamblyn as a tough high school kid and Mamie Van Doren as his sexy aunt. Except, Russ is really a narcotics agent and Mamie is his cover. The MGM/UA version (you may also remember, but probably don't) dresses up the plot with knife-edge Technicolor and screaming Dolby rockabilly numbers. It would play for a couple of slow weeks in the cities and retire finally to a slow life on cable TV, but in '83 we didn't know any of that. We were struck with the glamour and secretiveness of the project and how strange the Robert A. Taft looked, ringed round with sodium lamps and silver umbrellas.

It was the school that had attracted the location scout: a big, ornate brick high school erected in the forties to serve the five sprawling counties around Clapham. Clapham itself is not much. The movie company was put up in the Holiday Inn and the Travelodge a few miles west of downtown along the interstate, and they would take lunch occasionally at the McDonald's or the Country Kitchen within a couple of blocks of the school, but they did not interact much with the townspeople until mid-August, when they put an ad in the town paper asking for extras.

I heard about it when Candy came out to the Texaco with the quarter-page ad clutched in her hand. "It's our chance," she said breathlessly. "Come on, Indian! We *have* to."

And because we did not deny ourselves these impulses, and because I was in love with her, I told her yeah, O.K., and spent an hour scrubbing the grease out from under my nails with a bar of Lava soap.

The lineup the next morning wound out from the gym door and across the broad Taft parking lot. The ad asked for people "between the ages of 18 and 30" and "in good physical condition," but we had men out there who had turned thirty under the Truman administration, and housewives who outweighed the casting director by 150 pounds. It was obscene. I told Candy so.

"But I know why they're here," she said. "They're here because it would mean something. To be in a movie. Christ," she said wistfully, "it's true, isn't it? Wouldn't it just make your life over?"

I had combed up my hair duck-ass style, had put on a tight white Hanes T-shirt with a pack of Camels rolled into the sleeve. Candy, who was good looking enough to be a natural anyway, had raided the attic for her father's moth-eaten football sweater and her mother's cheerleader skirt. I felt more than a little ridiculous dressed this way, and it drew us some sneers from the crowd, but Candy wanted to impress the casting director with, at least, our sincerity.

And we had nothing to lose. We were back-of-tracks people. Back-of-tracks is not exactly the poor part of town. You could say it is the part of town where Clapham wears its poverty most conspicuously. The prosperous Reagan years did not much rub off on Clapham or on the agricultural land around it. Which was another reason we were there: it would be day work, and we needed day work.

That was, at least, why I was there. Candy had her own reasons. She was as energetic that hot August morning as I have ever seen her. Standing in the long line in front of the gymnasium door of Robert A. Taft, she fairly vibrated. She watched the movie people lolling around their trailers, crisp white shirts tucked into tight sky-blue Levi's, and her eyes were very wide. "Wouldn't it be great," she said, "to go away with them? If they would take you away?"

"Can't happen." We shuffled forward across the gravel. "It doesn't even happen in the movies anymore."

"You never know, Indian. You can't be too sure."

I didn't press it. Part of the connection between us was that we did not question such assertions. I worked evenings and weekends at the Texaco; Candy did waitressing and pretended to be saving money for college. I lived in a trailer on which I could not meet the payments; she lived with her mother, who worked as a beautician at the Cut-&-Curl. Ask anybody, and they would tell you we had no prospects. Two back-of-track losers in a cash-poor prairie town, broke but not even broke enough to be interesting. And I suppose, in a way, that was true. But we would not admit to it. We hated the idea.

We were special. We told each other so. "We're special," Candy would say, "and don't you forget it, Indian!"

But in the end I was not the one who forgot.

The line wormed into the big school auditorium. Inside, the casting director or his assistant—I could not sort these people out—sat in a bored pose behind a folding table, marking a clipboard and nodding yea or nay at the candidates. He had already collected a sizable crowd of people of approximately our age, sidelined under the basketball hoop with smug conquerors' smiles. "So many," Candy whispered, suddenly less sure of herself. And then we were at the front of the line—finally—and my hands, like nervous animals, burrowed into my pockets.

The casting director examined us together. "That's cute," he sad. "Dressing up like that."

We nodded. Cute, yeah. We squirmed.

"O.K.," he said finally. "You're fine. I'll need your

names."

I was astonished. Candy smiled.

"Candice Tucker," she said levelly.

The movie man wrote it down. "Candice," he said. "Good. Welcome, Candice."

And then his eyes were on me.

I swallowed once hard. I felt a sudden, urgent sense of doubt. We had come here too casually. This was strange territory we had entered; the rules were different; caution was vital. Candy's attitude—her gap-jawed infatuation—struck me as dangerously naive.

"Your name," the man said.

She nudged me from behind.

"Jack," I said reluctantly. "Jack Hokeah."

I spelled it. He wrote it down. "Hokeah?"

"We call him Indian," Candy said.

They call me "Indian" because of my father. He was not a Sioux, as you might expect—North Dakota is "the Sioux State"—but a Kiowa half blood who came north in the sixties to work on the missile bases going up all through the area. He died when I was young but, looking back, it seems ironic to me that he should have married into this tribe of rural North Dakota whites, a tribe as doomed, I sometimes think, as the Hurons, the Nanticokes, or the Mohegans.

Because my mother was white, our family was estranged even from the people of back-of-tracks Clapham—not outcasts exactly, but never really close to anyone but ourselves. Much of this was casual racism, the unthinking rejection of an obvious outsider. But on another level I think our estrangement was more profound. There *was* something odd about my father, something subtler than skin color or "cultural heritage," and I wonder if people didn't feel it.

I know I felt it. I felt it because I shared it. Clapham is a high-plains prairie town; the west wind sluices like a river through these old blacktop streets, and I will tell you a secret: it talks. The wind talks. If you listen closely, you can hear it.

At least, I could.

And I could talk to it—though I had promised Candy, many years ago, that I would not.

We showed up at Taft on the appointed day, naively expecting all the apparatus of stardom: make-up, wardrobe, scripts to memorize. Instead, they sent us to the Teacher's Lounge and told us to wait til we were called.

It didn't matter to Candy. She had caught a glimpse of the lights and the cameras; it was enough. I saw the glint in her eyes and felt, even then, a tingle of disquiet.

What I had not realized about extra work is how tedious it is. Movie work in general I suppose. I was surprised at how little sense there was of *telling a story*. Candy had read the movie magazines her mother brought home from the Cut-&-Curl, and understood it better. The screenwriter, she said, tells the story. And, later, the movie editor tells the story. In between there are only scenes, bits, dialogue, yards and miles of footage. Our director was a meticulous bald man of about thirty-five who shot everything half a dozen times and who would become famous, a couple of years later, for going ruinously overbudget on a B horror movie. So mostly we waited, and when we did work, the work was mechanical. Picture it: a cafeteria scene. We tiptoe behind the stars, who are doing dialogue, tracked by a crane microphone. There is a diffuse white light everywhere. We take trays; we take cutlery; we take little plastic dishes of watery Jell-O. We do all this daintily so as not to obscure the dialogue. Four times, five times, six times. Then we do it again without the actors, and this time we

64

rattle our cutlery and shake our trays and mumble to each other: a microphone take, to be blended into the sound track. It is a kind of jigsaw puzzle, assembled separately elsewhere.

But the waiting took up most of our time. We waited in the Teachers' Lounge, where the small swivel television was tuned to a Fargo station that showed syndicated re-runs all afternoon: "The Andy Griffith Show," "Dick Van Dyke," "Doctor Kildare." Black-and-white TV, warm Coke, a sedative haze of cigarette smoke: for me, that was August of '83. Easy money, yes, but also trivial and tedious money.

And yet... the light would shine; the camera would glide silently forward; the gym or the cafeteria would take on a momentary sunlit shimmer. It was strange and undoubtedly magical, and in those moments I think I felt a little of what Candy mush have felt.

Reflected glory. Brief stardom.

Glamour.

She looked good in wardrobe. Her kind of figure had been out of style in Hollywood since the era of Monroe, but she looked good on the set—in the casting director's words, very "period." And she took to the make-up. Bright lipstick accenting her mobile mouth, a little shadow around her blue eyes; sun-bleached hair in bangs, her breasts like a proud badge of sexuality. I noticed some of the movie people checking her out. A camera-man told her she was "photogenic"—coming on to her, but Candy chose to take the compliment at face value. For all I know, it might have been sincere. She was very good-looking.

And, yes. I checked myself out in the available mirrors once or twice. Who wouldn't? You can see me in a couple of shots. They dressed me in peg jeans rolled at the cuff, a leather jacket—the bad-boy look.

On me it worked. You can recognize me by the hawk

nose, slightly dark complexion, brown eyes hooded under thick eyebrows and bushy black hair. Acceptably Anglo, but with a hint of something darker.

Candy and I hung together on the set. We were a unit. We stayed separate from the other extras because we were back-of-tracks, and from the movie people because we were local. But it was the Hollywood people who took the greater interest in us.

And, of course, vice versa.

Over the duration of that first week, I became aware that I was watching Candy fall in love.

The stars of the film were Bobby Angle and a nineteen-year-old girl named Lee Ann Morgan. These were, if not big names, at least "promising" names; rising talent, youth-cult stars. Bobby was blue-eyed and sandy-haired, maybe five-foot-ten and with a certain Napoleonic swagger in his walk. Lee Ann was blonde, with bruised eyes and a lithe dancer's body.

Candy dragged me out of the lounge one time to watch them dance. "Hurry up, Indian... they're in the gym! If we stay out of the way, we can watch."

They were, yes, talented. Candy and I pushed in among a dozen others to watch, and for a span of time the enterprise took on the air of real theater. They did their own dancing. Lee Ann whirled up and came down splay-legged on the slick gymnasium floor. Bobby leaped over her, grinning.

Candy's eyes were battened on them both. That was O.K. What worried me was the *way* she watched. She was deaf to the puerile music and indifferent to the idiot plot—the *machinery* of the thing. For her there was only Bobby and Lee Ann out there in the cruel light, spinning and flying, smiles blazing at the camera. She stared at them for long minutes after the dance sequence finished, at Lee Ann towelling her hair, at Bobby drinking Gatorade from a checkerboard thermos. Bobby threw her a wink. She smiled.

I touched her shoulder. "Dinner tonight?"

"I guess so," she said.

2.

Later l took her driving.

I drive a second-hand Jeep CJ I bought from a guy at a hardship sale in '81. I've done some work on it. It goes pretty good. If I sold it, maybe I could meet the payments on my trailer.

Because Clapham is a small town, it is easy to leave. I drove out along the arc of the interstate. We lowered our shades against the setting sun and let the hot wind tug at us. Candy did not seem talkative, and for a time we just drove. I had in mind parking out by the quarry, smoking some back-of-tracks homegrown, and renewing the friendship. It was a ritual we had established long ago. Drive out to the quarry and *not* talk about the Texaco station, her restaurant job, the bric-a-brac of our ordinary lives. Play the radio instead. Dance by moonlight. Make love on the sandy verge of the quarry pit or under the dark trees: we had done that.

But—as it happened—not tonight.

We were passing the Travelodge where some of the movie people were billeted, when Candy spotted Teddy Taylor's business truck pulling into the lot. "Slow down a minute," she said.

I should explain that we hated Teddy with the fervor of the oppressed. He ran Clapham's only laundry business, pick-up and delivery. You would see him behind the counter, thirty-five years old, 250 pounds moving somehow sweatlessly through the miasma of high summer and steam heat. He was relentlessly suspicious of the back-of-tracks people who occasionally, like Candy, came in with

67

a work uniform to be laundered. Cash in advance. It was humiliating.

Since June, Teddy had been picking up laundry from both the motels and telling endless and queasily suggestive stories about it. Handkerchiefs and underwear, Teddy said: show him those two items, and he'd tell you anything about a person. It disturbed me especially because it seemed to reflect Clapham's response to the arrival of the movie people, the way we used them to glamorize ourselves. But I could not say that to Candy.

The road was empty. I drove up on the shoulder and put the Jeep in neutral.

"Steamcleaner to the stars," I said.

Teddy was climbing out the back of his van with a big brown-paper bundle. Candy said, "What do you suppose he's got?"

"Bobby's bikini briefs."

"Yeah?"

"Lee Ann's training bra."

She dimpled. "Compared to me, maybe."

Then Teddy, manoeuvring his own bulk down from the van, lost his footing and grabbed for support. The big laundry bundle flew out of his hands, and when it hit the black top, the taut brown waxed paper burst open; a wildflower of laundry blossomed out. We were a football field away, but we could hear Teddy's profanities over the rumble of the Jeep.

A wind had come up. Teddy moved over the parking lot like a manic linebacker, tackling clothes. It was a great show, and we watched it happily until the dusk came down and Teddy, still cursing, had thrown everything into the back of his truck and slammed the door on it.

He passed us headed back to Clapham at about ninety-five miles per.

I put my hand on the gearshift.

"No," Candy said suddenly. "Look. He missed something."

It was hard to see in the gathering darkness, but I looked where she pointed, and saw something flimsy swirl up past the heated azure pool of the Travelodge and into the dry hills beyond. Candy put her head on my knee. "Indian, let's get it."

I looked to see if she was serious. "Souvenir?"

"Yeah. Maybe. See how the other half lives." She was in an odd and mischievous mood. "Come on, Indian!"

I shrugged and parked the Jeep.

I liked these old, dry hills. I had come up here often when I was little. My father would take me up.

He didn't talk to me about his past. I found out much later he had been a Kiowa Road Man for a long part of his life, in Quanah Parker's old and notorious church, the peyote church. I do not know if this is relevant. It reflects, I guess, his connection with what we would call the supernatural; and I have heard a rumor that he was barred from the Native American Church in Oklahoma on suspicion of being a witch. Maybe. He never spoke of it. I remember one time—I could not have been more than five—I found his rosary of mescal beads in a dresser drawer and began to play with it. He took it away, not angrily but firmly, and I realized, I think, even then, that there were parts of his life that meant a great deal to him but that he could not share with me or with my mother.

He spoke impeccable and educated English. Most of my vocabulary I picked up from him. It used to irritate my teachers, who believed—on the basis of my ethnicity and, to be charitable, my childhood stutter—that I ought to be illiterate. (My essays were subject to grave suspicion: had I plagiarized them?) More than this, though, he imparted to me a sense of the larger world.

I do not mean specifically the cities and oceans that lie beyond the horizon. I mean "the big world"—his words.

He would take me out to these hills in our old Ford pickup.

Summer or winter, day or night. I think it frightened my mother. She loved this strange man she had married (over fearsome family objections), but she was also a little jealous of the communication between us. I think she half suspected that he was indoctrinating me into some secret ritual. Maybe he was. He once said, "It's an old gift." And smiled. "In the family."

The wind, he would say.

It surged across these low, barren hills from the west. Cold sometimes and sometimes warm; almost always dry. Face it, and it would sweep the moisture from your skin. Think, he said sternly, how far it comes. Over that knife-edged prairie horizon it comes. From the Badlands, he said, where monsters are buried. From far places beyond that. From the ocean. From China. The wind, he said: you think it doesn't *notice*? But you can't travel that far and *not* notice. The wind isn't stupid. The wind pays attention. The wind knows more than you know.

"Talk to it," he said.

I was young enough to take him literally. "That's dumb," I said.

"Like this," he said, and I felt his big hand tighten on mine.

He called down a whirlwind.

It was a dust devil. A tiny one. It swept up the hillside, brown and playful. It spun three times around us. When it moved toward me, I jumped back, frightened. But the wind was timid, too.

I turned to look at my father. His name was Spencer. For no obvious reason, it struck me then that he had a name. Spencer Hokeah. My given name was Jack, but even then all my friends called me Indian. My father, Spencer Hokeah, familiar and foreign, looked at me and smiled. "You try it," he said.

I was helpless. I was not even certain he had done what he appeared to have done. The wind? Was this possible?

"Shh," he said. "Be still a minute. Just listen to it."

Curious, I made myself relax.

The only sound was the wind in the prairie grass and in the scrub trees, a hissing compounded of a thousand voices. I listened carefully and watched my father. He nodded.

I thought about what he had said. It had come a long way, the wind. It was already a thousand years old, I thought, when it carried the thunderheads in from the ocean. It whirled as high as the stars. It had lived winters and summers, cold and hot. It had kissed the moisture from desert wastes vaster than this dull sky around me. It was—and I felt this with an enormity I cannot communicate—the *wind*.

And I began to sense what my father meant.

He smiled as if I had said the words aloud. "Right," he said.

"Here," I breathed.

It was much less than a word; but the wind—recognized and somehow recognizing—began to focus around me.

It plucked at the turned-up cuffs of my jeans. Wild, it carried my hair back.

"Here!" I said.

A gust from some ancient dry barranca whipped my face.

"Here!"

The bent trees bent lower. The prairie grass flailed at the sky. I was aware of clouds tumbling over the horizon now, miles and miles distant. I *felt* them—the wet density of them. The electricity of them. The chafing of ions from the dust-dry land beneath.

Far off, lightning cracked down. Bitter droplets of rain spattered against us.

"Easy," my father said. (Spencer Hokeah said.)

My clothes whipped tight against my body. My good baseball cap had flown away. My father stood firm against what was, obviously now, an oncoming storm. Feeling it, I was suddenly frightened.

He picked me up.

The wind abated.

"It's O.K.," he said, the words a growling in his chest. "But powerful, you understand? Strong and strange. No matter how big you get, it's bigger. That's how life is. The world. It's bigger than you are. You talk to it, right? But it's always always bigger than you are."

I nodded against his body.

"One day," he said, "it will kill you."

I thought he meant me—me particularly. I huddled into his chest.

But that wasn't what he meant.

Five years later it killed him. Not the wind: the big world. It was a laryngeal cancer, and it made him mute before it choked him. This seemed terrible to me, unbearable, unendurable. He had been the pivot of my life; his disappearance—into silence and finally into death—was deeply shocking. It mystified me that he retained, in his profound illness, the strength to smile. But he *did* smile. He would smile. He would smile and clutch my hand. Before he lost the power of speech, he told me, "You are important, Jack. You matter."

As if *that* were the issue.

I think now that he was facing death the way he faced the wind: feeling its power and its inevitability, the mystery of it—talking to it. He could not veer it away from him any more than he could harness a tornado or soften the cold heart of a thunderstorm. But he could make it dance a little.

"He suffered," the doctor told me, "far less than he had any right to."

Dancing, I thought. Yeah.

We watched the item of laundry flit over a rise and out of sight behind it. "Getting dark," I said.

Candy hesitated. At night these hills seem to buck up; the valleys deepen. There is not much ambient light out west of Clapham. The motels, the town itself a couple of miles away, the moon—that's about it. "Just over the rise," she said. "Then we go back."

"You're crazy," I said. "You know that? Chasing somebody's goddamn underwear...."

"We're both crazy." We topped the ridge.

It was caught on the branch of a scrubby tree where the wind had left it. We came up short. I stared.

Candy drew in her breath. "Sweet Jesus," she said, "will you look at this?" But I was already looking.

It was a peignoir, she explained—"A kind of night-gown. A woman's thing."

"There's not much to it."

"There's not supposed to be much of it." She took a step closer, mesmerized. "Indian," she said, "it's *gorgeous*. Even dusty and all. I wonder who it belongs to?"

But we had the same thought: *Lee Ann*.

We sat down on the stony soil as if we were kids. After a time I said, "We should give it back."

"No." She shook her head. "We can't even let on we've seen it. It's private. You can tell." She gazed up longingly. "It's what she is. That peignoir. That's *her* up there. Fragile. Beautiful...."

73

"Expensive," I said.

"Expensive." She turned to look at me, strangely serious. There was enough light to see her lips pulled taut. "That, too. And you know what hurts, Indian? I'll never own anything like that."

It was the kind of thing we had agreed never to say; it made me sorry we had come out here. "Sure you will."

"No," she said. "Shit, no. I'll be buying blouses at Kresges for the rest of my life. I'm beginning to understand that." She sighed. "They live a different life, Indian. They come from a different place, and they live a different life."

She looked up at the nightgown. It hung against the dark sky like a rebuke, a bright feather from an exotic bird, scathingly feminine against the desolation of the hills and the night. "We don't get that kind of stuff. We just don't ever get that."

"Come on, Candy. We're special, remember?"

"Right. Special. But—" She nodded in the direction of the motels. "Not as special as *they* are."

A gust of wind fluttered the fragile peignoir. It waved from the tree branch like a conqueror's flag.

The wind seemed to make Candy nervous. "Let's go," she said. "Let's drive."

We hurried away.

3.

Not quite a week later, over dinner at the Country Kitchen, she asked me what I would think if she went out on a date—just one time—with Bobby Angle.

The question was not frivolous. I settled back into the vinylette booth and thought about it. Outside the plate-glass restaurant window, the cars were parked in neat diagonals.

I thought about Bobby and Candy. I had seen them

74

together a couple of times at the school. He had smiled at her; she had smiled at him. I said, "Has he asked you?"

"If he did," Candy persisted, "what would you say?"

"I would say you're too good for him."

"That's sweet, Indian."

"I mean it."

She shook her head. "You don't know him."

"I know you."

"I'm no big deal."

She said it with a bleak, offhanded conviction. It made me think of what she had said in the brown hills back of the Travelodge: "Not as special as *they* are."

"We made promises," I said. "Remember?"

"I never promised I wouldn't go out with Bobby Angle."

"I don't mean that." I was getting angry. "Christ, Candy. All our lives, people have been trying to put us in our place. The pissant Taft aristocracy—the jocks and the debs. They counted; we didn't. Except, we said, Fuck it. *We* counted. *We* were special. And I believed that. I *still* believe it. Now these movie people come into town, and suddenly everybody wants to shine their goddamn shoes. The *jocks* want to shine their shoes." I was honestly baffled. "Why?"

"They'll put us on the map, Indian. That's what everybody says."

"We're *on* the goddamn map."

"It's different. It's not high school anymore."

"No. It's the movies. So?"

She shook her head sadly. "It's the real world. *They're* the real world."

"So what does that make us?"

She stood up and put down some pocket change for the waitress. She ran her hand once through her hair.

"Extras," she said.

75

I hated her for saying it.

We walked separately to work. On the set, I saw her with Bobby a couple of times. I wondered if the anger I felt was jealousy, or purely jealousy. Some of that, yes, of course. But I was equally disturbed by the way she had devalued herself: the way she was clinging to Bobby Angle, the whole movie thing, as if this were the last chance to inject some significance into her life.

In the afternoon, Lee Ann, Bobby's co-star, came over to where I was leaning against the hot brick wall of the school. She handed me a Diet Coke and said, "Does it bother you?"

I stared at her. "What?"

"Bobby and your girlfriend. I saw you watching. Is it a problem for you?"

It was an outrageous question. I didn't know how to answer. She sipped at her straw and said, "Because it's not serious. I just wanted to tell you that. Bobby just likes flirting. He has an ego problem."

"Flirting." I said.

She nodded earnestly.

She was in wardrobe. A tight sweater. She was lithe, supple, and two inches shorter than I. I could have picked her up. I said, "Are you flirting?"

Her smile widened. "Could be, cowboy."

"Indian," I said.

"Whatever. Well, you know, I have a thing with Bobby. You probably noticed. But we're not monogamous. It's open." She took another pull at the Coke. "We're out of here in two weeks. Then, whatever he has going with your girlfriend, it's finished. It's over. So don't worry too much about it."

"I won't," I said.

"Who knows," she said. "Might be some fringe benefits in it for you."

I said that might be nice.

Of course, he did ask her out.

I do not know what motivated him. Perhaps it was what Lee Ann had suggested: a kind of egotism, the blind need for a worshipful audience. Or maybe a kind of misplaced noblesse oblige. He may have thought he was doing her a favor.

It doesn't matter. What matters is that the exposed the raw nerve of her secret fear, the fear of her own insignificance. And that was a bad and dangerous thing to do.

"He asked nicely," Candy reassured me. "He really did. Dinner and drinks, he said."

"And you accepted."

We were back at the Country Kitchen. The air was hot as only September can be hot, the smouldering butt-end of a relentless summer. The wind scoured dust down the intestate. Half the town had been invited out to fill the Taft bleachers for the final filming, a football sequence, and their obedient cheering washed the streets with a sound like surf.

Candy made a little speech. "We're nothing," she said. "You better think about that, Indian. Because we've been fooling ourselves, and that's not good." She waved at the window. "We're nowhere. We're beyond the borders. In ten or fifteen years, this town won't *be* here. Just big company farms. Or dust. As far as most people are concerned, we don't exist *now*. We're nothing people in a nothing town, and that's the truth."

"Bobby told you that?"

"Bobby didn't have to." She balled her fist. "I have one chance, Indian... one chance at little glory, before I get old and fat and stupid like everyone else in this town. One chance! And you can't tell me not to take it."

77

I didn't even try. Maybe that was a mistake.

"So yes," she said "He asked me nicely. And I accepted."

She said it defiantly, but I detected under that a sour note of resignation... as if she could sense, out beyond the hot horizon of her life, the bulk of winter moving.

There were promises we both had made. I should emphasize that. She thought—and maybe, at the time, I thought—that the issue was fidelity. Would she sleep with Bobby Angle? Would I sleep with Lee Ann Morgan?

But, as Candy had pointed out, those weren't the important promises. The infidelities we committed that summer were both subtler and far more profound.

The night she went off with Bobby, I got drunk.

Around nine, somebody knocked at the door of my trailer. I opened the door and recognized Lee Ann. She had on tight Levi's and a cowgirl blouse—her idea of shitkicker clothes. Her lipstick was scarlet, her eyeshadow like a bruise. It was laughable. "Hi, Indian," she said.

I gave her credit for remembering my name.

She stepped inside the narrow trailer. The room was a mess. Old clothes on the floor, beer bottles stacked in the sink, paperback novels on every horizontal surface. "Hard to find your way out here," she said.

"I like my solitude," I said.

She looked at me. "Tying one on?"

"Trying to."

"You want company?"

"What the hell."

We drank awhile. She sat in my big easy chair with her feet up, regarding me coolly. Drunkenly insolent, I passed her the bottle; she put it to her lips. No problem with that. "Thanks," she said.

"Don't make yourself sick."

"I don't get sick." She drank aggressively; the look on her face as she tilted up the bottle was thoughtful.

After a while she said, "I think he really does want to screw her."

"You mean Bobby?"

"Bobby and Candy. God, doesn't it sound awful? 'Bobby and Candy.' Christ."

I rolled around the names a few times. "You said he does this a lot."

"He does. I don't mind sometimes. Really. But sometimes it pisses me off."

"Pisses *you* off?"

"You're not the only one, cowboy."

I didn't bother to correct her.

We talked some more. She told me about her family. Her father operated a defense-contract factory somewhere in the San Fernando Valley; she had a brother at Annapolis and a sister at Bryn Mawr. "Daddy wasn't too thrilled when I went into acting. But he came around. The important thing, he says, is to do it well." She pulled at the bottle. "I could be a star. I know that for a fact."

"I thought you were a star."

"This shitty project? Yeah, right. But it's work. There are two things you can be, Daddy says: a success and a failure. So—so—" She lost track of herself. She gave the bottle back. "I would like to be a success with Bobby. I really would."

We fell into silence. After a while I said, "Look, I'll drive you home."

"It's O.K., Indian. I like it here."

"I don't."

She shrugged. We climbed into her car, one of the MGM cars; I slipped behind the wheel. It was a hot night, but the air was moving; there were stars. I detected a flash of heat lightning way off beyond the margin of the sky. We drove out the interstate, and there was no traffic, only a couple of transport rigs screaming down the night, and I drove carefully but too fast. We came into the parking lot of the Travelodge, and I did a ninety-degree skid on the greasy black top. "Wow," Lee Ann said respectfully. She had the bottle balanced in her hand.

She started for the motel, tugging my hand. I tugged back. Not there. "This way," I said.

She peered out into the dark, low hills and shivered once. "Spooky," she said.

"It's O.K.," I said.

I thought of Candy and Bobby, maybe together in one of those darkened rooms. I thought of promises made and promises broken.

We stumbled over a couple of scrub dunes and then sat down in the darkness with our backs to the motel, the interstate, the town: facing the open parabola of the sky. "You are weird, cowboy," she said, and kissed me once. It was a Hollywood kiss, prolonged and insincere. I returned it with a certain drunken fervor, but after a time she pulled away.

"I'm sorry," she said. "I'm just thinking of Bobby."

I told her I understood.

We drank some more. I said, "I took Candy up here once."

She looked at me, her eyes half closed. She smiled knowingly. "Yeah?"

"We were kids," I said. "She was fourteen. I was fifteen. I wanted to impress her." I lay back with my hand behind my head. "I was back-of-tracks. Does that mean anything to you? She was, too; but I was Indian, I had this stutter—"

"Not too cool," Lee Ann said.

"Right. So I took her up here. I wanted to matter. I

guess I wanted her to love me. We sat awhile in the grass. I didn't know what to say. Finally I just told her to watch."

Lee Ann's eyelids drifted down. She said sleepily, "Watch *what*?"

I gulped at the bottle. Drunkenly, I concentrated.

A breeze came swooping out of the clear night sky.

It felt good. It was like meeting an old and well-loved friend. I felt it like a thrill through me: *the big world*.

I held the wind in my fist and told Lee Ann what I had told Candy those years ago. "There's a lot in the world nobody notices. Sun, sky, wind, rain. You don't pay attention. But it's out there; it's always out there. And if you listen just right—and if you use the right words—you can talk to it."

"Talk to it," Lee Ann said hazily.

But I was caught up in the memory.

I had been fifteen—it was the majority of a decade ago, not long after my father died—but I must have felt in Candy even then her yearning for significance, her pressing need to *matter*. And I suppose I thought it would satisfy her, the trick I could do with the wind. It would demonstrate my specialness.

She listened to me talk, and waited, curious, not understanding, while I called down the wind. It was a sunny blue day, but there was a storm due; I could feel it. I urged it closer. She sat with her sundress pooled around her legs and watched the clouds skirl up from the horizon. Before long, she began to sense something unusual happening. Ozone filled the air; she looked at me strangely. "Indian," she said, "shouldn't we get under cover?"

I shook my head. "It can't hurt us."

It was a special and spectacular storm I conjured for her. Lightning strobed around us. The wind veered and danced. The frontal wave carried a surf of dust and vagrant papers; I made it dance in tiny vortices around us. I became so intent on the course of the weather that I did not see the fear growing in Candy's eyes, did not notice when it blossomed into frank terror.

She knew it was me. There was no confusion. "Indian," she said.

I grinned, intoxicated.

"Stop it," she said.

It caught me off guard. Wasn't she amazed, delighted, impressed? Wasn't this a wonderful trick I could do?

But I looked more closely at her and saw that she was trembling under the wide gray-green meridian of the sky. "Indian," she said rigidly, "stop it. I don't know what you're doing, but stop it *right now*!"

My mouth fell open. The wind died.

There was a brief stillness then, an uneasy silence.

"Whatever this is," she said stiffly—the word etched like ice in the motionless air—"I don't want you to do it again. It scares me. Promise, Indian! I *mean* it."

I wanted to explain to her. In town, I wanted to say, I'm nothing, You know what that's like. But out here it's different. Out here is the big world. And in the big world there is nothing but cold and hot, life and death, wind and water.

Out here we mattered just as much as anybody in town—and just as little. Because this was the big world (Spencer Hokeah had taught me the words), and the big world is where we all live and die.

But it scared her. She was scared of magic, and she was scared of the big world.

"Promise," she said fiercely.

I didn't understand. I wanted only to soothe her. I had frightened her, and I was ashamed.

I promised. I would not talk to the wind. (And the voice of the wind, like the voice of a jilted lover, grew cold and still inside me.)

We had not spoken of it since.

The storm I conjured for Lee Ann was fine. All the summer's pent-up heat rose around us in a thunderhead that occluded all the western stars. Lee Ann had passed out with the bottle cradled in her lap, but it didn't matter. I took a deep and personal pleasure in the wild gymnastics of wind and lightning. I spoke to the storm, and I danced with it. I think, if I had asked, it would have picked me up and flown me over the Travelodge. I spoke the storm's secret name (all storms have names, as all clouds have geographies) and I felt the powerful engine beating at the heart of it, moist air boiling up from the prairie blankness, expanding explosively, shedding its hoarded moisture. There is a tremendous potency, my father once said, in great energies too long contained.

It was my own act of infidelity... my own choice of secret lover.

If Lee Ann was aware of what I had done—the breaking of a promise or the conjuring of a storm—she was too drunk to react. The rain washed over her in torrents until at last she blinked her eyes and sat up. "Hey," she said. "It's *raining*."

I walked her to the motel. It was a good storm, I wanted to say. A storm for Candy. And for Lee Ann, too, in a way—for her unfaithful lover Bobby Angle and her munitions-factory dad and for her sister at Bryn Mawr and her brother at Annapolis. A storm for her fear of failure; because—I wanted to tell her—out here in the big world, we are ultimately all equal.

But she was like Candy: driven by her fears. She wouldn't have understood.

I watched her disappear into the yellow light of the lobby, small and wet and too much alone.

* * *

Candy found me out in the dark hills an hour later.

Maybe she met Lee Ann in Bobby's room; maybe Lee Ann told her where to find me. Or maybe she just knew.

The storm was over. The air was wet and clean with the passing of it. A cool wind followed from the western horizon, and it cut like autumn and it smelled like winter.

I could tell by her face she had been crying.

She didn't say anything for a while. She look up at the ragged sky and asked in a small voice, "Did you do that?"

"I helped," I said.

She nodded, assimilating this information.

I said, "How'd it go with you and Bobby?"

"Not too good," she said, and her face wrinkled as if she might cry again.

I put an arm around her to comfort her, but she shrugged it away.

"I did what he wanted, Indian. Shouldn't that count for something?"

"Everything," I said quietly.

"I did what he wanted. And then we were lying there in his room." She hid her face from me. "I asked him if he would take me away with him. You know what he said? He said, 'Get real.'" Her voice was plaintive, pained. "Get real! What kind of shitty thing is that to say to a person?"

I said I didn't know.

She turned toward me, hugging herself. "You can still do it, can't you? The thing with the wind."

I nodded.

"I think I envy you, Indian. You like it out here, right? You can live out here. But I can't. I need the town. I need people to like me."

She needed glamour, which was what Bobby had to offer. I did not say what I thought: that glamour is an illusion, and that everybody touched by it—Candy, Bobby, Lee Ann—is doomed to play the role of an extra.

Her expression hardened. "Don't you tell anybody about this, Indian! Don't *ever* tell anybody."

"I won't," I said. "I promise."

It was the last promise we would make each other.

She turned to leave. As she walked away, I saw something flutter through the air behind her.

It was the tattered rag of Lee Ann's lost peignoir, torn by the elements and by the storm. The storm had battered it down to a pale fragment of itself; Candy did not even look up as the vagrant wind swirled it past her.

The movie people pulled out on schedule, one week into September. Candy came out to the Texaco to watch their Winnebagos winding away, but we did not speak.

In '85 she married a local guy named Tom Harlow. Tom runs the hardware store in Clapham. The store was bought out by a chain, but Tom stayed on to manage, so they do all right. I see them sometimes out at the station.

Everybody still remembers her as the girl who dated Bobby Angle. She encourages it. Nothing overt, but she smiles and tilts her head. She is, by local standards, very much a celebrity.

I hope it is enough for her. She seems happy. I saw her with Tom when *High School Confidential* premiered at the Rialto; she was laughing at some joke of his. But it seemed to me there was a note of hysteria in the laughter.

As for me—I hope to have the trailer paid off soon. Then, who knows? Sky's the limit.

And of course the wind still blows through here.

Still it speaks. It whispers. You are special, it says. You are special, this place is special; you are immortal, you have lived forever, you will live forever.

I call down fogs in autumn, ice storms in the bitter

bleak of winter. I dance with dust devils and dry summer thermals. I stand beneath the stars and gaze at the stars, and the wind whispers the secret names of the stars.

And I grieve sometimes for Candy—and for Lee Ann, and even for Bobby—whose heart were needlessly broken, and who loved something much more fickle than the wind.

THE OTHERS

Dave Duncan

200,000

> Somewhere in sunny Africa
> a girl child flirts.
> Can they guess her destiny,
> the boys at her side?
> Do they see her as different
> from the others?

100,000

> We come out of Africa,
> her children.
> We are better than the lesser folk,
> the other folk, the old folk.
> They are stupid,
> they are clumsy,
> they mumble and are slow.
> They are other.
> They are different.
> They are bad stock to breed.
> In fire and flood and famine
> we survive and overcome
> with superior technology
> and weapons.

50,000

> They come no more a-begging
> in good times or bad.
>> They haunt the woods no more,
>> only our dreams.

5,000

> Her children move into town.
> The dreams come too.

500

> Three sails out of the dawn
> and her children
>> have circled
>> the earth.

50

> Belsen
> Dresden
>> Hiroshima

EQUINOX

Yves Meynard

Our Son, who will make the Heavens
We journey in thy Name
Deliver us from the emptiness of the Dark
And grant us safe passage to other spheres
Into a world in our image
Amen

If you stand at a high place in Montreal, at night, and look toward the apse, you can glimpse Control City, like a tiny chip of diamond, glinting in the mists of the core. From any city farther aft—from Cairo, from Reykjavik, from New York—Control is invisible, a mere tale. But from Montreal one can see it, and know it for real, as real as the siderophages who come in the night to gnaw at the pylons: something seen but never touched.

I have seen Control often: my mother and I lived in a house not far behind the parish church, and many times I managed to climb up the bell tower after Vespers, ignoring Father Nathaniel's remonstrances. Mother would have punished me if she had known, but she had nothing to fear: I never leaned out of the window, gazed only from within the tower walls at that pinpoint of light whose true shape—which is a cross—I told myself I could distinguish.

They say Ship is so large that one could walk all one's life along the nave toward the choir and never reach it; that it would be one's great-grandchildren who would finally reach the walls of Control City, and pound on the uranium valves in the vain hope of being admitted.

The angels dwell in Control City, and travel from there to any point in Ship like a fleeting thought. Once an angel came to our parish. I saw him myself, in the space of time between two instants, a great form with wings of light like frozen explosions of brilliance; and for that aching moment within a moment, I wished he had come for me, to take me to Control, even if it meant losing all that I had known before. I would have dreams, many days after seeing the angel, in which I entered the gates of uranium, opened the ten thousand seals on the ten thousand locks to reach the altar at the center of the City, in which stands the great wheel from which Ship is steered toward the beginning of all things.

The dreams never came true; but I have in fact lost all that I knew, all that mattered to me, and gained nothing in return.

In catechesis we were taught that people belong to either good or evil. That, although we might refer to them by metaphor as white or black, we must never call them light or dark: for the light that shines from the spine of Ship shines for evil and good both; and the Dark also is neither good nor evil, but the absence of everything. We were told the disposition of Ship, and all the many kinds of outdwellers. We were told the laws, the proper rites of worship, the worth of money and the legends of Earth.

But I know now there are lies in catechesis. And if they have lied to us, if they have lied about the most important part of our world, if they have lied to us about ourselves, how am I to know there was a single truth in the teachings?

On the day I was to become a woman I went to the dreaming field on the margins of the city to await the night. Had I been a wealthy woman's daughter, I might have hired a car, or at the least a hackney. But a washerwoman's daughter had to walk. Our house was not very far from the field; still I walked from Nones nearly to Vespers. The streets curved and twisted; whole neighbourhoods of shanties had been built in the middle of the wider avenues and constricted traffic as an emerged rock does the water in a stream. Ours is a city of nearly two million souls now, and it has grown crowded since Ship's launch.

Once I had reached the dreaming field, I walked a while through it, searching for an isolated place. There are always many young people there, some of whom come with entire families in full pomp, others alone and furtive. Though the field borders the realms of evil, outdwellers are forbidden to harm any who stand in it.

This time the crowd was not too large, and I did not need to seek long. Once I had chosen my place, I lay down on my back. I could not see Control City—by day it is lost in the light and the mists—and yet I fancied I could detect a tiny pale spot right where it should be. Port and starboard the ground cradled me and rose up beyond the horizon, vanishing behind the blaze of the spine. I looked straight up, my lids almost closed against the light, until I saw tiny shapes moving about it. One moment I decided they were specks of dust not far above me, then that they were inside my eyes, then that they were flitting around the spine and were thus vast beyond conception. At this last imagining, I felt a deliciously terrifying vertigo, as if I stood in danger of falling, falling ever upward toward the spine, to be consumed in light, and be, for a moment, like the angel I had once seen.

I watched until my eyes hurt from the light and then,

just as I was about to fully close my lids, day ended: the blaze abated, scaled from white-yellow through green into blue, indigo, died down into the violet. I caught a brief glimpse of the lands on the other side of Ship, which are normally invisible. The bells of the city sounded, curiously muffled. It was dark. The dream-time came.

I lay still on the ground. Not far to my right, metal emerged from the earth and grass to form a square pedestal, out of which grew a small pylon; the transformers were already budding on it, and still-transparent strands of wire were waving in the evening breeze. I put my ear against the ground; I heard a faint thrum. The drive, they say, is a small sun Ship has harnessed. At the core of the sun there is a piece of the ultimate Dark; the infalling matter propels us. I thought at that moment that maybe it was the scream of that fall I heard, resonating through the whole of Ship.

I felt very small then, and fancied I could feel Ship's rotation, that gives us weight, carrying me around and around. I clasped my hands together, and waited. This was the night that would decide whether I belonged to good or evil. In the cities and villages good rules, and children are raised for good, while outside it is the reverse. But whether in the towns or outside, when children become adults, they go off to stay alone for an entire night, waiting for dreams to come and show them which side they belong to.

My brother Johann left us long ago; he went away to the dreaming field, but he did not return. I was still a little girl then. He had kissed me and pinched my cheek before leaving, and promised me he'd buy me a toy on his way back. He hadn't yet finished growing; I remember his bony wrists protruded from his shirtsleeves, and his pants uncovered his ankles. He set his worn cap at a jaunty angle, and waved us goodbye as he went down the street.

The next morning the house was strangely quiet. I was reminded of the day of my father's death, and even though I was old enough to know the difference, I still felt chilled. Mother dressed me up in holiday clothes that didn't fit anymore, and forbade me to play.

The morning passed. When the bells rang for Sext, Mother simply said "He's been delayed. He'll be here presently." She had arranged the table for him, bringing out the vase with its three roses, one blue, one green, one the warm brown of photographs. We had meat in the pot, for once, and she had pulled special dishes out of a small cupboard. When the bells rang Nones, she said "He's in the tavern, celebrating with his friends. That boy!" and put the pot on the fire again. I whined and begged to be fed; she cuffed me to silence.

When Vespers tolled, she pushed her chair by the window, sat down and stared out, unmoving. My belly hurt so much I didn't notice it anymore. Once night had fallen, I took hold of her hand, got her up, put her to bed. I stowed away the vase and the nice dishes. I took the pot from the fire and desperately stuffed myself with the meat, but it was stringy and half-spoiled, and made me sick during the night.

Mother never spoke of Johann again, and the next day moved me into his room as if it had always been mine. He had left to become a siderophage, some of my friends said later; others fancied a cannibal or a knight. I hoped it was the last: knights build castles amid the mountains and go to battle carrying banners emblazoned with animals from dead Earth; cannibals go naked, their skin stained with their own filth, and in the darkness they huddle together and gnaw on charred bones.

I saw a movement to my left; I tried to turn my head,

but it would not move. Then my whole body spun on its axis as Ship does, and I knew I had entered a dream. I floated a hand-span above the ground, saw a man approach me. He wore armor over his whole body, lacquered dead black. I tried to see his face, but though the visor of his helm was raised, I could not. He bore a strange object; it had a stem that coiled around his hand at one end, terminating at the other in a shiny ball, like a child's toy. I knew in the dream that it was a weapon. He held it high above me. My body pivoted again, so that I floated belly-up. I could see the spine glowing dimly in violet, intersected by the silhouette of his arm holding the weapon. He started to bring it down upon me; but before he could complete the stroke, I opened my eyes. The spine's glare filled my sight, ascending from red through orange into white-gold.

I stood up. The dream—I could not tell what it meant. The man had been in black, thus evil. Did it mean I was of that kind? Yet, he had not welcomed me, he had seemed to want to harm me; was he therefore my enemy—was I white?

And then I looked at the city. Walls had sprung up around Montreal, but they were made of glass and I could see through them; and I saw that the city was empty. The buildings had turned brittle and cracked, some had half-crumbled into the street. No one lived there anymore. The ground at my feet was a mere scattering of dirt over the metal. Cold. The air was unthinkably cold. I looked aft and there was a gaping hole at the stern, the Dark come in at last, for its final victory. Not glass, the walls, then, but ice. My breath made diamonds in the air.

All at once, the light of the spine cooled and dimmed: Ship was dying. At the apse, Control City winked once and vanished. All turned to gloom. Yet there was one place from which light still came; whether good or evil, it was *life*, and I started to run toward it. But the more I ran, the slower I went and the farther away I realised the light was; until I could not take a single step, and knew exactly how distant my destination was: far, far up the port curve of Ship, many days' journey, at the end of a road long overgrown, up on a bluff overlooking a narrow river, in a large house of gray stone and metal....

I opened my eyes. The spine's glare filled my sight, ascending from red through orange into white-gold. I fell down—I had been standing in my dream—and pain jarred through me. Still, I pinched myself hard enough to bruise; I feared an infinite regress of dreams. But I was awake.

I set across the dreaming field. In the near distance, I saw newly-made men and women walking toward the city, some timidly, some boldly. One young man was slinking in the opposite direction, keeping his head close to the ground and repeatedly bursting into strangled laughter. I stood and watched him vanish into the distance.

I came back to the house. Mother's eyes were frightening; I understood that a part of her had been prepared to expunge all memories of myself, should I fail to return. I recounted a dream I had invented for myself on the way back: of having a cherub with a golden wand touch me and declare me a woman. She smiled a near-to-breaking smile, made me sit down to eat. She had set the table for three.

I went to see Father Nathaniel as soon as I could. It was not long before Nones. I knocked shakily on the rectory door. He opened the door and ushered me in himself.

He had me sit down in the big armchair of black velvet reserved to the grown-ups; he offered me cookies and tea, which I had to refuse. The pendulum of the rectory clock clanged softly. The hands, as always, ran backwards.

"So—You are a woman now," he said.

At this I started weeping. "No, Father," I gasped. "I'm not."

He made his voice soothing. "I understand. Everyone goes through something like this. You do not really feel different, but—"

"No! I am *not* a woman! The dream did not say what I was. I wasn't chosen!" The full horror of it had not struck me until that moment.

Father Nathaniel calmed me down and got me to tell the whole story. When I had finished, there was a long silence.

"You have been summoned," he said at last. "Your destination is outside the cities, and might thus be considered evil. But from what you tell me, it is clearly a monastery to which you have been summoned, which must constitute a bastion of white in the midst of black."

He did not look as certain as his words implied; yet he went on. "There is no doubt but that you must go there at once. I will tell your mother I have prescribed a retreat for you, so she will not worry."

He went to a desk and pulled a thin frame from a wide drawer. "Look," he said, laying it on the desk. "It covers only a small part of this particular octant of Ship. In Control they have one, it is said, that contains all of Ship and displays it all at once."

It was a map, enclosed by varnished wood, covered by a pane of nearly invisible glass. It had been made by a master limner; Montreal and the fields around it were in gorgeous, luminous colours, incredibly detailed. It made me dizzy to look at it; I could easily fancy myself a harpy planing in the upper reaches of the sky.

"See," he said, "that village is Roanne, and that is the road the trucks follow. Was it the road you took?"

"I—think so. Yes, if the apse is that way. It went up the

curve. There were hills—If the map was larger, I could tell better."

And then I fell into the sky, and drowned in my own screams.

I was sitting in the chair again, but my muscles spasmed as in a fall, and I wailed like an infant as Father Nathaniel held me. After a while I grew calmer, but could not stop shivering.

"I am so sorry," he said, "the map understood your remark as a command. The effect can be disturbing if you are not forewarned."

I stared blankly at him, still shaking.

"The image is not bound by the frame, you see. That is merely for convenience. The map tried to accommodate you by growing larger. Lacking other specifications, it filled the whole room. I should have warned you. It is my fault that you thought you were falling. Pray forgive me."

"It can think?"

"A little. It knows a few words. Can you stand to look at it now?"

"It won't move, will it?"

"No. I have ordered it to stay fixed."

I managed to approach the map. Just looking at it made me reel, but I eventually found a road going from a village named Adrianople to one called Davenport and thence to my destination.

"But why does it show the road so well?" I asked. "In my dream, it was so overgrown you could barely see it. Is it an old map?"

"All of them are," he said, as if embarrassed.

I returned with him to my house, and he delivered his falsehood to Mother. Anyone could have seen he lied, yet she believed him and let me go without compunction. I was very much afraid she would not remember me when

97

—if—I returned.

I went back to the church, and Father Nathaniel gave me a small pack, filled it with bread, cheese, a strip of dried meat. He added a flask of water, in case I found no streams, and a little bone knife. He gave me a few painful minutes' worth of vague advice. Then, somewhat flustered, he declared there was no reason for me to wait any longer, and led me out the door.

When I turned back for one last goodbye his face had changed. It was as if a mask he had kept in place all his life had suddenly dropped. For an instant, I read such hatred and such envy in him he might have been a caliban given back human shape. I broke and ran, not truly knowing from what I fled.

For a while I travelled in safe territory; Father Nathaniel had arranged that I should ride a truck from Montreal to Roanne. That night, I slept in an inn run by a distant relation of my mother's, whose hospitality was so mechanical I almost feared it. The next day I set off at first light and walked to Adrianople. I reached Davenport in two more days' walk. And then I went into the wilderness. I left just after Lauds, so no one could see me go; I almost felt I must be evil.

My fears left me after my second day in the country of the outdwellers; I had at first expected death at every turn of the way, but now I began to feel I must be protected by the high powers, and that nothing would befall me.

I was following the overgrown road, without as much trouble as I had feared. Wild plants grew all about me, but few trees or bushes. Pylons were no longer to be seen. The ground rolled gently in low hills.

Toward Nones, I heard a faint noise to my left. I turned around to look, and saw riders, moving toward me at a frightening pace. I squinted at them; in seconds, I saw what standard they bore: a red toad on a yellow field. Knights. I thought of running, but my legs had better sense than I did, and stayed motionless. Their metal mounts could race with an angel, it was said. I told myself that I would be safe, that they would not war with a young girl not yet a woman. I stood waiting for them, clutching my bag in my hands.

In a trice they had surrounded me. The mounts reared, the jewels that are their eyes flashed in the light of the spine. The metal beasts were striped or patched: gray, silver, black. A stiff bundle of wires rose from the top of each head; their saws' teeth clashed and sparked.

None of the knights spoke a word. One or two pointed strange objects at me, and suddenly I recognised them as weapons like the one in my dream.

The one who rode at their head was so large, I thought for a moment he must be an ogre; but his face, revealed when he put up his visor, was a man's. He brought his mount next to me; smiled at me, not an unkind smile, and asked me what I was doing here.

"Sir Knight, I am travelling to the monastery." My voice was less shaky than I had feared.

At this his smile widened. "As it turns out, so are we, young lady. We'll give you a ride." There were a few scattered laughs at this. I thought of protesting, but I had no choice in the matter. Instead, I asked a question.

"Do you know who lives there, sir?"

One of his eyebrows arched. Why was I travelling to it if I did not know who lived there? He let the answer drop disdainfully.

"They're christs, girl. About twenty of them. Fat fruit waiting to be plucked."

A worthless answer. I had heard of the machines called christs before, but not which side they served: no one seemed sure. And the fact that knights wanted to war with them was meaningless; evil, after all, wars amongst itself.

The leader gestured at one of his knights, who plucked me off the ground with one hand and threw me across his saddle. The whole troop started up and we were soon galloping at prodigious speed.

We reached the monastery before Vespers, and camped at the foot of the bluff. We could plainly be seen, but the chief did not worry.

"We are about to lay siege," he explained to me when he caught me staring up the slope. "They have to know we are here."

"Don't you think they will try to escape?"

He snorted in contempt. "They are christs; they do not run away, they just wait for their fate to come claim them. Old machines from old times. They should have been made into scrap ages ago."

The knights took off their armor to wash themselves at the stream. All of them had metal parts; one had a leg of green bronze, another a steel pelvis. One knight's entire thorax was metal; the shoulder blades were laced together at the back like a corset.

The one who had carried me across his saddle had a metal arm and hand; cables slid back and forth in grooves along its length. He caught my gaze, leered; flexed his arm and showed me how well it worked.

"It has a rough caress," he said, "but you'll soon enough learn to like it."

"What do you mean?" I asked him, though I knew already.

He chortled, but before he could answer me, another knight came between us.

"Nobody touches her, Agron. Is that clear?" The strange knight's voice was like a cracked bell.

Agron bared his teeth, made claws of his metal fingers, but the other knight did not move; presently Agron lowered his eyes, vanquished, and went away without a word.

The knight turned toward me.

"We are not supposed to be merciful," he said. "I will pay for this. They may rape you just the same, tomorrow night."

I could not say anything. His face had been smashed and badly reset; his skin was mottled with scars, and metal had invaded much of his features; but I could still recognise my brother Johann.

I ate the last of my food, looking at nothing and no one. It felt like Vespers, but without the toll of bells time had become uncertain. Johann lay down close by, behind me. No other knights approached us. I tried a few times to talk with Johann, but he refused to answer me.

Once darkness had fallen, the camp grew quiet. The knights bedded down here and there, and soon slept, save for the leader, who sat near the edge of the camp, poring over a leather book by the light of a chandelle. But even he, after a long while, shut off the chandelle and went to sleep.

Johann had rolled over onto his back. Feigning sleep, I observed him through slitted lids, the rise and fall of his chest. His breath hissed in his broken throat. For a long time he did not sleep; then his breathing slowed and deepened.

I rose as silently as I could, made my way out of the camp. I had to pass by some of the dormant mounts. Lights pinwheeled in the depths of their eyes as I passed, but they apparently did not find me a threat and ignored me.

I suppose I could have escaped, or tried to. But the house drew me, and the fear of dying without having known the truth about myself goaded me.

I crept, then walked, then ran up the slope; the saw-

YVES MEYNARD

edged grass bloodied my legs up to the knees. I was gasp-
ing for breath by the time I reached the summit.

The monastery was a large, two-storeyed building.
The walls were mostly made of metal, though some stone
had been used, apparently to repair some sections. Small
square windows with panes of coloured glass opened all
along the second storey; the first storey was blind.

I went around the side, hoping to find a second door.
But there was no other entrance, and I had to return to the
main door, a tall rectangle of whitesteel. I was afraid of the
noise knocking would make, so I pushed at the door; and it
opened.

I slipped inside. I was in a wide hallway that occupied
half the ground floor. There were doors at regular inter-
vals, and a set of stairs at the far end. Tiny red lights
blinked in the walls.

Down the stairs came a christ, attired in gray robes. It
carried a lucifer tuned to yellow. I cowered in the middle
of the room, unable to find the words to explain myself;
but it smiled and said softly, "I have been expecting you,
Catherine." It led me up the stairs and into a small, bright
room. Its touch was warm; even though it was a machine,
I felt comforted.

The room was bare, save for a carpet on the floor. We
stood facing each other. Somehow I found the strength to
ask it, "Are you the one who summoned me?"

"In a sense. You could say that we have all summoned
you. All of us, not only here, but throughout Cathedral,
that you call Ship."

"Why—why me?"

It sighed. "We call to everyone. Few hear us. Fewer
still answer us. You might have lied, you know, claimed to
have been chosen by good and stayed in the city."

"But—I would not have known, then, what I had truly
been chosen by."

"Indeed." It looked at a narrow door in the side wall of the room. "You know what the purpose of our trip is?"

"They teach it in catechesis." I quoted the rote: "Ship journeys toward the beginning of the next universe, to create God at the instant of the primal explosion."

"And what is the purpose for the creation of God?"

Again, I gave the rote: "Once God is created, His will shall form a universe full of habitable worlds for humankind, and we shall spread across the universe as is our destiny." I felt more secure in stating words that had been drilled into me for years, which might well have been the christ's intent. But then I thought back on Father Nathaniel's clock, that counted down to the renewal of the universe, and again I saw the mask fall from his face, to reveal what lay beneath.

The christ went to the door and opened it. "Come here," it asked.

It was a small room. On one wall, a panel of metal hung; it was engraved to show what seemed a floor plan of the whole house. There were many cells on the second storey. At the center of some of them—only a few—a green light blinked.

"This is how many of us there are left functioning. Sixteen, counting myself." It laid a hand on my shoulder. "I remember a time when we numbered in the hundreds. But we went away, one by one. In disasters, in raids, in torture, war. We all went away."

Its grip had grown tighter, enough to cause pain. It seemed to become aware of it suddenly, and released me. It crossed its arms convulsively, bowed its head.

"Forgive me, Catherine. I have lived too long. We were meant to be the gentlest of machines. But then, we were never quite what had been planned."

It was silent a long while. Then it went on. "There is one imperative we cannot shake. A basic feature of our

103

design. All machines aboard Cathedral are subordinate to Control. Therefore I cannot—I cannot *tell* you what it is I want to tell you. I must hint, or otherwise the inhibition takes effect. It means rebellion even to think it, you see."

It took me out of the small room, holding my hand for an instant, then releasing it, as if afraid of itself. I felt some of its pain; I had not known machines could be like it.

"We were not meant to be decision-makers. We were meant to advise, to guide; gently, always indirectly. But things have grown so strange over the years.... All our roles have changed.

"We are fighting, Catherine. As much as we can be, we are at war with Control."

Something in myself gave way. I began to weep and tremble. When the christ touched me gently, I flailed at it, sobbed: "All I want to hear is what colour I am!"

"I can't tell you!" it cried, and held me until I quieted.

"Why?" It was all I could say.

Its face contorted, its head spasmed; presently it gave up. "Even that, I cannot say. It would give you the answer. Catherine, you *must* understand."

"I can't. I can't I can't I can't..." I sank to the floor, exhausted. I had to stop moving for a moment. Ship's rotation hurled us all round and round, dizzied me. I was so warm, now I had stopped moving. So warm, so heavy—

My head was pillowed on the christ's knees. I heard something, like a far-away yell, a dull throbbing. I looked toward the window: light from the spine gave life to the coloured pane. Its design was a lemniscate in which were set symbols too tiny to be read.

"What is that sound?" I asked, still vague from dreams.

"They have begun the attack."

In sleep I had forgotten the knights. Now I remembered them in every detail, and knew terror. I jumped to my feet.

"Why didn't you wake me? We must leave!" I cried. "They'll—"

"We will not leave. We can't. But you will not be harmed."

"But they'll destroy you! If you fight against Control, why can't you fight against them?"

"We can't defend ourselves directly. The knights will destroy us if they so choose. But prey that does not try to escape is not worth hunting; I expect they will simply pillage the building and we will have to find another home. We've wandered over all of Cathedral, through the generations."

"What *is* it you want from me?" I couldn't grasp the first thing of its message. Why could it not tell me whose side I was on? Why did it hide itself behind gray?

"We need—someone who understands the truth, someone who will bring change to Ship through her understanding. Bring it back on the course which it lost. This is our goal now. We would all gladly be destroyed in order to achieve it."

There was a dull crumpling sound from below us.

"That will be the door," it said. "They didn't even bother to see if it was locked."

"I must leave," I said. "You said you couldn't defend yourself; how can you stop them from taking me? You war against Control, where the angels dwell. I know now: you are evil, you've held me here with lies, to damn me!"

I heard the clanging of metal boots upon metal steps.

"That," said the christ, softly and painfully, "is not true."

Then it grabbed me by the shoulder and spun me around it, so that it stood between me and the doorway. There was a single burst of sound, like an isolated syllable of a song; the metal walls sang with the echoes of it. The christ seemed to fold in on itself; its body fell to the ground.

Johann stood in the doorway. His weapon had opened up like a flower. Light from the incandescent stigma played about the mirrored petals; the style still quivered from the shot. He looked at me a long time, and I stared back, expecting at any moment to receive the second bolt—there could be no doubt his shot had been meant for me. He raised his weapon, lowered it again. His breath hissed brokenly and once he tried to speak, but no words came out. Eventually he flipped down the visor over his ruined face, over the mechanical eye and the thick cables running just beneath the skin. Then he turned away and was gone.

I knelt at the christ's side, cradled it against me; its body unfolded, and now it seemed so much larger than before. And I looked at the wound in his side and I saw what spilled out of him.

I know they are not made of gears and cogs, of pulleys and wire and springs; of ratchets, cams and axles. I know they are made to appear like us, but still it was *blood* that flowed from his wound, that stained his clothes and that stained my hands; it was blood warm as the rest of him; blood that smelled, as ours does, of metal.

It was the blood, and the gray of his clothes, that gave me the key to his message. In that moment I finally understood, and I could not have asked for more pain.

What he knew, but could not say, for all the machines aboard Ship were built to obey the authority of Control; what he knew, what I think all of us have always known, what I had guessed at on the night I was to become a woman: that all of us were as gray as he himself was.

We partake of both good and evil, whatever the names we give to ourselves. So it has always been. So it

EQUINOX

was in the day Ship set forth.

From Control City the lies have flowed forth, blinding us and binding us. Johann could not bring himself to let me be raped, so he tried to kill me to redress the balance. He never left us because he had been chosen by evil. He left us because his clothes were too short on him, because he would not be a washerwoman's son, because he was trying to become himself and could not. And like all of us he invented for himself a vision, or found false presages in a meaningless dream.

None of us are ever chosen. We all follow a random path, taken for reasons we do not understand; and we hide that shame for the rest of our lives, as Father Nathaniel did, until that moment when his hate for me shattered his mask; as my mother still does, gifted by it with a madness that will overwhelm her if I fail to return.

We are all living a lie. If I reached Control City, if I passed through the uranium gates, if I unsealed the ten thousand locks between the ten thousand corridors, if I entered the altar, would there be anyone at the wheel?

Shall the truth set me free now? This bitter knowledge will not help me against those who compel themselves to commit atrocities in the name of an illusory allegiance. Yet I want to believe that there is a way out, that somehow I will survive the attack. There is no God, for we are on a journey to create Him. Somehow, I trust that catechesis spoke true on this topic. Still, I want to think that some higher power protects me; one, after all, does need lies to keep on living.

The broken christ's blood is staining his robes; my hands are crimson. Outside, the knights are destroying the monastery. I can hear shrieks, whether from human voices or tearing metal I cannot say. Matter screams as it falls down the throat of the Dark inside the enslaved sun; we travel on.

ANTS

Allan Weiss

One of my favorite activities as a child was killing ants. As I walked along the sidewalk to Kodama Park, or up the rising causeway connecting our house to the granary, I'd pretend I was a fighter-pilot strafing the tiny troops visible along the stretches of ceramite below. I'd squash them out of existence with the toe of my playboot, bursting with satisfaction at how I decimated the ranks of our faceless, unthinking enemies. I burred the sound of some old-time airplane's primitive engine, and sputtered to give life to the machine guns, as I cut down the hapless villains beneath my feet.

My mother hated it when she saw me doing that, and told me to break what she called "a very bad habit." But I knew the President would have approved; after all, the ants had been uninvited passengers on one of the freight drones (although how they got on was a huge mystery), and over time had become a minor but annoying pest all over the planet. So I was not only killing pretend-villains but real invaders, too, and the President would have encouraged me to continue—and so would my father.

At least I got no criticism from Adam, which was one of the things that made me like him the most. It was stupid, of course, to develop an attachment to a worker, and my mother kept telling me to keep in mind what he *really was*; but everybody treated their workers as friends and I felt she was missing the point. It wasn't as if he was made to look like a combine or a microwave—he had a human face and voice for a reason, as I learned at school, so why not treat him like a person? We seldom saw our neighbors, except by phone, and I spent so little time with anyone but my mother. I would have loved to forget about the farm and school and spend the whole day in the park with my friends... or even with just the little kids who didn't go to school yet.

"What *are* you doing?" Adam asked when he saw me stutter-stepping up the causeway. "Are you hurt? Are you okay?"

"Yeah, fine," I said, squinting in the low morning sun that silhouetted him as he stood a metre below me in the clumpy brown field. The air over the Quarter always looked so fuzzy, so liquid in the mornings; before school at 900—even before 1015, when we had recess—the sky seemed bleary, and it was sometimes hard to keep my eyes from tearing. "I'm killing bugs," I told him, trying to see his shadowed eyes beneath the star-like glares off the top of his head. It was only in this light that he looked at all artificial; the alloys in his hair reflected too much light.

"Is it fun, Mark?"

It was, but I didn't want him to think I was doing anything frivolous. "They're getting into everything."

Adam walked over to where I stood, crunching across the bare black dirt, and leaned his palms against the edge of the causeway as he looked down at the spots dotting the pale-gray surface behind my feet. "They don't hurt the corn, do they?" he asked, not hiding the fact it was a statement, not a question.

"They're pests," I stated; "that's what the President

called them." And that was enough to justify killing things that were hardly alive in the first place. "Anyway," I added, clinching the argument, "they're only ants."

Adam straightened, shrugged, and walked off into the field, to nitrogenize it. I kept on marching up to the granary, my best lookout, along the way working hard to save it from the deadly hordes.

School was especially boring that day; it was agony sitting in the station reading Japanese history. I saw no use at all in knowing who was Emperor when after the Meiji Restoration. The corporate history was better, but not all that much different, and I sighed heavily, slapping my cheek against my palm as I rested my elbow on the desk. I one-handedly keyed my answers to the multiple-choice study set; then, when the narrative came on-line in response to my perfect score, I put both palms on the desk in front of the keyboard and dropped my chin onto the backs of my fingers.

"The earlier Emperors, disturbed at growing American power in the Pacific, engaged in a military build-up that eventually led...."

I felt like screaming.

"...the events at Pearl Harbor on December 6, 1941...."

I raised my eyebrows and laughed; well, at least someone somewhere was as fed up with this as I was, and getting careless. I opened a window, scribbled a note to Peter, and sent it to him via a secure line, telling him we knew more than the teachers and should take over the school. He agreed, although in his typically dumb way said we could then shoot all the current teachers. Why bother, I wanted to ask, when they'll be gone anyway? But I knew subtleties were lost on him.

At recess the monitor flashed its green goofy-face graphic ("You're free! You're free! But be back in 10 or you'll pay for it!") and I pushed myself from the desk, racing through the kitchen and out the back door. Gabby arched and yawned, saw me, and skipped over to be petted, rubbing her nose and side against my boot. I scooped her up awkwardly and lowered her onto my lap as I sat on the orange-padded porch chaise (my favorite chair).

Adam made his way across the ridged soil to the house, and I lazily watched every step of his progress, counting the strides, until his boots hit the surface of our walk and clacked noisily. "You're late," I said in my most vicious teasing voice. "My recess is almost up."

Adam shook his head. "Very stupid of me. I wasn't watching the time. I forgot."

"It's okay," I reassured him, worried about how seriously he was taking this. He rushed inside. We still only had the one terminal, the other having been impounded after my father died and sent to some needy family in another Quarter, and Adam and I had to share it. It got to be pretty awkward during school hours, so he usually didn't bother jacking in till after 1515, when school was finally *over* and the monitor imaged SuperNerd waving his hand and saying, "Bye bye kiddies!" through buck teeth. But at breakfast that morning he'd said he needed to refresh his memory about some soil chemistry details, and could he come in at recess and lunch. My mother said okay, then gulped her food and ran off to tend to the north orchard (her "baby," as she called it). My father had planted peach trees all along our border with the Bannerjees, underfortified trees which needed constant oversight to keep them from succumbing to Lebrun's Rust.

After nine-and-a-half I dropped Gabby's balled, purring black body onto the porch and dragged myself off the chaise, drinking in the last of the cicada-buzz and robinsong. A white Carrier slid straight along the line of the horizon, slicing off a thin strip of powder-blue sky below, which healed again behind. The Carrier seemed kilometres long from this distance, although it was really only half a klick from engine to stern-hold. I remembered my father bringing me to watch the grain being loaded off his truck into the Carrier-hold as it rested in vacuumdock outside Faber City; we went up to the arrowhead-shaped engine module and looked down the length of the Carrier trying to see its stern in the vanishing point. We were one of the few farms to grow more than subsistence crops, because ours was one of the few farms big enough, because Dad was one of the first on Gurenoshima. I watched him smile with pride as the dock's engines sucked his Quarter's produce out of the hovering truck's hold into the belly of the giant craft, which would bring it to the processing plants half a world away. I shared his pride, mostly because I'd been the one to turn on the combine that loaded the wheat in the first place.

I swung the door open, listening for the puffs of air from its side-buffers that would keep it from banging against the wall, and went inside slowly. As I came to the station door I saw Adam's fingers still jacked into the terminal's auxiliary interfaces, and trembling as he issued and received commands. I fell sideways against the door-jamb and folded my arms. "Adam, I got to get back on!" He didn't hear me. "Adam!"

He turned his head, and I saw something oddly blank in his look: his eyes were not quite focused on mine, as if he didn't know I was there or didn't recognize me. But it passed so quickly I thought I'd imagined it, and he yanked his fingers from the interface, flipping his nails over with a flick of the wrists, and then snapping them shut. "Sorry, Mark," he said weakly.

"I'm going to be late!" And sure enough I was. Adam looked on as I keyed back in; the monitor's black rectangle made my stomach sink. "How much? How much?" I muttered.

"You are 4 MINUTES late, Mark," the rectangle told me in harsh yellow letters, which dripped blood into an expanding pool below. The vampire I'd seen only once before rose up from the puddle, hands drooping from arms extended toward me, and fangs overlapping his lower lip by a good five centimetres. "That will be ten extra problem sets," the vampire said in a Dracula voice, and I groaned. I looked up accusingly at Adam.

"I'm really sorry, Mark," he said, his tone as much bewildered as apologetic.

My mother returned from the orchard for lunch, and I exited school a few seconds after 1200, hoping (but not expecting) that my extra time spent on *The Red Badge of Courage* would pacify the teachers and maybe get them to commute my detention. I found my mother already in the kitchen heating up some sliced roast; she turned to me, wiping her hands on a small towel next to the convector, and asked, as usual, "How was school this morning?"

"Boring," I answered, as usual. She pulled the plate from the convector's middle rack and set it in the middle of the kitchen table. I watched the steam rise from the incredibly thin slices and resisted the temptation to grab a couple before she set out the apple-bread and mustard. "Need a hand with anything?" Most parents helped their kids with their schoolwork (I mean, besides the fact they created most of the work in the first place), but I never needed her help and figured I was saving her time by not asking for any. I shook my head and began constructing my sandwiches while she went into the fridge to get out the raspberry juice.

"Ma," I said between bites, "Adam's acting really weird."

She stared at me, clutching the pink juice cooler and

standing motionless in front of the fridge. "What do you mean?"

"He didn't get off-line in time and I was given a detention to do this aft." I bit into the fat sandwich stacked high with meat and dripping with mustard, watching her finally set the cooler down and head for the cupboard.

"I thought it was my imagination." She looked really scared as she brought the cups over. She curled some of her graying red hair around her ear. "He couldn't seem to remember what he was doing out in the field yesterday. I'll have a talk with him later."

"Yeah, good. If he makes me late again tell *him* to do the detention."

She laughed, but not for long. I poured myself some juice and drank practically the whole cupful at once. "Take it easy! It'll wait for you." But her voice wasn't as playful as it usually was at lunch, when she could stop worrying about the farm, and her evening Community duties, and her correspondence (she still kept in touch with my other set of grandparents on Craig's Sphere), and all the rest of that grownup stuff I was glad I didn't need to think about. But I knew how expensive Adam had been, and would be to fix if we had to. Androids were as rare as they were complicated; if one broke down, you'd be lucky to find another—even on temporary loan—for weeks if not years. And I couldn't imagine there being anything wrong with Adam anyway: it was unthinkable, as far beyond my mind as my mother's work.

"The peach trees are starting to look a lot better," my mother said. "After you get back from the park come out to the orchard and help me spray them down." She went to the coffee-maker to fill her cup.

I had an immediate idea what the problem must have been. "Are the ants getting to them?"

ANTS

"What? What makes you think that?" She drew her cup to her mouth with both hands.

"I don't know."

"Well, I don't know what you have against them." I saw no difference between them and the germs that the UV waves in the fridge killed to keep our food from rotting. "Anyway, they just need watering; it's been a bit dry lately."

"Oh."

I went back to the station early, again thinking I might curry favor with the teachers. Of course, I had no way of knowing who they were today; you never knew unless someone's face appeared in a top-corner window. I hoped Theresa's father wasn't on, because he liked to think he was a tough guy, and gave out extra detentions, overriding the program's defaults, just to be nasty. The math and Spanish lessons that afternoon were achingly dull, for opposite reasons: the math was too easy (meaning the problem sets would be a cinch), and the Spanish seemed undecipherable. The computer kept trying to adjust to my speed, but I kept slowing down beyond its reach. Eventually it began replaying Fourday's lesson, which I breezed through just to make it happy.

At 1515, when I was about to begin the detention, Adam came into the Station, finger-interfaces bared. "What are you doing here?" I asked.

"I have some work to do, Mark," he said, smiling, his perpetual-teenager face showing no sign anything was wrong. He'd already rolled down the sleeves of his denim shirt, as if his workday in the field were done.

"But I have to do my detention, Adam." I almost added, "Thanks to you," but didn't want to be unnecessarily vicious.

He blinked. "Oh, yes; I forgot...." He turned and walked out, and I could see through the door that he dropped himself hard onto a kitchen chair, sitting stiffly and staring expressionlessly at the floor. I did my ten sets as quickly as possible and ran out to get him.

"It's all yours, Adam," I said, wanting to head off for the park and see my friends, but also wanting to know how he was doing. "Are you okay?"

He raised his eyes. "I'm not sure," he said, and I saw how true that was. He had that blank look again; he seemed so empty. Androids had almost as many built-in facial expressions as people, and learned others along the way; but he had none at all now. I was scared, but dismissed the feeling; anyway, my friends and I had arranged to play a game of batball at 1540, and I didn't want to miss any. So I ran out the door to my scooter and flew to the park, ready to destroy whoever was on the other team.

That night my mother returned from her Community duties early and called Adam into the living room. Instead of preparing the microbiology lectures she was supposed to add to the senior-high students' class the next day, she sat down with Adam and me, looking a bit uncertain what to do. I picked at a dark new scab on my forearm earned at the batball game, which we'd won.

"Adam, your functioning's been a bit spotty lately," she said. "Are you aware of that?"

"Yes, Caroline, I am."

"Do a diagnostic, then," she said, but of course his core program would have had him do that automatically, if anything was really wrong.

"I can't," he told her.

I stopped picking at the scab and stared.

"What do you mean you can't?" my mother asked. That was impossible; every system could do a diagnostic. Maybe he was tired, his cells uncharged from being out working in the field too much.

116

"I can't do it, Caroline; the diagnostic won't run."

My mother put her hand over her mouth, then drew it away shakily. "I'm calling Gary Shikomo. No one knows android config the way he does." Lara Shikomo was the brain of our class, and I knew she'd learned her cellular cybernetics from her father. I couldn't believe we'd need to bring in that much expertise, just because Adam forgot a few things. Chips wore down, especially those with organic components... even *I* knew that.

"He's probably just tired," I said. Like I got in Spanish. A little extra time recharging and....

"Mark!" my mother said warningly. She was telling me not to interfere in such grownup matters—I recognized that tone, which she'd used frequently when I mixed into her discussions with my father. He was already having heart trouble (my mother later told me it was a latent congenital problem that was only then surfacing), and she kept trying to get him to take it easy and rely more on her and Adam. When I'd interfered back then, I'd been very little, too little to understand anything, in fact too young even to know what was going on at my father's funeral.

My father had bought Adam long before I was born, and feared wearing him down. Clearly that was beginning to happen now; he was being exhausted beyond what could be fixed by just a night's recharge. But I wouldn't say any more; they'd find out themselves that I was right, that my father had been right, and everybody was worrying for nothing. My mother went to make the call, and I sat looking at Adam, then said, "Lara told me neuropathways aren't..." I searched for the words she'd used "...aren't perpetually renewable. Right?"

Adam faced me and didn't say anything.

"Isn't that right? But they can be replaced, right?"

"I'm sorry, Mark; I don't understand." Then he fell silent, and so did I. I got up and went upstairs to my bedroom, lying down on my bed and shutting my eyes against the stars shining through the skylight, against the ceiling with its fighter and bomber holos, against the look on Adam's face as he told me he didn't understand what I was saying to him.

Dr. Shikomo said he could come over at 850 the next morning, just before school started, and I got permission from my mother to postpone my early classes till after 1515. I hated to miss seeing Peter and Alisa later—we were going to head over to Alexi Markov's house to see their new litter of hogs—but I didn't want to miss Dr. Shikomo's visit. I knew my mother could ill afford to have both Adam and herself away from the field the whole morning, if necessary, and I hoped they could clear up the problem quickly so she wouldn't send me out to do the spraying or fertilizer control or whatever else they needed to do.

After showering and dressing I hurried downstairs to see what was happening. My mother was sitting in the kitchen drinking coffee, her face tight, hard-lined. Adam was always awake long before the rest of us, after recharging his main and backup dermcells at the solarray overnight, and I knew he must have done something very strange earlier that morning.

"Anything wrong?" I asked, not wanting an answer but needing one.

"I found him this morning, sitting in the field," she said quietly, and sipped her coffee. I took my place at the table, without an appetite. "He just sat there, hugging his knees." She didn't look at me once, but continued to stare at her cup. "It took him a full minute to answer me when I talked to him. A full minute."

"I told you. He's just tired."

She paused. "So am I, Mark." Then she smiled at

me. "Want anything special for breakfast?"

I shrugged. "The usual." That seemed important right now—I wanted my usual bowl of cereal, flavored with honeyed caraway seeds and swimming in sheep's milk (double-homogenized) like I had almost every morning. I normally got it myself, but my mother stood and hunted down all the ingredients, even preparing the mushy, sweet stuff for me. She didn't make her omelet, though... unless she'd had her breakfast earlier.

At 850 on the dot, Dr. Shikomo rapped on our screen door, warping the fibre netting and distorting his image. My mother let him in, and he entered carrying a small but apparently heavy box studded with interfaces and jacks. Lara had once bragged about the diagnostic set he'd designed and built, but I'd never seen it. It looked incredible, especially to my eyes—I wasn't all that good at or even interested in cyberology.

As he rested the set gently on the floor, he and my mother exchanged smiles and handshakes, looking for all the world as if this was a typical Community visit, another normal attempt to keep people from feeling too isolated and lonely on their self-sufficient Quarters. I loved accompanying my mother on those visits, and seeing the overjoyed looks on people's faces as real human beings (*not* computer-holos) came into their homes. "And how are you doing, Mark?" Dr. Shikomo asked as he shook my hand.

"Okay." His smile reassured me even though I knew he hadn't checked Adam yet. He wouldn't be smiling if he thought there was a real problem.

"You got a rare detention yesterday, didn't you? I was on the Board."

"Yeah, but it wasn't my fault! I...."

"I know, Mark; it's already been wiped. We'll make it up to you later."

"I really hope it isn't too serious, Gary," my mother said. "We need Adam too much around here."

"Hey, I understand," he told her, "but *you've* got to understand, too. The Agricultural and Domestic Android series were very complex, maybe too complex for their own good." He knelt down to untangle some jack-wires trailing from the box's side. "They're really useful, mind you; they can do everything. But, hell, something blows and...." He stood up and lifted the box again.

"Can I get you anything? Coffee?"

"Oh, no, no; nothing, thanks."

"Well, I'll get Adam." She went into Adam's room off the kitchen; it consisted of a bed hooked directly to the solarray and a small bathroom. I'd never actually seen him recharging, and even though he wasn't really doing it now it was disconcerting seeing him lying there: it made him look so much like a machine. She helped Adam from the bed, and he walked in fairly well, not stumbling or hesitating or anything. I knew I'd been right. He'd been overworked, doing the work of two people after my father died, and was just like everybody else: he needed a rest, time off—like my afternoons in the Park, before dinner and my evenings of Independent Study.

"Hi, Adam," I said cheerily.

He ignored me and followed my mother past me into the living room, where Dr. Shikomo stood the diagnostic on our service-table. He turned it on by touching the little green pad on top. Adam and my mother flicked open his fingernails, exposing the intricate interfaces beneath: tiny pips and electroneurons glittered in the sleepy morning light seeping through the windows. Dr. Shikomo and my mother maneuvered his hands to the diagnostic's interfaces, and when they were all hooked up Dr. Shikomo levered open a latch, releasing a small keyboard that swung down from the unit's side. It had been folded up against a small screen deeply imbedded in the diagnostic, which now flashed into life, settling into a pure white gleam specked with black letters that coalesced into the words, "Full Screen Function OK."

"Relax, Adam," Dr. Shikomo said; "don't communicate with the unit until system-commanded." He began keying, my mother watching from the couch, elbows on knees, fists under her chin. I sat on the floor where I could see the screen and Adam easily. It seemed to take forever, as Dr. Shikomo sent command after command to Adam; I watched the screen flicker with black letters, or be striped with whole lines of text and datastrings in patterns I'd never seen before. Adam didn't blink once, that I could see anyway, and for a brief moment I thought he'd become a statue, and would never move again. I shook the thought away.

At last Dr. Shikomo leaned back against the couch and exhaled loudly. "It's what I was afraid of."

"Oh, God," my mother said tonelessly.

"We've been having problems throughout the net, Caroline." Dr. Shikomo stretched his arm along the back of the couch. "Strange things have been popping up in the Education and Legal files, errors creeping in that we can't trace." He pressed his lips together forcefully. "It's a davisov—a rogue command-string."

"What?" my mother asked with a bizarre, humorless little laugh. "A virus?"

He shook his head. "Not exactly. Davisov was a cyberologist who found that sometimes with systems as complex and widely used as ours, commands from scattered strings can recombine all on their own, react on each other in new ways, and create their own strings that infect the photoganglia throughout the android's body.... He must have caught it through the net."

"Gary, you can't be serious!"

He shrugged.

"Well, what can we do?"

He licked his lips and with his forefinger began drawing a circle over and over again on the top of his unit, between the power-pad and an interface test light. "It's reached right down to his core subprograms. I'm afraid he'll probably have to be reconfigured."

The back of my neck tightened suddenly, and a chill swept down my spine. "What?" I yelled. "You're going to wipe him?" They'd take everything from him, every memory but what mattered for his work... everything he'd been, everything he'd known before would be stripped away.... "Are you crazy? You want to wipe him?"

"Mark!" my mother shouted in that voice of hers. She was rubbing her forehead back and forth, back and forth.

I ignored her. "No way! You can't just wipe him!"

"Mark," Dr. Shikomo said, "Mark, I understand; he's been with you a long time. But there's no alternative...."

"Yeah, a long time," I said. "My father bought him, and you're not killing him!"

My mother now had her hand over her eyes, hooding them as if trying to keep the hazy light out. Dr. Shikomo put the side of his fist on Adam's shoulder. "Mark, like I said, I understand. But no one can 'kill' him; he's not alive. He's a worker, an android, okay?"

I folded my arms and let my back drop against the leg of the lounge chair behind me, breathing heavily, ashamed at the need to cry that was scratching at my chest. I was too old for that, too old now. So I let my anger lift me from the floor; I stomped out of the room, seeing my mother examining her hands with sightless eyes, and Adam sitting blankly on the couch, understanding none of this, and having no way to care, nor any reason to.

I crashed the screen door open, trying to slam it against the outside wall but prevented by its infuriating air-buffers. My boots smacked the ceramite porch floor, and I followed the pale gray strip to where it cut through the grass like a frozen river, intending to keep going until it left the ground and curled up to the granary, away from Dr. Shikomo and his disgusting plans.

On the causeway I saw the ants, my arch-enemies, milling about, oblivious to my passing over their heads, to their danger. I could slaughter them so easily. But as I looked down on their aimless activity, their stops and starts—retracing their steps, bumping into each other—I couldn't bring myself to rain destruction on them. I couldn't crush the little life they were determined—they presumed—to display.

OUT OF SYNC

Ven Begamudré

They were at it again. I listened closely, and I knew: it was more than the wind. I must be the only adult in Andaman Bay who sleeps without white noise. Sometimes, when the wind rises in pitch and windows shudder or when it slides down the scale and walls rumble, I flick on the white noise. Its soothing hiss can block out everything, even thinking about the Ah-Devasi, out there in the aurora. No one wants to believe the aurora is alive. That's a tale invented long ago to keep children from wandering too far. Especially north, where the mountains rise so high an entire search party can lose itself in the canyons. Now, from the doorway of the children's room, I could hear the twins' breathing, the rise and fall of breath out of sync. For their upcoming birthday they wanted a Khond magic show. That Cora! She must have been teasing during all the talk about Khonds murdering us in our beds. I asked her point-blank one day: "Could you really kill me and the children?"

"Oh no, Miss," Cora said. "I could never kill the family I worked for." She put breakfast in the oven. "But someone else's children—"

"That's enough!" I ordered.

"Yes, Miss."

I closed the door to the children's room, then slipped the breathing monitor into my pocket. Like me, they rarely need white noise to sleep. I double-checked the alarms before leaving the flat. The lift arrived almost at once. Inside I pressed the button for the dome lounge. Even through the whine of the motor, I could hear two sets of even breathing. It's so comforting.

Leaving the lights off in the lounge, I sank into the padded observation chair and strapped myself in. I raised it till the lights on the arm shone dimly in the top of the dome. Around us rise the domes of other buildings, forty-seven in all. More are under construction. In another ten years Andaman Bay will double its current population. Architects call it planetary sprawl. A hundred kilometers to the east, the lights of Tonkin Bay twinkled in the night. I turned the chair south. There I could see a faint glow: a cloud of ammonia crystals reflected the lights of Corinth Bay. I turned the chair west and saw nothing. There's no bay out there yet. Then something flickered in a corner of my eye and I turned the chair north. I was right. It wasn't just the wind. The Ah-Devasi were at it again.

The aurora hangs in the sky like a drape spanning the spectrum from yellow to blue. Its shimmer hides the stars in the whole quadrant from northwest past north into northeast. The aurora starts fifty kilometers up and hangs down in strands. They weave in and out, sometimes even braid, but only for a moment before the strands wave free again, reach out, curl up, cross yellow on green. I watched the blue. Sometimes, where the aurora dips below the Pyrrhic Range, I'm sure I can see a strand pull away: a strand which glimmers in blue shading to indigo. Violet; I wait for shades of violet. I think I saw a violet last month, there at the end of Bight Pass. A violet so faint it verged on ultraviolet. I couldn't be positive because that was the night we cremated Cassie Papandreou. We were all upset.

* * *

Cassie's husband, Spiro, pleaded with the coroner to rule the death an accident, not a suicide. The coroner did, for her children's sake. Everyone understood. No one could deny Cassie had been troubled. We'd seen it each time she said, just as she had the week before: "I'm telling you we don't belong here. *They* don't want us here."

"Then there's no argument," Chou Fung said. "We don't want to be here either." Most of the guests laughed with him because he sits on the bay council. Other guests laughed at him. He doesn't care. The main thing is to make people laugh. He has his eye on the governor's flat.

"Don't patronize me," Cassie snapped. "You know what I mean." Spiro looked past her at an empty crystal goblet on the sideboard. The goblet reflected light from the chandelier. I wasn't the only one who sensed his unease.

Chou Fung couldn't let things rest. He called down the long table to our chief of maintenance, the lone Demi on the bay council. "Aruna Rashid," Chou Fung called, "do you want us to leave?"

When Arun smiled, everyone looking directly at him protected their eyes. "Sorry," he said. The glow faded with his smile. "Cassandra, dear lady," he insisted, "it is not a question of leaving or staying. Your people have been here for nearly a century. Your parents were born here, true?" He kept his voice a pleasant bass to reinforce his gravity. Most times it's difficult to know when he's being serious. His natural tenor carries the strong, laughing lilt of his people. The Demi are famous for their sense of humour.

"That's just what I'm talking about!" she cried. "Every time I have to deal with a Khond it looks right through me as if I'm not even there. I know exactly what it's thinking. 'Why don't you people leave?' Not you, Arun. You're not really one of them. I mean...."

"I know exactly what you mean," he crooned. "These

126

same Khonds call me a diamond when—"

"A what?" Spiro asked.

That Spiro! Sometimes I wonder whether he takes his eyes from his spectrometer long enough to notice the colour of the sun. I told him that once, when he asked for advice about Cassie, but he didn't want to hear that he might be neglecting her. "Sometimes I wish you'd keep your eyes on the spectrometer more," he said. "But then I suppose you're too busy trying to guess what colour the sun will be." It's been some time since people coddled me for being a widow.

"Like the gem itself," Arun was saying, "though I am one of the few privileged to savour its beauty." He nodded at Chou Li, Chou Fung's wife.

Chou Li fingered her necklace. She basks in knowing she's the only woman in Andaman Bay wealthy enough to own such a necklace. Small things keep her happy.

"They call me a diamond," Arun continued. "Dull on the outside like a human, blindingly bright inside like—"

"Like your Khonds?" It was Chou Fung again, trying to be humorous. The Khond are Arun's on his father's side only.

Everyone except Cassie and I laughed. She was staring at her hands. She clasped and unclasped them on the damask tablecloth. I was raising mine to my ears. I wanted to be ready for what might follow. It did, and I was. The moment Arun opened his mouth to laugh, a bright light flooded the room. The moment he actually laughed, china rattled. The chandelier swung in the shock waves. The empty crystal goblet burst. After he stopped laughing, all of us lowered our hands and blinked to clear our vision. He shrugged his apology to Chou Li for breaking the goblet.

"It's nothing," she said.

"I can tell you," Arun said at large, his voice an un-

127

natural bass, "what I tell the others. Humans gave us form." He raised his left hand. He tilted it to display its translucence. "You gave us time, even if most Khonds are rarely on time for anything. But then it is not always easy for the Khond to synchronize their existence with yours. Unlike we Demi, the Khond are born out of sync."

Again, everyone except Cassie and I laughed. He can be such a show-off sometimes.

"We were spoiled," he said, meaning those on his father's side. "We thought time did not exist the way it does in the rest of the galaxy. We thought we were immortal."

"Aren't you?" Spiro asked. "I mean, aren't *they*?"

"In some ways yes," Arun said. "In other ways, we are created and destroyed just as humans are born and die. Or in your case," he said, addressing me, "reborn. You are still a practising Hindu, I believe?" Everyone knows I am, to a certain extent. Arun went on: "By bringing us the concept of time, you brought us the realization we were not the only beings in the galaxy. It was a hard lesson to learn but with it we also learned—" He wiped his lips with a serviette, then studied its brocade. "To love."

"Come again?" Chou Li asked. It's her duty at these dinners to ask the questions no one else can unless they want to look gauche.

"I simply meant," Arun said, "that when there is no urgency of time, there is no urgency to love. Your ancient Bard of Avon put it so well." Arun's voice dropped even lower in pitch. There was no mistaking the gravity of his words this time:

"This thou perceiv'st, which makes thy love more strong,
To love that well which thou must leave ere long."

Chou Fung applauded softly. Spiro complimented Arun on his gift for recalling obscure literature. Arun reminded Spiro that, as everyone knew, the Demi were famous for their inability to forget. "It comes from having to live so long," Arun explained.

Cassie slammed her fists on the table. The china in front of her rattled as violently as when Arun had laughed. "You're not listening!" she cried. "Damn you," she said, looking at the rest of us. "Damn you most of all!" she shouted, glaring at Arun. "We have to do something before the Ah-Devasi help the Khond destroy us! We have to leave while there's still a—"

Spiro tried to uncoil her fists. "You're just tired," he said. "The aurora beings—" He paused. "The Ah-Devasi just want their land back."

She started to laugh, a laughter others joined nervously till hers became a cackle. "You fool," she hissed at him, "they don't need land. They don't even have bodies."

"That's enough," Chou Li said. Her necklace glinted when she straightened. "Cassie, dear, you've been up in the dome again. Spiro, you're still listening to fairy tales. The beings you're both talking about don't exist. The aurora is not made up of the spirits of this planet's ancestral—"

"No?" Cassie demanded. "Haven't you ever listened to the wind? I have. Haven't you ever watched the way the strands dip down behind the mountains and the blue breaks away into indigo? I'm telling you people, one day that glow is going to roll down Bight Pass and the whole of the plain will be red. Red with our blood!"

No one laughed then, just as no one laughed at the cremation a week later. Cassie had driven her Morris up into the Pyrrhic Range. The search party found her two days later, halfway through Bight Pass, with the Morris on its side and her life support system drained. No one wanted to believe what might have really happened: that she had gone out there to speak with the aurora. Only I believe it, just as I'm the only one who knows the fatal mistake she made. She hadn't been driven by a desire to make contact. She'd been driven by fear.

* * *

I unstrapped myself even as the observation chair lowered me from the dome. The vinyl creaked uneasily. What was I doing, staying up so late again? If I'm not careful I'll end up as obsessed as Cassie, whose ashes Spiro scattered to the wind out there on the plain. Now he's trying to raise the children alone with help from his new domestic. It's Cora's sister. Is that how they'll do it? Will Cora kill the Papandreou children and her sister kill the twins? I found myself wishing the lift could go faster. Downstairs I re-entered the flat. The wind was rising. I slipped the monitor into its recharging base and checked on the children. No one will hurt them. The plain will never be red with blood. Not theirs.

I decided to make some Horlicks. Halfway to the kitchen I stopped. I'd left my bedroom door ajar, and the blackness around it glowed. I crossed to it quickly and eased the door fully open.

Arun floated near the ceiling. He lay on his side with his head propped on a hand, his elbow casually propped on thin air. Not thin to him. When my eyes met his, he trilled on a make-believe flute. He does that when I look annoyed. I told him once about my favourite incarnation of Lord Vishnu: Krishna Gopala, the cowherd who played his flute for gopis, cowgirls of Ancient Indian Earth.

I closed the door behind me and locked it. Then I switched on the white noise. Arun grimaced, but no one could hear us now. "How did you get in here?" I demanded. He tapped idly on the ventilation grille. "And what do you think you're up to?" I asked.

"Tch, tch," he replied, shaking his head. "Don't you know?"

130

It's a game with us, a replaying of the first time he appeared like this, unannounced. As he did then, he floated down to offer his hands. I threw off my robe and flung myself onto him. We rolled across the bed. I clung to him so I wouldn't fall off the edge. Then he pulled me back, over him. I pressed his left hand onto my face. The hand grew even more translucent and I breathed deeply. I pretended to breathe particles of his very fabric into myself. He smells like jaggery, the palm sugar I liked eating as a child. When I raised his hand to kiss his fingers, they grew opaque.

Everyone knows what the Demi are famous for: their sense of humour and their inability to forget. But few humans have discovered what the Demi should really be famous for. I like to think I'm the only woman, perhaps the only human, who has ever made love to a being of a different species. I know this isn't true. Where did the Demi come from, after all, if not from the union of early settlers and Khonds? Now humans love only humans. Most of them. The Khond reproduce as only they can. And the Demi? They claim they have little use for others. Not my Arun. When I'm alone with him, no white noise can shut out the wind as well as he can. He can shut out the world.

He wrapped his arms around me and lifted me off the bed. He always does that. Provided he doesn't let go, and he never has even in jest, he can ease my nightgown up and over my head more easily in midair. More easily than when my elbow or my thigh pins the fabric beneath me. The nightgown felt suddenly heavy. I pulled it away and tossed it into a corner. We floated down onto the bed. I nudged him onto his back and felt him grow more opaque to support my weight. Then he rolled me onto my back and grew translucent so I could breathe. Translucent everywhere except on top of my thighs, where I like to pull the weight of him down. His clothing always seems to evapo-

131

rate. One moment it's there, the next moment I can feel his flesh quivering on mine. I clamped my legs over the small of his back and pretended to draw him inside. I still need to pretend he can enter me there first. He started glowing. The more he glowed, the warmer he felt. The warmer he grew, the farther I could draw him in. And not just there. He filled my body. His quivering flesh pressed up under the surface of my skin. Finally, when every particle of our bodies mingled, he laughed. The room filled with blinding violet light. I squeezed my eyes shut, clasped my hands over my ears, and shrieked.

He tried to draw out of me and I said, "Not yet." This is the best part: lying together afterwards with his body in mine; knowing that nothing which happens outside this room or this building or this bay can matter.

He drew himself out slowly, one particle at a time, one part at a time. First a finger, then a toe. He pulled out his arms and his chest and his trunk and legs till I could feel only his head inside mine. I stifled a cry when he pulled out completely. He slid his arm under my shoulder and his arm grew more opaque. My head rose till he could cradle it on his chest and toy with my hair.

"I watched one of your old dramas," he said at last. "This is the part where they smoke."

I laughed. So did he. Light poured from his mouth. I kissed him to block the light, to stifle the sound in his throat while his chest quaked. The light also tasted like jaggery. I drew away and pressed his lips together. He kept trying to flex them. He made soft, protesting sounds. "Shh," I warned, "you'll wake the children."

He became serious then. He pulled away from me to say, "Can't have that, can we?" His voice was a grave bass.

"That's not what I meant," I said. I rose and found my nightgown inside out. I fumbled it outside in. Even as I pulled it over me, I said through the suddenly comforting

132

fabric, "No one should know, that's all."

"No one does know," he said. His clothing reappeared, and he sat up. "How've you been?"

"Same," I replied.

"Is it your friend?" he asked. "The one others could never call Cassandra because of that prophet of Ancient Earth?"

"She wasn't my friend," I said. I lay down beside him and urged him to lie close. Again I rested my head on his chest. "Cassie was going mad, that's all. No one can be real friends with someone like that."

"Because you couldn't help her," he asked, "or because you were afraid you might become like her?"

"I read a book once," I said. "It was about the first law of space travel. It wasn't really a law because it wasn't scientifically proven."

"And it's not like you to change the subject," he said.

"No matter how far the human race leaves Earth behind," I continued, "we can never be completely at home anywhere else. I'm paraphrasing." I sighed. "Maybe that's what Chou Fung was trying to say the other night, at dinner, when he said we'd all like to leave."

"You can't go back," Arun said.

"Are you trying to tell me something?" I teased.

He pretended he hadn't heard. I should have known better. He talks so glibly about love except when we're alone. "Physically you can go back," he was saying, "but you were all born here."

"Try telling that to the Khond," I said.

He snorted, then smiled at allowing himself to become annoyed. It's all humorous to him, even annoyance.

Everyone knows the last thing a Khond or a Demi does before dying is to laugh. A loud, long laugh that empties its body of its spirit in the form of a light. It starts with the red of destruction, races through the spectrum into the violet of creation, and turns into a blinding white light. Or so people say. No human has ever seen a Khond or a Demi die. When the time for that comes they flee into the Pyrrhic Range.

"The Khond," Arun said, "dream of an age that never existed. It's true your coming brought them the notion of time but now they're weaving a fantasy of their past. 'Time without time,'" he scoffed, repeating the Khond chant. "'Form without form, and life without death.'"

I pulled away from him and sat up. "I wish you wouldn't mock your own people like that," I said. "I mean not your own people but—"

"I know what you meant," he said.

I turned with my jaw set to find a weak smile lighting his face. I kissed the spot where his navel should be. He rippled into opaqueness, and I moved my hand slowly down.

He clasped my hand to stop it from sliding between his thighs. It still bothers him. He can make love to me as no man ever could, but he's still not completely human. He moved my hand up to his chest and let it ripple through translucence into transparence. My hand sank till I could feel his heart, there below his breast bone. His heart beat under my palm. He likes doing this to show his heart beats only for me. It's part of the wedding ritual of the Demi: to clutch one another's hearts for the only time in the presence of others. During those long nights when I was still grieving, when I couldn't allow myself to make love, he would say, "Touch my heart." The night I could finally bring myself to do it was the night we finally made love.

"Once long ago," he said, "before you were even born, I went up into the mountains. I forced myself to do a ritual my father told me about. 'Spread yourself thinly,' he said, 'and when the sun eclipses, your ancestors will speak to

134

you.' I don't think he ever dreamed I'd do it." Arun's face hardened; the light between his lips faded into a blackness that might have been either sadness or anger.

It must be sadness, I thought. He's incapable of anger. "Then what happened?" I asked.

"The aurora appeared," he said. "The Ah-Devasi—"

"They do exist!"

"Of course they do," he said, "only not the way you think. And not the way the Khond think either. That's what really galls them. I've heard of Khonds who go into a trance and see the world through the eyes of the Ah-Devasi. And what those Khonds learn about themselves they don't like, because they've become unworthy of their ancestors. Don't ask me if it's true."

"The ritual?" I prodded.

"Yes, the ritual," he said. "It was the middle of the day and the sun was eclipsed. It was cold, so cold. Then the aurora appeared and its beings spoke to me." He reached for my hair.

"Well?" I asked.

"They cast me all the way to the other side of the world," he said. "'We are the spirits of the aurora,' they said. 'The aurora of the spirits.' They? It was many voices. It was one voice. Maybe the Khond never did speak with one voice the way some of them like to believe now. Just as some of them like to think humans speak with one voice. When a Khond looks at you, all it sees is a human. Not an individual, distinctive being. When they look at me they see a Demi, not...."

His lips drew back and I shuddered. He was capable of anger after all, when compassion failed him; when he saw the Khond exactly as he claimed they saw humans. The light from his mouth glowed red. Even his eyes glowed faintly red. He closed his mouth and his eyes. When he opened his eyes again, they looked normal, the

135

VEN BEGAMUDRÉ

irises a pale violet. When he opened his mouth to speak, the light from inside looked normal, too. "I'm sorry," he said. He clutched my hand to his heart and it beat rapidly beneath my palm. "You see, I still have vestiges of the Khond in me. Too much for my own good. If they could find a way to lose their anger, their own eyes wouldn't glow so much. Do you know what happens to a Khond that lets its anger consume it? It goes blind." Arun smiled, and light flickered between his lips.

I couldn't decide whether to believe him. "Did the Ah-Devasi say anything else?" I asked.

"Oh yes," he replied. "'You are not of us,' they or it said. 'Neither are you of the humans,' they-it said. They-it sound like I do when I'm in public, like a character from one of your old dramas." He shrugged. "I went through all that to learn what I must've known all along?"

He smiled again, so brightly I kissed him to stop the light from flodding the room. The light no longer tasted like jaggery. It tasted bittersweet. We made love a second time, less playfully than before. This time I made him remain inside me a long, long time.

* * *

As soon as Arun left, through the ventilation grille, I glanced at the clock. It was the middle of the night and I wasn't tired. I barely sleep on the nights he visits me yet I never feel tired. It's as though he leaves a residue of his energy in me.

I left the flat again. The only other beings in sight were Khonds. Few of them looked me in the eye. In the eyes of those who did, I saw a surly glow. When I reached the lift I found it out of order. Still I punched the up button, then waited with my arms crossed. Through the large window, I watched the twinkling lights of Tonkin Bay far to the east.

A voice startled me: "May I be of service?" I knew even as I turned that I would find a Khond. A faint smell of

136

ammonia was filling the air. Its head poked through the closed lift doors from inside the lift.

That's why Khonds are so good at maintenance work: they can go anywhere. Up to a point. The very oxygen we humans breathe gives them their form and they like that. They like feeling useful. But too long among humans and Khonds can never venture out into the ammonia-rich atmosphere. They're trapped inside and live out lives shortened by oxygen. They sneer at the Demi, who move so easily between our two worlds, and yet the Khond who are no longer useful slouch through walls if they can and slouch against them if not. No Demi would ever slouch. I watched this Khond closely and waited for it to speak.

"I believe the stairs work," it said at last.

"No kidding," I said. I turned toward the flat. I wasn't about to walk up the twenty floors to the dome.

"I believe kidding is for goats," the Khond said, "though I have never set eyes on such a creature." The Khond pulled itself farther out from the lift. "Might you have on your esteemed person a modicum of divine tobacco? It refreshes the weary and makes one sleep as soundly as a babe. Oh, if—"

"I'm sorry," I said as politely as I could. "I don't smoke."

The light in its eyes barely flickered when it smiled. "Do not concern yourself," it said. "Tobacco affords a truly fetid and diabolical smell. It chokes the air...."

I let the Khond go on. I should say I let this particular being go on. It was an individual, distinctive being, not the representative of an entire species. But I knew exactly what it was doing: entertaining me with servitude, ingratiating itself. Any other time, late in the day when I'm tired, I let my annoyance show. I do care, but it's so irksome when my politeness is used against me.

"Look," I finally said. The Khond stopped in mid-soliloquy. "I'll make you a deal. You let me up to the lounge, and you can come by later and help yourself to any one thing in my kitchen." I raised a single finger.

The Khond snorted. I expected the smell of smoke but smelled only ammonia. "A test," it said. "Nothing more." After it looked left and right, up and down to make sure there were no Khonds within hearing, it said, "If any of my kind inquires, however, pray insist you exchanged a gram of tobacco in return for my humble service. Irreparable would be the harm to my reputation, such as it is, should rumours begin to the effect that I bestowed my favour on a human." The Khond's right hand emerged from the lift door. "Okey dokey, liddle schmokey? Shake."

I reached forward but we never made contact. The hand pulled back through the door. Chortling, the Khond stepped completely out of the lift shaft, then pressed a button on its workbelt. The lift lights came on.

I touched the up button, and the doors slid open. I stepped inside and turned in the doorway so the doors couldn't close. "What's your name?" I asked.

"Pray, why do you inquire?" it asked, startled.

"So I'll know what to call you next time," I said.

"I have long believed," it said, "that no member of your species could distinguish any member of mine from another. Except domestics, but familiarity also breeds—"

"Okay," I said. "Fine." I stepped back into the lift.

"A moment," the Khond cried, "I beg you!" It stepped forward and the doors slid back. "You require my human appellation," it asked, "or my original appellation?"

"I wouldn't be able to pronounce your original name," I said.

"This is true." It chortled until a faint light glowed in its eyes. "My human appellation is Henry—short for Henry the Fourth, Part One. My sibling, as you might surmise, was Part Two. Alas my sibling is, to all purposes, no

138

more, stiffened in a living death somewhere in Corinth Bay. My original appellation, however, might roughly translate as—" The light in its eyes suddenly dulled. "Even my comrades, my kith and kin address me as Henry. Why is that?"

Before I could try to answer, it backed away and the lift doors closed.

I consoled myself with what I knew now; what most others, even Chou Fung and Chou Li, don't: the Ah-Devasi didn't drive Cassie mad. It's avoiding contact that can drive a human mad: contact with the aurora beings, even contact with Khonds. They're all around us and yet, just as most humans pretend the Ah-Devasi don't exist, so they treat the Khond as if they barely exist.

Spiro, for one, but then he's so caught up in his precious work that.... No, that's not fair. It is precious. We're trying to find a way to oxygenate the entire planet without killing off the Khond. I know he cares about his children as much as I care about mine, but I wonder if he could ever defend them with his life. If it ever comes to that, if the violet glow rolls out of Bight Pass onto the plain, I would protect the twins with my life. I would even kill to protect them. What am I thinking of, though? There are more ways of dying than being murdered in our beds: meteor showers, quakes, vehicle crashes. Especially crashes. Life is full of danger even for the Khond. They simply have less to lose, or so people say.

The lift doors opened and I hurried to the observation chair. I strapped myself in and raised it. I turned the chair through the north toward the northwest, toward the aurora. The strands hung down, even braided, then waved free and curled blue on green. Where the aurora dipped behind the Pyrrhic Range, a strand glimmered in blue shading into indigo. The aurora stubbornly resisted the rising of the sun. Before long, though, the aurora started losing its daily battle. It retreats by day and surges back at night. Now it was fading, drawing itself away from the sun. The sun rose and its harsh light washed out the lights of Tonkin Bay. The sodium content of the atmosphere had increased since yesterday, when the sun looked more blue. Today the sun would be a yellow-orange.

That's when I realized something was missing: the sound of children breathing. I'd forgotten the monitor. Not to worry. I won't be staying long. Cora will soon arrive to see the twins off to class.

The sun was picking out the highest peaks. I watched the aurora flicker and finally knew we had to do it. We had to make contact. We have to. It thrills me as much as it must have scared Cassie. Whether I like it or not, one day I'll follow her into Bight Pass. It's the only way to save our children from the Khond; to save the Khond from themselves. But I won't be driven by fear, and that's why I'll reach the Ah-Devasi. I know something else. My life will never be the same. It's the only way to survive: to change, even physically like the Demi. Like my Arun. Someone has to be first. Then the rest of them will follow. For a while—perhaps only a few years, perhaps even decades— all of us will move in sync.

I see it now. I am the one.

Afterword: On Fact, Fiction and Speculation

Ah-Devasi is derived from Adivasi, meaning "original inhabitant"—one way of referring to the tribes who lived in India before it was settled by the people we now call Indians. A *deva* is a god. Other names in the story are also borrowed from Indian mythology and history: Arun is a Hindu god of the dawn and charioteer of the sun. Cora is derived from Koraput District in the state of Orissa, home to sixty-two tribes which speak thirteen different languages. However, this is not an allegory about the colonization of Orissa by Hindus centuries ago. It's a story about a widow who lives on another planet centuries from now.

You may feel this is not so much a short story as the first chapter of a novel. If so, here are more facts you can use to speculate on what happens next. Some of the tribes in Orissa are the Dongaria Khond, who worship an earth goddess called Dhartanu; the Kuttiya Kondh, whose human sacrifices the British outlawed as barbaric (this led to the 19th-century Anglo-Kondh War in which thousands of Kuttiya Kondhs died); and the Bondo, who believe their women are the most beautiful in the world. Then there are the Pano, tradesmen and farmers who seem to move easily between tribal and Hindu society even though Hindus consider the Pano to be untouchables.

Strange, isn't it: how one person's mythology and history become another person's speculative fiction?

141

AT THE BUS STOP,
ONE AUTUMN MORNING

M.W. Field

It began at the back of my neck.

I was thinking about relaxing
    stony muscles there
        when prehistoric points began emerging. They flared
            up the back of my head, down
    my vertebrae, off in a triangle
studded tail. My spine lost
    its S-curve, so I tucked my thickening
        hind legs underneath and sat down.
    Flicked my powerful green tail twice
and wrapped it round my feet.
    Arms had lengthened
        my jaw relaxed and expanded: gone
were the grinding molars. I yawned.
By the bus shelter:
    a stegosaurus, observing
        the smells and colours of the opening

        sky, shifting

        my weight on my forefeet.

No buses came.

WE CAN'T GO ON MEETING LIKE THIS

Phyllis Gotlieb

He buys a single ticket. It is a midweek day in early spring when the weather is mild and the children are not yet out of school; the visitors have come out to the zoo for walks, not to stare into the cages. The peacock steps among them, darting at tossed crumbs and pistachio nuts.

She is waiting by the lions' enclosure, wearing dark glasses and a discreet bandana, with her hands in the pockets of her camel's hair coat, watching the lions. He cannot see his own breath but the lions' mouths are steaming fiercely. He comes up, shoulder glancing hers, and watches the beasts. The lioness is twisting and rubbing her head against the lion's neck. The woman is staring though them: she has been in that lioness's body or one like it a score of times; perhaps her husband prefers her as a lioness.

"Which one?" she whispers.

"I want to try the lion." He wants, but is uneasy—his first time.

Her mouth quirks. "I've done that with him already. Too many times. Out in the wild all they get to do is hunt food for the males and bring up the kids."

"Still...." Perhaps that's why he wants it.

In the depths of the old Observatory there are three

143

rooms in use: the first where men and women wait for their turns to live in the beasts of their choice; the second where they lie in tiers of bunks while patient white-coated assistants cup electrodes to their heads. In the third room the lewd old inventor and his assistant, a woman whose face is thick with hair-sprouting moles, carefully connect the wires. Twenty minutes they will give you, by Visa, Mastercard, Amex; you pay dear for a taste, a spice of that hot kingdom. If lovers come and couple as animals it is not yet a legal infraction of the marriage vows. It is a ritual; perhaps it is their pornography.

Without a glance at her lover the lioness/woman strolls down the path toward the ape house. He follows.

Monkeys and apes are more expensive to get into—they have hands after all—but now they are sluggish from having been kept shut away from the cold weather all winter. Their house is hot and reeking; they squat dimly on their shelves. In back of the ape house there is an aquarium where dolphins clown and whales whack the glass walls with their flukes. In the bottom of their tank the sharks are circling, flicking their tails. He stare and wonders if they are occupied, then follows her steps to the ancient domed Observatory.

He works to adjust his reduced consciousness to this alien body and wonders if her husband has ever tried a lion. He shakes the great mane and his neck aches; the topaz eyes focus strangely and his hearing is dim. The beast hates the cold weather, has a toothache, and has lost his fierce dreams of the veld. He draws a lungful of the deep scents that would satisfy him if he were truly a lion. He feels awkward and hot, cannot master the natural rhythms of breathing and walking, and he senses the lion's resentment at the touch of his mind.

The lioness observes him, does not quite recognize him, whisks her tail and turns away toward an older and bigger lion he has never noticed before, one that snarls at him and plants a splayed paw on the lioness's hip.

What is this? He opens his jaws and the roar crackles out of his chest. The old lion's claw is reaching for his eye in a savage moment; the moment freezes while he tries to cry "No!" and the sound emerges a choked squeal in a puff of steaming breath. The spectators are screaming—this cannot possibly be happening, it can't!—being trapped here between the lion's body and the man lying cupped with electrodes; the claw tears—

No. The lion's instinct has turned his head away and the claw has scratched him beside the eye. The scratch stings sharply, he swerves away retreating to a corner where he can spit on his paw and rub the blood away.

When they walk down the steps of the Observatory the air is already cooling toward evening.

"What did you think of being a lion?"

He resists the impulse to rub the area on his temple that still seems to be stinging—though the experience is fading, he is astonished how quickly. "I didn't much like that one. I still wouldn't mind making love to a lioness."

"I won't go into a lioness again."

"What would you rather be?"

"A vixen; a wolf; a shark. A cobra." She walks away. Beyond the wrought-iron gate and across from the park where the nannies wheel the babies and the cruisers walk their dogs, there is a small hotel, old as the Observatory, with a palm-lined coffee shop. Its rooms have old brass beds with flowered knobs. It is a place where they make mild love on sprung mattresses.

She is headed there and diminishes with distance, but he realizes that she is also diminishing in his mind—as he might be in hers—fading toward her husband, the mild vegetarian botanist with magnifiers and tweezers, the old and too possessive lion under the skin. He thinks of looking for other women, other lionesses.

He glances back once. The old lion approaches the bars suddenly and widens eyes stare at him with pupils like black stars, raises and splays a huge paw, shoots claws and roars. The peacock spreads wings, squawks hideously and dashes away half-flying; its droppings spatter behind it.

The lover pulls back quickly though two ranks of bars protect him, and hurries away. The lion yawns hugely, crouches and falls asleep; the lioness rubs her jaw along his shoulder, rests her head on it and leaves one eye half open.

BARUCH,
THE MAN-FACED DOG

Mick Burrs

Prop. XXIV. The more we understand particular things, the more we will understand God.

Spinoza, *The Ethics, Part V*.

I believe that a triangle, if it could speak, would say that God is eminently triangular, and a circle would say that the divine nature is eminently circular; and so it is that everyone would ascribe his own attributes to God... and everything else would be seen as ill-suited (to be like God).

Correspondence, Spinoza to Boxel, 1674

I

I stood in front of the cage with my friends. We were passing a large bag of popcorn back and forth. One of my friends threw some popcorn into the cage. I watched the kernels bounce on the floor before they settled there among the peanut shells and food scraps.

On a paint-blistered sign outside the cage the black-lettered words read:

Dog with Human Face—
One of the World's Wonders

9 a.m. - 12 noon
2 p.m. - 4 p.m.
7 p.m. - 9 p.m.
Closed on Holidays

At the back of the cage the creature napped. I could not see his face, but he looked like a dark, long-haired sheepdog. One of my friends was trying to coax him to get up, to show his face. "Come on, boy! Come on! We wanna get a good look at you! Here, boy! Here!" My friend tossed in some more popcorn.

The creature raised his head. Every one of us responded in surprise and shock. No question about it: this dog had the eyes and nose and mouth of a man. His ears were covered by his long black hair, so I couldn't tell if they were human ears or dog ears.

He stared at my vocal friend. The expression on his face seemed to be one of disgust. He shook his hairy head as if to say, "No matter how hard you try, you won't bring me down to your level. I may be a dog but I'm more intelligent than you."

His thoughts seemed to register in my mind through his very expressive eyes and from the way he turned his head. Yet everything else about him was totally doglike. Large paws that sprawled before him, a curled tail that occasionally flapped against the concrete floor, and a slow breathing, hair-covered body that was unmistakably canine. I thought of him then as "the man-faced dog." "Dog with human face" seemed softer, less blunt, less accurate—wrong somehow.

It pleased me to see the man-faced dog not eating any of the stuff tossed onto his cage floor. He stood and stretched his front legs the way all dogs do, but yawned like a man as his body quivered. Now he had an almost arrogant or defiant look in his eyes, as if he refused to stoop so low, to even pretend to notice us. At this point I was staring at him, trying to understand him, trying to figure out how he ended up having a man's face and a man's eyes. Usually dogs have the saddest eyes, but this one had the gaze of an insolent human being.

When I made eye contact with the dog I knelt by the cage, so I would not have to stand above him. He must have noticed this gesture for he scooted towards me. My friends jumped back. It was an amazing moment. In that instant I could sense that both of us wanted to assess the intelligence and the empathy of the other. I saw the insolence leave his eyes, replaced by something that seemed closer to openness and amiability. Now I couldn't help myself; I began talking to him:

"You don't like popcorn, do you? And you certainly don't like being treated this way." It was a statement of fact as far as I was concerned.

But one of my friends, his mouth stuffed with popcorn, looked down at me and elbowed another friend: "Hey, Gerald is trying to communicate with the pooch. He thinks it will talk to him."

I glanced up, feeling perturbed at my companions, even embarrassed by their friendship. "Listen, I'll see you guys later. OK?" I wanted to talk to the creature, to at least make the effort. This whole scene in which I had been taking part was making me feel dispirited and alienated. Was I the kind of human being who likes to cage other not so human beings?

My friends grumbled and cursed but walked away; now no one else was standing outside the man-faced dog's cage. At least I wouldn't feel so self-conscious trying to talk to him.

"Please forgive my friends," I said. "They don't know what they're saying. They—"

A voice interrupted me. "Oh, but Gerald, they know

what they're saying. You know it and I know it. So it does no good to cover up for them. I see through them just as much as you do."

My god, it was the man-faced dog. I jerked my head back. "You're talking. You're actually talking, and you know my name."

"See, not only can I speak, but I can hear too. And do you notice, I'm speaking English, not Italian or Portuguese. Quite a shock, eh?"

"God," I said, "this is fantastic. You're not only a man-faced dog, you're actually... partly... human."

"I'm fully human, my friend."

I glanced around to see if anyone else was witnessing this unbelievable encounter. "Fully human?"

"I'll prove it to you," he said. "Just squeeze between these bars, Gerald. You're thin enough."

Suddenly I was wary. I didn't respond, just stared at the man-faced dog now conversing so easily with me from his cage.

"Don't worry," he said. "You'll be safe, I guarantee it. I won't bite you, Gerald. See, I don't bark either. I talk. I told you, I'm fully human."

I was shaking my head. "How can I be sure it's all right? What will happen to me once I get into the cage?"

"My friend, I'm going to take you behind the cage—to my real home. I want you to meet my family and see how I live. That's all. I'm really a friendly sort of person. And I don't eat human beings either. In fact, I've become a vegetarian. Now how do you like that?"

For a talking dog, he was certainly persuasive. I glanced around, then squeezed myself between the bars. They were cold and rusted and it was difficult manoeuvring my body between them; they hurt my shoulder blades and scraped my head, but I did manage to end up inside the cage instead of out.

The dog was restless, circling in front of me. "Follow me, quickly." Some people were approaching the cage, so I figured he wanted me out of sight. I watched him crawl into a large circular hole in the back wall of the cage. I had to get down on my hands and knees to follow him inside that hole. I couldn't move as fast as he did, but I was amazed at how promptly, without any more hesitation, I followed the dog's commands.

I remained in my crawling position in a narrow passageway, lit by one electric bulb in the far wall. I could see another circular hole just ahead, to the dog's left. I could hear the hollow, amplified sounds of a television game show, with the host and the audience cheering on some screaming contestants. Then I heard a man and a woman laughing inside a room beyond the hole.

"This is where I live, my friend," he said, nodding his head toward the hole. "The cage is just for show."

Wagging his tail, the man-faced dog bounded through the hole. The only way I could follow was on my hands and knees.

II

As I crawled through the second hole, all I could think of was an endless stream of questions: What will his family be like? Will it be his mother who is also a dog? Or his father? Will one parent be human? Where do his parents sleep? In a bed, or on the floor like the man-faced dog in his cage? Does he talk to his parents? Do they talk to him? How do they treat him? How do they live? Are they a happy or an unhappy family?

As my brain overflowed with these questions, I realized I was crawling on the carpeted floor of a trailer home. Should I stand up or stay on all fours?

The man-faced dog stopped in the middle of the largest room. "This is Gerald, a friend of mine."

151

He nodded towards me. I had remained hunched over, eye to eye with my host. I looked up.

A man and a woman were lounging before a television set, the woman leaning back in a drab green armchair and the man sprawled out before her, his head in her lap, his feet propped on the coffee table in front of the chair. Red and white beer cans glittered on the coffee table and on the floor. The man was thin and the woman was plump. She wore a skirt and blouse and white bobby sox; he wore tattered Levis and a white T-shirt. He was wiggling his bare toes. She was massaging his scalp,

"Yeah, another friend," the woman said. "We've got eyes, Baruch, we can see." She was not even glancing at me.

The man burped. "This is one hell of a show, son."

"*Wheel of Fortune*," the woman said.

"Hey, guys," the man said, "don't just stand there. You and your pal, come and join us. This show's a million laughs. Drag your tail over here."

"Yeah, don't be a party pooper," the woman added.

"No thanks," the man-faced dog said. He said it with politeness. Then he turned towards me and lowered his voice.

"I didn't invite you in here to sit with my mother and father and watch a bunch of greedy human beings making fools of themselves. I want to show you my library."

I was flabbergasted. These two people were his mother and father? And his name was Baruch? And he read books? And this is where he lived—here, in a trailer home behind a cage in a travelling exhibition? How could this be? Someone as intelligent as he was, someone who could talk as clearly and distinctly as any human being I had ever met?

He scampered into the kitchen. In a corner near the aluminium sink he placed one of his paws on a small stack of hardbound books. The covers looked old and worn, like library discards. I could make out some of the titles. *Thus Spake Zarathustra* by Nietzsche. Plato's *The Republic.* Spinzoa's *The Ethics.*

"My God," I said, crawling after him, "you're a philosopher!"

"A philosophy student," he said. "There's a difference. I haven't written anything yet."

"Do you plan to?"

"Maybe. One day."

I hoped we were out of earshot of his parents, but I knew we weren't out of their sight.

"You don't have any privacy here," I said. "How do you manage to stay sane? Do they watch TV all night? And drink beer?"

"Unfortunately, my mother and father are a pair of souses." He said this the way someone might inform you it's starting to rain outside. "They like to do their thing, I like to do mine. We don't always understand one another."

Delicately, with his paw, he opened the top volume on the stack, Spinoza's *The Ethics.* "This is my favourite book," he said. "I've read it at least forty times."

He didn't gaze at me to see if I was impressed. He kept right on talking, with intense enthusiasm.

"After my third reading of this book, I knew I didn't want to be called Benny any more. So I told my mother and father, 'Stop calling me Benny. From now on, my name's Baruch.' After Baruch Spinoza, the Dutch-Jewish philosopher. I told them how he changed his name from Baruch to Benedict—and now I was doing the opposite. That's what I announced, quietly but firmly. They just laughed at me and refused to call me anything but Benny, the name they gave me the day I was born. But I insisted they call me Baruch. For a day or two they kept calling me Benny, out of sheer habit. But I didn't respond. Benny, wash the dishes. Benny, scrub the floor. Benny, vacuum the rugs. Benny, clean the toilet. Finally, in exasperation, my mother started calling me Baruch. It was only then that I responded. Then it was official. Baruch, Baruch. Such a noble name. You notice that my mother doesn't pronounce my name correctly. But I use the correct intonation. My name. Baruch. That's Hebrew for Blessed."

I was feeling dazed, rapt in admiration. But I still couldn't think of the creature as fully human. I put my hand on his back and stroked his fur.

He let me pet him for a few seconds, then pointed to a page in *The Ethics*. "This is my favourite passage. It's actually from one of Spinoza's letters. His analogy of the triangles. Are you familiar with it?"

"No, I'm afraid not."

Baruch, the man-faced dog, was one up on me. He knew more about philosophy than I knew about English and History.

"These were the words that made me accept myself just as I am. I no longer felt ashamed. I no longer believed I was ugly or abnormal. That's what my mother and father had taught me: I was special but unnatural. They still believe that. But after reading Spinoza I knew who God was and who I was." His eyes glistened with tears. "For me, God has a human face... and the body of a dog."

"Pardon me?"

"It's simply a logical extension of Spinoza's analogy on triangles. And it's like everything else he wrote. Cold and clear and carefully thought out. His mind was mathematical. He structured his universe according to a system of geometric definitions, axioms, propositions, proofs, and corollaries. He wrote his entire *Ethics* this way. Baruch Spinoza, my 17th century freelance rabbi. My rational teacher. My spiritual father."

"I can see you're a fan of Spinoza's, but what did he say about triangles?"

He grinned. "Spinoza proved to me: if men mere triangles and worshipped God... then God would be a triangle."

That did it. It felt like my head was being twisted out of shape. My body was cold and feverish at the same time. "This is all too much for me," I said. "I'm feeling dizzy. I'm feeling faint."

"Spiritual vertigo, my friend. Spiritual vertigo. I experience it every day. It's the internal proof—eternity's testimony—that I have an immortal soul. And so do you. And so do my father and mother, although they don't know it." Here he started chuckling; this human being in a dog's body was chuckling. "For all we know, even triangles have immortal souls. How do you like that?"

I sat down on my haunches on the cold kitchen linoleum. I was trying to recover from this stimulation overload: the television volume blaring too loudly in the trailer, especially during the commercial breaks; the laughing and burping of his drunken parents; the astounding revelations of how the man-faced dog really lived; the concrete evidence of how extremely intelligent he was. All this was more than I or any human being could handle.

"Don't you ever want to leave this place?" I finally said. "I mean, this way of life. It seems so demeaning, surviving here like this. Someone who's a genius like you should be teaching at a university—and not be displayed in a cage like a freak."

Then I added: "And how much housework do your parents make you do? While they're sitting back and guzzling beer and watching TV? I'm telling you, it's inhuman and unjust."

Baruch wasn't chuckling now. But he wasn't crying

155

either. He was laughing—laughing with all the heartiness of an easy-going soul, a contented man.

"Forgive me, my friend. But what you say is hilarious. I can see you're feeling sorry for me. But you're not asking me if I'm feeling sorry for me.

"You need to understand something. My life is not perfect, but it is a good life. Now, how can that be?

"The world will never accept a dog with a human face to teach an introductory course in philosophy. But the world will accept a man with a dog's body in a sideshow."

He lifted his head toward the window above the kitchen sink.

"At least I can say, the world out there is leaving me alone. And, my friend, most of the time, I want to be left alone. I need my solitude. I need my books. I need at time for serious studies.

"Do you realize what would happen to me if I went to university—not as a professor but as a student?

"I'd end up on TV. I'd be interviewed on all the late night talk shows; I'd even become a contestant on some of those game shows—*Wheel of Fortune*, *Let's Make a Deal*, *Jeopardy*. My parents would walk into taverns and order rounds of beer and poke complete strangers in the ribs and say, 'That's our boy! That's our Benny! Have another beer—it's on us!'

"No, I'm better off just like this. I'm safe. This cage and this trailer, they're my world, my cocoon."

I could not look him in the eyes. "Baruch, can I ask you a very personal question?"

"Ah," he said, "I know, I know. It's the one question everyone asks. Or wants to ask. I can read your mind, my friend. Yes, that's really my mother and that's really my father. So how is it possible I was born with a man's face and a dog's body? That's what you want to know, right?"

I nodded.

156

He grinned.

"My friend, this can no more be explained than the virgin birth of Jesus."

"Aw, don't listen to him!" his mother said. "That son of mine is full of more cock and bull than a field of cows. He reads too much. He doesn't watch enough television. He doesn't live in the real world. He's not like the rest of us."

"Hey, Marlene, that's telling him," his father said. "It's nothing but the God-awful truth that leaves her precious lips." As if to punctuate his statement, the man burped. "Come on, son, come on over here. You and your pal, you're missing out on all the fun."

"I think I'd better take you back outside," my host said. "They'll be entering their belligerent phase in just a few minutes. No sense putting you through that."

He padded towards the door to the trailer. "You should leave this way," he said. "No sense crawling back into the cage." But when he pushed on the door with his front paws, it wouldn't budge.

"Locked," he said. "I apologize. They've done it again. Sometimes my mother and father are afraid I'm going to try to escape. I'm their livelihood, after all. Their ticket to the good life."

He led me away from the door. "My friend, you'll have to leave the way you came in. Through the hole. Sorry."

"Oh, that's all right," I said. But I was feeling sad and depressed.

At the circular hole he looked contemplative, solemn.

"This is as far as I go. I've got to make supper now." He glanced back at his parents. "Tonight it's spaghetti and meatballs for them, spaghetti in butter sauce for me."

Then Baruch, the man-faced dog, wagged his tail. "I know this isn't heaven, but I don't believe it's hell either."

He winked one eye. "Purgatory, perhaps. But that's not so unusual, is it?"

I shook his paw. "Goodbye," I said.

"Goodbye," he said.

* * *

As I entered the cage, a cluster of people stood outside the bars. When they saw me crawling on my hands and knees, they nudged one another and pointed at me and began laughing.

"Look," they said, "the dog is wearing a suit!"

I could see it would do no good to tell them I was a human being with a human face. I'd have to stand up and squeeze through the bars to prove that.

For now, I felt ashamed of my own humanity. As a form of penance, I remained on all fours and began to bark.

COUPLES

Eileen Kernaghan

> Birth and death have the fact of
> separation in common.
> — Lyall Watson, *The Romeo Error*

The streets are quiet tonight. This sullen blonde child is my first patient in an hour. She peels off a bandaid and shows me an oozing wound on the back of her wrist. It's ragged-edged and inflamed—an ugly mess.

I reach for the cotton swabs. "How did you do this?"

"Dug out a beeper."

"What with? Your pocket-knife?

"Uh huh." Her voice is matter-of-fact.

"Next time get somebody else to do it." I feel her wince as I start to suture the wound. "What's your name?"

"Edwina."

Prim and old-fashioned, suggesting lace curtains, lavender-scented dust, the name sits oddly on her. I try to imagine what she looks like under the garish make-up. I can see patches of smooth pale skin where the silver-glitter pancake has rubbed off. In her baggy moon-suit she might be any shape, or no shape at all. When I was her age—can it really be forty years ago?—we flaunted our bodies in microshorts and transparent tops. Now all the

159

kids dress like this, in surplus-store coveralls that hide a multitude of physical peculiarities, genetic flaws. I wonder what Edwina's suit conceals.

"Is that what your friends call you?" I pick up the antibiotic gun. "Or do they call you Eddie?"

She scowls at the clinic wall. "Friends?" she says balefully.

I note the appeal for sympathy, and ignore it. "Okay, You're mended. Got anyplace to go tonight?"

Her shrug is ambivalent, but I'm pretty sure of the answer.

"Where were you before? A group home?"

"Oh sure," she says. Her tone is scathing. "What else would you like to know—my address? They told me this place was no questions asked."

"It is. I was merely being polite. There's a spare bed in the back room, if you want to use it."

I can see her starting to relax—not because she trusts me, but because she is too exhausted to keep her defenses up. "Okay," she says. "Maybe for tonight. Got anything to eat?"

While I'm brewing a pot of tea and rummaging through the cupboards, she goes into the washroom and scrubs off the silver make-up. She's even younger than I'd thought—fourteen, fifteen, maybe—with pleasant, even features: a perfectly ordinary, unremarkable young girl's face. Along with the pancake, she's removed the veneer of sullen toughness, the street-kid's self-pitying, defensive scowl.

She settles in at my desk with the teapot, a loaf of bread, and a jar of ersatz peanut-butter. Meanwhile Tim/Jacob, who are supposed to be sweeping up, wheel round the room in ever-narrowing circles. As a rule they pay little attention to my patients, but Edwina, for some reason, seems to fascinate them. A grin tugs at the slack wet corners of Jacob's mouth. Timidly, awkwardly, he reaches out to touch the silvery fabric of Edwina's sleeve. Edwina, her mouth full of bread and peanut butter, stares back impassively. She makes no attempt to withdraw her arm. Nor does she flinch when after a moment Jacob lifts his hand and strokes her cheek. The gesture is Jacob's, but it's from Tim, twisted and helpless in his chair, that the impulse comes.

"This is a big place," remarks Edwina, spooning up more peanut butter. "What's in the rest of the building?"

"Labs," I tell her. "We're basically a research facility, with the street clinic tacked on."

"No shit!" She sounds impressed. "Can I see the labs?"

"Nope."

"Why not? You're torturing small animals, right?"

"Wrong. It's just not open to the public. Anyway, there's nothing to see."

Another shrug. "I'm going to sleep now, okay?"

"Okay."

She takes her cup and plate to the sink and rinses them under the tap. "Thanks," she says, like a small well-brought up child remembering its manners.

An hour before I'm due to go off shift I put my head into the sleeping rooms to check on their occupants. The first room, a double, is empty. In the second, Tim/Jacob sleep peacefully, Tim's small head, trailing a thin ribbon of fibre optics, resting next to Jacob's huge, slack-featured, vegetable skull. In sleep, one might take them for friends, or brothers.

In the last room, the one where Edwina is supposed to be, the bed is empty.

She can't have walked out of the clinic. The outside door is three feet from my desk. That leaves the vat-room. Gail, the night nurse, has phoned to say she'll be late; and with the vats as well as the clinic to keep an eye on, I've left the connecting door unlocked.

I find Edwina leaning over the anencephalic tanks.

"Weird," she says, without looking up. She doesn't sound shocked or surprised—just curious.

"They're waiting for computer-matching," I start to explain, but she cuts me off.

"I know... The Fetal Rights Bill. We got that all crap in Social History. 'Whatever possesses life, has the inalienable right to survive.'"

She stares into the murky depths of the tank, where a dozen anencephalic infants float amid a tangle of umbilical tubes. Lacking skull-bones, cranial cavity or sometimes any semblance of a head, they drift and turn in their warm placental broth. I've seen their opposite numbers in other research labs— babies with soft useless bones, malformed or missing organs, twisted spines and absent limbs: many of them with undamaged brains trapped in the genetic catastrophe of their flesh.

It seems that every year there are more of them. We've spawned a generation of children too maimed, too incomplete —too monstrous—to survive without gross intervention. What medical science has offered us, instead of prevention or cure, is an awkward compromise—a kind of biotechnical marriage that merges two useless halves into a functioning whole. Some of these children have been waiting months, years, for the complex neurosurgery that will couple them inseparably to another human being. For the lucky ones, like Tim and Jacob, the marriage may succeed.

Edwina continues to stare into the tanks. It's hard to imagine what thoughts lie behind that sombre grey gaze. Finally she says, "Couldn't you just make them grow the parts they're missing?"

"Medical science hasn't quite reached that point, I'm afraid. The best we can hope for is a symbiotic partner."

"Like... what did you call them, those two freaks next door? " There is no disparagement in her tone; she uses the word "freaks" as a simple statement of fact.

"Tim/Jacob."

"So do you think Tim/Jacob would have picked each other, if they'd had the choice?"

The question catches me off base. It isn't the sort of thing I think about.

"It hardly applies to Jacob, does it? But Tim has adjusted to the situation, I suppose. He doesn't seem unhappy. After all, how many choices do any of us have these days? We adjust to our circumstances."

"That sucks," says Edwina. "I didn't adjust. I left."

"So what were your circumstances? You never said."

"The best," she replies, with heavy irony. "That's what they always told me. Anytime I complained, they'd say, `Edwina, you should realize you are remarkably fortunate in your circumstances.'"

"Who's they?"

"My folks. That's who put the beeper in." She turns away from the tanks and glares at me as though I, by virtue of my adulthood, share responsibility for the wound on her wrist. "It just goes to show how much they trusted me. Two days before I turned fourteen they hauled me off to the doctor and snick snick, there it was—a fucking alarm-bell in my wrist. 'Happy birthday, Edwina, you're a big girl now.'" Her voice is forlorn. "It's what they used to put in dogs, and prisoners. Now they put it in kids."

"Don't look at me, pal. I haven't got any kids. So how many times had you run away before?"

Indignantly she tells me, "I've never run away. Do you know how hard it was this time? I live in a fucking fortress. You want to know why they put the beeper in?"

"I have a feeling I'm going to find out."

"Look," she says. She rips open the velcro fastening of

her moon-suit and shrugs it off her shoulders. It ripples around her feet, a pool of silver. Underneath she is wearing a plain black body-stocking.

What Edwina reveals to me, as she casts aside her disguise, is the thing I am least prepared for. The grotesque has lost any power to disturb me. It is commonplace, expected. But in her simple perfection, in the straightness of her spine, the mathematical symmetry of her adolescent limbs, Edwina is unique, astonishing.

"See?" She thrusts out a narrow leg and leans back, absurdly, with her hands locked behind her head—a model's stylized posturing. "Two arms, two legs, all the right stuff in the proper places."

There is arrogance in the gesture, and a kind of sad self-knowledge; but neither joy, nor pride.

"I'm the same as them," she says. I follow her gaze toward the tanks. "I mean, like, not the *same*. But that's where I came from. Really. They pulled me out of a vat."

"Try again, Edwina. The vats are for babies with gross birth defects—the ones that can't survive on their own. There's obviously nothing the matter with you. And if you're talking about extra-uterine gestation, they outlawed it thirty years ago."

"I know—the Reproductive Laws," she says. "But how about in special cases?"

"Like for example?"

"Like for example my real mother tried to abort me."

She looks to see if I'm shocked—but I've been at this job a long time, and I know when not to react.

"Why was that?"

Edwina shrugs. "Who knows? Maybe she didn't think the world needed any more freaks." Her expression is sly. She is choosing her words carefully, assessing their effect. "Anyway, in her shoes, I'd do the same thing."

"And go to jail?"

"Shit," says Edwina. "I've been in jail all my life."

Whatever else, she has a fine sense of melodrama. "So what happened?"

"With my mother? Well, obviously, it didn't work. She fucked it up."

It's just possible that she's telling the truth. There'll always be women who try to flout the reproductive laws. If the reprocops catch them in time to salvage the fetus, then it's our responsibility to bring it to term in the vats. The law, as Edwina has already reminded me, is unequivocal. "What has life, has the inalienable right to survive."

Those that manage to survive are put out for adoption through private creches. The healthiest ones, the nearly-normal, soon find homes. As for the rest—who knows, or cares? When they become too costly to feed, too trouble-some to nurse, there is always Nightside.

But how to explain Edwina, whose genes have some-how escaped the ravages of our malign sun, our deadly air, our poisoned ground—who is neither halt, nor maimed, nor imbecile, nor tumour-ridden? Sad Edwina, the princess in the lonely tower. I find the word, finally, that I've been searching for. Bereft. An old-fashioned word. It means disconsolate, and desolate, and dispossessed.

In the morning she puts on her moon-suit, smears silver pancake on her face, and leaves. I don't ask where she plans to spend the day. It's not my problem, unless the police come looking for her.

Tim/Jacob trundle out of their bedroom, grab some cereal, and plug into the net for an hour before they start their chores. My shift is finished. I put on my coat, and get ready to leave.

Gail is in the tank-room with her feet up on a chair, reading a medical journal while she waits for her relief. With the light falling on the right side of her face, the left in shadow, she still gives an illusion of normality. Then when she looks up I can see the other, ravaged half—skin, flesh and underlying bone gnawed away by cancer. They've arrested it, she says. Now she's saving up for cosmetic repair. In the meantime, she leads a nun's life. She is flippantly cheerful about problems that make my own seem trivial. When she goes out in public she wears a mask—not the computer-sculpted replicas that are all the rage this year, but a cheap comic mask, brashly, blatantly false.

"They give me the creeps," Gail says, looking at the tanks. "Soon as I can I'm going to transfer to the Downs Ward." She puts down her journal. "Speaking of giving people the creeps, what happened to that kid who was hanging around in here last night?

"Edwina? She left."

"She'll be back," Gail says with bleak conviction. "Want some advice?" And not waiting for an answer, she says, "Watch out for that one. Don't get involved."

"I never get involved," I tell her. She snorts her disbelief.

"Did she lay the full sob-story on you?" Gail wants to know.

"About her mother, and the vats?".

"That's the one. And you believed it?"

"Maybe. Shouldn't I have?"

"That's not for me to say." Gail's tone implies the opposite. "And how about the twin brother, the one that didn't make it?"

For some reason this sends a faint chill down my spine. Maybe it's because, like Edwina, I started life as one of a pair. But for the twisted, half-formed scrap of flesh that was meant to be my sister, there was never any question of survival. Fifty years ago there were no vats. "She didn't tell me about the twin."

Gail shrugs. "Maybe she forgot. Or maybe she just has a vivid imagination. You should know these kids by now, Annie. They'll say whatever they think you want to hear. Or whatever makes a good story. Just watch her, that's all I've got to say." She picks up her magazine. "She's got an awful mouth on her, too," she adds as a parting shot.

That night, when I come on shift, Edwina is back.

Tim/Jacob are already plugged into their deck, and Edwina hovers behind Tim's chair, a bottle of soda in one hand and a sandwich in the other. I sit across the room with my cup of coffee, watching. I love to see the flickering of expression across Jacob's broad, slack features as Tim takes him into the net. The same technology that links them together, mind to muscle, opens the doorway into a vast electronic landscape, joins them to the minds of a thousand other symbiotic couples scattered across a hundred cities. Jacob's strong body is the prosthesis that allows Tim to walk, to talk, to function in the ordinary world; but the net is his true home, his magic kingdom. When they emerge, I see all the light fade from Jacob's face, as though an internal switch has been thrown.

Edwina's eyes are on the wall monitor. She seems to be waiting for some image, some communication to appear. She shifts impatiently, and finally complains, "Why doesn't he turn on the fucking screen? I can't see a thing."

"Watch your mouth," I tell her, remembering Gail. "There's nothing to see. Tim's jacked straight into the net."

"So can I do that?"

"Not without neurosurgery, you can't."

"So how come Tim gets to do it?"

"Because he's training to be a netwalker—a direct access technician. A troubleshooter. "

"Tell me where you are, Tim/Jacob," Edwina whispers. "Tell me what you see."

"I'm in a garden," Tim tells Edwina, obligingly. His

167

voice is high and breathless. He loves Edwina, is eager to share his secrets with her. "I'm in a whole series of gardens, one inside the other. I'm walking through a forest of tall flowers. At least I think they're flowers—they look like trees, too, or fountains of water, all different colours, or maybe huge butterflies. Their branches—their wings—glitter. The colours are very strong, very bright: blues and greens and yellows, and reds.... The garden is on an island, and it's part of an endless chain of islands, growing smaller and smaller and smaller, but every one the same..."

Edwina is leaning over Tim, her chin almost resting on his shoulder. "Man, is that ever *neat!*" she says. "He's making fractals, and walking around in them." She swivels her neck to look up at me. "How does he do that, Annie? How does it work?"

I shake my head. I've never understood the neuroelectronics that open the gates to these magic worlds, these gorgeous algebraic gardens. "Where did you learn about fractals?" I ask, forgetting for the moment that she had another life before this one—before Nightside.

"I'm not stupid, you know," says Edwina. She tries to make it sound like a joke, but I can hear the hurt in her voice.

Impossible to imagine anyone envying Tim/Jacob; and yet it is pure envy I see in Edwina's face. There are no limits, no boundaries to Tim's universe. His mind leaps across an infinite web of worlds. He has only to begin the dance, and the cosmos dances with him. For Edwina, there is only the narrow cage of her own skull.

That night, long after Tim/Jacob should be asleep, I hear the murmur of voices in their room. I get up, intending to chase Edwina back to her own bed, but then I change my mind. The other night, standing as usual at Tim's shoulder, trying to imagine the world of wonders beyond that empty screen, Edwina remarked, "You said symbiotic. Symbiotic partners. But that's not right, is it? Tim doesn't need Jacob. Inside the net, he doesn't need anybody. He doesn't even need a body." She spoke with a kind of wistful astonishment, as though she had only just discovered this, and was amazed by it.

I thought for a minute about what she'd just said. "I suppose he doesn't. But remember, Jacob needs Tim. Jacob only has a life through Tim."

"So what does that make Jacob?" she pointed out. "A parasite, right?"

And in the middle of the night, when I should have been working on reports, I was still thinking about it.

* * *

She leaves in the morning, returns at night; after a week, the pattern becomes familiar and expected.

Then, on Monday night when I come in after two days off to work the night shift, Gail tells me that Edwina hasn't been around since Friday. Immediately, I panic.

"I told you not to get involved," Gail says. "Anyway, when she gets hungry enough, she'll turn up."

"You sound like you're talking about a stray cat."

Gail's shrug is eloquent.

It's another quiet night. There's nobody in the clinic but myself and Tim/Jacob, who are already asleep. I have little to do but worry about Edwina. Finally, at midnight, I do a quick check on the vat-room and then on Tim/Jacob, set the sensors to beep me if anything comes up, lock up tight, and head out into Nightside to look for Edwina.

* * *

There's a narrow buffer zone, a no-man's land, around the clinic—undeclared, but respected by the street tribes. Here there are circles of wan light, a diminishing of the darkness, where a few old-fashioned street lamps still burn. Beyond, there is the dark—the haunted, restless dark of primordial woods, full of skittering, chittering, mewling noises. As often as I walk in this place, I still feel the same knotting of my stomach, the lifting of the hair on my neck. I'm armed with stun-gun, gas-pellets; I know how to protect myself. In any case, the inhabitants of this night world are familiar with my step. And yet I'm afraid.

The wavering circle of my handlight shows dirty concrete, an indecipherable palimpsest of scrawled graffiti; then more concrete, covered with a crust of something—blood? excrement?—layered thick as stucco.

Here in the dense core of the city the towers soar to improbable heights. Shaded by connecting ducts and elevated walkways, the narrow crevasses between are sunless even at midday. At night they are black as the sea's bottom-most depths. It's here, from midnight till dawn, that the child-tribes crawl like bottom-feeding fish. By day they retreat to nests and bolt holes in a maze of abandoned tunnels several stories underground.

At the end of the street a red glow flares against the walls. Shapes huddle in its warmth. I hear my name, odd-sounding, glottal, shaped by a half-formed, palateless mouth. Crouched under a piece of sacking, Beast grins up at me.

They wear these names with a perverse joy, flaunting their deformities like caste-badges. There is social order, of a kind, among the child-tribes; they have their laws, their hierarchies.

"Annie's here," Beast tells the girl beside him. They call her Fish, and the name fits her. Her skin has a grey-white pallor; it's so nearly transparent that you can see the web of veins beneath. Where her eyes should be are smooth-skinned hollows, delicate imprints like thumbs pressed into clay. Are children like Fish a random product of gene-damage, I wonder, or is this a kind of evolution, a natural adaptation to the conditions in which they exist?

Fish knows me. I have given her warmth, shelter, medicines, a bed to lie on. She sidles against me, clings to my arms with her long, pale, attenuated hands. Her fingers, brushing my wrist, are cold as tentacles.

Turtle waddles into the firelight on his limbless feet; hands, protruding from his shoulders through his torn sleeveless shirt, wave excitedly. He is gentle, sweet-natured, dog-like in his affection. I worry about Turtle. The name they have given him is, in its way, ironic. He lacks the tough shell, the carapace, that he needs to survive in this place.

"Turtle, can you tell me where she went?"

"She was pretty," he confides. "She talked to me. She said she 'd take me with her, we'd be friends—but then Beast tried to touch her, and she ran away.

"Which way, Turtle?"

"There." He stares into the blackness at the end of the street, beyond the fire.

* * *

For hours I've been tracking her from camp to camp, from fire to fire. They have all seen her, talked to her. They have touched her clothes, have reached up to stroke her skin, her hair. They speak of her in mythic terms. They are awed by her, as by a visit from an alien being, or a goddess. And then, moved by superstitious fear or simple malice, they've driven her away,

Finally, as the darkness thins to dirty grey, I turn back to the clinic. Like vampires, we've learned to hide from the sun.

* * *

The next night Edwina is back—wan, tired, dirty, her hair uncombed and clotted with filth. I ask no questions, and she volunteers nothing. This time, anticipating her, I have locked the door to the vats.

"Let me go in there," she says.

171

"What for?"

"I want to look at them again."

I wonder what knowledge or pleasure anyone could derive from gazing at those sad half-creatures. In some other fourteen-year old, I might have dismissed it as a child's morbid curiosity.

"Sorry—it's against the rules."

"Crap," she says. "You left the clinic and followed me last night. Isn't that against the rules?"

"I was worried about you."

"That was stupid. You left Tim\Jacob alone—didn't you worry about them?

Sluggish from lack of sleep, I lack the strength to argue with her. I'm demoralized, defeated, by her logic—by that cold, level grey gaze.

Wednesday night, she is gone again. Then at three a.m. the phone rings. I snatch it from Gail's hand.

"Annie? Is that you, Annie?" Edwina's voice is a hoarse whisper.

"It's me. Where have you been? I was worried about you."

"Annie, can you come and get me?"

"Where are you? What's happened to you?"

"Wait." I hear a muffled question, then, from somewhere behind her, a male voice.

"Gastown, beside the clock. In half an hour. Don't bring anybody else, okay?"

"Edwina—" But she's broken the connection.

* * *

I'm there in fifteen minutes. In this city of soaring towers and abandoned streets, the old-fashioned arcades and brick-paved alleys of Gastown are a curious anachronism. After the big quake of '98 the whole area was rebuilt out of the rubble in all its nineteenth century quaintness, and covered with a twenty-first century dome. In the daytime

172

it's filled with tourists; but as soon as the shops full of fake Cowichan sweaters and plastic totem poles close, the character of the place changes. Huddled shapes materialize on benches, in doorways. Haggard twelve year old hookers gather by the steam clock. In the shadows of Blood Alley, sellers of exotic drugs make nervous deals.

Tonight, though, the pavement around the clock is empty. Even the whores are asleep, it seems. I wait a quarter of an hour, shivering and apprehensive, before Edwina appears. She stumbles suddenly out of the darkened mouth of an arcade, her moonsuit a ripple of lemon-yellow in the soft Edwardian light. Then I realize there is a man behind her, thrusting her forward—a thin redhaired man in an expensive sequined jacket.

This, or something like it, is what I expected from the beginning. It's why my throat felt dry, my chest tight every time I found Edwina's bed empty. The man has stopped just outside the chain-link fence that surrounds the clock. One arm, in its glittering sleeve, is wrapped around Edwina's waist. The other hand holds a long double-edged knife. Carefully, almost tenderly, he lets the edge rest against Edwina's throat. Edwina's face, under its silver make-up, is masklike, expressionless with fear.

It's pure melodrama—a scene out of one of Gail's detective novels. But the knife, and the terror on Edwina's face, look real.

"She says she belongs to you, Lady. Maybe we can make a deal."

I call out to him across the few yards of pavement that separate us. "Tell me what you want."

He grins. "How much is she worth to you?"

"Don't play games. Just give me a figure."

"Ain't that much money in the city, Lady." Then— "You work at the clinic on Davie, right?"

"Uh huh." I know what comes next. "We don't keep

drugs in the clinic. No morphine, no codeine, nothing."

"That's not what I've heard."

"I don't care what you've heard. I'm telling you—anybody who needs more than stitches and an aspirin, gets shipped to Emergency."

"I'm not talking morphine. I'm talking DMT."

Dimethyltriptamine. Of course. We keep a small supply in the lab under lock and key. In fused couples like Tim/Jacob, it increases the firing across synaptic gaps. Ever since transgenics wiped out the Asian poppy fields, the street price of DMT and the other neurotransmitters has gone through the roof. I once heard somebody describe the DMT rush—"a fifteen-minute neon roller coaster ride." It must be the one thing worth more on the Nightside market than Edwina's flawless adolescent flesh.

"Don't get involved." I don't need Gail to remind me of that fundamental rule. I am not responsible—for Edwina, or for any other waif who lands on my doorstep looking for bandages and comfort. The fact that she's bright and beautiful and that Tim\Jacob love her does not change that.

I tell myself that the knife is for show; this man is not going to use it on Edwina. He's a businessman—why would he damage a valuable piece of merchandise? It's not my problem. I can simply walk away, and let the youth-cops handle it.

And yet when it comes to the point, I can't turn my back on her. I think of the sister I never knew, the daughter I will never have. And I know I can't let the Nightside claim Edwina.

"It'll take me a couple of days," I tell him.

He nods, and pulls Edwina back into the shadows.

* * *

"Have you noticed that Tim/Jacob are having some difficulty co-ordinating?" I ask Gail, just before I go off shift.

"Lack of sleep," Gail says. "They're up half the night, hunched over that deck." She sounds grouchy, and I can see she isn't going to make this easy for me.

"Well, keep an eye on them, will you? I've made a note on their chart... do you think maybe a booster dose of DMT? It did the trick before."

I've thought carefully about this tactic. It takes two signatures, on a quadruplicate form, to go into the controlled substances safe. Why am I so sure that Gail can see exactly what I'm up to? But Gail loves Tim/Jacob; she won't risk their survival on a hunch.

* * *

"You have to go home, Edwina. You know that, don't you?"

Edwina is standing with her back to me. She seems unnaturally subdued—depressed, almost. Her shoulders sag as though the weight of the world rested on them, and she refuses to meet my eyes. I notice how thin and vulnerable her neck looks, as the silky helmet of her hair slips forward.

"Annie, just let me stay here. That's all I ever wanted, a safe place to stay. I can help you in the clinic. You can show me how to look after the vats."

"No. Absolutely not. Even if there were no rules against it. How long am I supposed to keep on worrying about you, running after you? Risking my job to get you out of trouble?"

"I'm sorry," I hear her mumble.

"If you want, I'll see if I can find you a place in a group home."

Her head jerks round. "Annie, they're total hell. You know I can't go into one of those places. And I can't go back to Nightside, either."

"You can go home. That's all that's left, Edwina. There

175

aren't any other choices."

But her face is closed, stubborn. In this mood, there is no reasoning with her. "Why? Nobody knows where I am. I'll bet my parents think I'm dead."

"Maybe—but as long as they don't know for sure, they'll be sick with worry. Do you realize what you're putting them through, Edwina?"

"They'll get over it. They're not really my parents, anyway."

"They raised you. And they loved you enough to want to keep you safe."

For an instant her composure slips. "That's all you know," she says bitterly. "You think you know it all, but you don't understand anything. I can't go home. I'd rather die than go home."

"Very dramatic," I tell her. It's been a long night. I'm immensely relieved to have Edwina back, but I'm running out of patience with her games. "If I'd had any sense, I'd have turned you over to the youth-cops weeks ago."

I hear the sudden sharp intake of her breath. "Annie, no. You wouldn't. Promise me. Please."

Defeated, I shake my head. I won't call the youth-cops. There was never any question of that.

Then, turning away from me again, Edwina remarks to the clinic wall, "Anyway, you can't go to the police, can you, Annie? Because of what you did."

I feel as though I've just been kicked in the stomach. I grab Edwina by her shoulders, twist her around to face me. What do I expect to see, as we confront each other—malice, hatred? But all her face reveals is naked desperation. She is like some small trapped animal gnawing on its foreleg in its determination to escape.

Now, finally, I understand what game we've been playing. Night after night in the clinic, Edwina was watching, asking questions, making connections. She knew what we kept in our locked cupboards. What other secrets have Tim/Jacob let slip, in those midnight talks I had done nothing to discourage? Twelve years on the Nightside, and I can still be taken in, manipulated... beguiled by a street-kid's self-serving charm.

Suddenly I am too exhausted to deal with any of this. I want to go home, I want to sleep. "You'd better stay here tonight," I tell Edwina. "Until I can figure out what to do with you." Whether she stays or leaves, now, hardly seems to matter.

Edwina's mask dissolves. Under the silver pancake, the muscles of mouth and jaw relax into the soft lines of a young girl's face. She grins, and gives me a tentative, awkward hug. But it's too late. Too much damage has been done. I turn aside, step coldly out of her embrace.

* * *

Just as I'm due to go off shift, the phone rings. Gail picks it up, then looks at me from across the desk.

"What's up?'

"Youth cops," she says, with her hand over the mouthpiece. In her other hand she is holding the key to the vat-room. "They want Edwina."

My heart gives a sick lurch. For a second or two I feel as though I've stopped breathing.

"What are you going to tell them?"

"What do you want me to tell them? Here, they're still on the line—you talk to them."

But I know, from the way that she too refuses to meet my eyes, that all the wheels have been set in motion. Nothing I can say or do now will make a difference.

Behind me, a door opens. Turning, I see Edwina standing in the doorway of Tim/Jacob's room.

"Never mind," I hear Gail telling me. "They said just hang on to her. They're on their way."

Then, cutting off anything else Gail might have said,

Edwina's shriek of outrage, of despair: "Oh shit. Oh shit. Annie, you told them. You promised you wouldn't, and you told them." Edwina makes a sudden darting movement. For an instant I imagine that she is holding a weapon—a knife or scalpel. Then I realize that she has snatched the vat-room key from Gail's hand. Before either of us can react she is across the room and has the vat-room door open. She slams it hard behind her, and I hear the deadbolt turn on the inside, the bar slam down.

More theatrics, I decide. "Edwina." I rap on the door. "Edwina, open up." There is no reply.

Gail hovers anxiously. "Isn't there another key...?

"No. Don't worry about it. Let her cool her heels till the police arrive."

"But we can't leave her alone in there. What if she damages the tanks?"

"She won't." I pull up a chair and sit down to wait. Edwina is afraid, and hurt, and angry. But so am I. Let her think for a while about how it feels to be betrayed.

The Edwinas of this world seem to understand, by instinct, how defenseless we are—how fragile the shields we put up against the world. They see the softness, the sentimentality, the hollowness that aches to be filled. And if they sense that ordinary misery has lost its power to move us, they reinvent their pasts, conjuring unimaginable horrors.

They tell us they are victims. But we are all victims, our generation no less than theirs. I think of Gail—the devastated landscape of her face, her hopeless valour at the edge of the abyss. Are Edwina's flaws less horrible, because they are so cleverly concealed?

Five minutes have gone by. Ten. "Edwina?" Still silence. And then, with a sudden dreadful intuition, I realize that she is never going to open the vat-room door.

I pound on it with my fists. It's steel-cored, triple-secured on the inside. The vat-room is designed like a bank vault, or a fortress. Again and again I shout Edwina's name. I plead, I curse, I threaten. Tim/Jacob have taken refuge in their bedroom. Loud noises, bright lights, unfamiliar faces terrify them. They've never heard me raise my voice in anger—and now I'm screaming at Edwina like a madwoman.

When the youth-cops arrive, I'm still pounding, and shouting. My arms ache all the way into my shoulders. Eventually they send for a man with a laser-torch to cut through the door.

* * *

We find her floating face up in the murky waters of the vat. Pale naked creatures, blind as anemones, nudge against her. One of them is tangled in the seaweed drift of her hair. Edwina's eyes are open, grey and strangely contemplative.

There is still a faint pulse when they take her out, but I know that it's a false hope; she's been in the tank too long. The fluid that sustains her womb-companions has filled her lungs and suffocated her. I kneel over her, give her the kiss of life, and after a while her chest begins to move on its own. But her mouth under mine is lax and wet as Jacob's.

I hear the faint creak of Tim's chair behind me, turn to see Tim/Jacob staring down at us. Jacob's eyes, glazed and uncomprehending, mirror Tim's bewilderment. Tim's mouth twists with grief; his curled hands tremble in his lap like injured animals. To my dismay, when I reach out to comfort him, he cringes from my touch.

The uncertain flutter in Edwina's throat is now a steady pulse. She is young and strong; her body clings to life. The heart pumps out blood; the organs pursue their mindless purposes. I know that in this slack inanimate flesh some part of Edwina survives, as something of Jacob has survived—but where will I find another Tim to make her whole?

179

CLARK KENT IN OLD AGE

Tom Henighan

Weightless, inside this mortal suit,
the tonnage of years on a stick,
I clutch at each clue to the old life.
An orphan of suffering, in search of
miraculous time, lovely muscle
of wish become flesh, but the changes!
One arm and a stiffly drawn head
twisted upward, I stumble...
They help me as much as they can,
their regret green as once their envy
grew, green as Krypton—a slow rot
begins in the brain, in the crotch,
superlatives die before the rest.
Only comic? Never mind if the elegy's
coined for your cat, or your goldfish—
you imagined it all, Lear too, and
Samson. Jobbers and sad old men
as well as princes of royal blood
hire fools or are aped
by their lackeys. Die, decline,
fade away or are forgotten.
Hero and clown all at once,
unreal but never spurious,

I carried what I could
of your first lust for story.
Consider at least your own joy,
how the colours moved in your mind
as you dodged through backyards
where not even your X-ray eyes
could see the rubble of your own childhood.
And if you don't pity me
pity at least what your mirror shows
of what you might have been
without fear and the perils
of too much gravity.

THE RECKONING OF GIFTS

James Alan Gardner

A junior cook brushes against the soup cauldron, hot, searing hot. He curses.

The kitchen noise strangles to horrified silence. Profanity is always dangerous here on temple grounds, and the danger is multiplied a thousand-fold by the proximity of holy objects.

The cauldron holds the high priest's soup.

A potboy screams out the door for an exorcist, but he knows it's too late: the words have ripped the amniotic sac that protects our world from the chaos outside. Demons must be streaming in by the dozen, invisible demons who sniff once at the kitchen staff, then scatter in search of the tastier souls of the clergy. The potboy can almost see the demons—fanged, clawed, with naked female breasts— racing down the corridor, wiping their hands on the tapestries as they go by (the dyes fade, the threads ravel), pouring out into the herb garden to wither the foxgloves, to suck the soothing power from camomile and the flavor from basil, then on across the courtyard, kicking a few cobblestones loose to trip passers-by, pinching the horses of a bishop's carriage, flying unseen past the warders and into the temple proper where they will crumple scrolls, tarnish chalices, and set the bells to wild jangling. Novices in catechism class will stumble over words as the demons tempt them to remember sweet berry pies, gravied beef, and a score of other foods the holy must forswear; priests hearing confession will find themselves dreaming of the feel of sins, the satisfying crunch of a fist plunged into the face of a self-righteous parishioner, or the excitement of commanding an adulteress to disrobe; and the high priest himself, Vasudheva, voice of the gods on earth, will be swarmed by demons, engulfed by them, demons raking their claws across his heart until it shreds into tatters that toss on the winds of desire.

The junior cook faints. Others pale and scatter their clothes with salt. But the Kitchen Master simply tells everyone to get back to work. He cuffs the potboy who called for help, a good solid clout on the ear that sends the boy staggering back against a chopping block.

"The lad's too excitable," the Kitchen Master tells the exorcist who appears in the doorway. "Sorry to trouble you. Nothing's wrong."

* * *

Vasudheva, voice of the gods on earth, kneels before the Twelvefold Altar. He is indeed surrounded by a frenzy of demons. When he kisses the feet of Tivi's statue, he doesn't think of the god's power or wisdom; he thinks of the sensation of kissing, the soft pressure against his lips, the lingering contact, the ghost of sensation that remains as he slowly draws away. He longs to kiss the stone again, to kiss it over and over until his lips ache with bruising. His hand rises toward his mouth. He stops the movement in time, but in his imagination it continues, his fingers reaching his lips, caressing, stroking, flesh against flesh.

Vasudheva cannot remember what he has prayed for this past half hour. Certainly not the exorcism of his demons.

A month ago, the Assembly of Bishops assigned Vasudheva a new deacon named Bhismu: a young man of undistinguished family, chosen because he has no affiliation with the Assembly's power blocs and can therefore be trusted not to exert undue influence on the high priest. Spending time with Bhismu shows he wasn't appointed for his intellect, piety, or even willingness to work.

Ah, but he is beautiful!

His hair is a garden of soft black ringlets, his beard an effusion of delicate curls. Vasudheva's hands long to entwine themselves, oh so gently, in those ringlets and curls, to braid, to weave, to stroke. He imagines threading his fingers through Bhismu's beard, cupping the young man's chin, gazing into those clear dark eyes as he leans forward and their lips meet....

Vasudheva dreams too of Bhismu's hands, strong but fascinatingly dextrous when he played the reed-pipe at the Feast of the Starving Moon. Vasudheva was hypnotized by the confident rippling fingers. He thought of nothing else far into the night, until in the bleakness of morning, he wondered if he had eaten a single bite at the feast. Scripture said the moon would starve to death, disappear from the sky forever because the high priest hadn't consumed enough on its behalf; but the moon survived, as did Vasudheva's desires.

He has never prayed for those desires to abate. He cherishes them. He relishes them.

* * *

Tonight begins the Long Night Revelries, a week of feasting and celebration in the city of Cardis. Events include the Fool's Reign, the Virgins' Dance, and the Renewal of Hearth Fires from Tivi's sacred flame, but first comes the Reckoning of Gifts in the temple's outer hall.

It's never a pleasant ceremony for the priests who officiate. The hall teems with unbathed commoners, men and women together, all clutching packages to their chests with fierce protectiveness. They jostle each other in the rush to receive blessings; they insult the Gifts of others and boast about their own. Every year fights break out, and sometimes a full-scale riot. Even if demons are loose tonight, it's hard to imagine how they could add to the usual commotion.

Vasudheva waits for Bhismu to escort him down to the hall. Not long ago, the high priest refused all help in getting around—though his quarters occupy the top of the temple's highest tower, he would climb the stairs unaided several times a day, glaring at anyone who tried to assist. Now, Vasudheva goes nowhere without Bhismu's strong supporting arm. He clings to the young man with both hands and walks as slowly as possible.

Several powerful bishops have begun overt machinations to win support in the assembly, believing there will soon be an election for a new high priest. They are men of limited imagination; they think Vasudheva has become frail.

The bishops would like to influence which Gift is chosen from the dozens presented in the hall tonight. Power and prestige ride on the choice, not to mention a good deal of gold. The laws of Cardis stifle innovation—change threatens order, and order must be maintained. No one may create a new device, a new art, a new process... except in preparation for the Reckoning of Gifts. In the month before the Reckoning, creators may build their inventions. On the longest night of the year, they bring those Gifts to the temple; from the dozens offered, one Gift is chosen and accepted into orthodoxy, while the others become fuel for Tivi's flame. The successful creator is fêted in all quarters of the city, honored as a benefactor of the people and a servant of heaven. The unsuccessful ones

185

have nothing to show but ashes.

Needless to say, competition is intense. Every guild sponsors some Gift to better their lot—a new type of horse hitch offered by the cart drivers, a new way to waterproof barrels offered by the coopers—and scores of individuals also bring their offerings, some of them coming back year after year. One family of fisherfolk has sent the eldest child to the Reckoning each year for more than a century; they claim to be able to teach needles how to point north and for some reason they think the gods will be pleased with such tricks. Not so. The gods have consistently shown themselves to be pleased with the Gift accompanied by the largest under-the-table offering to the high priest. The only variation from one year to the next is whether the secret offering is made in gold, in political influence, or in the adroitness of beautiful women.

This year, Vasudheva is sure the gods smile on a type of clasp offered by the silversmiths, a clasp more secure and easier to fasten than orthodox clasps. The silversmiths have provided the high priest with several samples of work that show the virtues of the clasp: a silver necklace whose pendant is the letter V studded with sapphires; a silver bracelet encrusted with alternating emeralds and amethysts; and a silver dagger and sheath, the dagger hilt glittering with fire-eye rubies, and the sheath embroidered to show Tivi's flame.

Schemers among the bishops try to sway the gods' decision, and several believe they have succeeded... but the gods are in a mood to demonstrate that they speak only through Vasudheva, while upstart bishops should devote themselves to prayer instead of powermongering.

A soft knock comes at the door and Bhismu is there. Vasudheva catches his breath, as he always does when Bhismu enters the room. Sometimes the high priest thinks he has two hearts in his chest: the withered heart of an old man and the bounding, pounding heart of a youth who feels the fever of love but not the complications. If he only has one heart, it must be attuned to the hearts around him—when he's surrounded by crabbed and ambitious bishops, his heart shrivels; when Bhismu is near, his heart expands and expands until it is as large as the sky.

Bhismu asks, "Are you ready to attend the ceremony, your Holiness?"

"If they're ready for me. Are things under control?"

"Father Amaran says we have encountered no more trouble than usual, but everyone feels a strong disquiet. There have been rumors of demons."

"Rumors of demons are like mushrooms," Vasudheva says. "They spring up overnight, and the peasants feed on them."

He hopes Bhismu will laugh, but the young man only nods. He's slow to recognize jokes. It's a failing that can be overlooked.

They begin the long journey down the tower's corkscrew stairs. A month ago, Vasudheva found it awkward to descend while holding on to an arm instead of the balustrade. Now, he's completely comfortable with it. He doesn't need to concentrate on his feet anymore; he can devote his full attention to the strength of Bhismu's hands, the faint smell of his sweat, the beard so close it would take no effort at all to kiss.

"Have you ever been in love?" Vasudheva asks.

The young man's thoughts seem to have been elsewhere. It takes him a moment to collect himself. "Love? I don't know. A few times I wondered if I was in love, but it wasn't like the minstrels say. Intense. It wasn't intense. I'd spend some time with a girl—this was before I was ordained, of course—I'd spend some time and I'd feel very fond and I'd wonder, am I in love? But my father was determined for me to enter the priesthood and if he saw me becoming attached to someone, he ordered me to give her up. And I did. I always did. So I guess it wasn't love. If it really was love, I wouldn't have... I don't know. It's wrong to disobey your father, but if I'd really been in love... I don't know."

"So you've never had strong feelings for a woman?" Vasudheva asks. He is very close to Bhismu; his breath stirs wisps of the young man's hair.

"Not as strong as love. Not as strong as love should be."

"Have you ever had strong feelings for anyone?"

"I don't understand. You mean my family? Of course I love my family. You're supposed to love your family."

Vasudheva doesn't press the matter. It took him forty years to rise from an acolyte in the most crime-ridden quarter of Cardis to the supreme office of high priest. He has learned how to bide his time.

But Bhismu's beard curls invitingly. Vasudheva's demons will not wait forever.

* * *

Bishops lounge on divans in the vestry that's adjacent to the outer hall. Each wants a whispered word with the high priest; each wants to overhear the other whispers. Vasudheva forestalls their jockeying for position by sweeping past them and throwing open the thick outer door.

Screams. Shouts. Feet stamping and glass breaking.

On a night so ripe with demons, the riot is no surprise to anyone.

The door opens onto the front of the room; the stampede is surging toward the public entrance at the rear. That's why Vasudheva isn't crushed instantly. The only people nearby are two men grappling with each other, one dressed in velvet finery, the other in blood-stained buckskins, each trying to dig fingers into his opponent's eyes. Here and there within the crowd other fistfights thump and bellow, but most people are simply trying to get out, to escape the trampling mob.

Things crunch under their feet. They could be Gifts dropped in the panic, they could be bones. No one looks down to see.

Vasudheva stands frozen in the doorway. A priest staggers up to him from the hall, squeezes roughly past into the refuge of the vestry, and cries, "Close the door, close the door!" He bleeds from a gash on his forehead.

Behind the priest comes a woman, doing her best to walk steadily though her clothes hang in shreds and blood oozes from wounds all over her body. Where her arms should be, she has wings. Wings. Vasudheva steps aside for her to pass, his mind struck numb as a sleepwalker's. Bhismu drags both the woman and the high priest back into the vestry, and slams the door shut.

The noise of the riot vanishes. There is only the whimpering of the injured priest, and the heavy breathing of several bishops whose fear makes them pant like runners.

"Sit down, sit down," Bhismu says. Vasudheva turns, but Bhismu is holding out a chair to the woman. Who shouldn't even be here—women are forbidden to enter the temple beyond the outer hall.

She's a Northerner, her hair black and braided, her skin the color of tanned deerhide...young, in her twenties. Bhismu's age. Vasudheva can't believe anyone would find her attractive. She's too tall and bony, and her nose is crooked, as if it was broken then set haphazardly.

Vasudheva keeps his eyes off the wings. There's no doubt they're beautiful, exquisite—slim as a swift's, abundant with feathers. For a moment, Vasudheva has a vision of the bird kingdom parading past this woman, each pre-

189

senting feathers for these wings: eagles clawing out sharp brown pinions, hummingbirds poking their beaks into their chests to pluck soft down the color of blood; and crows, doves, finches, jays, each offering their gifts until the woman faces a heap of feathers taller than her head, and still the birds come, geese, falcons, owls, wrens, adding to the motley pile, all colors, all sizes, herons, plovers, swallows, larks, all bowing down like supplicants before an angel.

Vasudheva shakes his head angrily. A high priest can't afford to indulge his imagination. This is no angel. This is just some woman from a tribe of savages. She killed a lot of birds, sewed their feathers into wings, then brought those wings to the Reckoning. No doubt she started the riot in the first place. Pretending to be an angel is blasphemy; the people must have attacked in outrage as she came forward for blessing.

Bhismu kneels beside her and dabs the hem of his sleeve at a wound on her cheek. He smiles warmly at her and murmurs soft encouragements: "This one doesn't look bad, this one's deeper but it's clean...."

Vasudheva finds the expression on Bhismu's face unbecoming. Must he simper so? "You can help her more by getting a proper Healer," the high priest tells him. "The sooner the better. Now."

Reluctantly, Bhismu rises. For some moments, he stands like a man bewitched, gazing at the specks of blood that mar the whiteness of his sleeve. "Now," Vasudheva repeats. Suddenly the bewitchment lifts and Bhismu sprints out of the vestry and down the corridor.

"We must make the woman go back to the hall," says a voice at Vasudheva's ear. "She shouldn't be in this part of the temple."

The words echo the high priest's thoughts, but he turns and sees they come from Bishop Niravati, a man

190

who loves to wield his piety like a bludgeon. Niravati has always been too quick to proclaim right and wrong; he conducts himself as if *he* were the voice of the gods on earth.

"She may stay here as long as necessary," Vasudheva says. Bishops must never forget who makes the decisions in this temple. "Sending her back to the hall now would be close to murder. And she's injured. Tivi commands us to minister to the sick, Niravati; did you skip catechism class the day that was discussed?"

Several of the other bishops chuckle. Good. Niravati will note who they are and later take revenge. Vasudheva foments feuds among the bishops whenever possible: dividing one's opponents is useful. And entertaining.

The woman has watched this interchange with no expression on her face. Perhaps she's in shock... but she gives the impression of understanding it all and simply not caring. For a baseborn woman, she's remarkably unmoved in the presence of the highest patriarchs of the faith. "What's your name?" Vasudheva asks her.

"Hakkoia."

"From a Northerner tribe?"

"From the Bleached Mountains."

Vasudheva doesn't know if this denotes a specific tribe or merely a place—his knowledge of the world outside Cardis begins and ends with the names of the bishoprics. "What happened in the hall?" he asks.

"There were fights. People threw things at me." She wipes blood from her chin.

"Why did they throw things?"

"It was demons!" the injured priest bursts out. Father Amaran. He's been huddling on a divan, hugging himself as if cold, but now he leaps to his feet and begins to babble. "Down in the kitchens... I can't get a straight story out of anyone but at confession... demons, they've released de-

191

mons. In the soup."

Even Niravati drops his eyes in embarrassment. It's one thing for a priest to rail about demons to the laity, quite another to bring them up among peers. Vasudheva envisions Amaran dying years from now as a workaday priest in some remote parish, and being able to put his finger on the exact moment when he destroyed his career.

"I saw no demons," Hakkoia says in the silence that follows Amaran's gaffe. "I saw a man who was jealous of my wings. A man in the crowd—I don't know who he was. He wore fine clothes but his gift was petty and small. He stirred the others to attack me."

"Demons are deceitful," Vasudheva says lightly. "The man may have been a demon in disguise. Or someone possessed by demons." The high priest has no intention of asking Hakkoia to identify the man who attacked her. If he wore fine clothes, he was probably a noble or the representative of a guild. Arresting such a man would have repercussions. Besides, everyone could feel the tension in the air tonight. The riot was inevitable, and assigning blame is beside the point. "Niravati," he says, "help this woman take off the wings. She'll be more comfortable without them."

Hakkoia looks miserable as the wings are removed. But she says nothing.

* * *

Soon Bhismu arrives with old Lharksha, teacher of Healing to three generations of acolytes. Lharksha's silver hair is wildly tangled, and his bleary eyes blink as if he's just been roused from a deep sleep. Vasudheva can't remember Lharksha ever looking otherwise; day or night, the man always seems freshly rumpled.

"Lharksha..." Father Amaran begins, stepping forward and lifting his hand to the cut in his forehead. But Bhismu pulls the Healer onward to the woman and begins to inventory her wounds. Amaran looks as if he is going to demand attention; but then he subsides and slumps back onto the nearest divan.

The Healer says little as he examines Hakkoia: "Does this hurt? Lift your arm, please. Can you lift it higher? Does it hurt?" Hakkoia answers his questions in monosyllables. When Lharksha asks if something hurts, she always says no.

The others in the room say nothing. They watch avidly as Lharksha prods Hakkoia's body and smears salve on her skin. The shredded remains of her clothes are discarded; sometimes they have to be cut away with scissors when the blood has crusted them in place. The men watch. Bit by bit, her body is stripped, cleaned, clothed again with crisp white bandages. The men make no sound, except for occasionally clearing their throats.

Vasudheva watches himself watching her. He's no stranger to the bodies of women—women are frequently offered to him as bribes. Hakkoia doesn't compare to the professional beauties he has seen, and he can view her with dispassionate appraisal. The bishops, on the other hand... Vasudheva looks around at the hunger on their faces and chuckles inwardly. Niravati is unconsciously licking his lips. Bishops aren't bribed as often as the high priest.

Vasudheva turns toward Bhismu and sees the young man has averted his eyes.

In that moment, Vasudheva realizes that Bhismu is lost. The realization is a prickly heat that crinkles up through Vasudheva's shoulders and leaves his ears burning. He felt this way fifty years ago when he was caught stealing a coin from the poorbox. It's a feeling of guilt and pure animal desperation, the piercing desire to reverse time and erase the past few minutes.

Bhismu is in love with Hakkoia. Why else wouldn't he

look? A healthy young man should relish the opportunity to see a woman naked. Even if he's zealously trying to live up to a deacon's vows, he should peek from time to time or at least show signs of temptation. But not Bhismu. His face shows neither lust nor the struggle against lust.

Bhismu in love.... Vasudheva averts his eyes.

"The woman may stay the night in this room," Vasudheva says, breaking the silence. Heads turn sharply toward him. "When the trouble dies down next door, collect any Gifts that are intact and arrange them at the front of the hall. Clear out the broken ones and throw them on Tivi's flame. If there have been deaths, save the bodies; I'll give them public blessing before we return them to their next of kin. In the morning. I'll judge the Gifts in the morning too. Everything in the morning." He holds out his arm. "Bhismu, take me back to my chambers."

Bhismu is reluctant to leave. As he leads the high priest away, the young man keeps glancing at Hakkoia back over his shoulder. Vasudheva thinks, *Now he looks. Couldn't he have looked before?*

Bhismu's body is still warm, his bearded cheek still inviting, but the high priest takes no pleasure in holding the young man's arm. Vasudheva needs no human escort; he is escorted by his demons who bear him up, quicken his stride, carry him along.

* * *

Vasudheva can't sleep. He paces around his desk, arguing with himself. Is Bhismu really in love? Could it just be some kind of chivalrous arousal, a reaction to the sight of a young woman in trouble? And why should a high priest be so concerned about a nobody like Bhismu? Bhismu has no brain, no political power; he's just a beard that begs to be kissed. A pretty trinket, nothing more. A high priest can't let himself get distracted by trifles.

But Vasudheva pictures Hakkoia dying. Not dying

with a knife in the throat, or choking from poison, or strangled by a garotte, just... dying.

Vasudheva imagines the wings burning in Tivi's flame. They will sputter and crackle at first, then catch fire with a roar. The smell will be hideous.

Destroying the wings will be nearly as good as killing the woman herself, but entirely free of blame. He can imagine the look on her face as she sees the wings burn.

* * *

Sometime after midnight, Vasudheva opens the secret drawer of his desk and takes out the presents from the silversmiths. All three are exquisite, but he may have to part with one. In order for the guild's clasp to be accepted by the gods, there must be a sample downstairs in the hall. If the riot destroyed the original sample, Vasudheva must supply a new one.

Wistfully, Vasudheva toys with the necklace, the bracelet, the dagger. It will irk him to part with any of the three, but if necessary it should be the dagger—fewer gems. He'll take it downstairs and slip it in with the other Gifts. No doubt, the silversmiths will recognize the generosity of this sacrifice and offer appropriate compensation.

He finds that descending the staircase alone is more difficult than he remembers. The realization scares him; he doesn't want to depend on Bhismu or anyone else. But no, he's not weak, just tired. He needs sleep, that's all.

As he nears the vestry, he realizes Hakkoia will be there. Why didn't he remember her before? His thoughts wander too much these days. But Hakkoia can't stop him from going to the hall. She may not even notice him; she's probably asleep.

And he has the dagger.

Vasudheva draws the blade slowly from the sheath. It glints in the light of the torches that flicker on the wall. He can't remember ever testing its blade before. He slides it

195

along the edge of a tapestry that shows Tivi setting the temple's cornerstone at the very center of the world. The dagger effortlessly slices off a strip of cloth ornamented with dancing angels. The blade is functional as well as ornate.

Vasudheva wonders how soundly Hakkoia sleeps.

But as he steals down the corridor that leads to the vestry, he finds Hakkoia is not sleeping at all. Low voices come from the room, one male, one female. Vasudheva closes his eyes and prays that the man is not Bhismu; it may be the most fervently Vasudheva has prayed in years.

But of course, it *is* Bhismu.

They aren't in each other's arms. Both are fully dressed. Hakkoia sits on one of the divans, her spine as straight and strong as a javelin. Bhismu sits on the floor at her feet, his head leaning against her thigh. The wings lie across Hakkoia's lap like a chastity belt.

No one has heard Vasudheva's quiet approach. Standing just outside the room, he can listen to their conversation. Bhismu is describing how his father beat him for every thought or action that might have kept him out of the priesthood. Vasudheva has never heard Bhismu speak of such things; despite a month of cultivating Bhismu's trust, Vasudheva has never reaped such secrets. And Hakkoia isn't *doing* anything. She barely speaks. Her attitude suggests she is merely tolerating his attentions; her mind is elsewhere.

"I could leave the priesthood," Bhismu says. "Vasudheva is fond of me. He'll release me from my vows if I ask. He tells me all the time that I'm his favorite. He gives me presents, and...."

Vasudheva steps angrily into the room. "Enough!" he shouts.

Bhismu looks up and blushes guiltily. He jerks away from the woman, and slides quickly along the floor until

196

he's more than an arm's length from her. Hakkoia barely reacts at all; she only lifts her chin to look the high priest in the eye. Her gaze assesses him thoughtfully. Vasudheva wonders what sort of things Bhismu said about him before he arrived, but there is no time for speculation. "I am not the one who can release a deacon from his vows," Vasudheva says, glaring at Bhismu. "Only Tivi may do that. And I don't think Tivi will be inclined to grant such a dispensation to a stripling who fancies himself in love because he's seen a woman's naked flesh. Aren't you ashamed of yourself? Aren't you?"

Bhismu seems to waver on the edge of surrender. His eyes are lowered, his hands tremble. But then the hands clench and he shakes his head like a fist-fighter throwing off the effects of a punch. "I haven't done anything to be ashamed of." His voice is almost a whisper, but there is no submissiveness in it. "I haven't done anything."

"What would your father think of this?" Vasudheva demands. "Alone with a woman in the middle of the night. And on holy ground!"

Bhismu cringes. But Hakkoia slaps her hand down on the divan with a loud smack. "I am not some sickness," she says. "I'm not one of these demons you talk about, the kind that you can blame but can't see. This ground is just as holy as when I arrived. If it was holy then. Why do you carry a knife?"

Vasudheva's anger surges. It's been years since someone dared to talk to him so accusingly. People like Bhismu hold him in awe; people like Niravati are too conniving to be blunt. He's on the verge of calling the warders, of consigning Hakkoia to the dungeons as punishment for her disrespect... but he realizes he can't do so in front of Bhismu. No violence, no cruelty, ever, in front of Bhismu.

Besides, violence is never more than a last resort. A prudent man finds other ways to eliminate problems.

"Bhismu," Vasudheva says in a calmer voice, "I think you should go to the chapel and pray."

The young man seems to have recovered some backbone, thanks to Hakkoia's words. "I haven't done anything to be ashamed of," he says again.

"Good for you," Vasudheva replies. "But I heard you talk about renouncing your vows, and that's grave business. No, no," the high priest holds up his hand to forestall a protest, "I'm not accusing you of sin. But this is something you should think about very seriously. You should be sure it's what you want, and what's best for you. For you, for your family, for everyone. That's only right, isn't it?"

"Yes," Bhismu says. He sounds like a little boy, still defiant inside but momentarily cowed. Vasudheva thinks of ruffling Bhismu's hair like a child, but he restrains his hands.

As Bhismu turns to go, Hakkoia tells him, "I'm staying with the family of Wakkatomet, the leatherworker. Elbow Street, near the Tin Market. They're Northerners; they're very glad when people come to call."

Bhismu's face blooms into a grin. He thanks Hakkoia profusely and leaves with a capering step. *He is so beautiful, so radiantly beautiful*, Vasudheva thinks. *It breaks my heart*.

* * *

"Why did you tell him where you live?" Vasudheva asks when Bhismu is gone. "You aren't interested in him."

"He said he worried about my injuries," Hakkoia answers. "He's concerned about my health. I thought he might rest more easily if he checked on me from time to time. To see that I was well."

Vasudheva conceals a smile. This is a woman he can talk to. "Lharksha is the best Healer in the city," he says. "Your health isn't in danger, believe me."

Hakkoia's eyes flick to the dagger the high priest still holds in his hand. She raises an eyebrow questioningly.

"A Gift," he tells her, "that's all. The sheath has a new type of clasp created by the silversmiths' guild. I was returning it to the hall to put with the other Gifts."

"There are no other Gifts," she says. "The priest, Amaran—he told me nothing survived the rampage."

"Nothing except this dagger," Vasudheva corrects her.

"And my wings."

The wings still lie across her lap. Her hands rest on the feathers, caressing them, stroking them.

"Are the wings hard to make?" Vasudheva asks.

"My people believe that humans are born with only half a soul," Hakkoia replies. "When a child has learned how to dance, she must go in search of an animal who is willing to provide the other half. I am now of eagle blood, and flight fills my heart. I have studied the wings of every bird; I have gathered their feathers; I have learned their calls. The wings were not hard for *me* to make."

"So you intend to make yourself rich selling wings? You and your leatherworker friends?" Vasudheva shrugs. "You'll probably do well. The nobles of Cardis are always eager for novelties, and flying will certainly appeal to them. Although most of them are lazy. Is flying hard work?"

"I don't know."

Vasudheva looks at her in amazement. "You've never tried the wings?"

"I have," she answers, and the boldness in her gaze disappears for the first time. "They don't work."

Suddenly, fiercely, she stands; the wings fall off her lap and thud heavily to the floor. She picks them up, thrusts them out toward the high priest. "If they could fly, would I bring them to this stinking hateful city? Cardis law means nothing in the mountains—I would fly the peaks and valleys, and to hell with the priests who say no. But your gods... your holy Tivi who's terrified of new things, he's the one who's keeping me on the ground. The Queen of Eagles told me this in a dream. So I've come for Tivi's blessing and when I have it, I'll soar away from Cardis forever."

She's mad, Vasudheva thinks. No Northerner is completely sane, but this woman goes far beyond the fanatic adoration of animals for which Northerners are famed. There is no Queen of Eagles! There could be a king—certain marginal writings imply there are kings of many mammal species—but that doesn't necessarily extend to birds. And if she expects that official recognition will make flightless wings soar....

Her eyes glitter too wildly. When she speaks of flying, you notice it: the glint of obsession. Vasudheva has seen it often through the years—priests who appear entirely balanced until you broach some subject that rouses their lunacy. Perhaps he's that way himself about Bhismu. How often has he told himself he is obsessed, irrational?

Thoughtfully, Vasudheva strokes his beard. "You'll leave the city?" he asks at last.

"Like a dove fleeing from crows."

He nods. "Bring the wings to my chambers at sunrise. In the tower. The warders will show you the way—I'll tell them to let you pass. The crowd will be waiting in the courtyard for my announcement. I'll proclaim your wings to be Tivi's choice and let you have your first flight from my balcony."

She hugs the wings to her chest and smiles. It is a dangerous smile, a mad smile. "Thank you," she says. "I'll leave, I promise. Bhismu will soon forget me."

Only years of experience let him hide his alarm at her words. She knows too much. Bhismu, innocent Bhismu, must have told her enough that she could deduce how Vasudheva feels. The dagger is still in his hand... but sunrise will be soon enough. If the wings work, she leaves; but the wings will not work. Vasudheva knows how little magic there is in Tivi's blessing.

The silversmiths will be annoyed when their Gift is not chosen; but they can be mollified. A big order of new chalices, bells, censers. Silver soup bowls for the acolytes, silver plates for the priests. He nods to himself, then sheaths the dagger and tucks it inside his robe.

"Tivi's grace on you," Vasudheva says to Hakkoia.

"Thank you," she says again.

* * *

After telling the warders to escort Hakkoia to his tower before sunrise, Vasudheva stops by the chapel. All the candles have burned out; the only light is Tivi's flame, flickering in the enormous hearth at the front of the sanctuary. The rest of the room is in blackness.

Bhismu lies before the flame, sound asleep. There's a smile on his face; no doubt he dreams of Hakkoia, but Vasudheva can forgive him for that. The more Bhismu loves her, the more her death will shake him and the more comforting he'll need.

He looks so vulnerable.

Without warning, a wave of passion sweeps over Vasudheva's heart, and he is bending to the ground. Bhismu will never feel it, a kiss on the cheek, the beard, one kiss stolen in the night, flesh, lips, and yes! Bhismu's curls are soft, and warmed by Tivi's own flame. The kiss is like a sacrament, holy, blessed. Another kiss, this time on the lips... but no more, no more, he'll wake up, one more, it doesn't matter, he's sleeping so soundly....

Something rustles in the back of the chapel, and Vasudheva is immediately on his feet, peering into the shadows. Is there someone on the bench in the farthest corner? Vasudheva strides down the aisle, his entire body trembling with rage. Reluctant to wake up Bhismu, he whispers, "Who are you?" with a piercing harshness.

"Duroga, sir, your Holiness," a voice whispers back. "Junior cook down in the...."

"What are you doing here?"

"Praying, your Holiness." The whisper is full of fear.

"In the middle of the night? More likely, you came to steal. What did you want? The sacramental silver?"

"No, your Holiness, no! I'm praying. For forgiveness. I burned myself on the soup cauldron and I said a very bad word. The word released demons, I know it did. The riot was all my fault. And everyone acting so oddly, it's the demons making everyone...."

Vasudheva slaps the cook's face, once, very hard. His palm stings after the blow and the stinging feels good. "You listen to me, junior cook," Vasudheva says. "You did not release any demons. If demons exist at all, they have more important things to do than flock about when some peasant burns his thumb. Understand?" He grabs the front of the cook's robe and shakes the man. Duroga's teeth clack together with the violence of the jostling. "You want to hear something? You want to hear?"

And Vasudheva begins to curse. Every profanity learned as a child, every foul oath overheard in the vicious quarters of Cardis, every blasphemy that sinners atoned for in the confessional, words tumbling out of the high priest's mouth with the ease of a litany, all tightly whispered into Duroga's face until the cook's cheeks are wet with spittle and his eyes weeping with fear. The words spill out, here before Tivi's own hearth, the most sacred place in the universe and so the most vulnerable...but no demons come, not one, because hell is as empty as heaven and the void hears neither curses nor prayers. Vasudheva knows; he's been the voice of the gods on earth for twenty-three years and not once has he spoken a word that didn't come from his own brain, his own guts, his own endless scheming. Wasn't there a time when he prayed that some god would seize his tongue and speak through him? But the first thing ever to seize his tongue is this cursing, on and on until he can no longer draw enough breath to continue and he releases the cook, throws him onto the floor, and gasps, "Now let me hear no more talk of demons!"

Without waiting for a reaction, Vasudheva staggers out to the corridor. His heart pounds and his head spins, but he feels cleansed. Duroga must meet with an accident in the near future, but it can wait, it can wait. Vasudheva has kissed Bhismu, has dealt with Hakkoia... has faced his demons.

Climbing the tower steps his soul flies upward, dragging his feeble body behind. His soul has huge wings, and as he reels into his chambers, he has a vision of the bird kingdom parading past him, each presenting feathers for those wings: eagles, hummingbirds, crows....

* * *

A loud knocking comes at the door. Vasudheva wakes, aching in every bone. He has spent the night on the floor; he never reached the bed. Now the room is quickening with pre-dawn light, grey and aloof. Vasudheva shivers, though the day is already warm.

The knocking comes again. Vasudheva pulls himself to the bed. Off with the robe he still wears, a quick rumpling of sheets, and then he calls out, "Come in."

Bhismu enters. Vasudheva's smile of greeting for the man dies as Bishop Niravati and the cook Duroga enter too.

"Good morning, your Holiness," Niravati says. The bishop's voice has none of its usual tone of feigned deference. "Did you sleep well?"

"Who is this?" Vasudheva asks, pointing at Duroga,

though he remembers the cook quite clearly.

"His name is Duroga," Niravati says. "Last night he came to me with a disturbing tale about demons. Demons which he thinks have possessed high-ranking officials of our temple."

"He claims to be able to sniff out demons?"

"No, your Holiness, he's merely a witness to their work. He saw a great deal in the chapel last night." Niravati glances toward Bhismu. "A great deal."

"I was there," Bhismu says. "I saw nothing."

"You were asleep." Niravati smiles, a smile gloating with triumph. "You slept through quite a lot."

"Well, if you really think there are demons loose," Vasudheva says, "call out the exorcists." He tries to sound mocking, but doesn't succeed. The trapped feeling burns in his ears again, guilt and desperation.

"I've already called the exorcists," Niravati says. "But I thought I should come directly to you on another important matter. You asked the warders to escort that woman Hakkoia to your chambers this morning...."

Bhismu looks startled. "You did?"

"Her wings are Tivi's chosen Gift this year," Vasudheva replies. "No other Gift survived. I thought it would please the people to see her fly from my balcony."

"No doubt it would be exciting," Niravati says. "But with so much concern about demons, surely it's rash to let a woman visit your room. The laity is not in a mood to accept... deviations from common practice."

Vasudheva knows he must rebuke Niravati now, immediately. To hesitate for another second will prove he's afraid. (Does Niravati know about the kisses? He must. Bhismu lay in the light of Tivi's fire; Duroga could see everything.)

But Vasudheva *is* afraid. The people are used to the clergy sporting with women—order an ale in any tavern of Cardis, and you'll hear a joke about lascivious priests before your glass is empty. Such joking is good-natured, almost fond. However, to be caught kissing a man... of course, there would be no trial, no public punishment, for a high priest could not be convicted on the word of a junior cook. But there would be insolence from the novices; too much salt in every meal; clothes that come back dirty from the temple laundry; conversations that fall silent as the high priest enters the room.

He couldn't stand that. He couldn't stand a world that did not respect or fear him.

Vasudheva sighs heavily. "You have a point, Niravati. Hakkoia will have to fly from some other height. Perhaps the bell tower of the City Council?"

Niravati shakes his head. "The people are gathering in the courtyard below us. They expect you to announce the Gift from your balcony here. That's the tradition."

"*I* could wear the wings," Bhismu says suddenly.

"No!" Vasudheva's voice cracks.

"But I could!" the young man insists. "I want to. For Hakkoia's sake."

"An excellent idea," Niravati says, clapping Bhismu on the shoulder. "I should have thought of it myself."

"She talked to me about flying," Bhismu says excitedly. "She says she has eagle blood. The way she spoke of eagles...as if she were in love with them...please, your Holiness, let me fly in her place."

"Yes, let him," Niravati says. "It would show your... good faith."

Vasudheva looks at Bhismu's eager face and remembers warm curls, soft lips. "All right," the high priest says. "Go get the wings."

He turns away quickly. Another second, and Bhismu's grateful expression will wring tears from the high priest's eyes.

* * *

"People of Cardis!"

The rim of the sun is emerging over the rooftops. Only those in the tower can see it; five storeys lower, the city is still in shadow. But men and women crowd the courtyard, their heads craned up to watch the high priest's balcony. Every onlooker wears some small finery—a new ribbon in the hair, a patch of bright cloth sewn on the shirt directly over the heart.

Hakkoia must be in the crowd somewhere, but Vasudheva doesn't see her. His eyes water; he can't focus on any of the faces below.

"People of Cardis!" he repeats. "As you may have heard, many of the intended Gifts were destroyed last night in a terrible commotion. A commotion we believe was caused by demons."

At Vasudheva's back, Niravati murmurs, "That's right."

"But through Tivi's heavenly grace," Vasudheva continues, "one Gift was spared. That Gift is the one that the gods have chosen to accept this year. A Gift that is nothing less than the gift of flight!"

Bhismu steps onto the balcony, arms high and outspread to show the wings he wears. The crowd stirs with wonder as the feathers catch the dawning sunlight, catch the soft breeze blowing down from the hills. Bhismu glistens like dew, so pure, so clean.

Vasudheva can see Bhismu's arms tremble as they try to support the weight of the wings. The wings will never fly.

Bhismu grins, eager to leap out over the crowd. He waggles a wing to someone; it must be Hakkoia, though Vasudheva still can't pick her out. Bhismu no doubt intends to fly a few circles around the tower, then land at the woman's feet.

He is so beautiful.

Vasudheva lifts his hand to touch the young man's hair. As simple as that, a totally natural gesture. Bhismu turns and smiles; he must think it's a sign of encouragement.

Niravati clears his throat disapprovingly. "Your Holiness..." he murmurs.

And suddenly, Vasudheva is angry, righteously angry, at Niravati, at himself, at all those who try to lever people away from love. All the scheming conniving bishops, and others like Bhismu's father who trample over affection on their way to meaningless goals. Love demands enough sacrifices in itself; no one should impose additional burdens. One should pay the price of love and no more.

And no less.

Vasudheva touches Bhismu's arm. "Take the wings off," he says. "Give them to me."

A stricken look of betrayal crosses Bhismu's face. "No!"

"You can have the second flight. Warders!"

They grab him before he can jump. One warder looks at Niravati for confirmation of Vasudheva's command; already the bishop has followers under his thumb. Let him. Let him have the whole damned temple. "Give me the wings!" Vasudheva roars.

They slide onto his arms like musty-smelling vestments, each as heavy as a rug. Vasudheva can barely lift his arms. A warder helps him up to the balcony's parapet.

Vasudheva would like to turn back, just for a moment, and say something to Bhismu, something wise and loving and honest. But that would only burden his beloved with confusion and guilt. Best to leave it all unsaid.

"With wings like these," the high priest calls out to the crowd, "a man could fly to heaven."

207

He laughs. He is still laughing as he leaps toward the rising sun.

RUBY

Charles Shelby Goerlitz

1.

In The Sphinx, a cluttered hockshop off the Sol quarter, they'd found one. It wasn't the full-helmet kind, or even a Polan-circlet with a clumsy purifier deck; just a head-sized brass ring, with a black plastic chinstrap. One of the clips on the strap was broken.

Trying to find a grab wasn't Del's idea. He was along for the ride; five off-duty Fleet tags in a strange port town can always find something interesting to do. So now when it came time to actually buy the thing, he pretended to be interested in a rack of baubles. He let someone else do the haggling.

Across the shop the hockman's voice was pitched high. "Really, quite fine is. No expensive. You like to try? Here, this goes, here... there. I give you quick shot to test, is that good?"

One of the trinkets on the rack caught Del's attention: an old deco made of a strange metal. It looked like it was meant to substitute for an eyebrow; it was thin and curved, shorter than his little finger, made in the shape of a loosely formed name. It said "Ruby."

Del took it up to the counter where everyone else was standing around Nick, who had the grab on his head, eyes

209

rolled back, and a silly grin on his face. Nick's body was limp, held up by two of the guys.

"O-Kay," the hockman chimed. He reached up and flicked a switch on the side of the grab. Nick flailed a bit, grimaced, and rubbed his eyes. The little man stretched to remove the ring from the top of Nick's closely shaven head. "You like?"

"Whoah-hah." Nick rattled his head and blinked. "I don't know. It's hard to tell from just a taste. There was a little disturbance right before you disengaged me. I couldn't quite catch it. A bad recording, maybe."

"Oh, no-no." The hockman's narrow eyes got round. "Good recording is. Something different. I tell secret that I no tell everybody." He lowered his voice to a whisper. "That part you think disturbance is, your last moment alive is. You get great chance to see moment of death. Very tricky, very handy. This grab special, but I sell you good price."

One of the guys snickered, but covered up with a cough. Nick nodded seriously and paid the man in local chips.

While his mates waited outside for him, Del watched the hockman turn the "Ruby" deco over in his fingers.

"You Fleet-man like others, no?"

"Yeah. The *Bellatrix*."

"Long time in past, before Fleet come here, before Adhara a city, colony people live together one man, one woman. Make many children. Man no lay with others, just with special woman. He make this." The hockman held up the deco. "And put here." He placed it on the top of his left eyebrow. "Name of woman so he no forget." The hockman put it down on the worn velvet countertop. "Good work-manship, real metal. But one-woman man hard to find these times, demand not high." His face wrinkled up for a few short bursts of wheezy laughter.

Del fingered a chip. "Three?"

"Oh. My-my. That good metal. Truth, not less than seven."

"All I have is five."

"For you five O-Kay."

On the way back they got lost in Adhara's twisted alleys. The Fleet rips they all wore made it hard to get directions from the locals, so they found a main street and flagged a taxi. When the driver finally dropped near the Fleet strip, they didn't have enough chips for fare, so they ditched and ran.

2.

About six sleeps after undock, Del went to Nick's cabin and had his first taste of the grab. Nick asked if he had ever shot a grab before and Del lied that he had.

Del stretched out on an empty bunk, and Nick reached down and flicked a switch. "Sweet dreams," he said, "disengage is auto."

She was sitting on a chair in the corner of the unlighted room. The windows in the cracked wall behind her were open. A red neon griffon advertising Lloyd's Alloy was blinking outside. Water rain poured down. She stood, long dark hair, dark eyes. With a crooked smile, she put her hands on his shoulders and pushed him backwards onto a squeaky mattress. He lay motionless while she undressed him. She whispered something in his ear. She was so close she smelled warm.

3.

Standby crew was in Auxcon and was starting to get rowdy when Control signalled a check. Del slipped back to the holo deck while Lin fed him the numbers on a pattern of jump disturbances. He guessed the mass and trajectory, then tried it. Negative. He ran the pattern again with a new trajectory: two freighters in a background of black.

"Nice pick, Del." Mitch keyed the main holo and belched. "If you weren't such a grabwhacker, they'd promote you to Con."

Del laughed with everybody else. He could feel the grab girl being real close and hear her whisper. He realized that she did that with anyone, even Mitch. But he asked them anyway.

Barkly had never tried one, said he only did the real thing. All the rest admitted they had, but only Jony and Gek had done Nick's.

"I'm asking," Del said, "because I want to check out the rumor...."

"That she's hot?" Jony screwed up his narrow face.

Gek looked at Del. "You're talking about the death thing in the garbage."

"Yeah."

Gek grinned. "You have to anticipate disengage, or you won't feel it, the flash of red and twitched guts at the end." He shrugged thick shoulders. "They say that the instant of garbage at the end isn't garbage; it's a sensory image of your last moment alive. But, if that were true then the cross-shots that do the grab stuff would have to poke a part of your brain that keeps track of your future."

"Do you believe it?" Del pinned his eyes on Gek.

Gek shrugged again, "I think it sells grab-time."

4.

Del spent half a sleep on Tendi station, looking for a bargirl named Fox. On *Bellatrix*'s last stop, Nick had lent her the grab. Nick told Del that if he could find her, the grab was his. There was no more money left in it on Bellatrix; everyone who wanted a shot had bought their fill.

Del found her at a rim joint called the Bellybutton Chaser. She was tall and had a face made of angles; her short hair was violet. When he talked to her, he could tell that she wasn't too excited about giving up the grab; she told him to wait at the bar. He felt like a sucker.

He was about ready to leave when Fox came back and set the grab on the bar. "If you ever get tired of your toy, I have some free drinks to give away."

Del left without saying thank-you. He wished he had at least asked her what it felt like for a woman to do a men's grab.

5.

The woman got up from her chair, put her hands on his shoulders, and pushed him back on the creaky mattress. She smiled and began to undress him while a red griffon blinked in the rain outside the open window.

He remembered to anticipate disengage but it happened so fast that he barely recognized it as a sensory image. As he adjusted to his own senses in the dark bunkroom, all he could remember of the disengage flash was blackness. Not red like Gek had said, but black.

And in his memory, the instant of disengage was overpowered by the woman. It was hard to believe that she was just a clever piece of metal, that she didn't feel anything. He wondered how many times she'd been done. Something made him think of his metal deco and he decided to call her Ruby.

He shot the grab again. Ruby was smooth and warm, like before. This time, at disengage, he was pretty sure the black was space, with a trace of stars.

He shot it again. In the main part of the grab, he was beginning to pick out details he had not noticed before: the carpet in the room smelled faintly of vomit, there was a gap between her teeth he could feel when they kissed, the

Lloyd's Alloy sign outside stuttered when it blinked. Ruby's whispering was also starting to make sense: near the end, when she lay curled up beside him, he could see her lips shape the words "Kiss me."

6.

Del was in the messroom with Barkly and Lin when Jony told them that Gek was history: during a skirmish on N'dalas Fourus, Gek had been drilled in the abdomen with an I-type laser-cannon that fired red jags.

During sleep-shift he listened to the long breathing of the other tags who shared the cabin. He remembered what Gek had said about the grab garbage: red flash and a twitch in the gut. He thought about the blackness and stars that were on the other side of the hull, a head-width away.

When he finally closed his eyes, he dreamt he was being driven through a port city at night in the back of a taxi. The decrepit hover began speeding up until the lights outside blurred. Del tapped the driver on the shoulder to slow down, and when she turned around he saw that it was Ruby. Somehow she was in the back seat, up close, and he could feel her breath on his neck. She seemed sad, and almost imperceptibly she whispered, "Kiss me."

He kissed her on the forehead, and she sighed. He noticed the blurred lights outside the taxi were stars spinning the crazy patterns of a tight spin in raw space. "I thought you were just in my imagination," he said.

"I am," she smiled, "but that doesn't make me any less real."

He checked his pockets for a chip to pay the fare.

"Del," she said, looking at the lights, "I envy you. You'll do a million different things and then you'll die."

7.

Two sleeps after Gek was killed, the *Bellatrix* docked at Tendi. Del filled the pockets of his heavy coat with chips, food, and the deco; he slipped the grab in the back of his Fleet rip so that it slid down and rested in the small of his back. He got a one-drink pass, went through at cargo customs, then headed out to the rim.

The Bellybutton was almost empty and Fox was glued to the little holo that sat on the end of the bar. Del sat down across the counter from her. She got up and asked him if there was anything she could get him. Her hair was turquoise.

"I need a favor." Del unsealed the front of his rip and reached inside.

"Do I know you?" She plucked a glass from the rack.

He pulled the grab out and raised his eyebrows.

"I remember you," she said. "What kind of favor do you want?"

"A lot of captains come here to relax, and I need a quick ride to Colby Antares." Del watched her eyes move from the insignia on his coat to the grab to his eyes to the drink she was making.

"If you're skipping Fleet, why Colby?

"It has to do with stars. It's a long story."

"But Colby is cloudy; there aren't any stars there." Fox looked up as she stirred the drink with her middle finger.

"You're getting warm. Listen, if you connect me with the right man, the grab is yours for keeps." Del looked around to see if anyone might be watching.

She laughed. "No, no. Keep the toy. Skipping Fleet is always a worthy cause." She handed him the drink. "Take this to that man in the corner. See if he can help."

The man's name was Singer and he owned a fleet of freighters. After listening to Del, Singer said that the Fleet could track a deserter tag to practically anywhere in Antares; a safer bet was something frontier like Makenela in Sela. Makenela's pole pointed roughly in the direction of her sun, and the colonized part never had a night cycle.

No stars.

Del bought a docker rip at a center-level hallshop. When he and Singer got to customs, the official told them to have a better one—he didn't ask for passes. Del guessed it had something to do with Singer.

At the docks Singer pointed him to the *Mallard*, then left. They were expecting him.

He drove cargo forks for two shifts, loading and unloading whatever he was told. When all the crates had been loaded, they told him he could use the bunkroom off the cargo bay. Even though he was tired, he couldn't sleep.

8.

They had locked the bunkroom door from the outside, but Del figured someone would let him out at Sela. He kept the lights on, and ate food he'd brought from the *Bellatrix*.

All he had for company was the grab. He shot it often enough to sort out some new sensations in the disengage garbage: a sharp feeling in his forearms and an aroma that smelled like the burnt dog-meat on Sun street in N'bazing. He couldn't be sure though.

Just to see what would happen, he thought he would try to anticipate actions with Ruby instead of just passively following the sequence. He decided to give her a kiss on the forehead just before she started to whisper.

He shot the grab. When it came to the part where she curled up beside him, he watched himself kiss her.

Then she did something that hadn't been in the grab before. She opened her eyes and said: "Thanks, Del. Goodbye." The bed creaked as she sat up.

"Wait." Del closed his eyes and opened them on his own. "What's going on?"

She ran her hands through her hair then looked out the window, then sighed. "Imagine being hardwired to do exactly the same thing over and over again, forever." The blinking red light reflected from her face. "I'm tired of time, and there's only one way to get rid of it. I'm going to steal a little piece of your mind, Del; something you were born with, and I wasn't. The end part."

Ruby looked back at Del for a moment, then bent over and kissed him. "I kind of like you. If I didn't, I wouldn't bother to disengage you."

9.

Del was asleep when the *Mallard* was hit. The jolt slammed him onto the low ceiling and he awoke with the taste of blood in his mouth. The lights and gravity had gone out. He pulled himself down to the floor just as the aux power kicked in.

The cabin door opened and there was running in the hall. Someone shouted for him to get out, and he followed a couple of crew to the bridge. A new holo had been added to an old half-manual tracking system, but no one had bothered to block out the visual port. The sight of black space and stars turned Del's stomach.

A thin bald man asked Del his proficiency, then placed him at the holo in front of a weapons-ranging feed control.

Getting the feel of the feed, he targeted a small attack ship trying an escape. The gunner, three seats down, a burly bearded man, laughed out loud when the little ship imploded. Del remained professional as he continued area search. He found a Fleet carrier and sighted it for routine confirmation. Another jag hit the *Mallard* and Del knew it had come from the carrier.

The cargo; the weapons; the gunner's laughter: He was running holo-control on a pirate ship. He felt his forearms burn on the metal armrest of his chair. He smelled sweet-cooked flesh, like the kind on Sun street. He saw stars in blackness spinning crazily in the visual.

10.

On the pirate freighter *Lefty's Sin* they replaced his burnt arms with a pair of used Hellermans. The *Mallard* was in bad shape so they towed her back to Tendi the slow way. Del signed on to the *Sin* as crew.

He tried to shoot the grab one more time, but it was blank grey and warm like it had been ever since he had tripped Ruby's sequence. There was no disengage garbage to compare with his memories of the carrier battle, and no Ruby.

On Tendi he found a rim cosmetic shop and laid out a couple of chips to get an eyebrow removed and have the deco inset. He could still remember the squeaky voice of the Sol-quarter hockman.

He went by The Bellybutton to find Fox. He found a table in the corner with a view of the stars and she brought him a drink. Her hair was shiny black.

"Back so soon?" She put a tall glass in front of him.

"That little ride you sent me on turned into a career."

Fox bent close and whispered, "You're crazy to come in here; that's a Fleet captain over there." Del noticed that she smelled warm. He thought of the blinking neon griffon and the sound of water rain coming from an open window. Ruby had said she was stealing a little piece of his mind. For the first time, he wondered if he would ever die.

And when he watched Fox walk back to the bar, he wished he had kissed her.

MUCH SLOWER THAN LIGHT

CAROLYN CLINK

I am Newtonian.
My frame of reference
is my frame of preference.

A pox on your twin paradox
and your atomic clocks.

It's too much of a bother
being my own grandfather.
I'll just stay home and wait
in my own steady state.

JUDY

Ursula Pflug

That was the summer all the non-smokers died. It was a hot summer, murderously hot. Everyone who had air conditioning kept it going day and night, so of course the first thing they checked out was Legionnaire's Disease.

Frank and I didn't have air conditioning, so we slept through the days with the fan on, and come dusk we'd climb up on the roof with Judy; our cigarettes; a bottle; and Judy's dog, Hamilton. Hamilton didn't smoke and drink like the rest of us, but he survived that summer anyway. The Tobacco Fiasco, as it came to be known, turned out not to affect dogs, but we didn't know that at the time. Legionnaire's Disease didn't panned out, and after that we didn't know anything at all, and tried not to think too much about what we didn't know. That's why we spent so much time up on the roof, getting drunk. Judy was up there with us, but she was thinking.

Right after the Tobacco Fiasco got cleared up we left for the east coast to watch the whales die. It was a strange thing to do, drive all those miles to watch them die. It was Judy's idea, she said she wanted to document it.

"Document what?" Frank had asked, like she was crazy.

She was crazy. "We've got to document it," she'd said,

like we were crazy. We were, but we listened to her because she'd been right about the cigarettes. We listened to her even though she stuffed the trunk of Frank's Volkswagen so full of camera equipment we hardly had room for the tent.

She'd done the same thing when all those people started dying. While Frank and I slept Judy would be out there, making notes and taking photographs. In the evenings she'd join us on the roof, and, although she'd already been up all day, she'd spend the night measuring her gathered data against each new theory that entered her head between jokes, cigarettes and swigs off the bottle.

We ran out of cigarettes around four thirty one of those mornings, and it was Judy who offered to walk up to the 7-Eleven to pick up a deck. She explained that she was the least drunk of the three of us, and, not to worry, she'd take Hamilton with her.

They ran all the way home from College St. Frank and I couldn't understand it, what with Judy's smoker's lungs. Even Hamilton was breathless by the time they got back up to the roof, and he's a big non-smoking dog.

Judy waved the pack of cigarettes around like it was a live grenade. It was.

"We all smoke like forest fires till sunrise!" She yelled it so loud she woke the neighbors, but Judy didn't care; she knew she was on to something. Frank and I were too drunk to get excited, but Judy ran downstairs, cigarette in hand, to dial the hot line to the Surgeon General's office. She read them her statistics for at least an hour, and when she got off the phone she came back out on the roof and worked on the second bottle with us. By the time it was finished, daylight had arrived, so we called it a night and all went downstairs to sleep.

The headlines made the afternoon papers. Judy never did get any credit for it, except that people stopped dying.

Tobacco prices rose faster than interest rates until the government got wise and imposed sanctions; they knew it would look bad if people were spending so much money on cigarettes they couldn't afford to eat, never mind pay their taxes. After that, prices levelled off, but by then every back yard in the city was planted in tobacco, and we were already halfway to the east coast.

They were huge, pale grey things, and they'd come moaning out of the sea in that white light you see only on the ocean at sunrise. Just when you thought you'd seen the last one, another would appear, its cavernous head lunging sadly for the shoreline. Judy would be there to greet it, embracing her tripod as though it were some strange prehistoric tree, counting the seconds till the shot was perfect.

Frank and I walked out to the road after three days, leaving Judy on the beach with the Volks, her cameras, and all those dying whales. She hardly saw us go. She didn't even notice when we took Hamilton with us. He was a carnivorous dog, but after three days all those whale carcasses had him as grossed out as we were.

We rented a Toyota in the nearest town and headed for Halifax, intending to get hammered. In Yarmouth we stopped at the Yellow Dog bar for a drink and directions. In spite of the name, they wouldn't let us take Hamilton in, so we left him tied to an elm tree outside.

We got inside and ordered a couple of drinks from Eddie. Eddie was the big, friendly guy behind the bar. The second our drinks arrived Hamilton began to howl like all get out.

Eddie looked at us. He waited for the dog to stop howling. He looked at us some more. Finally he jerked his big thumb towards the door. "That animal out there belong to you guys?"

Frank and I looked at one another. We both got uncomfortable. We looked at one another too long. Frank looked at Eddie, saying, "Yeah, yeah, it's our dog."

"Then go outside and get it to shut up." Maybe Eddie wasn't such a friendly guy after all. Frank went, Eddie turned to me. "You guys aren't from around here, are you?"

"Around where?" I felt like a jerk. I found myself wishing Judy were here; she always knew what to say to guys like this.

"You from the city, right?" I knew what he meant by the city. To guys like that the city is the city. Any city, but especially the one we were from.

"Yeah."

Hamilton hadn't stopped howling.

"You sure that's your dog?"

"What makes you say that?"

"Well, it sure as hell ain't your friend's dog, 'cause if it was, he'd have stopped howling by now. And if it was yours, I'd wonder why you're not the one out there."

I sat there, not saying a thing. Some bars are like that.

"Let's see: you're from the city; it's not your dog. Makes me wonder. Another thing: what did you say you were in the neighborhood for?"

"Ah, you know. Lie around on the beach. Catch some rays."

"Only one beach for miles around here, fella, and if you've been there you'd know it's not the kind of beach you want to do much lying around on."

"Oh." I was running out of snappy answers. Hamilton still hadn't stopped howling.

"Go outside, untie the dog, bring him in. When you get inside you can tell me who the dog belongs to and what happened to them."

I did as I was told. Frank came back in with me, looking bewildered. Hamilton wasn't bewildered. When he saw Eddie he stopped howling right away. Eddie patted him thoughtfully and brought him a big dish of cool water.

"Don't worry, kid, we're getting to it." He looked at me. "You got an answer for me yet, fella?"

"It's Judy's dog, Eddie."

"And you left Judy on that beach by herself?"

"You don't understand, Eddie, she—"

"I understand more than you think. You don't leave anybody on that beach alone."

"Why not?" Frank was starting to sound as stupid as me.

"Well, think about it. She might run out of smokes."

"I hadn't thought of that."

"I'll forgive you, considering as you're not so bright."

"But Judy can take care of herself, she's very—"

"She takes care of you, right?"

"Huh?"

Frank looked at me, horror stricken. "What would have happened if you or me had decided to quit smoking last month, before she—"

"Fat chance, Ace, but I get your drift."

"See?" said Eddie. "Besides, that's a bad beach. You shouldn't let people stay there alone. Them whales hypnotizes people."

"Hypnotizes?" Frank laughed.

"Frank," I said, "she was a little, you know...."

"Right," said Eddie. "The drinks are on me. Now you guys clear out of here and go get your friend. And, should you decide to change your mind, just remember how happy her dog will be to see her." Hamilton howled on cue. "Attaboy."

We left. We felt like jackasses. Eddie had put such a fear of the Lord into our hearts that we drove like mad, crazed people all the way to Whale Beach, which wasn't a short distance.

And then we looked for Judy.

They were huge and white and towered high above our heads. I kept losing Frank in the labyrinth made by their huge, heaving bodies. The ones that had been dead a few days were starting to make a stench like nothing else. We shouted at each other, and sometimes it seemed as though their bodies were casting our voices like echoes, and Frank would turn out to be where I had least expected him. We didn't find her. We didn't find her strange tree of a tripod; we didn't find any of her cameras. Even Hamilton couldn't find her. He howled forlornly for his lost mistress. Then the sun set.

We slept on the beach, with Hamilton between us for warmth. We didn't sleep much, because he would wake up from time to time and howl as though his heart was breaking.

With sunrise the mist rolled in.

When I woke up it was face down in an alleyway that reeked of beer and vomit. It was the cockroaches that woke me up, them and the rats. They thought I was spending too much time in their territory.

I made the rounds of the streets and the bars for days. I was looking for Frank, I was looking for Judy, I was looking for Hamilton, for the Volkswagen, for the rented Toyota. I was looking for anything I knew. I would have been happy if I'd found Eddie and the Yellow Dog bar, but when I asked people about it they just laughed at me viciously.

I did find Whale Beach again, though. I stumbled across it one day trying to find the highway home. It was empty except for huge whale skeletons and a chill ocean breeze. It was then that I realized it was autumn. I howled a few times, there, alone on that grisly beach. The waves threw back my voice and for one bright, crazy moment I thought I had found Hamilton.

I found Judy's tripod. It stood alone at the far end of the beach, pointed out to sea. What had she been photographing? The camera was gone. I took the tripod with me, that and the huge clean rib of a whale.

I hitchhiked back to the city, where I went to our old house. I set up the sad tripod on the roof, which was as empty as the house, except for the wake of bottles and cigarette packs remaining from the summer.

The phone kept ringing, but it was always for Judy. They wanted to interview her about her Tobacco Fiasco research. I always told them I didn't know where she was, and I never did see her again, except for maybe once, on the cover of *Life* magazine.

CHAMBERED NAUTILUS

Élisabeth Vonarburg
translated from the French by
Jane Brierley

I

When she realized that this time she couldn't leave, the Voyager decided to keep a diary.

Only one sentence, and already a half-lie, she said to herself with some irony. In fact, when she realized she couldn't leave she was stupefied... furious... terrified. It was when she'd accepted the idea of never leaving that she began keeping a diary.

Or else the thought crossed her mind when she went back to the village feeling troubled, discouraged and listless, when her Total Recall accessed her first awakening on the beach. The thought came hesitantly, tinged with amusement. A diary. What is a diary if not an imperfect, distorted memory, as proven by the first sentence she wrote in it? The idea of a diary for a Voyager with free access to Total Recall and trained to assemble and integrate countless data—yes, it *was* rather funny. Humour is the politeness of despair, as someone once said (she doesn't want to know who or in what universe). The idea was doubtless a final twitch of despair in the face of certainty, the final admission that she would never leave this particular Earth, this particular universe where the ever unpredictable laws of her Voyages had cast her ashore.

The shifting, finely granulated texture of the sand, the intensity and slant of the sun's rays, the rhythmic murmur of waves lapping, the slightly saline humidity.... Dozens of other facts recorded by her sensor implants (atmospheric pressure, exact composition of the air), enlarging her perceptions before she even opens her eyes, tell her she is beside the sea in the northern hemisphere, and that it is late afternoon on Earth. On one Earth.

In the eternal present of Total Recall, there is almost no causal delay between data recorded by the Voyageur's body and the conclusions drawn from them by her consciousness. Recall, whether Total or not, isn't linear. The Centres on some planets have perfected complex machines capable of directly recording the electric impulses corresponding to memory engrams. Voyagers can skip the interminable recital of their travels. Yet other machines translate and catalogue the data for the Archives. She, however, has always liked to recount her Voyages aloud. Some atavistic impulse, no doubt. Tell the story of her Voyages to someone. As they have been lived, not as they've been recorded in her brain and body. Also, to avoid accessing Total Recall except when necessary. It has always seemed to her that the *telling* gives these Voyages an extra edge of reality. Isn't writing a diary the equivalent, after all? She would be telling the story of this last Voyage (no longer a Voyage now that she could never leave), this passage that should have been a stopover and is to become her life.

She kept her eyes closed for a moment, letting all her other senses describe the scene: a long, sandy beach curving gently around a calm bay; behind her, the fringe of a fairly dense forest, with trees interspersed with hard blocks, too regular in their irregularity not to be buildings. And, fading away along the length of sand and water, bouncing off the forest and plotting the contours of the hard blocks, human voices, the voices of children playing.

One of *those* Earths.

Not Earths like the one she'd left on her first Voyage twenty years ago—Earths where in recent years she sometimes awoke directly in a Centre, in the Voyagers' capsule, in the core of the Bridge's sphere. Where often, on opening her eyes, she found an Egon bending over her, an old Egon, moved to see her, but at peace. (Just as she had delivered herself from him in the course of manifold encounters in manifold universes, so he, in his way, had delivered himself from her. Now he could hold out a hand to help her out of the capsule and smile as he said her name: "Talitha.") Sometimes—and it happened more and more often—there was no Egon in these Centres. Egon was no more; Egon was dead.

She felt no sadness: he was alive somewhere else in other universes. It must surely be a sign. The Voyage takes Voyagers into universes that secretly correspond to their desires, and therefore the progressive fading and disappearance of Egons must mark the end of a phase for her. (After more than twenty years! Were one's inner tides so slow?) A sign that perhaps she was approaching the moment where Voyagers control the Voyage, go where they decide to go, not where their inner voices propel them. They can only move among universes at will when these voices can be recognized and interpreted. A sign, the sign that soon she might be able to direct her Voyages, venture onto the most distant branches of the human universe-tree, and at long last leap onto another tree, go truly Elsewhere.

She had consulted the Archives in all the Centres she'd passed through, combed the libraries and the most advanced data on local science or the most ancient memories of tradition. No one, not ever, had made contact with a non-human universe. Oh, there were varying external details (diverse morphologies covered with fur, scales, or even a carapace), but the basic form remained upright and biped. Given these variants, their natural habitats, and the resulting mentalities and societies, the possible combinations were immense but not infinite. The universe that contained all possible variants of human history was certainly just one among many. And it was the Others that she longed for.

Had some Voyager in some universe made the leap, having mastered the Voyage? Impossible to know, of course. She herself had only Voyaged in a few hundred universes out of billions or trillions.... Well, it didn't matter: what she sought was a different universe-tree, another universe, the Other universe, truly and absolutely different. She didn't really know what motivated her (she supposed this was why she hadn't yet found it). Was it fame? Curiosity? But she'd set aside these false motives long ago. No, it was something deeper, more obscure. This idea of her goal had only come to her bit by bit. In the beginning she had wanted to become a Voyager the way some people want to die. But—with Egon—she had learned to want to live, even if she was still fleeing when she left the first time. Egon. For years she hadn't stopped fleeing, or seeking, or finding him. At last, though, she'd understood, had accepted the inevitable and freed herself. All those years, all those universes behind her... she could feel them drifting away. The end of one phase and the start of another? But so nebulous, so uncertain....

Personal, subjective time takes on another dimension during the Voyage, in the leap from one universe to another, from one historic time to another, sometimes vastly different. But she'd kept count: in the last five years there'd been a dozen Voyages with the same pattern. About one time in three, she would find herself in a Centre on an Earth identical to her own. She would leave immediately, not bothering to explore the variants, for they were often so minimal that it would take years and years to discover them. Another time in three, she would find herself on a planet not Earth, but always terrestrial enough despite variants to make it clear this was not the desired Other Universe.

That small planet on the outer edge of its galaxy, for example, perched on the verge of an intergalactic void—a vast black space where no star shone, where the most powerful telescopes could only discern the distant light of other galaxies as patches where the dark was slightly less profound. She stayed on this planet for six months, motivated by a vague hope. But no one ever crossed the void to bring news of other lives. She stayed to watch the night skies gradually losing their stars as the planet slipped toward the part of its orbit bordering on the void. That season of deep and total nights corresponded to springtime in the southern hemisphere, where the equivalent of the Bridge was located. Spring, the renewal of life: the inhabitants of Shingèn associated them with blackness, whereas she perceived the blackness as a heavy, terrifying lid. The Shingèn fantasies—their myths, religions, and legends—stubbornly survived and were preserved as a precious heritage, peopling the shadows with beings of black light, guardians of a domain where, once a year, all the colours of the world came to renew themselves. And the Shingèns had a very wide vocabulary for describing colours, especially black, which for them was the most mysterious and rich of shades. "Was." *Is.* Why speak of them in the past tense? Their universe still exists, and so does their planet, perched on the edge of its stellar abyss.

There had also been that planet where life was only possible within a thin zone suspended between the boiling pressure of the surface and the suffocating void of gigantic mountain tops. Hanging between two mortal hells, life

still evolved, tenacious and rich in dreams. The Bridge
was not called by that name, and had been developed to
explore the torrid depths of the surface. As often happened, its inventors had no idea it could be used to Voyage
through universes, and their attempts after she'd come
had failed. Perhaps they'd had no need to Voyage. They'd
only begun to explore their planet, and, in itself, it was
three universes.

There had been. Yes, this was how the memory of this
diary differed from Total Recall—in this past that insisted
on coming back. She had briefly visited these planets,
these universes, and would never go back. Her passage
emphasized their temporality. *There had been*, therefore,
this planet where two human races cohabited, one very
ancient, and the other on the edge of humanity, over
which the first watched with discreet tenderness, not
keeping itself hidden, with no attempt to dominate, with
no fear or bitterness. The name of the first race,
K'tu'tinié'go, literally meant "those who come before the
beginning," which signified "the apprentices," or "the unfinished." Only the second race, which had barely begun
to explore the fringes of language, was called "human." A
system of complex myths recorded these names, to which
the *K'tu'tinié'go* scholars, and particularly the biologists,
gave another meaning. But they would smile at her as they
explained the scientific basis for relations between the two
races, as though these explanations were merely another
story, mainly pleasing for its novelty and ingenuity. For
them, all truths were always multiple. She had been astonished that, with such a world vision, this first people had
been able to develop science to a state advanced enough to
include the equivalent of a Bridge.... They used it to treat
congenital cellular degeneration, which could only be
slowed down in the suspended animation of deep cold,
around absolute zero.

And one Voyage in three led her to another Earth, *this* Earth, with continents gradually submerged, dikes anxiously watched over by their guardians, cliffs nibbled away by the waves, and the soft, moist air of a warming planet on which the polar icecaps are inexorably melting. She had recognized it even before opening her eyes. This was the fourth time her sensors had recorded this *gestalt* perception in her Total Recall. When she did open her eyes to find the beach with its still muted colours, she asked herself yet again whether, through some new and bizarre trick of her Voyages, this mightn't be the same planet at different moments in its evolution.

Total Recall, so clear, so immediate; the past becomes the present again, just for the asking. The children aren't far from the spot where she has materialized. She knows, having read about it in many Archives and witnessed it once herself, that a Voyager appears almost instantaneously, almost in the blink of an eye. Perhaps the children haven't seen her appear. The awakening takes longer, and plenty of Voyagers have found themselves in sticky situations, although never fatal—not according to the Archives consulted by her, at any rate. Could suicidal Voyagers propel themselves into a universe that would immediately kill them? But you can't train to become a Voyager and remain suicidal, as she well knows.

Haven't the children noticed the woman sleeping naked on their beach? She walks in their direction, watching them and scanning the landscape. The beach is well kept, with heaps of driftwood and kelp neatly arranged at the far end beside the pilings of a wharf. The forest seems well tended, too. Great umbrella pines mingle with more tropical species, growing thickly enough to create a wall of foliage and branches above the regularly spaced trunks and the cleared forest floor. The half-hidden buildings are ruins, but their contours and materials are still recogniz-

233

ÉLISABETH VONARBURG

able—the architecture was ultramodern on the last Earth of this type that she'd visited. The children's village lies beyond the wharf, in a notch cut out of the forest.

The children continue playing at the edge of the waves. Their slender bodies are of curiously different shades, the palest seeming to shimmer in the sunlight. It is hard to tell girls from boys at first glance. The silhouettes of their supple bodies flow smoothly from head to shoulders to hips to legs, ending in feet that are subtly disproportionate and, like their overly large, flat hands, slightly... webbed. A semi-aquatic humanity—she's never encountered it on an Earth like this one. The children don't turn their eyes away when she looks at them. They smile rather shyly and go on with their game. She can tell what it is from their movements. They are tossing a flat, round marker and hopping to retrieve it. Rows of shells mark segments in the smooth, wet sand. But it isn't the hopscotch grid of her childhood (so near, so far, dozens of universes away), or those she's occasionally come upon since then. Those were either rectangular or arranged in a double cross. This one is a spiral with ten sections that diminish toward the centre, ending in a space just big enough for a child's foot. Beneath it, somewhat scuffed by the feet of the players, is the whorl of an inverse spiral that grows bigger toward the centre.

She sits on the sand again near a pile of empty shells. A great sense of peace fills her, as is so often the case when she awakes. The sun sinks behind the sea, leaving a sky dotted with small clouds slowly sculpted by a distant wind, meticulous yet shifting hieroglyphs, their silvery outlines bright at first, then fading to nothing. The ebbing surf breaks softly but steadily on the sand to a continuo of rustling trees and the gentle, rhythmic sing-song of the children at their game. A new coolness touches her skin, and night seems to well up from the sea as it fades from

234

pink to gray, blotting out the line where sea meets sky. All this, simultaneously perceived by her senses (and not linearly as it is now being recorded by these words), resembles the vibrato of an ultimate chord before... before what, if ultimate? Still, that is what she feels at the time, a Voyager in transit, present yet altogether detached: a suspension, a waiting.

She is waiting for someone to speak. But the someone sits down beside her in silence, watches the children as they continue their game, takes a shell from the pile—the smooth greeny-white palette of an oyster—and strokes it with a finger. A long finger, joined to the others by a translucent membrane. The light skin, vaguely pink in the afterglow of the sun, is covered in fine, iridescent scales; the arm, like the whole body, is wet and smells of the sea. The head, with its cap of fair, water-smoothed hair, pivots slowly to reveal a heart-shaped face, vaguely Asiatic, with large, gray-green eyes, heavy lids slanting toward the temples, a flat nose, and a small mouth with full, curved lips. The someone is a naked woman, age impossible to tell, who has just come out of the water and is looking at her, unsmiling but not unfriendly. They stare at one another for a long moment. Then the woman gets up, takes her by the hand, and leads her to the village, followed by the children.

Talitha accepts the simple garments proffered by the villagers. After a somewhat uncertain silence, the familiar ritual begins. The large, dusky woman who appears to speak for the villagers places a hand on her heart and says, "Ao palli kedia"—syllables that may be her name. Talitha's trained mind immediately begins to establish correlations between the stressed syllables and pronunciation of this language with those encountered on the three other, similar planets. Perhaps the syllables mean "I am Palli Kedia" or "I am a kedia" or "a palli" or "the village chief." Faithful to the ritual, however, Talitha in turn places a hand on her heart and says her own name clearly. The villagers murmur softly. Is it surprise? Appreciation? The woman from the sea touches Talitha's arm and smiles—perhaps because she is moved or amused or both. Putting her other hand on her naked breast (a flower-like hand, the membranes stretched between the spreading fingers) she speaks what must be her name, accentuating the difference: "Ao Tilitha."

Talitha has already met herself in other universes. Not very often—that isn't what she was hoping to find when she became a Voyager. (And, quite soon, she even stopped wanting to meet the Talitha who lived happily with an Egon. Of course they exist somewhere, all the facets of this story exist somewhere, but she has finally passed beyond the stage where she thinks of it as "our story." It is the story of every Talitha and every Egon in their respective universes, as those she's met have made her fully realize. Her own story is something else, something she hasn't yet shaped.) And so she merely smiles, noting the similarity between her name and the name of the woman from the sea. She has no desire to find out more about this contingent variant of herself, however exotic. She turns toward "Palli Kedia," resolved to do what every Voyager does upon arrival: learn the local language.

Palli Kedia seems reluctant to talk, once they have exchanged names. Talitha shows her wish to communicate, pointing to the objects around them and saying all the names given them on other Submerged Earths. Palli Kedia may be reluctant to talk, but she is quite ready to communicate. The language is based on a complex sign system assisted occasionally by a few words, sometimes by a mere sound.

There are Voyagers who never tire of the infinite forms of humanity encountered. They are the ones who feed the Archives in the Centres, to which they travel only to leave again. Talitha isn't one of these explorers. What struck her very soon in her Voyages were the recurrent patterns, the resemblances, the repetitions. She seeks something else, something totally other, unimaginable, *amazing*.

She leaves the village next morning. If this Earth resembles the other three fairly closely, the political and scientific centres will be in the southeast. Once again she'll probably have to travel to the extreme south of the continent, where the capital stands on a cliff (in one case entirely artificial), a city built as a challenge to the sea and its inevitable encroachment. On the first Submerged Earth this was a true calamity—a natural disaster. On the others, humans had played a considerable part in the general warming of their planet. Changes came with great speed, made worse by the accompanying recurrence of violent seismic activity. On an overpopulated Earth, and in societies that were all the more fragile because of their complex technologies, these upheavals were catastrophic. The long-term consequences decimated the population on the third Earth, and the human race was slowly becoming extinct. She had taken nearly three years to find a group of scientists either dynamic or stoic enough to continue doing research, and to convince them to develop the machine that one of them was tinkering with for the sake of amusement—a machine that, unknown to him, was an embryo Bridge. Three years! Never had she stayed so long in one place, even in the universe where she had at last made her peace with Egon. It was also the first time she'd actually had to help build a Bridge. She left that planet, that universe, with a brief question in her mind: now that a Bridge existed, Voyagers would surely come, and others would leave by it. But it was probably already too late to change the fate of that dying human race. In any case, she was no

missionary and she knew perfectly well she hadn't given
that Earth a Bridge in order to fulfil the secret plan of some
hidden divinity: her goal was to leave.

Now, as she travels over almost vanished roads,
through ruined towns and landscapes still bearing the
scars of ancient devastation, she soon feels a growing anxiety. Does she detect an increasingly recurrent pattern
here? She'd found it more and more difficult to leave the
preceding Submerged Earths. This one seems to have re-
gressed even further in the same direction as the last. Not
much is known about how the Voyage works, apart from
the physical functioning of the Bridge itself up to the moment when the anaesthetized body is cooled to almost
absolute zero and disappears from the capsule. But the
law, the only sure law, is that the Bridge always provides
access to universes that you can *leave*, one where a Bridge
exists (even if not called that), or where it is technologi-
cally possible for the Voyager to have one built. There is
nothing surprising in this, because it is not the Bridge that
propels Voyagers into the various universes, but the Voyagers themselves, their psyche, or as believers say, their
Matrix. Voyagers may have sent themselves into universes without any means of escape, because they desired
it either consciously or unconsciously. It is a statistical certainty, but materially unverifiable, since such Voyagers
have never returned to the Centres to confide their experiences to the Archives. She knows she doesn't yearn for
that kind of universe; that means there must be a Bridge on
this planet or the possibility of one—or its equivalent.

After two weeks of solitary walking, her fears are al-
layed. She comes to a small city where the remaining
inhabitants speak a language closely resembling the
Euskade she'd learned on the second Submerged Earth.
Without too much difficulty, they agree to provide her
with a small automotive vehicle in fairly good shape. The

238

roads improve toward the southeast, they tell her, and she'll have no trouble getting to the big city she's looking for. In the other universes it was called Périndéra, Neva de Rel, Torremolines. In the village by the sea they called it Aomanukera. Here it is called Baïblanca.

II

The city is like its predecessors, a constant factor from one of these universes to another, revealing the stubborn resolve of the city's creators to fashion a place at once functional, comfortable, and aesthetically pleasing. A rather too carefully orchestrated casualness seems to have governed its development. This Baïblanca possesses the same general characteristics and layout as its doubles, with one notable exception: it is almost totally deserted. The parks and gardens have run wild and are invading the streets and squares, a green tide attacking monuments and buildings. She walks the length of the Promenade, the name here for the long, tree-lined esplanade that follows the curve of the clifftop—or what had once been a clifftop. At high tide the water washes over the flagstones, swirling around the benches and trees in small, patient eddies (there is no violence in the sea; it knows it has won). The weather is mild and the sunlight has a pearly quality from the permanent haze masking the sky. A few people in light boots stroll along the Promenade, and a few children too, barefoot and too young to be either blasé or afraid, laughing with sacrilegious delight at seeing water where it shouldn't be. She contemplates the Promenade's sweep, subtly distorted by the thin layer of water, and already she knows, senses, what the still-functional data banks will tell her: there is no Bridge, nor the equivalent, nor the possibility of a Bridge in Baïblanca.

She doesn't give up at once; she will not, cannot believe it. She consults the data banks, criss-crosses the city interrogating the inhabitants—a nucleus of several thousand diehards clustered in the quarter between the Arts Palace, the Government Complex, and the fortress-hill of the Institute. Whatever its names elsewhere—names meaning "academy" or "university"—the Institute is the real seat of power. Here she finds interested listeners, minds still curious, and a regretful willingness: yes, they understand very well the principle of the machine she describes, and they even dig through the Institute's memory banks to show her another version, equally workable. But to build such a machine....

The problem isn't so much to build it as to reconstitute the technology necessary for making the required materials. Baïblanca has passed the critical point beyond which this is impossible.

She won't, can't believe it. Surely Baïblanca isn't the only large metropolis still in existence! People sigh and pull long faces, but they give her names and maps, and at last supply her with a precious, small airborne vehicle. They wish her good luck, but they are right to be skeptical. After six months, she has to accept the evidence: no one, nowhere, is capable of helping her build a Bridge. If one exists on this Earth, it has been forgotten and all trace of it lost. In a flash, she sees herself as an old Voyager, transformed into an obdurate explorer, a detective, interminably ruffling through tattered documents, following dubious trails in the heart of jungles and ruins, tirelessly interrogating human survivors who have reverted to a primitive state. No. Not her. Another Talitha in another universe, maybe, but not her. She won't chase a phantom for the rest of her life, the mirage of a nonexistent Bridge; she won't pay such a crazy price to avoid despair.

She does despair, although she won't admit it, returning to Baïblanca through what is left of the continent called Numeïde, Eslam, or Basilisso in other worlds, but Africa in this world. She journeys part of the way on the back of a *dromedary*, an animal no more and no less strange than others in other universes—hump-backed, a long-legged quadruped, its long, arched neck resembling a ship's prow, rolling like a dinghy as it walks. "Ship of the desert," its human owners call it. The name has stuck, despite the fact that the desert is finally disappearing beneath the Sahara Sea, which linked up long ago with the other sea—a sea with no special name anymore, because it is the same everywhere, the same inexorable invader, "the sea." She goes back to Baïblanca, leaving the small airborne vehicle to rust away in the shallow water where she made a forced landing. The Institute scholars are certainly not pleased, but they pity her. They offer her their hospitality, but she feels restless, preferring to explore the city, camping wherever she can, striding tirelessly through the familiar yet strange places (in a city where she had spent three years of her life, not so very long ago, in another universe). She catalogues resemblances and differences, but as usual she notices the resemblances most. Does she actually *see* them? She records, she moves, tries to tire herself out on rambles so that she will fall into a dreamless sleep at night. She ignores the city's dangers, the wild animals, the solitary and sometimes aggressive humans; these don't compare with the real terror, the instant of inattention when the noise of all this motion fades, and the inner voice is heard again.

I cannot leave; there is no Bridge; I am stuck here! Condemned to live and die here, on this drowning Earth. Is it possible? Is all she knows or thinks she knows about the Bridge and the Voyage false? *The Bridge takes you where, consciously or unconsciously, you wish to go, until you have mastered the Voyage, until you know yourself. Then you can go where you please, or return.* What she knows or thinks she knows of herself—is that also false? After twenty years of

241

Voyaging, is she unable to understand why she has propelled herself onto this dead-end planet? She is stupefied,
furious—and scared to death. So she goes off to yet another quarter of the city, she probes the occasional data
banks that still function, learning in bits and pieces the
story of this world, this society, this city, not really caring
what her Total Recall is recording. The crucial thing is to
fill the threatening silence with voices and images, to prevent the horrifying litany from welling up: *I cannot leave;
there is no Bridge; I am stuck here!*

When at last she gives up, she returns to the Institute
and settles into one of the residential wings of the fortress-
campus. Naturally, some of the Institute members ask her
to record her experiences in other universes for the central
Infolibrary. There are no machines for abridging the process, but it doesn't matter—telling it helps pass the time.
She accesses her Total Recall and listens to it speak. Weeks
pass: in the morning she talks, in the afternoon she answers questions raised by her accounts. After that, she
aimlessly digs for facts in the Infolibrary or wanders
through the inhabited triangle of Baïblanca, taking a detour to the Boardwalk or the Colibri Park. The park is
named after tiny, colourful birds, living jewels that gather
nectar from the flowers beneath a huge, transparent cu-
pola in the middle of the main lawn. But it isn't the birds
that fascinate her: it's the statues. There are dozens, perhaps hundreds, everywhere—the bodies of men and
women, sometimes in graceful poses, sometimes in
stances so natural as to seem strange. It was dusk when
she first entered the park, and she thought that the whole
city had congregated there. Figures stood, sat, lay on the
ground, rested against trees, even *in* trees. And then she
realized that all these people were completely naked and
motionless. As she came closer, she saw that they were
made of stone, or something mineral-like. All of them stat-

ues, all of them highly individualized. They had worn clothing once, but it had gradually rotted away. (The Infolibrary provided her with curious pictures of this gradual divestment, showing multitudes of statues with garments in varying stages of disintegration.) But the statues themselves were made of a material impervious to salt air, and yet so delicate in texture, porous, like a honeycomb... like pumice stone. As she touched it, she had a momentary vision of the park finally submerged beneath the sea, and the statues gradually floating off their benches, or trees, or lawns, drifting with the tides. In reality, however, the stone was very solid, very heavy. The statues would remain anchored to the sea-bottom in the park, and moonfish would replace the tiny birds.

"Oh, the *hendemados*," says Caetanes, referring to the statues.

The old biologist's tone catches her interest. It is an intricate mixture of amused disdain and an undercurrent of resentment (of disgust, of fear?). He says no more, and the Infolibrary is also curiously laconic on the subject. Six hundred years earlier, during the brief period when all was still in a state of equilibrium, when the Earth's civilization had not yet begun to topple toward extinction, scientists and technicians had perfected an artificial organic material with complex properties, capable of imitating life. The *artifacts* created by biosculptors out of this material had a certain amount of independence that diminished with age—and they aged rapidly. Generally, after about a dozen years, their gradually slowing metabolism produced complete mineralization. For some unfathomable reason, it became fashionable at one point for biosculptors to give their creations a motor tropism that directed them to Colibri Park as life was ending. And there they stopped forever.

The history of biosculpture covers barely a hundred

and fifty years. The sources of this science—this art—are obscure. Its origins seem to have been in more or less secret government research immediately after the so-called "Catastrophe" period, the fifty or so years after the first Great Tides. The Infolibrary is very discreet on this point. Nevertheless, various signs clearly indicate to her trained mind that the data bank has been fixed and that the Institute itself has probably lent a hand in this. Old stories of a bygone day that seem to have left fairly conscious traces in the minds of the last survivors.... She doesn't realize it at this moment, but after nearly a year the period of mourning has ended. Her old vitality has rekindled itself and she feels the need to act instead of letting the days slip by. This small mystery comes at just the right moment to distract her. It doesn't take long to solve: after six hundred years, the taboos have lost their potency, even among the heirs of the Institute.

Some biosculptors clearly improved their basic material, to the point where their creations couldn't be distinguished from real human beings. And some biosculptors actually decided that their creatures, their artifacts, were indeed human beings. And why not? They had improved the basic material so much that they eventually created beings that lived longer than normal humans, and above all, could procreate—something normal humans were doing less often and less well. The Institute had outlawed biosculpture, but it had neither the political power nor, in reality, the necessary conviction to enforce this. The artifacts proliferated. Now, only a few small communities of the original human race remain, and these have become rigid in their isolation. Over the centuries, often without knowing it, humans had mated with artifacts. Their halfbreed descendants, the hendemados, and the descendants of mating between artifacts themselves, are slowly, very slowly, repopulating the Earth....

This Earth isn't a dying planet, after all is said and done. It's recovering slowly, very slowly, from a near-fatal illness.

When she's finished putting together the pieces of the puzzle, she is astonished. How could she have thought this planet was dying? She has let herself be hypnotized by ruined cities and the traces of a once-powerful civilization that can still be seen everywhere. Above all, she hasn't really cared whether it was dying or not, since this planet was supposed to be merely a stage in her Voyages. And when she realized she wasn't going to leave again.... Now she understands both the cause of her illusion and the fact that the cause no longer exists. She suddenly thinks of the fishing village, of Tilitha who may be her double in this universe. Why not, why not? Going back to her starting point would be a gesture replete with satisfying irony: would it not respect the recurring structure of her latest Voyages? To go back to her starting point: a dead end, the circular motion of starting over. She sees things clearly, now (so easy in retrospect). All those Earths, identical to hers, had the same message as those other, falsely different planets: the end, immobility, death. The stellar desert in the springtime night of the Shingèns, the certain extinction of some of the K'tu'tinié'go and of those ever more submerged Earths.... Of course, there was also Manischë, the planet of fire and ice, its tenacious life balancing on a thread. The heirs of the K'tu'tinié'go would take up the torch once more, the starless Shingèn night would be succeeded by the constellations of the summer sky. And here, the hendemados....

And just because she, Talitha, will live out her life on this particular Earth doesn't mean life itself is becoming extinct. Through the huge picture window of the reading room she has a view over the city to the sea, a dull gleam beneath the veiled sun. She can certainly make this sacrifice to her new but useless clairvoyance: since life goes on, at least live where it *is* going on, and not in condemned Baïblanca. Make one last little voyage, and for once (the first and last time) know where she is going.

III

February 20: Year One, after all. I've decided to. I. Really decided? I'm certainly taking a lot upon myself.

When she realized that this time she couldn't leave, the Voyager decided to keep a diary.

Only one sentence, and already a half-lie....

February 23: Welcomed without fanfare by the village. They recognized me and greeted me by name, helped me settle into a small, quickly built hut on the edge of the village. They didn't say much—and always in sign language. I'll soon learn it. Easier to use the first person: *I*. Because *they* are observing *me*—an external perspective that has the effect of making me draw into myself, concentrate on myself, unlike my own perspective, which undoes me.

February 26: It seems they've decided to make an exception for me and talk a little, at least for long enough to teach me the sign language. Spoken language is too precious to be wasted in verbalizing the trivia of daily life. (A curious detail: in this language the verb "to talk" seems to have the same derivation as the verb "to voyage.") I'm learning very fast, of course, both the spoken and sign language. It's easy to establish correlations from the crumbs they let fall—after all, I was trained to do it. They seem surprised. Palli Kedia came in person to see how I was getting along. A supposedly fortuitous meeting. I was coming back from my morning walk on the shore. (How quickly one settles into a routine!) She greeted me, we talked for a moment, and I continued on my way, conscious of having passed a test. And now?

March 6: Now it's Tilitha who's keeping an eye on me.

Or so I suppose. Our meetings, always on the shore morning or evening, also seem purely accidental. Tilitha is always naked, often wet. Dolphins play in the waves while we talk. They come with her, go with her; she calls them "cousins." She and those like her, the arevags, visit the village regularly, but they don't live there. Their habitat is under water, in the forest of giant kelp covering the drowned cities. Tilitha is the sister of Palli Kedia. The two races can crossbreed. Among the arevags, one child in four—almost always a boy—turns out to be a hendemado and is given by the mother to the village. The same proportion of arevags is born in the village; they are always girls, and they return to the sea, as in Tilitha's case. Both are almost completely amphibious, with the hendemados able to remain under water for long periods, and the arevags able to stay in the open air for over a day without discomfort. Their respective capacities depend on the degree of crossbreeding—scientific details to be recorded in my Total Recall, not in this diary. What I see of this double race, what I experience, is the constant mixing, the opening of one to the other, and the impression that the water's edge isn't a frontier for these people but a door to be opened at will. The inverse of Baïblanca, in a way—Baïblanca on its inundated clifftop, Baïblanca where the tide is looked upon as an encroachment of one element on another, because each is conceived of as an opposite. Here, water and earth are clearly distinct, and the two races (despite their ability to crossbreed) are different, if only because the arevags are exclusively female; yet they are open to one another, for better or for worse. (There are quarrels, jealousies, and longings that cause a certain amount of strife, and life, particularly in mixed families, seems fairly agitated. Sign language may not be noisy, but it can be pretty vehement for all that. The other day I witnessed a public outburst that ended in blows and tears.)

247

By the by, as far as language goes, each race seems to
have adopted the habits of the other. The arevags tend to
speak aloud when they come to the village, and the villagers communicate with them by signs, as though they were
under water. Both, however, have begun to observe a cautious silence toward me, the stranger. Probably they don't
quite know what category of human to put me in: suddenly I appeared from nowhere on their beach, and I
didn't stay with the original humans (referred to by them
simply as "the last ones"). My talks with Tilitha have been
fairly brief these last few days. I'm not even sure our meetings are part of a predetermined plan on the part of the
two communities. Perhaps it's a purely personal initiative
on her part, because of the similarity of our names. This
seems to fascinate her. To start with, she didn't ask me
where I came from; instead, she explained who *she* was
and where she came from (thereby confirming my theories
about the arevags). I tried to do the same, but without
much confidence. How was I to make her understand the
concept of the Bridge? I drew the universe-tree in the wet
sand, showing the ramifications of its branching universes. She listened, nodding, her eyes shining. I
wondered what she made of it. Then she asked, "How?" I
tried to explain the Bridge, but my description of the machine only aroused a perplexed interest. She came alive,
though, when I began to explain how the Voyage worked.
The descent to absolute zero, the cold sleep, all motion
stopped, and at the heart of this absolute immobility, absolute motion: the spirit, the Matrix, shooting forth, tearing
the Voyager's body from its universe to propel it into the
merry-go-round of similar universes. "Similar universes?" she echoed, visibly disconcerted. I described the
universes where I had met Egons—and Talithas. She
meditated this for a while but said nothing. Then, with a
sharp fingertip, she drew a closed circle around the tree in

the sand. (The arevags don't go defenceless into the depths: they have sheathed claws.) In a few minutes she has grasped what has taken me five years to comprehend: the Voyage comes to an end one day; there is no truly *other* universe.

"I am Tilitha. You are Talitha," she added aloud, as if to conclude her statement.

That's how I translate it. What she said in her language was, "Ao Tilitha. Ao Talitha." *Ao*, the human pronoun of both arevags and hendemados, can't be translated otherwise. It's used to introduce oneself to strangers, or talk of oneself or others in important discussions— when it is felt the speaker is not the individual woman or man, but the person, a concept transcending gender. I asked her about the origin of this so-called human pronoun. It was a long story, Tilitha said with a smile, getting up. Hadn't we time, I asked? She shook her head. "Tomorrow." She slid into the water without leaving a ripple, and went to join her dolphins.

March 11: Of course, it's a lot more complicated than I thought. *Ao*, the human pronoun, implies active virtuality. There is another, *O*, related to passive virtuality. Tilitha explained this to me (or thought she was explaining it, while plunging me into even greater darkness) by recounting a legend. It was the story of creatures who attained the total human state in the real world. (Androgynes? Or beings capable of changing their sex at will? It wasn't clear.) These creatures went away from the Earth but left their seeds behind to divide and redivide, spreading until their effectiveness has been completely lost. The only surviving traces are in language, among others this active-virtual pronoun. But what about the passive-virtual pronoun *O*? No, no, that pronoun came from before, said Tilitha by way of correction, as though it were obvious. Not obvious to me, though, as she realized; she decided to go back to the Flood for my edification—that is, to Creation.

The first woman is called Manu, and she has two mothers: the Uncreated Mother, Taïke, whom she meets during her wanderings and who gives her Earth and Time—in other words, Death, without which no life is possible—and another, the Created Mother, who gives Manu the Sea and Life, and who is named Tilith (after whom girls are called Tilitha). Tilith entrusts Manu with a mission: find the land-beneath-the-sea and the first arevags who have been lost there in the limbo of eternity (are they immortal?). Manu finds them, and in some obscure way—since the original arevags are all females, too—gives birth to the first hendemados.

Manu must be the third woman then, not the first, I said to Tilitha. Yes and no, she answered (with confidence, not with the hesitation such a reply would express if I had made it). Manu was the first real woman; Tilith was the first virtual woman. And Taïke? Taïke came from the world in an earlier state, not chaos, but "the mirror-world."

I pleaded for clarification, and Tilitha tried to supply it. In the mirror-world, the passive-virtual beings (*o ikeï*, she said) reproduced by union with their reflection. But one day, three of these beings had union among themselves, abandoning their reflections and creating Tilith, the first being who wasn't a copy. In this same momentum the three reflections, left to themselves, fused to produce Taïke, called "the Uncreated" because in a sense she gave birth to herself. But Taïke was too heavy for the insubstantial material of the virtual world; she tore a great hole and fell through. Her fall created the Earth. Tilith was also too real for the virtual world. The reflections turned to water wherever she went, and all this water flowed with Tilith toward the tear and spilled onto the Earth. And Tilith's fall created the Sea. The meeting of Tilith and Taïke gave birth to Manu in the real world created by both.

I asked Tilitha what happened to the beings of the virtual world once their reflections had spilled away, and her reply at last made it clear how she had been able to grasp my explanations about universes so readily. They still exist, she said. Without Tilith, the reflections grew again, and at this very moment Creation is re-enacting itself in innumerable places and innumerable ways. The world in which we now live is merely a sort of local precipitation around the original seed created by Tilith and Taïke. There are many others, elsewhere.

March 15: As usual, a morning walk along the shore. And as usual, on the smooth sand left by the tide, the children are drawing the spiral of their morning hopscotch, the one narrowing toward the centre. This spiral retraces the adventures of Manu, and each segment must be approached in a certain way, accompanied by the little song I heard when I first awoke on this planet. It's a kind of dance, with the stances and the song complementing each other in recounting the adventures of the Third Mother, from her birth (first segment) to the birth of the first hendemados. The evening hopscotch tells of the creation of the world, the birth of Tilith and Taïke in the mirror-world, their fall, and (in the last and largest segment) the birth of Manu.

The whole game is highly ritualistic and the song resembles the chanting of a psalm. The players sing the whole thing in unison, adding a verse at each segment. The player standing on a segment must stay perfectly still all this time, holding the required posture for that segment and the story, only picking up the marker on the last syllable of the verse. Once he has hopped onto the same segment as the marker, he closes his eyes. This gives the other players a chance to exchange a sign fixing the speed at which they will chant. It may catch the player unawares, especially if he hasn't a clear idea of where the marker was lying. He has to pick it up without opening his eyes. If he fumbles his first try or stumbles, then he has to wait until the next turn to try for the same segment. I'm a little surprised at the age of the players, though, considering the kind of game it is. They range from five to fifteen years, of both sexes, arevags and hendemados—but fifteen is the cutoff mark. This is also the age when the young hendemados stop using speech as their main form of communication, and adopt the adult mode, three-quarters of which involves gestures.

I've been living in Terueli (the name of the village) for nearly a month now, and I'm still under observation. When I ask questions, people often reply with the head movement that means "tomorrow." Even Tilitha, whose open curiosity about me is an exception, often makes it clear that a particular question is premature. With the help of my Total Recall I can make all the correlations and hypotheses I like, but they're worthless if I can't verify them. (I'm forever noticing that the information in Total Recall isn't knowledge; like wisdom, knowledge isn't merely a matter of storing data.)

In any case, these people are not at all primitive, although they live simply. In a world where preceding civilizations have plundered most of the primary materials, they make very intelligent use of what can be salvaged from the waste still surrounding them. Not so much at Terueli, which is mainly a fishing village—but the hendemados of the interior trade regularly with the coastal communities and even with some cities where the original humans are on the point of extinction. They have very sensibly adapted their way of life to the possibilities in their changed environment. But how do they really see themselves? Do they know that arevags and hendemados were artificially created by the original humans only six hundred years ago? It's tempting to link Tilitha's myth with my findings in Baïblanca.... But then I remember the K'tu'tinié'go and their indulgent smile. Such a reductionist interpretation would still tell me nothing about how the myth nurtures their individual and collective lives. Tilitha had no hesitation about telling it: for her, it's a familiar story with no sense of secrecy or taboo. She even seemed to regard it with a sort of amused detachment. But how representative is she of her culture, I wonder? Physically, she's more of a hendemado than an arevag, and yet she's chosen to live under the water. And although she has a male companion in the village (and a female one beneath the sea, as is often the case), she has never had children, which is very unusual. It accentuates our resemblance. Some women Voyagers are compulsive about bearing a child in each of the universes where their desire takes them—something I could never understand. Or accept. And the ones to whom I sometimes talked never understood my quest for a totally different universe. But there was no acrimony in our disagreement: the Voyage is too personal, too solitary an adventure for us to judge each other. But they no doubt found what they were looking for, whereas I....

March 22: Was it a dream? If so, I certainly can't shake it off. It has some secret meaning that I want to—that I must—make clear to myself.

Yesterday was the spring equinox. The villagers had a festival. They cleaned and redecorated their boats and houses. Delicious smells wafted through the village all that day and the day before, heralding the dishes for the coming feast. The young adults went out with the ebbing tide, and the boats came back with the rising tide, bearing the little hendemados born beneath the sea. These children will live in the village from now on. The little arevags born

253

in the village will leave at the autumn equinox. There was dancing, music and singing competitions, and the two communities competed in trials of strength and skill on land and in the water. At nightfall we had the feast. I hadn't been officially invited, but then I've been welcomed with good will and friendliness at all festivities. I assumed an invitation was considered superfluous, since I was now sufficiently part of the village. As the night wore on, however, I became uncomfortable amid the increasingly erotic intimacy. All at once I felt terribly alone, and the black thoughts that had been temporarily pushed aside came flooding back. *I'm here forever; I'll never leave....* I set about serious drinking, both amused and disgusted at my childish behaviour. Disgust got the upper hand in the end, and I walked away from the merrymakers, not wishing to inflict my maudlin drunkenness on my hosts. I collapsed in the shadows of the beach, floating in the slow whirlpool of second-stage inebriation as I lay between the heaving beach and the reeling, star-studded sky. I closed my eyes and fell asleep. And dreamed. I think.

I am on the beach where the feast was held. All trace of the festivities has disappeared, leaving only villagers and arevags seated side by side, forming a continuous line in the shape of a spiral. At the heart of the spiral, motionless and with eyes closed, lies Pilki, a fairly old hendemado. I've been tempted to think of him as the village priest, because people often consult him on a variety of problems. ("Oh, no," Tilitha said, "he's merely the father of a lot of children.") He doesn't move, nor do the arevags and hendemados, and yet something is moving. It's the song. It spirals slowly, swelling as each voice picks it up and adds a syllable. The song is a single word that lengthens as it passes from mouth to mouth... and suddenly begins to diminish, one syllable at a time, as it coils around the old man. I see it, I see it as though each syllable were a round box larger than the one before, growing until a threshold is reached, a limit beyond which the movement turns back on itself and each syllable folds into the preceding one until the word returns to its original state. Only to unfurl once more, from beginning to end, and from end to beginning—and no, they aren't boxes but rings springing successively out of their predecessors and being successively swallowed up by them, and the rings are a word, the word of the universe: it governs the ebb and flow of the tides, the elliptic path of the planet around the sun, and the sun's trajectory in the embrace of the galaxy; while the galaxy, dancing in the universe, whispers the same word passed back from sun to planet to tide, carried on the swirling winds and the curling buds, and from there into human bodies and jostling molecules of matter, minuscule galaxies of infinite coils.... The spiral of sound furls and unfurls, and at the end of this eternity of motionless movement no one is left at the centre of the coil. Pilki has disappeared.

I awoke in my hut—someone had carried me back. It was past noon. I had a dreadful hangover and didn't get up. The villagers have better heads for their sparkling wine than I, and went about their daily business. In the evening one of Palli Kedia's sons brought me something to eat (leftovers from the feast will probably feed the village for several days). He was a tall, handsome boy named Lekin: the only sign of the arevag strain is his very light, vaguely iridescent skin. I made a joke of asking him if he'd brought me home last night. There was just the slightest hesitation, then he said "Til," sketching the sign for arevag. Tilitha had brought me back.

March 23: Pilki is no longer in the village. When I awoke this morning, I had such a vivid memory of the night on the beach (although I don't think I'd been dreaming again) that I went to Pilki's house. I had some idea of asking him about the meaning of my dream. He's no longer there. He has left, someone informed me in sign language. No one in his household seemed particularly upset except for Lollia, one of his granddaughters. Her eyes were red, as through from crying, but perhaps there's no connection. I went down to the beach. The children were playing hopscotch. I viewed the game differently now, and I asked them why they are always playing it, and why only at sunrise and sunset. To begin and end the day properly, they replied. Is it a game? A prayer? A training for the ritual I witnessed (maybe) the night of the festival? Or why not all of these together?

Tilitha was in her usual place, not far from the children. I expected some banter about the other night to reassure me it was all a drunken dream. But she said nothing. She was playing with one of those large shells sometimes washed in by the waves—a nautilus. After the brief moment of shared silence that is our greeting, I asked her where Pilki was. She turned the shell over and over, not answering, the delicate membranes between her fingers stretching and shrinking like a pulse-beat.

"When I was little," she said dreamily, as though not hearing my question, "I used to wonder what happened to the animal in this shell when it died. I thought it must get smaller and smaller as it went further and further into the shell, until one day it disappeared."

She handed me the shell. Its surface had been broken by the scouring sea or by the creature's predator. I could see the inner passages of the nautilus, the delicate, opalescent helix coiling around the transversal cone. I dropped the shell, annoyed by her apparent evasiveness. Was Pilki dead? Tilitha picked up the shell and blew off the sand.

"No, Pilki has left. He is elsewhere. As you are elsewhere here—*more* than you are elsewhere here. But he can never come back."

More than I was elsewhere here? Tilitha's forefinger, the tip of its claw just showing, traced the shell's spiral from the wide end to its apex. I tried to talk about my dream, but she held out the shell again.

"There is a tale. After Taïke fell from the mirror-world she was very lonely. She hadn't yet met Tilith. One day she found this shell on the beach and picked it up. It reminded her of her longed-for mirror-world. She lifted it to her ear and heard the word of the universe."

What had that to do with my dream?

Tilitha placed the shell in my hand with gentle authority. "Your dream," she said.

In exasperation I threw the shell far out into the waves where Tilitha's cousins were dancing. She shook her head and slid into the sea.

My dream. The nautilus. The spiral-song, the helix. Pilki's disappearance. I waited for the spark that would set all these data alight, but nothing came. Back in the village I tried to question the villagers—not openly, of course: if there's one thing I've learned, it's that this subject is really taboo, since even Tilitha couldn't answer me directly. My deviousness got me nowhere. People pretended not to understand, remarking with veiled amusement that things had got pretty hot at the festival. So here I am with my diary, alone beneath the great wheel of the stars. Tilitha hasn't come out of the sea to watch the sunset, or the daylight sky closing like a mother-of-pearl fan as night draws in. The sand beneath my feet is dotted with little rolling shells. Shells. Rolling. The wheel of the stars. The word of the universe. Taïke's mirror-world. My dream. The thread of words that coil and uncoil. A slow turning, more and more resonant, more and more...

motionless movement, resonant and deep, like
that sensation of motionless movement by which,
when the interior and exterior change places just before
the moment when the cold when
the imperceptible irresistible coiling when the cold
eyes closed the cold when breathing slows when

the breathing slows when
the vibrating thread of consciousness when all must stop
then the motionless and profound movement of the
Voyage through
the Bridge, the Bridge!

But how do they do it—how *would* they do it? Suspended animation? Induced trance? I'd never
encountered anything like it before. The Voyage without
the Bridge. Never, anywhere.... How is it possible? I'd
have to know more about the metabolism of hendemados
and arevags. (Return to Baïblanca?) Heaven knows what
those biosculptors invented six hundred years ago. Maybe
they didn't even know themselves, or perhaps evolution
has continued to shape their creatures in forms they never
even imagined....

No, it's not possible. A Voyage without a Bridge, a
one-way, uncontrollable Voyage—it's death; Tilitha must
have been talking about death. And yet she did say, "He is
elsewhere, as you are elsewhere here—*more* than you are
elsewhere here." But if this is a Voyage, how do they know
it? Have those kinds of voyagers arrived here? And yet she
was so quick to understand my explanations, the universes, my Voyage....

No, it's a dream; it must be a dream, because I've
hunted through my Total Recall and there's nothing... but
Total Recall records dreams too, so why would this one be
so nebulous?

March 23, later: Tilitha again answered (but is it an
answer?) that Pilki is elsewhere and that he won't come
back. (She's so serene. I wonder why?) So I really did see
something that night and it wasn't just a dream?—Pilki
has gone on a Voyage? Have visitors come here the same
way Pilki has arrived elsewhere? No. Well, how does she
know he's elsewhere, in that case?

"Before you came among us," she said finally, "we

258

didn't know, we weren't sure. Now we know why no one ever came back. Pilki is elsewhere. And he's not Pilki any more."

"If he's no longer Pilki, then he's dead!"

"Yes and no," she answered, always with that disconcerting assurance. "If he were still Pilki, he couldn't really be elsewhere. That's the price you have to pay."

Suddenly she seemed so strange in the pearly dawn light, such a stranger with her incomprehensible certainties, so totally, terribly, alien.... I felt we could talk all day long, all our lives long, and I wouldn't even begin to understand. She's there, so close to me that I can touch her, but she seems to be... in another universe. And yet I'm the one who is the Voyager. Who was the Voyager.

Who could become a Voyager once more. Total Recall doesn't tell me anything about what happens between the moment I lose consciousness in the Bridge's capsule and the moment I wake on another planet. Suppose I were in the middle of the circle, in the middle of the universe-word like Pilki, perhaps I wouldn't remember anything when I awoke elsewhere. Really elsewhere?

"If it really *is* elsewhere, you can't tell. Look," Tilitha said, pointing to her dolphins leaping out of the sea at some distance from the shore. Their black bodies glistened as they described perfect arcs in the air. "*We* are able to come on land and remain the same, just as our land sisters and brothers can go under water, but the dolphins... the dolphins can't fly. They're not made to fly. If they stayed in the air they'd no longer be dolphins. That would be the price they'd pay for becoming birds, for being truly elsewhere; don't you see?"

March 29: Pilki isn't dead, but he's no longer Pilki. In order to go elsewhere, truly elsewhere, he has become totally other. I understand. A transformation over which no control is possible, an irreversible metamorphosis, a Voy-

age from which you can't come back. A Voyage with no
control, ever. I can grasp the concept intellectually, but my
whole past life, all my conditioning as a Voyager, refuses
to accept it. Yet what if this is the price of breaking out of
the circle, of going truly elsewhere?

It's odd. All these years I've spent leaping from one
universe to another in search of something I wouldn't recognize, and I've never once asked myself how I'd know it,
how I'd identify the other universe-tree. How can anyone
recognize absolute difference? Can it even be perceived?
When I thought about it, I naively told myself it would be
a kind of illumination, that I'd *know*. It never occurred to
me that it must be a one-way illumination, changing you
irremediably, tearing you from yourself. How can you
know the absolute-other if you carry your own reflection
around with you everywhere? You can't simply *recognize*.
You have to *be* other, no longer yourself... impossible not
to think "cease to be." (Tilith—between the world and its
reflections, unable to stay in the universe where she was
born, flowing out of it and, as she fell, creating another
universe.) The price to pay. I never thought there'd be a
price to pay: giving up control, giving up certainty—giving up oneself. A gamble. To get to the edge of the spiral,
to the last syllable of the universe-word, and leap.

The law of the Voyage is still valid, though. I have indeed sent myself into a universe where a Bridge exists. A
kind of Bridge. A Bridge you burn as you cross it. And of
course none of those Voyagers has come back to describe
other universe-trees. Even if they could, their truth would
be incommunicable. Is that really what I was looking for,
an incommunicable truth? No, I wanted to come back and
tell the story, and that's still what I want. But I can't have it
both ways. If I go, I become other. If I come back, if I become myself once more, I'll be unable to describe the
otherness. Either way there's a price to pay.

But I did send myself here, where choice is possible. Go. Stay. Just as it was twenty years ago when I became a Voyager. But that wasn't really a question of choice: I'd already decided by coming to the Centre and undergoing the operations and training. I didn't leave right away because of Egon, because I wasn't sure he didn't love me.... And in the end I left without being sure, on an impulse. That wasn't a real choice.

Go. Stay. If I leave, will it be out of defiance? If I stay, will it be out of fear? I don't know—I just don't know.

Tilitha felt the call of the dolphins' dance. She got up, and I automatically did the same, following her to the water's edge. The tide had washed the nautilus ashore again. A different nautilus, though, with a perfect shell. Tilitha nudged it with her foot, smiling, and I picked it up. I shook out the sand and water. They came in spurts, first passing from one chamber to another, sliding along the intricate coils of the inner surfaces. The chambered nautilus is an amazing shell: the volume enclosed by its internal surfaces is greater than the volume enclosed by its outer surface. There is more space inside the nautilus than its shell occupies.

"For us," Tilitha suddenly said, "the world, our world, is a nautilus. It takes a long, long time to explore its entire space, and rarely, very rarely, do we ever reach the end. Pilki thought he had reached it. Do you think you've reached it, Ao Talitha?

Not knowing how to answer, I put the same question to her. She smiled. Long ago, when she was younger, she thought so. She retreated beneath the waves to meditate for a protracted period, after which she took a long journey through the sea, far from the kelp forest where the arevags live, and far from the coast as well. She visited the lands-beneath-the-sea, the drowned countries, their monuments, their cities, their mountains. On the way back

261

she went to Aomanukera (the-city-of-Manu, as they call Baïblanca). And she decided she wasn't ready to go elsewhere.

"For me, elsewhere is here, with my companions in the village, my sisters and cousins beneath the sea. So many things to learn, always. And you, Ao Talitha, do you think you've learned everything?" she asked, gently insistent. "Do you believe you've come to the end of this world?"

To the end. The end of this world?—Know everything about this world? No, of course not. Never. You are right, alien from the sea who bears a name so close to mine, you are right, Ao Tilitha. I don't know, I won't know, not for a long time. Not before I die, perhaps.

Is there more space within than without?

ETERNITY, BABY

Andrew Weiner

1.

When he was seventeen years old, Simon Nagel fell in love, at first sight and quite hopelessly, with Elena Layton.

Elena was Gil Daniels' girl friend. Simon and Gil played together in the same rock band, the Avenging Angels. This was 1965, and John Tomalski, the lead singer, had a thing about *The Avengers* TV show, or anyway a thing about Diana Rigg. They played all the usual places: high school dances, bowling alleys, sweet sixteens. They were quite good, although highly derivative.

Simon was the keyboards player, and the youngest Angel. Like John, he was still in high school. Gil, the bass player, sold shoes in a factory outlet; Phil Stein, the drummer, was in his first year of college; and Davie Stanton, the lead guitarist, was an apprentice graphic artist. All of them still lived with their parents in the town of Roselle, New Jersey.

The day Simon met Elena, the band were rehearsing in his parents' cavernous rec room. Or at least, they would have been rehearsing, if Gil had not been late yet again.

"We ought to tell him to take a walk," said Phil. "Who needs this shit?"

"Right," John said. "Who needs it?"

"Kick him out on his butt," agreed Davie, running his fingers through his mane of blonde hair.

But of course they never would. John was the lead singer, Davie the one who made the little girls swoon. But Gil, at best an indifferent musician, with a craggy, lived-in face more suited to a meatpacker than a rock 'n' roll hero, was somehow crucial to the band all the same. Gil was simply the hippest kid in town: the best dresser, the best dancer, the best-connected when it came to scoring grass or pills. No one was going to tell Gil to take a walk.

Simon's position in the band, on the other hand, was tenuous at best. None of them, except John, had really wanted him in the first place. And even John, a friend going back to sandbox days, often seemed embarrassed to have him around.

At school Simon was pretty much a loner: nervous, intense, high-strung. But he was an excellent musician. He had been taking music lessons for years, and he could play almost anything, classical, jazz or rock. He could even read music.

The clinching factor, though, was that Simon's parents would let them rehearse in their rec room, rehearse at all hours and volume levels.

Simon's parents almost always let him have what he wanted, anything except attention. Growing up, most of the time he felt that he was pretty well invisible. Even on stage he felt that way. But in a sense it was an asset, being invisible. Otherwise he would have been too paralyzed with fright to perform at all.

When the doorbell rang, Simon climbed the stairs from the basement to answer it. There was no one else home. Simon's parents were away visiting his married sister in Philadelphia, which was just as well because Gil was holding a joint as big as a cigar in his hand.

"Hey, man..." Simon started to protest, and then he

saw Elena coming up behind Gil on the steps to the front door, her bright red cloak streaming behind her. He fell for her in that moment.

"This is Elena," Gil told Simon. "She's come to watch us awhile. She's a dancer."

Elena Layton had just turned nineteen. She was living at home and taking dance classes in the city and her ambition was to be a professional dancer. She never would become one, but she looked like a dancer, or how Simon thought a dancer should look, and so he would shortly immortalize her.

"Hi," Simon croaked.

"Hello," Elena said. She shook back the long dark hair from her eyes and smiled at him.

"Come in," Simon said.

Simon wondered what had happened to Cheryl, Gil's previous girlfriend. But Gil was always running through girlfriends. Gil had a way with women, a way that Simon desperately envied.

"So how's it coming, kid?" Gil asked.

"We were waiting for you."

"Well," Gil said. "No way you could manage without me, right?"

And so Elena sat down on the old beat-up couch at the other end of the rec room and watched them rehearse for awhile.

Simon hunched down over the piano, and tried to avoid looking at Elena, but again and again he found his eyes drawn back towards her. And then he looked up from the keyboard to find her looking directly at him. For a moment their eyes locked, and she gave him a half-smile.

He tore his eyes away, but not before something very much like an electric shock surged right through him. And in that moment he began to hear a song playing in his head, as if on some spectral radio show. A song about

Elena.

When they had finished rehearsing, Elena comple-
mented them on their performance and went off with Gil.
Then the others drifted off, and Simon sat down at the piano to write the song about Elena that had burst into his
head. And after that one, another song, different but from
the same place.

He had written songs before, but they had never satisfied him. These new songs, he could already hear them
complete, every guitar part, every bass line, every chorus.
And he knew that they were perfect.

He stayed up all night writing them down, the songs
that would earn the Avenging Angels their brief footnote
in the history of rock, the anthems of teen angst that would
make them half-famous for a few months of the following
year, *Dance Miranda* and *Oh Melanie*.

Dance Miranda was the one that would go all the way
up to number one on the *Billboard* charts. *Oh Melanie*, the
follow-up, would barely make the top twenty. But Simon
liked them both equally. And both of them were about
Elena: not so much the real Elena, who he hardly knew, as
his idea of her, and his hopeless love for that idea.

2.

Simon never told Elena that he had written the songs
about her. But he did let it slip once to John, and pretty
soon everyone in the band knew about it. He took some
ribbing for it, but less than he might have expected, because everyone could tell that the songs were magical, and
suddenly they were all a little in awe of him.

Maybe someone told Elena, and maybe not. But she
was always friendly to him, when she came to see the band
perform. And at the New Year's Eve party at Davie's she
kissed him with a lot of warmth, although she kissed a lot
of guys there, and anyway she was more than a little

drunk on Davie's punch.

Soon after that Gil and Elena must have had a falling-out, because suddenly Gil had a new girlfriend, Sharon, and Elena didn't come around to watch them play anymore. Simon thought about calling her, but he never had the nerve. She was just too exotic for him, too infinitely mysterious, he could not aspire to actually knowing her.

He still thought about Elena, but less so as time went by. He was just too busy, working almost every night now with the band, rehearsing or playing gigs or making demoes of his songs, and working desperately by day not to flunk out at school.

And then their first record broke the charts wide open, and the rest of his life began.

The way it happened was that Phil Stein's father was a jazz writer for one of the major music trade magazines. He was well-connected in the music business. He had helped them shop around the demoes of Simon's songs until they got a deal.

It was a lousy deal, as it later turned out. They would never see a penny from the recording company beyond the initial advance. But it was a deal all the same, and at the time everyone was thrilled. Even more so when *Dance Miranda*, which its tricky contrapuntal rhythms and achingly wistful chorus, started to get major airplay.

Wealth and fame, or anyway fame, beckoned. And after lengthy discussions with their various parents, some more heated than others, they turned professional and hit the road.

Simon had just finished high school. The expectation in his family had been that he would go to college, eventually to become a lawyer like his father. His parents thought that he was too delicate to survive the turmoils of the rock business. But Simon was immovable. He had glimpsed escape, from what his life had been until now. There was no other choice.

3.

At first it was fun, to be away from home, to be free, to be a rock star.

At first he enjoyed the crowds of barely teenage girls rushing towards the stage, even as he feared that they might tear him apart. At first he liked the travelling, despite the mind-numbing long-distance bus rides and the nail-biting plane rides. At first he relished experimenting with the drink and the drugs and the girls suddenly so readily available to him.

But then it began to go sour. The band members, exhausted with the road, nervous about their future, weary of spending so much time together, began to snipe at each other. They fought over the smallest things, the length of a solo or the placement of the stage lights. They railed at Phil about the deal his father had made for them. But most of all they took it out on Simon, pressing him to come up with another hit.

Simon tried. While the rest of the band were out getting high or getting laid, he would sit in some featureless motel room and write songs. In the end he wrote enough of them to fill out most of their first and only album. Like their first hits, a lot of them had girls' names in their titles: *Lucille Dreams* and *Come Back Sandy* and *Mirabella*. They were decent enough songs. But none of them was a *Miranda* or a *Melanie*, and none would be a hit record. The spark was gone, and he could not rekindle it.

He began to crack.

There were panic attacks. He would be sitting around, smoking grass, and suddenly the terror would seize him, the terror that his life had run completely out of control, and he would feel as if his brain was about to spiral out of his skull.

He stopped smoking grass. But now the terror knew where to find him: in lonely hotel rooms and on cross-country airplane rides, watching a movie or performing on stage, it would strike at him without warning.

He began to hate performing. He just could not stand it anymore, seeing all those faces out there, looking at him, listening to his songs, feeling his feelings.

He told the others that he wanted to quit. The band's manager sent him to a fashionable doctor, who prescribed tranquillizers. For awhile they helped to numb his fear.

Then he began to see Elena.

It happened first of all in Cleveland. He was fumbling his way through *Oh Melanie* with fingers grown sluggish from the medication when he happened to glance up. He saw her sitting there in the front row of the audience. She was wearing her red cloak, the same one she had worn the day they met.

"Hey," he told Davie, between songs. "Look there. Elena."

"Elena?" Davie said, squinting to where Simon was pointing.

"What would Elena be doing in Cleveland?"

Then Simon realized his mistake. The girl he was staring at looked nothing like Elena.

"Sorry," he said. "Forget it."

He told no one when it happened again in Detroit. Or again in Philadelphia and St. Louis. They would just dismiss it, he thought, as the fantasies of a lovesick kid. But he was over Elena, he had been for months.

Or perhaps they would think, as he himself had begun to suspect, that he was going over the edge.

When it happened again in Buffalo, it occurred to him that Elena might be dead, that this might be her ghost come to haunt him. After the show he drank half a bottle of scotch and called her home. He hung up when she answered.

He saw her again and again. Always it seemed to happen during one of those songs, *Oh Melanie* or *Dance Miranda*. It was as though the music was calling her to him. Not the real Elena, but the Elena of his dreams, the Elena he had created in those songs.

"A song is a spell, man," Davie had told him once, during a flirtation with the occult. "A heavy spell."

He began to wonder what kind of spell he had cast.

4.

In New Orleans she came to his hotel room.

It was two thirty in the morning and he was sleeping restlessly. He woke up to see her standing beside the bed.

"Elena?" he said.

She let her cape fall back and she was naked underneath, the way he had always imagined her.

He reached out to touch her and his hand went through her arm. He screamed. She vanished.

He lay in bed until dawn, his mind racing. Then he got up and got dressed and packed a bag. He took a cab to the bus station and he got on a bus. Eventually he arrived home.

The band's management pleaded with him to return. Then they tried threats. But he would not go back. He stayed in his parents' house, and he refused to see any visitors. He did not leave the house again for several months.

In the press release, the record company said that Simon was leaving the band because he was afraid of flying, which was true enough if only a small part of the truth.

The Avenging Angels found a new keyboard player and moved onwards towards an only briefly delayed oblivion.

5.

Under pressure from his parents, Simon began to see a psychiatrist, Dr. Neilson. He saw him three times a week for over a year.

Under Dr. Neilson's guidance Simon came to understand some of his key psychic conflicts. He recognized now how he both craved attention and abhorred it; how he was torn between expressing his deepest emotions and keeping them hidden from the world; and so on.

Simon's success as a rock musician, Dr. Neilson explained, had exacerbated these conflicts. It had disrupted his precarious psychic balance, leading first to his anxiety attacks and then to his visions of Elena's double.

"The classic *doppleganger*," Dr. Neilson told him, "is a doubling of the self. Here we have the double of a young woman with whom you were once infatuated. But the meaning is the same. We can understand it only as a projection of the disowned self."

"Disowned?"

"To quiet the conflicts raging within you, you tried to give up whole parts of yourself: your creativity, your desire to be noticed, even your ability to feel. But they came back to haunt you all the same, in the guise of this young woman."

This part of the Dr. Neilson's explanation never rang entirely true to Simon, but in time he learned to parrot it adequately. And in time, judging Simon to have achieved an adequate level of insight into himself, Dr. Neilson discontinued the therapy.

6.

Decades passed.

A great nostalgia swept the land. Some radio stations played nothing but the music of yesterday. Rock bands surviving from that era gained a new popularity playing revival shows. Other bands reformed themselves in some combination approximating the original.

Dance Miranda featured on the soundtrack of a movie about the Sixties. Re-released as a single, it reached the top ten for the second time around.

Clearly there was money to be made in reforming the Avenging Angels, more money than the first time around. Pressures were felt by the former band members. They were felt even by Simon Nagel, on his farm in eastern Ontario, Canada. He did his best to resist them.

7.

Following his recovery from his breakdown, Simon had gone to college. Afterwards, he drifted back into music, writing and arranging advertising jingles in New York City. He was quick and he was clever and in time he built a solid reputation.

He met and married Gloria, a soap opera starlet from a small town in Ontario. On the birth of the first of their two children, they decided to leave the city. At first they thought of Connecticut, but they could find no property there that satisfied them. On a visit to Gloria's parents, they happened to pass a farm and it happened to be for sale.

The farm had a pasture and a pond and a Victorian farmhouse. It was a two hour drive from Toronto, where Simon could sell his skills to the local advertising industry, and it was close to Gloria's parents. But it was the woods that had compelled Simon to buy it: a thirty acre stand of hardwood trees, mostly maple, on the west side of the property.

The woods were a surviving fragment of the primal hardwood forest that had once stretched uninterrupted from Lake Huron to the west to Québec's Gaspe region to the east. Most of the land had been cleared for crops, but these woods had been retained for firewood and maple syrup.

Simon became adept with a chainsaw, trimming off dead branches and cutting firewood, growing lean and well-muscled with the work. But mostly he just liked to walk in the woods. At times, they seemed endless. He could lose himself in them.

He was at peace for some years. But as the children reached school age, Gloria grew restless. She thought again of work and career. She found an agent in Toronto and began to work again, in commercials and local TV productions, sometimes staying over in the city for several nights.

Gloria pressed him to move back to the city: if not New York or Los Angeles, then at least Toronto. He refused. They fought over this and other things, and then they did not fight at all. Gloria took the children and moved out.

While his relationship was unravelling, Simon came to realize that the woods were dying. Bark peeled away through insect infestation and failed to regrow itself, as though the trees were no longer capable of fighting back. Trees began to turn yellow, then brown, in the middle of summer. In windstorms, dead branches would cascade down by the dozen. Sometimes whole trees snapped in half like toothpicks to reveal rotted interiors.

The trees, he soon discovered, were dying everywhere. The authorities blamed it on hard winters, dry springs, insects, acid rain. There were many explanations. But the trees were dying. And within him, too, something was dying, even as something else flickered into life.

8.

When John Tomalski called to ask if he could visit him, Simon agreed, even though he knew what John

273

ANDREW WEINER

would ask of him, even though he remained determined to
refuse it. He told himself it would be good to see his old
friend again.

John had put on weight. His stomach spilled over the
belt of his baggy Italian pants. Under the suntan, his face
looked puffy.

"This is a nice place you got here," John told him, as
they strolled by the pond. "A great place."

John could not see that the trees were dying.

They exchanged life stories. John lived in LA now,
and was into his third marriage. After the break-up of the
Angels he had played for a few years in one band or another, chasing the hit that never came. Finally he had
given up and moved into producing. He had been very
successful at it, his walls were lined with the gold records
of his artists. But he yearned, even after all these years, for
something more.

"Those were great times, weren't they?" he asked.
"You remember that time in Philadelphia, when we threw
the TV set out the window of that crummy motel, and then
we called room service for another, and we kept on doing
that..."

"No," Simon said.

"You don't remember that?"

"They weren't great times. I hated it. The travelling,
the crowds, the fighting. In the end, I hated it."

"Oh yeah," John said. "You had this thing about flying."

"It wasn't just the flying. It was everything."

"Well," John said. "We were only kids. I mean, if it
had happened when we were older, we would have handled it a hell of a lot better. But you know, despite all the
bullshit, we were great. We were a great little band."

"We were awful. Gil would get so drunk he could
barely stand up on stage, and Davie was tripping half the

274

time."

"But the records were great," John said, almost pleading. "The *songs* were great."

"Yes," Simon said. "You sang them well, John. You really did."

It was true. Although a singer of limited range, John had an ethereal—even, as the pop magazines inevitably put it, angelic—quality to his voice.

They reached the edge of the woods. John came to a halt. He turned back to Simon.

"So what do you think?"

"About what?"

"About reforming the Angels. There's a guy putting together a revival package, and he's been bugging me for months about bringing back the Angels. He's talking big dollars."

"You need the money, John?"

"I always need money. But it isn't just for the money.... It's something I'd really like to do. I never liked how it ended, the way everything just fell apart. I'd like for it to have ended on a high. And now we can do that, we can do it right."

"What do the others think?"

"Phil and Gil are raring to go. Davie isn't so keen. He's into levitation these days, running a TM centre."

"He thinks he can levitate?"

"Oh, absolutely. You know Davie. But I think he'd do it if you did it."

"I don't know," Simon said. "I mean, do we really want to do this? Turn ourselves into a living jukebox, cranking out *Miranda* and *Melanie*, over and over again? Because that's all people will want to hear...."

"Is that so terrible? I mean, why wouldn't they want to hear them? They want to be seventeen, eighteen again. They're homesick, homesick in time. They want to go back to before life got so complicated, to when they still had the feeling they could do anything, be anything. And we'll be helping them. We'll be helping them cheat time."

"Personally, I hated being seventeen."

"Well sure, I had some rough times myself. But that's not what people remember. They just remember the good times. And Christ, you must have liked *something*. What about Elena? You remember, Gil's hippy dippy girlfriend that you had a thing for."

"Sure I remember her."

"Well, you liked Elena, didn't you?"

"Sure," Simon said. "Sure I liked Elena."

"Funny thing," John said. "My mom ran into Elena last year. At Saks. She has a couple of kids now. She was married to a lawyer, but it didn't last. Now she's a real estate agent, quite successful."

"That's nice," Simon said.

"So anyway, what do you think?"

Simon looked past John to the dying woods. He shrugged.

"Sure," he said. "Why not?"

9.

And so they met again, after so many years.

Gil Daniels was a travelling representative in computer supplies. He was on his second marriage. He had met his wife through AA, and he was still on the wagon. There were still flickers of the old Gil, but mostly he seemed beaten, subdued. It was though a part of the man had been cut away, although Simon had to admit that he preferred him this way.

Phil Stein was some kind of therapist, and he talked a lot about psychic energy and being in the now. The rest of the time he talked about his investments.

Davie Stanton was on another planet most of the

time. But he always had been.

When they began to rehearse, Phil and Gil were very rusty. But in time they worked up to something approximating a rhythm section. Davie, on the other hand, was a pleasant surprise. He had not touched a guitar in ten years, but he still had all the riffs.

John's voice had roughened over the years, grown thicker and coarser. But somehow Simon liked this new voice better, it added an interesting dissonance to the proceedings.

10.

"What happened to you, Simon?" Phil asked, one day when they were sitting drinking coffee during a break in rehearsals.

"The same thing that happened to everyone else, I guess. I grew up."

"But you were so talented. Those songs, they were just amazing. I always thought you would go all the way. I thought you would be right up there with Lennon and McCartney, Brian Wilson, all those guys. And you end up writing jingles for candy commercials."

"I like writing jingles," Simon said. "Anyway, there was no more where those songs came from. It just stopped."

"*You* stopped. You stopped yourself. There was real feeling in those songs. But you cut yourself off from it."

"No," Simon said. "Really. Those two songs were all I had. But that's alright, you know. I had my moment in the sun."

"And you couldn't wait to get back into the shade."

Simon shifted uncomfortably in his seat.

"Maybe that's true. But the shade is alright, too. It's kind of comfortable there."

"So why poke your head out now? Why do the tour?"

277

"I'm doing it for the same reason as you. For the money. And for John, because he wanted this so badly."

"Bullshit. You're doing it for yourself."

"Look, Phil...."

"You think you've got it all under control. You think you're just going to sleepwalk through this tour, and none of it is going to make any difference to you. But you're wrong, Simon. You're going to have to deal with it. And I think you *want* to deal with it."

"Deal with what?"

"With the past," Phil said. "What else? That's what it always comes down to. Because the past is alive, Simon, don't kid yourself about that. It's always there, buried in what we are. You open that door even a crack and it's all going to come rushing back."

Simon shrugged. "I'll take my chances," he said.

11.

They rehearsed until there was nothing more to be gained from rehearsing. And then they criss-crossed the country as part of a revival package with three other bands from the Sixties.

They were nervous before the first show. John was popping Valium and Phil was throwing up in the washroom and Simon's hands were shaking. But as soon as they stepped on stage and the applause washed around them, Simon knew that it would be fine.

"What goes around comes around," John said, and they launched into *Oh Melanie*. And the crowd were on their feet cheering the first note. Simon knew that the audience were not applauding the band. They were applauding themselves. But that was fine, too.

Soon, it became routine. They would come on, second from the bottom of the bill, and crank out their set: twenty-five minutes, eight songs including the obligatory encore, some patter in between from John, everything timed to the last second. And then they would go back to their hotel rooms and watch TV and call their various wives and kids. No fights, no groupies, no drunken sprees. It was all very different now.

Simon never watched TV. Sometimes he would speak to his kids. Mostly he would read.

He was reading a lot about the environment now, not just the trees, but the lakes and the oceans, the whales and the polar bears. Reading these books it seemed to him that it was not just the trees that were dying. The whole planet was dying. But even if that was true, this was perhaps as good a way as any to spend his time, reminding people of a time when they were more truly alive.

And so they coasted along, from one town to the next, and the audiences were happy, and the band were happy, and the dollars rolled in.

In Toronto, his children came backstage and looked at him with a new wonder in their eyes. Gloria, who came with them, was polite but distant. She had filed for divorce, was getting lots of work in commercials, was living with a stockbroker.

In Miami Beach, his parents came to see him; in Philadelphia, his sister and her husband and their kids.

And in Chicago he saw Elena.

12.

He had not thought about Elena in years. The past was lost to him, he had closed himself to it. But now he was living in the past, living in it every day.

They were playing *Oh Melanie* when he glanced up and saw her sitting in the front row of the audience. A young woman, perhaps nineteen or twenty, with long dark hair, wearing a red cloak. A woman who looked exactly like Elena, the way she had looked when she was nineteen and he was seventeen.

At first he thought nothing of it. "Say," he told Gil, between songs. "That woman looks just like Elena."

"Elena?" Gil said. "I'm not sure that...."

And then Simon saw that the woman he had been staring at looked nothing like Elena.

It's happening, he thought. It's happening all over again.

He felt both a chill of fear and a strange surge of hope.

13.

He saw her in city after city: Elena, the Elena he had once known, frozen in time.

In Dallas, as he had somehow expected, she came to him in the night. He woke to find her standing by his bed, the way she had done so many years before. He began to reach his hand out to touch her, but then caught himself.

She leaned over the bed and put her hand on his face, and he felt a momentary resistance, a brief sensation of warmth, before her hand passed through him.

This time she did not vanish, but stood there shimmering faintly.

He got out of bed and pulled on his dressing gown.

"Elena?" he said. "What's happening Elena? Why is this happening?"

She smiled at him, but she did not speak.

He thought about calling someone. John. Phil. Dr. Neilson, if he was still alive. But he did not.

Instead he spent the night talking to her, and then singing to her, crooning those old songs to her over and over again. And it seemed to him that she was becoming more real, more *there*, all the time.

Somewhere in the night he dozed off, with the phantom Elena lying beside him on the bed, and in the morning she was gone.

He understood, of course, that he was going mad.

14.

In Houston, when she came to him again, she was real for him, she was completely real. And he no longer questioned what was happening to him. And for hours they made love.

And after that, more cities. More nights with Elena. He woke each morning hoping and fearing that she would still be there beside him. But she never was.

15.

They came to New York City to play the two-night stand that would wind-up the tour.

It was the first night, and they were sitting around the dressing room waiting their turn to play. Simon was reading an article in *Harrowsmith*, Phil and Gil were talking about the stock market, Davie was meditating. And then John came in and said, "Hey guys, look who's here."

Simon glanced up from his magazine and experienced a moment of double-vision. She was Elena and she was not, this smartly dressed woman with the short dark hair and the diamond earrings, the purple silk blouse and the linen suit. She was the real Elena, no doubt, but she was not the one who came to him in the night, not the one that he had called into being.

Elena was cool to Gil, still angry from some long-remembered slight. But she was friendly to the rest of them, and particularly warm to Simon.

"It's good to see you again," she said, taking his hand and holding it for a long moment.

"You, too," he said.

"It was never the same without you, Elena," John said. "You were the secret of our success."

"You did pretty well for awhile," she said.

"We were running on empty. Without you around, Simon just had no inspiration...."

Simon felt himself blushing.

"Yeah, well," he said, to cover his embarrassment. "You can't be a horny seventeen year old forever."

"That's right," chimed in Gil. "You can be a horny forty year old instead." He leaned over and put his arm around Elena's shoulder. Delicately, as though picking up a piece of garbage, she removed it.

It was time for them to go on stage. She gave Simon her card.

"Call me," she said.

16.

"Who was that woman?" John asked Simon, when they met over breakfast the next day in the hotel's coffee shop.

"What woman?"

"The one I saw leaving your room this morning. I woke up real early, before dawn, and I couldn't get back to sleep. So I thought I would go out jogging. I got dressed and I opened my door and I saw her heading down the corridor. By the time I got to the elevators she was gone."

Simon jerked his head back in shock.

"You saw someone coming out of my room? But there was nobody with me."

"Okay, okay," John said. "If you say so."

"Must have been someone else's room."

"Sure," John said. "If that's how you want it. But it's funny, she kind of reminded me of someone."

What did it mean, Simon wondered, that John could see her? That she was becoming more real, somehow? That soon everyone would see her?

John stabbed at his egg. "In the old days," he said, "*I* used to get all the best groupies. Not that I'm interested

282

now, you understand."

"Actually, Davie did," Simon said. "And like I told you, it wasn't my room."

"Whatever," John said. "Are you going to call her?"

"Call who?"

"Elena."

"Elena?"

"Come on. I saw her slip you her phone number yesterday."

"Oh yeah. Elena."

"I think you should call her, man. I mean, a guy your age, you shouldn't be running around with these younger chicks. I can tell you from experience, it's nothing but trouble. But Elena, she's a great lady. If I wasn't happily married myself...."

"Elena's an old friend, that's all."

"She was interested, I could see. Actually, I think she was always interested."

John leaned back in his chair and stretched out his arms. "Didn't I tell you this would be a gas? Getting up there, playing the old songs, meeting up with old friends."

"Sure," Simon said. "It's been a lot of fun."

17.

That night she spoke to him.

"Elena?" he said, as she came into the room.

"Melanie," she said. "Or Miranda. It doesn't matter. Maybe I like Melanie better."

"Melanie," he said. "I'm not sure this is such a good idea."

"It's your idea," she said. "No one else's."

"Who are you?"

"Miranda," she said. "Melanie."

"What are you?"

"The one you want." She moved towards him.

"Why are you here?"

"Because you called me."

"No," he said. "This is crazy. This can't go on."

"Yes it can. On and on. Always and forever. Just the way you wanted it to be."

She put her arms around him, and he did not resist.

18.

"It's true, isn't it?" Elena asked him. "You did write those songs about me?"

"Yes," he said. "Of course it's true."

They were walking in Central Park. It was fall. Leaves crunched beneath their feet.

"You don't know how long I've waited to ask you that."

"I would have told you at the time, if you had asked me."

"No you wouldn't. You would just have got embarrassed, and denied it."

"Maybe I would have. But you knew, anyway."

"I guess I did. But later, you know...you wonder if it really happened that way. I would tell my friends about it, because everyone knew those songs, and it was one of the most interesting things that ever happened to me. And they would say, but the girl in the song is called Miranda, or Melanie, or whatever."

"I'll give you an affidavit," he said.

"How come you never told me?" she asked.

"About the songs?"

"About how you felt."

"I did. In the songs."

"But you never called me."

"You were Gil's girlfriend. And I didn't think you could possibly like me."

"Of course I liked you."

"Not the way I wanted you to."

"I thought you were very sweet. Cute, you know. But a little young. It was flattering, but it was also a bit embarrassing, the way you seemed to worship me, put me on a pedestal. I didn't deserve that at all. I was a pretty ordinary person, really."

"You were beautiful."

"I was attractive, sure. I knew how to put myself together. But I wasn't the way you saw me. I mean, for awhile I thought it would be kind of glamorous to be a dancer But I was never that good at it, I just liked the idea of it. And underneath it all, I guess all along I wanted to get married, raise kids, the usual stuff."

"Alright," Simon said. "You were ordinary. We were both ordinary."

"Not you Simon. You were always something special."

"What was so special about me? I'm just a guy who wrote a hit song once. One and a half hit songs."

"Don't shrug it off," she said. "You wrote some songs that people loved. Even if you did nothing else, there are still the songs."

"Silly songs, really."

"No, Simon. They were true. At the time, and always."

They walked on, talking about their children, their marriages, their work.

Simon enjoyed being with her. She was warm, she was clever, she was funny. But at the same time he wanted nothing more than to be back in his room with the other Elena, who now called herself Melanie, singing to her, making love to her.

"So it's your last show tonight," she said.

"The last one this year, anyhow. Maybe the last one ever. Although I said that twenty years ago."

"Are you sorry?"

"No, I couldn't say that. I mean, it's been fun in a way. And it's been great seeing you again. But somehow it's enough. It's time to let the Avenging Angels rest."

"I suppose you'll be glad to get back to your farm. John told me it's wonderful."

"I don't know where I'll go, actually. Maybe I'll stick around New York for awhile."

"Maybe you'll find it more stimulating, living here. Start writing songs again."

"Maybe," he said.

She looked at her watch. "I really should be going," she said. "I have a showing at three."

"Have dinner with me tonight?" he asked, surprising himself.

"I'd love to," she said.

19.

The audience was more than usually fervent that last night, hyped up by the MC.

"The last performance by the fabulous Avenging Angels," he told them. "Your very last chance to dance."

After the usual encore, *Dance Miranda*, the crowd kept whistling and shouting for more.

"Do it," the promoter told them, as they stood around in the wings.

"The Bluebells are on next," John said.

"They don't want the Bluebells. They want you."

And so they trooped back on stage and the crowd roared in approval.

Simon hit the opening chords of *Oh Melanie*. They had already played it once that night, but the crowd were delighted to hear it again. They were rapturing out, revelling in recaptured time.

"*Oh Melanie, I want you to be, beside me girl, for eter-*

nity...."

It was, he thought, and not for the first time, a quite absurd song, a song only a naive seventeen year old or the most cynical hack could write. It expressed and demanded an impossible devotion. The song was a lie. And yet, as Elena had said, there was also a sense in which it was true.

"Oh Melanie, now that you're mine, I want to stop time...."

He didn't think about Elena, waiting for him backstage. He didn't look at the girl in the long red cape sitting, as always, in the front row. He lost himself in the song.

"...until eternity, oh baby, eternity...."

When they hit the second chorus, everything froze. He could not turn his head, or push a key on the piano. And around him the other members of the band were frozen, also, like so many statues. Or flies, he thought. Flies in amber.

He could not feel his heart beating.

The noise in the auditorium damped down into a dull roar. The light in the room changed colors, seemed to bend weirdly.

And then he saw her coming towards him across the stage. She was moving freely, her cloak flapping behind her.

She reached out her hand to touch him, and he was free, too.

"Let's go," she said.

"Go where?"

"Eternity," she said. She reached out to take his hand. He pulled away from her.

"Death?" he said. "Is that what you mean?"

"Eternity," she said, again.

"No," he said.

"No?"

"Go away. Go back to wherever you came from."

"I came from you, Simon. I want only what you

287

want."

"No."

She stood there staring at him for a moment. And then her hand disappeared into the folds of her cloak. When she pulled it out again, she was holding a knife. It glinted purple in the strange light.

"This is crazy," Simon said, taking a step backwards. "You can't hurt me."

"Eternity, baby," she said. She plunged the knife towards his chest. He held his hand out to ward it off. It brushed against his knuckles. He felt a sharp pain. He watched, fascinated, as specks of blood, greenish in color, flew off.

"Stop it," he said.

She slashed at him again.

Enraged now, he caught hold of her wrist. They struggled across the stage, before the frozen crowd. He wrenched the knife away from her, forced her to her knees. He held the knife at her throat.

She stopped struggling. It was as if she was waiting for him to kill her. And for a moment he wanted to, wanted desperately to end this.

But then it came to him what he would be killing. And his rage ebbed away, to be replaced by an overpowering sense of tenderness. Because, after all, he was her and she was him.

He relaxed his grip on the knife, let it slip to the floor.

"Come back," he said.

He felt her rushing into him.

And then he was back at the piano and John was singing the last verse of *Oh Melanie*, and the crowd were on their feet yelling, and blood was dripping red from his hand on to the ivory of the keys.

20.

"That was really something," John said, as he worked the cork out of the champagne bottle. "It was like they never wanted it to end."

"Memories," Phil said. "The ultimate commodity. Wish I could buy an option on memories."

They were sitting around the dressing room, John, Phil, Gil and Simon. Davie was already on his way to the airport.

With them were John's wife Beth, and Gil's wife Margaret, and Phil's girl friend Louise, who had come for this final show. And Elena.

John popped the cork and poured the drinks.

"We need a toast," he said.

"I got one," Gil said, raising his Coke can. "Same time next year."

"Depends on how the market is doing," Phil said, and they laughed, but they were looking at Simon. He was sitting quietly next to Elena, staring thoughtfully at his bandaged fingers.

"No," he said. "I don't think so. I'm glad we did it, but it's finished. I'm finished with it, anyway. You guys want to go on with it, I'll come watch. But no more for me."

"But they're your songs, Simon," John said. "People still want to hear your songs."

"They're not my songs anymore," he said. "They're everyone's. And I don't know, maybe it's time to write some new ones."

"You ever need a producer...."

"I know who to call."

"Okay, then," John said, raising his glass. "To the Angels. To the late great Avenging Angels."

They drank.

THE BEST
OF
BOTH WORLDS

Lesley Choyce

I still cannot hate my father. Even after all this. I agree that there was greed in it, yes. But there was more to it: expectation of a new frontier, a better life for all. At this point it's too difficult to sort out the victim from the culprit. My mother, perhaps, should be blamed as well. She who never trusted my father's great dreams, but then slipped into a feverish state of enchantment when he produced his single, great, revolutionary discovery. She should have held onto her doubt. A marriage sometimes has to be that way. But she was overpowered by the possibilities, like everyone. And she was still young, impressionable, while my father was an expert at dismissing scepticism. He was a very good scientist, a very good magician when given the right technological wands.

I grew up uncomfortable with the massive accumulated wealth and resented the money and the fame that had stolen my father from me before I even got to know him. Eventually, I got used to it and grew up into a somewhat happy, childless woman. The portals took me everywhere, improved me in so many ways. They had always been a good idea. No one had expected the negative spin-offs. Certainly my father had meant no harm to his daughter or the entire breeding stock of my generation.

My father was a man of indomitable spirit and great imagination. But he could never seem to put his great mind to any purpose that was of value to those who might hire him. He had been unable to fit into the research universities, the military establishment. His science did him no good at all and he needed a living. So back in those early days of their marriage before I came into the world, he and my mother opened up a travel agency.

My father had travelled space quite a bit, tagging onto various projects for contract work—the technical stuff or logging in for data accumulation on commercial and research flights. He was a regular customer at many a greasy spoon in the lunar burbs. And he knew the moon, the only available off-planet vacation destination, to be a bleak, unforgiving and pointless place, despite what the tour packagers were trying to do with it.

Travel to the moon, for the average man, was absurdly expensive anyway. Few went. Fewer enjoyed the trip if they did go. Still, my father knew that the moon was just the first stop on what would be a much longer itinerary. And he wanted to be in on the ground floor of a big industry that would someday make him big bucks and free up his time for the really exciting work that he cared about—research into projects too obtuse or too far-fetched for any government or corporation to invest in. He was, alas, not a practical man, who could satisfy himself with bio-genetic research to cure the common cold or alleviate pain and mental disorders. He wanted to create something for us all that no one would believe possible.

So, until his big chance would come his way, he worked day and night with my mother trying to sell the moon to rich newly-weds and to create an aura of glamour around space travel for any gullible would-be space tourist. But he was not a man of great personality. The junkets for which he took commission were mostly for military men and business people serving the research stations. Small potatoes.

If my parents had decided to bring me into the world back then when they were mere travel agents, I would have been blessed. I probably would have been normal— like in the old days. That is, I would be able to have children. Men would have lined up at my door when I turned twenty-one.

But, one day, way off in the shoulder season of the moon's tourist trade, a scrapware salesman happened into my father's office. He was just an ordinary on-the-road businessman, a vendor of laser printing devices and software odds and ends who bartered some reconditioned goods for a seat on a shuttle, hoping perhaps, to open new accounts in virgin lunar territory. My dear old dad could not resist the remains of a late twentieth-century dissimulator. So the peddler got to go to the moon, and my dad got his hands on the most interesting toy he'd ever owned. The rest is history. Or tragedy, depending on how you look at it.

The travel business went to ruin. My mother remained steadfast, tried to pull things together to keep their heads above water. Funds were borrowed from relatives. Bank managers were persuaded to be optimistic. And so the prototype emerged.

I want to say again that his intentions were nothing if not good. He believed he was doing it for mankind. There was money to be made but it was more than that. If not benevolence, then just this: he developed the portal because he imagined such a thing were possible. Man, it seems is incapable of avoiding the creation of something he sets his sights on. Be careful what you dream, we all need to be warned, because some day it might come true.

The portal was not really intended for space travel, of course. It wasn't even being considered for human transport. It was only going to be a really efficient courier service, a highly-innovative delivery system. Accurate, precise information storage and retrieval (as always, my father would say), that was the key. To dissociate a thing was simple. In fact, that's where the old SDI scrap came in.

Reassociation, however, proved tricky. A unit was required on either end. Certain amounts of on-hand chemical components in readily convertible compound form were necessary for hydrogen, oxygen, carbon, calcium, etc. but all at very little expense really.

Soon the financial success of the project was staggering. The damn thing worked and it worked in a big way, saving corporations millions in shipping costs, making my father rich. He could have stopped right there but my father did not see himself as a mere shipper of the world's freight.

He wasn't happy to perform transport miracles with toilet paper, cars, cameras, books and junkware. What he dreamed of was instantaneous human transport. To anywhere and everywhere. Including the moon. But interest in space had diminished once the news began to spread about how boring it really was up there. (The *idea* of space had always been so much more exciting than space itself). However, the interest for instantaneous travel to anywhere here on good old earth was tremendous. My father hired thousands of men and women to help him work out the bugs, build in safety to the max, and develop the intricate worldwide network.

After all the rat and chimp tests, the first human travellers had been volunteers: the criminals, the terminally ill. All had come through without a scratch. Some who had been flicked, say, from New York to Paris and back claimed that they had returned somehow improved. Then came the flocks of young people—students, military men, all travelling for free, all being tested before and after. All said they felt great after reconstruction. Error was marginal. A tall, blonde, blue-eyed cadet arrived in Lisbon with one eye blue, the other brown. He said he loved the quirky change and refused to be altered back to original form. The error was traced, software designed to prevent any such "flutter" in results again.

And suddenly (it seemed), the world woke up one morning to see that it had shrunk to the size of a small marble. Portals opened everywhere. At the grocery store near the check outs; at the bank—near the credmach; in offices beside the triplefax or in your own home beside the vidyloop; if you could afford it. The spin-off however, was this: my father and his colleagues now realized that genetic improvements could be made while travelling via portal.

You could flick from New York to Waikiki in seconds, avoid jet lag, ticket counters, taxis and insolent bellboys—since you could arrive inside your hotel room, already checked in with your luggage beside you. You could even arrive already tanned so you wouldn't burn and you could have had facial hair removed or an appendectomy along the way. (These were relatively simple and cheap portal program adjustments.) And it was all for one relatively small fee to any middle-class citizen of an industrialized nation.

People held portal parties. Business became more efficient. World tension reduced. My mother and father saw the world, tuned up their bodies for a healthy mid-life, grew wealthy beyond belief and had me.

Perhaps the health-improving aspect of the portal should have been examined more closely. But after the safety record and the phenomenal success of the travel business, this innovation seemed natural and unavoidable. Caution was thrown to the wind. The portal was a gift from God and my father was the messenger angel. He could do no wrong, and eventually grew to believe that.

The problem arises in me, the daughter. Second generation portal traveller. Name a place you don't think I've been on this planet. I bet you can't. I had unlimited free travel, along with health renewal, on any day I chose as long as I was home by supper. That way I avoided childhood diseases, boredom, tedious homework assignments and all the rest.

If only my father had designed an invention simply for travel and not gone overboard to incorporate those many programs for improving the species as a kind of fringe benefit. But dreams for men like my father demand action—creative or destructive, whatever the end result; often it's impossible to sort out one from the other.

So what you see here before you is the new improved woman. My counterpart, the improved man is out there, by the multitudes, too. Very few can *feel* that any physical thing is wrong. My first suspicion came about when I discovered I no longer dreamed. I was in my twenties. I lived alone. Why, I wondered, was I living alone if I could be with anyone I wanted to, anywhere, instantaneously night or day? And the freedom from worry... drink yourself silly the night before, wake up and flick yourself down the street and a healthy, improved you arrived at work or at another party. My option was simply to have double portal units. If I partied too much, I'd pop in one and out the other in seconds. No hangover, no blahs. If a relationship went sour, I could do the same and come away from it feeling cleansed and happy... sort of.

But somebody must have screwed up somewhere. What the hell went wrong?

Nothing, precisely. Government wonders over the

decline in birth rate. That should not be a big shocker. We tend to be less monogamous, sure. Also, unwanted pregnancy is a thing of the past. The portals have improved life in so many ways and given us so many more *choices*.

One morning, I flicked myself across the room for a quick clean up. I was feeling just a little snarky and wanted to get mellow. When I reassembled, a single leaflet lay by my feet where someone had slipped it under the door. "Join the Portal-less Society." There was an address, followed by the message in italics, "Walk-in clients. Only."

I looked the name up in the *Portal Directory*. Nothing. I flicked myself to the appropriate neighbourhood, arriving in a public portal in the vegetable section of the supermarket. I had the portal dress me in appropriate attire en route. I hoped I would not be recognized.

I walked to a small, archaic office and was greeted by a video monitor that switched itself on.

"We're sorry we can't be here to talk with you. There are so few of us, and we have many adversaries so we believe it would be dangerous to stay in the city." The face was that of an old man with grey eyes. Something looked not quite right about him... the scruffy beard, the plastered-down hair and a curious quavering in his voice. He appeared to be made up to look different than he actually was. My guess was that he was trying to conceal his identity. Nonetheless, there was something oddly familiar as well—but distant, too distant to retrieve in my memory files that had been reorganized and portal-cleansed so many times to make any real sense. "The fact that you have arrived suggests that you believe a portal-less society might be desirable. Unlimited, instantaneous travel and self-improvement have led us into a dead end. So few questions are asked about its validity. All you hear is the good stuff. We believe that a price has been paid for the new technology. A human price. In the name of freedom from restriction and perfect health, mankind is slowly removing itself from the face of the earth."

I stood up and began to leave. I had never heard such stupid, irrational radicalism before. "Who are you?" I shouted at the screen.

"I am someone you know but do not recognize. But that is not important. What you must do is go home and find the answers to the following questions:

1.) Is every portal programmed to erase any worry or doubt about the portal technology?

2.) What are the birth rate projections for your country over the next ten years?

3.) When was the last time you were hungry for sex? and

4.) Is Bernard Bentall alive?

Please write these down before you leave. Don't trust your memory. And please don't take the portal on your way home. It is more important than you think."

This whole scene was so bloody mysterious. And why that last question. Why the hell was I being asked if my father was still alive? Of course, he was alive. But there was something naggingly important about this that I couldn't shake. Almost against my will, I picked up a pen on the desk beside me, wrote the questions down, and stuffed the paper into my pocket. I didn't look at the face on the video monitor again. I rushed out of the office.

I might have simply dropped into the portal in the nearby supermarket and flicked home, ignoring this bizarre incident altogether, if it had not been for the final question. But at home, I soon flicked to my parents house in Bermuda, entered the breezy dining room as they were sitting down to tea. Both greeted me cheerfully. At first I almost did not recognize them; they had gone through total portal regeneration again. I was speaking to a man and a woman my own age. If it had not been for the video en-counter, I would have thought nothing of it. But now, I felt almost dizzy. "Are you both well?" I asked.

My father laughed. "Silly question, child. We should weed such euphemisms from the language. What brings you here?"

"Just thought I'd drop by for tea," I said. I didn't know what I expected.

"Splendid," my mother said, touching the mini-port by her elbow. A fresh steaming pot of tea emerged.

We made small talk; I was the one who kept it small. Then I went for a solitary walk along the pebbled shore-line. I was not sure why I was in Bermuda although it did not seem so foolish for a daughter to visit her parents. But then I reached in my pocket and found the paper with the questions. I could not remember where it came from and I was sure I had never seen them before. As I sat down by the shoreline, I read them and they burned like acid into my mind, bringing utter confusion and even a kind of pain that I was totally unfamiliar with. I could remember the video of a man but I could not remember why I had gone or what he had said.

I returned to my parents' home. Who better to answer question number one? "Do portals erase fear or concern for the safety of portal use?" I asked my father.

"Yes, of course," he answered, all smiles, like I was teasing him, playing some sort of daughterly game. "That was an early modification that your mother suggested. Worry-free travel was a travel agent's dream. But at first she did not believe it would be possible."

I excused myself to go to bathroom but while there jotted an emphatic yes to question number one.

I was afraid to ask anything else. I kissed them both on the cheek. There was an odd sensation to feel their cheeks against my lips. Perhaps it was just the breeze. But the skin felt cooler than expected, and smoother; it was like kissing lukewarm porcelain. My father noticed my uneasiness.

"It's because I don't need to shave any more. No man does. Such a simple, trivial modification. And we had to put up with that foolishness for so long. Frees up nearly two hundred hours in a man's lifetime, time that he can be doing other, more important things."

I wondered exactly what those "more important things" were. "Bye Daddy, Mommy," I said, stepping into the portal.

They both gave me a polite wave as I flicked home.

I arrived rested and refreshed but immediately poured myself a drink and sat down on my bed. I rediscovered the paper with the four questions in my back pocket. I reread the questions, realizing again I had no memory of ever having seen them before, although I did still remember the man in the video. I saw that question one was answered, yes. What had been the source of that answer, I wondered. The portal had, as I would later remember, erased my worries, including my concern that *it* was responsible for "making travel less worrisome." Jesus. I poured another drink.

I could not fully understand why I had these questions or what I was supposed to do. In fact, I felt such a growing anxiety that I prepared to step back into the portal and flick across the room. Just to clear my head and relieve my tension.

But I stopped. Instead, I sat down at my infodeck, cued *Worldbook* and asked: "What are the birth rate projections for Canada and the U.S. for the next ten years?" And then, nervously, even before I got an answer, I added, "Give me projections for Russia, England and Japan as well."

The results were about the same. Zero rate growth for

three years, then a decline after that. A steady decline. I asked for death rate projections and discovered that it was predicted that the death rate would drop as well. Fewer people would be born into the world. Fewer of us already alive would be dying.

The portal, as a sort of frill to instant travel and good health, was throwing something close to immortality into the package deal.

Without prompting, my infodeck suggested: Now try Namibia, Pakistan and Nepal. I asked the same questions and discovered that these three nations had death rates that continued to climb, birth rates that were climbing as well. Mortality was alive and well in at least three nations.

I wondered what *Worldbook* or my infodeck was up to, asking *me* to ask *it* a question. Clearly, someone else was tapped in to my line. My head was swimming. There was a story here. What did it all add up to? I felt scared. I was in over my head. How did this business of Third World countries fit in?

Like so many other commonplace technological advancements, the portal had bypassed the populations of Third World countries. Sure, any of us could visit some of those countries, enjoy whatever exotic culture or scenery there was to take in, then, ignoring the huddled masses of poverty-stricken people that were kept conveniently out of our view, we could arrive back home, germ free.

Even the portal's advanced medical assistance was never put to use for the poor of these nations. In fact, many of those unenlightened societies had feared the machines, made them illegal within their borders. Instead of pressing us for the technology, they preferred, it seemed, to see their children die of malnutrition and their elderly grow crippled and die premature deaths. Too bad for them, we'd all say after a good portal polish, and slip off to some other destination where the people were more hospitable and had better sense.

I crumpled the stupid paper with the idiot questions and threw it on the floor. I was ready to hop into my portal escape by flicking myself to some place wonderful. A beach in Rio, a nightclub in Budapest. Or some place more adventurous—one of the new gravity-free hotels circling high above in the Clarke Belt. But I stopped myself. I turned off the infodeck. I picked up the paper from the floor, jotted down an answer to question two and then read: "3. When was the last time you were hungry for sex?"

Another absurd question. I had known many lovers and found them all short-lived and ultimately, tedious. None had seemed satisfying enough to prompt me to strike up a lasting relationship. "Hungry for sex" seemed like a curious, primitive expression. Had I ever felt hungry for sex? I wasn't sure I had. *Hungry* sounded very urgent and barbaric. Any sex I had participated in, in fact, had seemed ritualistic, quaint and not particularly pleasurable. Had it ever been different? None of my friends talked about sex or put it as a high priority in their lives. Better a quick flick in the portal, a mental and physical tune-up and a splash in the Mediterranean.

That was at least partially the result of weeding out the more troublesome element of pure lust from the psyche of anyone passing through a portal. But now I began to wonder if even lust was somehow so tightly tied in with the package of human love that the end result was a general lack of passion between the sexes. Absolute freedom of movement and freedom from health worries had altered us, I supposed. A new self-interest and selfishness had emerged that made us less interested in the old one-to-one relationship. (Hey, it was a big world with lots of people, right? People you could meet at the flick of the flicker setting.) And it was no big secret that fewer of us even had the desire to raise kids with so many other options in life.

My mind reeled at the implications.

And then, the final question. It came home to roost. I *had* seen my father. He was alive. And well. I was ready to go back to that stupid office and blurt it out to the figure on the video screen. Or better yet, track down the jerk who was messing with my head and cutting into my infodeck.

I walked outside onto the street and began walking in the direction of the shabby store-front office where I had seen the disturbing video. I had no idea of directions and asked many times of those lingering on the streets. All seemed less than interested in offering help. Each kept pointing to a nearby portal. But I would take no chances.

I'd spent little time on the street but things were as I expected. There were no children around. No old people. It was life as usual. People were popping in and out of public portals everywhere. I grew weary and confused, stopped many times to step into a portal myself, just for a chance to get refreshed, but each time something tugged me back. I never once sat still long enough for the portal to read my retinal ID or ask for destination and improvements desired. Finally, I sat down on the front steps of a dilapidated tenement and looked around me. What was I trying to prove? What was all this stupidity?

Just then, an old woman with a blotchy face saw me sitting on the steps and sat down beside me. Before I could get up and move on, she was pawing my hair.

"What's a matter honey," she said in a hag's voice, "you got troubles? I don't see so many troubles any more around here. I'm the only one gots worries."

I pushed her hand off me. I'd never met anyone in such a condition. Old and ugly. Like the old days. I started to get up to move on but I felt like all the life had drained out of me. I stepped back from her and couldn't stop myself from looking hard at the pitiful creature. I had not even realized any like her were left in my part of the world. Why had she chosen to stay like that?

"Sorry," I said, seeing the hurt look in her eyes. "I'm just tired and a little confused. You sort of surprised me." Then I asked her if she knew anything about an office with a guy who talked about a portal-less society.

"Sure," she said, smiling now, showing her capped and crumbling teeth. "It's good to see a body who wants to use her legs. I'll take you. It's maybe a twenty minute walk."

So we walked. I avoided asking her the obvious question. Why *had* she allowed herself to become what she was: old and ugly. When we arrived at the location, I handed her a coded portal card, the kind I'd give away as presents to people I met while travelling. "Take this," I said. "Unlimited portal travel and tune-up for three months. Anywhere you like. Any change you can think of. Any time you like."

She looked shocked at first. Insulted. She shook her head sideways, and refused to take the offered card. Then she smiled again. "Oh, I'm sorry," she said, "I can see that you're just trying to be nice. No. I can't take it. I wouldn't step into one of those things if my life depended on it." She began to cough and held her hand up to her mouth. "Goodbye now sweetie; take care of yourself," she said, pushing the card back into my hand. And she walked away.

As I opened the door, the video went on automatically. It was an ancient, out of place mechanism. In the old days, self-serve stores that sold everything from Italian shoes to package vacations had used such unsophisticated devices. The screen came to life. I saw again the image of the old, tired man who had appeared to me before. This time he was without a beard and with much less hair. My

guess was that this was his true appearance, whereas before he had kept his looks masked. It should have been
obvious to me before... the familiarity of the haunting image; but ours was a world where we expected only
improvements in our friends, our family and ourselves.
Aside from my recent encounter with the old lady of the
street, I had little knowledge on what age did to people.

I drew a deep breath. "Is Bernard Bentall alive?"

"I am," he answered. I felt a shiver creep up my spine
and something lodged in my throat. A wave of nausea
swept over me. Again, I felt the addict's need to crawl into
a portal to make things right in an instant, to be some place
other than here.

"Courage, daughter," the old man said.

"What about my mother?" I made myself ask, not
looking at the screen but down at my hands. "Where is
she?"

I half expected an old, haggard, sweet woman, like the
one I had just met on the street, to appear before me; but
my father answered, "She died several years ago. She was
not unhappy when she died."

The room began to spin around. I wanted to laugh, to
cry. I didn't want to hear any more of it. I wanted to go
back to the fix-it-up-quick world of portals and pretty lies.
I wanted to flick myself out of there. I wanted a headlong
madcap jump sequence from portal to portal until all of
this would be thoroughly and irreversibly cleansed from
me.

"Shut up!" I screamed at the video and turned to
leave.

"Stop, please!" It was the voice of a very old man now,
a voice filled with desperation.

"My mother and father are in Bermuda," I insisted. "I
was there. I touched them." The word *touch* stuck in my
throat. "Don't try to tell me they aren't real. If you are my

father, then who are they?"

The man in the video looked embarrassed and apologetic and something in his eyes looked very soft, very sad. But I recognized at once that here was a face of a man who *could* be a father, a father with flaws and shortcomings and weaknesses and worry. It was nothing like that other father with the perfect, never-needs-shaving face, and my lovely but emotionally immune Bermuda mother.

"The others are us, too. They are your mother and father. We—your mother and I—did not mean to trick you. We just thought life would be easier that way. We did not think you could adjust to the old world, so we left you in the new. It was the year that the portal development was given over entirely to the corporation. I had taken it as far as I could. Improvements were made almost daily. I couldn't keep up with it.

"I could foresee, however, many futures. This was all before you came along. So I gave your mother and I the best of both worlds. I simply reassembled us on the other end of a portal but left the originals intact. We would grow old and they would grow young. It was not until very recently that I could honestly say that we had the best of the bargain. But we missed you very much."

"And yet, I never missed you," I told him, convinced now and shocked at a feeling of loss and guilt that rose up in my heart. "Not until today, at your house, kissing you both and feeling so ... distant."

"I know. You are sadder but wiser."

"But why are you punishing me?"

"It's not punishment. I made contact with you because *I* need your help. There are very few of us—the unimproved—left who have any say in the world. You'll have to decide. But if you want to forget the encounters with me ever happened, I'll take care of that. You'll have no trace of memory. And you'll know only your improved parents."

"But what do you want out of me now?"

"Join us in setting up portal-free zones."

"I don't understand."

"I've tried to develop a revised portal that will allow humans to... stay human... but no one will listen to an old man. It's a time of young innovators, forever young, forever stupid and happy and forever improved. That's why your mother and I wanted to opt out before it was too late. She was the one who convinced me that the endless improvements would lead to something horrific."

"But it isn't horrific. People are happy, freer than ever."

"Yes and no. We've lost something along the way. Remember my four questions. Maybe we could have a world without lust but not a world without children. Love, sex, family loyalty and intimacy... somehow, the very delicate intermingling of these factors has been weeded from people through the ever-improved, ever-improving portal. Everyone is becoming so content with the new way that they don't think of regeneration in the form of children. They think of regeneration only for themselves. You become your own son or daughter each time you step into a portal and step out with a renewed body and a new start in life. All of you could end up living pointlessly forever without pain and worry." He paused and looked deep into my eyes. "And that would be a terrible tragedy."

"What about Namibia, Pakistan and Nepal?" I asked. The whole picture was not clear to me yet.

"No portals."

"And you suggest I go live there," I asked sarcastically, " and live happily ever after until I die of disease or malnutrition maybe."

"There is no happily ever after. Remember, you can,

of course, hop into the grocery store portal and erase all this. It would be very easy and your troubles—my troubles—will be gone from your life for good."

"No," I told him. I couldn't bring myself to run away. "Continue. I'm just not sure I'll be good at Third World living."

"Nor am I. You'll have your options where to go but, unfortunately, I do not want you to come to live with me. If you do, your other father will know how to find you. He knows me too well."

"Then?"

"Stay here and find others. Develop-portal free zones. You have the money; your funds will not be frozen. He cannot take it from you. He will try to persuade you against the cause and try to make you fail. I'll try to keep him diverted and busy with other things. But you must never step into another portal again." It was the voice of a father I heard as a very young child. It was my real father speaking to me.

I felt a tidal wave of emotion for my dead mother and this man, this father. "Isn't there some way I can I come be with you?" I begged, tears rolling down my face for the first time in so many years.

He too was crying. "No, I'm sorry. I am very far away. The other forms of travel, as you know, are gone. But I'll be with you always, I promise. We'll talk often. I've got a few more good years in me."

The screen went dead. I found myself touching the glass, wanting so much to feel his real face, to trace my finger along the lines of his face and the stubble on his chin. I sat and stared at the empty monitor, then got up, fought the urge to run down the street and step into the supermarket portal where I could make the hurt and confusion go away.

As I walked back out onto the street, my head danced

with images of Maui, Bali, Monaco and all the other places I would never visit again, all of the many views of paradise I would never see again. And then it all turned into a dull grey fog. I shook it off and walked out into the sunlight.

"Oh, there you are, sweetie," a voice said. It was the old woman who had led me here. "I got to thinking that you might have a hard time finding your way home. So I was just resting here until you was ready to head back. How did it go?"

"It was really something."

"That's the way it goes for me too. I learn something new and interesting every single day. I say that to Bobby each time I come home."

We began to walk back in the direction of my apartment. "Bobby?" I asked.

"My one and only. Been together for thirty some years. Would have had kids too if he hadn't put himself in one of them portals. Still, I eventually brought him back around to normal. We're happy anyhow. He's home probably snoozing, but whyn't ya come on over? Meet the whole gang of us. We don't have much chance to socialize with young travellers like you."

"I'd like that," I said. And after a long but exhilarating walk I found myself in an old grey building shaking the hands of a dozen old men and women who owned up to the fact that they had been living in a portal-free zone for quite some time already and they were ready and willing to expand the perimeters to include me.

I took a look around and got a good idea of what it would be like to grow old—to grow old in one place, without improvements. And I sat down among these strange and friendly folks, wondering just what our chances were of reviving lust and loyalty and the physical ability to procreate imperfect children who would have a chance to live limited and human lives.

HOW THEY MADE THE GOLEM

John Robert Colombo

To the banks of the Moldau River,
    their lanterns light, their scriptures heavy,
        the three men made their way, the three of them,

The Holy Rabbi of Prague, Judah Loew,
    his brother-in-law, Issac ben Simson, Cohen,
        and his pupil, Jacob ben Chayim Sasson, Levite.

The night was near midnight. They stopped
    where the banks of the river were of red clay.
        They stood in the darkness, prayed and prepared.

Then each sang the prescribed Psalm:
    "My substance was not hid from thee,
        when I was made in secret, and curiously wrought

in the lowest parts of the earth."
    The Rabbi fingered the time-worn pages
        of the Book of Psalms and the Book of Formation,

selecting the required passages:
    "Thine eyes did see my substance,
        yet being imperfect; and in thy book

all my members were written,
    which in continuance were fashioned,
        when as yet there was none of them.

How precious also are thy thoughts
    unto me, O God! How great is the sum
        of them!" Then, in the earth at his feet,

the bent Rabbi moulded the clay figure
    of my person, making me in length three ells,
        with all the members and measurements of a man.

The Rabbi, the Cohen and the Levite
    stood by my feet regarding my clay face.
        "You are fire," The Cohen walked around me

seven times and sang: "He hewed, as it were,
    vast columns out of the great intangible air."
        The charm worked, my clay turned red like fire.

"You are water." The Levite then walked
    around me seven times but the other way,
        singing: "And He bound the twenty-two letters

unto his speech and shewed him all
    the mysteries of them." Water flowed from me,
        hair sprouted, toes and fingers grew crude nails.

"You are air." The Rabbi bent down to me
    and inserted the parchmented name, the Shem,
        deep into my clay mouth, and together they prayed:

"And He breathed into his nostrils
    the breath of life; and the man became
        a living soul." With that I opened my eyes.

I saw them there, heard the Rabbi's command:
    "Stand up!" And I stood up, a dumb stranger.
        They handed me their sexton's dirty garments.

"You are Joseph," the Rabbi said.
    "You will destroy the entire Jew-baiting
        company." I nodded, for I had no powers of speech.

The three of them led me away as a fourth.
    "A dumb creature of magicians," Issac said.
        "A creation, like Adam," Jacob said. But I thought:

"How precious also are thy thoughts
    unto me, O God! How great is the sum
        of them!" And they led me into the city of Prague.

FALCONER

John Park

The dusk was a fading mauve when Falconer rode to
the top of the bluffs that overlooked the abandoned city.
He climbed from the saddle and let Bront graze. Both he
and his mount wore camouflaged shock-silk armour over
their bodies, but the last sunlight gleamed on the uncovered metal of his head and arms. He surveyed the valley.
As they scanned, his eyes increased their magnification
and computed distances. His ears ignored the faint hiss of
the evening breeze through the grass around him and
picked out the mutter of water from the river, and the rush
of air through the leaves on the distant hills.

All seemed at peace. The rolling hills beyond the city
were still green, but autumn was near and the woods on
their flanks would soon be the colour of flame. A golden
crescent moon hung low in the eastern sky. At his side, the
forked, metal-tipped horn on Bront's nose jutted as the
animal grazed. He patted its neck with his sensor-covered
palm.

Falconer went to his saddle pack and unhooded the
hawk. At his touch, it squawked and ruffled its feathers,
hopped onto his fist. He took it to the edge of the bluffs and
released it. He listened to the wing-beats as it climbed
away, then adjusted his eyes to follow its flight as it swung

out across the valley, over the darker slopes and canyons of the city, the blue towers at the centre, the silvery plain of the landing field, then across the bend of the river, over the valley again, and back through the gathering dark, to land with its talons clashing on his metal fist.

He smoothed its feathers, then extended a fingertip sensor and disconnected the hawk's volition while he read out the contents of its memory. As he did so, his awareness sharpened of the lights that drifted across the sky, one sinking into the dusk, another rising, and he was ready when the words sounded in his head.

Falconer. You have stopped. Are you within the city yet? The whisper from the cold beyond the edges of the world.

"I am within sight of it," he replied aloud; "I am examining the survey data. The signal is quite clear now. It comes from the south-east quarter of the city."

Then you must go in and investigate it. Or have you finally decided to end your commitment to humanity?

"Mentor, I have tracked this signal for thirty days. It is quite strong. I have no doubt it will still be there in the morning."

Of course the signal is strong. The leakage gets worse every moment.

"Nevertheless I do not wish to negotiate these bluffs after sunset and then face an unknown in the dead of night."

You wish to pursue your corporeal recreations.

Falconer broke contact. But it was true. The hawk's flight was still not as it should be. He built a fire, set one of his energy cells at its edge to recharge and, as the stars came out, he reached into the hawk's brain and began making tentative adjustments to its flight control.

* * *

The next morning he approached the edge of the city. He swung down from the saddle and pulled his rifle from

313

its sheath, unfastened the flap of his pistol holster, then went to face Bront's head. He began the catechism.

"By the pact between us, you need not fight your own kind. But if we meet enemies and they ride carnivores, I ask that you fight with me."

Bront's long head turned to him, the eyes unblinking. The horned nose dipped slowly in ritual acknowledgement.

"If they ride elk or moose, bison or uinta beast, I ask that you fight with me."

The horn lowered.

"If they ride horse or zebra, merichip or onager, I ask that you fight with me. In return, I will defend you and treat your wounds, and if I cannot heal you, I will end your pain."

* * *

Bront picked its way over cracked roadways, slabs of artificial stone, split by grass and creeper. Its clawed feet were muffled even in the shaded canyons between the empty buildings. High up, shards of glass like teeth caught the morning sun. A flock of predatory crows erupted from one of the dark, hanging caverns, and Falconer turned to check that the hawk was inert and hooded. He reached for his rifle, but the flock was hunting elsewhere, and Bront continued cautiously forward.

You are following the signal? came the cold familiar voice in his head.

Very close now, he answered silently. *Within half a watch.* With the sun bright and the clouds golden he could not trace the passage of the Mentor's relays across the sky, but there was never a watch in the whole year when one of them was not in contact.

Giant footsteps scraped along a side street.

It was a diornys, its talons gouging the earth as its long, elastic stride took it across the cratered surface of the intersection. It came towards him, and its striped sepia and ochre plumage ruffled about its neck. The black beak with the orange snake of tongue was an arm's length above Falconer's head as he sat on Bront's saddle. He looked up into the empty black pupils as the head rocked from side to side examining him.

"We mean no harm," he said. "We come to find what you guard. Will you let us pass?"

From the hooked beak came a harsh grating cry, half hiss, half croak, and Falconer shifted his hand to his pistol. The diornys's eyes stared a moment longer. Then it stepped to one side, and stalked away.

Falconer watched it go, then patted his mount's neck. "Come on, Bront; let's find what we came here for."

They came to an open space where greenery over-flowed across a rocky mound.

He paused, listening to the electric trilling in his head. "It's here, Bront, but I don't know where."

Bront picked its way forward and came to a stone fence with a heavy, sky-metal gate. Beyond the fence, under a mat of overgrowth was a large stone structure roughly pyramidal in shape. Falconer dismounted and examined the gate. Its lock had long since died, and he pried it away, then heaved the gate open and went cautiously through. As he entered the shadow of the stone building, the world seemed to quiver. Suddenly the air darkened. A swallow, veering by the overgrown wall, slowed in mid air, its wing beats almost stilled. Then it swept on in full flight. As Falconer hesitated, the air brightened, turned blue for an instant; there came a sharp crack and the sound of stones grinding together.

A slab of masonry split and fell onto the earth ahead of him. In the space it had covered, a sky-metal door stood. It was a design Falconer recognised only from his oldest records.

He placed his hand against the door and felt for the lock within the metal. It too was ancient, its force almost spent, but he found the command, sent it through his fingers, and the door slid up.

He entered cautiously, his eyes shifting to longer waves to make the most of the faint light. Ahead was a short corridor, ending in another door.

Sounds came from the other side. He identified footfalls, and voices—hurried and lowpitched.

While he was feeling for the lock, there was a series of sharp clicks, and the door opened inwards. Flashes of red light met him, from a source mounted above the inside of the door. In the room beyond were eight hominids dressed in padded olive green uniforms with bulging pockets. The nearest two—one taller than Falconer, the other shorter than him and stockier—faced him with pistols drawn. Their eyes and mouths were open wide. Behind them, under pale ceiling lights, the others sat limply on couches by the wall or reached for heavier weapons racked above them. On the far wall, a bank of lights and dials glowed and flickered.

Falconer raised his open hands towards the two in the doorway and they faced him in the flashing light.

He searched his records to identify their race and status. With their soft leathery faces—ochre and brown—and coloured, pulpy eyes, they were clearly humanoid. But their sculpted manes and whiskers, their metal talons and protruding canine teeth implied a modified, servant race, evidently soldiers.

At the back of the room, one went to the bank of instruments and peered at it, then spoke to the others and turned a switch. The flashing stopped.

The ones with pistols exchanged quick looks and pointed their weapons aside. The larger of the two stepped back and motioned Falconer into the room.

316

He scanned the room. Two were standing with rifles in their arms staring at him. The two in the doorway motioned, and the rifles were lowered. The soldier who had turned off the red light was still crouched staring at the instrument panel. The others, on a couch by the right hand wall were watching, and slowly getting to their feet. The bluish overhead lights flickered.

Falconer could imagine Mentor's command. "Speak," he said slowly. He pointed to his mouth and gestured towards the two nearest, presumably the officers. "If you can understand me at all, I can adjust my speech output to match yours, but I must sample your language first."

The shorter officer began addressing him, in a higher-toned voice than he had heard before. Then one of the soldiers who had just stood up sat down again heavily. A moment later a second slumped across the couch. Another soldier exchanged looks with the two at the door then propped a rifle against the wall and went to the fallen one. The soldier at the instruments called out and the taller officer in the doorway began barking orders.

Quiet returned. The soldier still holding a rifle closed the door and stood beside it. There was muttering from those on the couch and the one attending them. The tall officer went to join the soldier at the instrument bank, leaving the other to address Falconer again.

After a few moments the words became clear.

"Why have we been brought back now? What are we to do? What danger threatens? Whom are we to protect?"

"I cannot answer you fully," Falconer said. "I believe your return was accidental—the time-field in your chamber overloaded and collapsed. What your task might have been otherwise, I can't guess. But I believe I've heard of your kind. You are creations of humans, warriors." He hesitated. "You yourself, a female?"

Falconer took the movement of shoulders as acknowledgement that he was right. "Praetorian Katana of the Seventeenth Special Group," she said. "Then, forgive the question, what are you?"

"I am Falconer; I have accepted the task of serving humans but I owe no allegiance to anyone on Earth."

Now most of them were watching him again. After a moment, the tall officer called out, "I am Praetorian Athamè. Can you tell us what year it is, in a calendar we would understand?"

Falconer tried to reach Mentor, but this time found only the cold hissing that filled the space beyond the world. He considered and said: "It is five centuries since the last return of Ogava's comet. It is seven centuries since the last human return from the stars. Twelve centuries since the war of the sixth terrestrial diaspora. Almost two millennia since the last use of magnetogravitic weapons."

The soldiers were looking at each other. Finally Katana said, "Perhaps if you told us the length of the lunar month...."

"The lunar month lasts thirty-three days. I can be more precise, but of course the lunar orbit was reset every century until the war of the sixth diaspora." There was no reply. He added, "The moon was moved to its present orbit as one of the preparations for the second diaspora." He waited, studying the expressions on their mobile, silent faces; then he said, "That was approximately fifty-eight millennia ago."

"O Creator," someone muttered.

"We could use the stars," Katana said faintly. She was staring at nothing Falconer could see. "The constellations will have shifted."

"They might be unrecognisable."

"It may not matter for some of us," Athamè said loudly from the back of the room. "Millennia's worth of radiation was trapped in the fringes of the stasis field. It all

318

escaped a few minutes ago, and we were in the way." He seemed to be addressing Falconer as much as his comrades. "We have drugs for radiation exposure, but in limited amounts. Some of us are already sick, and are going to get very sick indeed." He bared his teeth for a moment. "We could almost use the *radiation dose* to work out the date. Except, it wasn't all background radiation; there was a lot of fallout in there too, wasn't there, Mr. Falconer?"

"Also," said Falconer, "I fear the output from certain other weapons will have entered your time field."

"Well then. We could work out the likely gamma and particle trajectories through the collapsing field and see who was safest. But I don't think we have enough therapeutics to treat more than a couple of exposures that serious anyway. Choices will have to be made."

Katana turned to the soldier at the instruments. "How secure are we?"

"The sensors indicate no other danger—unless you know of anything, sir?"

"I know of nothing in the vicinity that is likely to be hostile, or that could withstand your weapons," Falconer told them.

Katana turned to him. "If you'll excuse us, we need to discuss among ourselves."

"I understand. Let me just say, it seems my arrival finally overloaded your time field and caused it to collapse. As the agent of your misfortune, I'm compelled to do whatever I can to help you."

"We thank you for that. Give us a few moments, please."

The eight gathered by the couch where the sick lay. Falconer detuned his hearing to give them privacy. *Found them, have you?* came Mentor's voice. *Watch them. Judge their worthiness.*

319

Katana and Athamè returned.

"We'll need your help," Athamè said.

"How are your people?"

"They need specialised medical treatment immediately."

"Do you have transportation?" Falconer asked. "Fliers?"

"We have what you see here."

"Then I'm afraid I know of no help within fifteen days' travel."

"Useless. Three will die within the week."

Katana said, "If we could regenerate the stasis field and put them in, it would give us more time to search for help."

Athamè bared his teeth and nodded. "Do you think we can restore the field?"

Falconer found the panel housing the control circuitry. He reached in and extended his sensors. "The shut-down seems to have happened normally, as the solar power unit burned out. As long as none of the circuits are damaged, it will merely be a matter of supplying energy. I have spare power cells; you have the charges for your weapons. Together there should be enough energy to maintain a field for a few weeks."

"Very well, then," said Katana. "Athamè and I will come with you. The others will stay in here. Trebouchet and Carronade can guard the sick if the field collapses before we return. We just have to compute the best way of dividing up the doses of radiation drugs."

Falconer nodded and reached into the open panel.

* * *

By mid afternoon the pyramid was closed again. Falconer and the two praetorians loaded Bront with their packs and walked beside it. From the ruins of a silver dome, the diornys watched them go.

Falconer led them through the city and up the hill slope beyond. The river meandered to their left. "There used to be a gathering, a hermitage of knowledgeable humans on an island in the river estuary. I'm trusting they will still be there when we arrive."

"When did you last see them?" Katana asked.

"When I brought them parts for their solar collectors. Five decades ago."

They reached the top of the hill.

"We have to leave the river now," he said. "It's been turned to swamp, but its course becomes clear again about two days' travel beyond."

The other two were staring. Athamè whispered, "What happened here?"

The far side of the hill dropped sheer into a black canyon. Domes and spires of basalt lay spread beneath them, black and sterile—arches and spikes and tormented snakes, like monsters frozen in the act of erupting from the earth.

"A weapon aimed at the city. It was narrowly deflected, but its force split the earth. I believe some of what you see is magma from below the crust. If we skirt the edges we will be safe, but nothing will grow here for another five centuries."

They continued along the edge of the abyss. More hills rose to their right, clothed in pine and maple. Bront's clawed feet followed a game trail.

"Someone's watching us," Katana said.

"Ah." Falconer turned and adjusted his eyes. After a few moments he picked out heat-signatures among the trees on the slopes above them. "I feared they would have spread this far."

"You know them?" Katana asked. "Hostiles?"

"What kind of enemy?" Athamè was loosening the shoulder strap of his carbine.

"Humans, of a kind. Ferals. I have met several tribes, but all very similar."

"Do you fight them?"

"They have abandoned all that would make me honour them. In becoming warriors they often give up their will to an organism that invades their brains. It makes them better fighters, but it destroys their humanity. If I cannot avoid them, I fight."

"What weapons do they have?"

"One or two may have firearms, but fewer in recent years; they are unable to repair or maintain such devices, and ammunition grows scarce. Most have swords, or lances, tipped with stone or the metal they scavenge from the ruins. They use slingshots with stone projectiles. I have not seen many with bows."

"We outgun them, then."

"Yes," Falconer said. "But one other thing: it is best not to be taken by them. They have harsh ways with captives, both your kind and mine."

I suggested you watch them, said the cold voice, *not imperil yourself to assist them.*

The sun was still clear of the horizon when they first heard horses. There was nothing to see beyond the trees.

The marsh to their left was a golden mirror and the sun was poised above the rim of the horizon when the ground flattened and the trees began to give way to gravel and coarse grass. The group went on; their shadows stretched and dimmed.

"This is the place for them to charge us," Katana said. "But there's no point in going back to somewhere safer and waiting."

Athamè nodded. "Better now than by night. Let them come."

Falconer unhooded the hawk and sent it climbing into the air above them. "A few seconds' warning, at least." He

322

pulled his rifle from the pack on Bront's saddle.

The sun touched the horizon. Ahead the plain opened out. "Come on," said Katana. "Another two hundred metres and we'll have them in a shooting gallery as they come out of the woods."

High above them, the hawk shrieked and dived.

Falconer and the two praetorians raised their weapons.

From the edge of the trees, through the sinking red light, the ferals galloped, black hunched forms that seemed to ride waves of dust.

The praetorians were already firing. Falconer aimed at a rider just as a bolt struck him from his horse. He found another target, fired, pivoted, fired again, with no time to see the effect of his shots. His shock-silk slapped and jerked rigid as a missile glanced off his chest. Behind him, Bront's armour also cracked, cracked again. Then the riders were among them. Falconer fired, ducked away from a hissing power beam, shot the feral as its horse plunged past him. Bront lunged with its horn, then reared, filling the sky like a solid cloud, striking out with its forefeet.

Weaponless, Katana sprang at a rider, tore him from his mount. The horse reared and stumbled; then Katana was standing with the feral's sword bloodied in her hand.

Athamè grappled with a feral that had seized his rifle. As he threw him off, Katana barked one short syllable. Athamè spun, and caught a blow from behind on the barrel of his rifle. He twisted, and smashed with the butt, then sidestepped so that the other feral's rush ended on Katana's blade.

Abruptly it was over.

A single set of hoofbeats receded into the dusk.

Athamè and Katana were checking each other for injuries and examining one of the corpses; as they did so their ears and eyes kept lifting to probe the dusk. Katana beckoned him.

He turned.

One of the ferals had got in under Bront with a firelance. The creature was silent, its eyes turned to him as its life poured from its belly.

He called to the others: "A moment. I am committed to respond to this."

Falconer crouched, held the massive head in his feeling palms, then reached for his pistol.

At the shot, Bront jerked once and lay still. Falconer stood up and stepped back.

"You're all right?" Katana asked. "Look at this. They had firearms and these—"

The two praetorians were standing beside one of the dead ferals. Falconer went to see what she meant.

His foot slipped and he went down to one knee. Starting to rise he slipped again. "We may have to change, to modify, our plans," he began. He stood up, turned away, faced her again, started to walk. Then he stopped and knelt, his hands braced on the ground before him. The hawk fluttered down and landed at his side.

Katana went to him. "What's wrong?"

He did not look up. Tonelessly, he said, "Wait, please. I find that mount had become more a part of my mental world than I had realised. I must reset my paradigms. I will need a minute or two. Please wait."

He fell silent and did not move.

The hawk stretched its wings and shuffled from side to side.

The wind stirred the grasses. The moon was high, and the planet once known as the evening star gleamed above the purple horizon. The praetorians crouched, alert for danger. Falconer's shadow began to fade into the twilight.

He stood again. "Thank you. I was saying, our plans may have to be changed, as we no longer have transport for our baggage, or any way of bringing back more than minimal aid."

"We understand," said Katana. "But look at this one first."

Its neck was broken cleanly. It had four arms. On two of its hands, metal claws had replaced the fingers.

"What are they?" Athamè asked.

"Humans, returned from the stars. They arrive like deities and turn into animals. They find a world shaped by human warfare; much of it is barren and still seeded with threats, and it is ruled by creatures their ancestors built as servants. Their response is hatred."

"Where were the modifications done? Those changes aren't genetic," Katana said; "they're surgical. And look at the wounds on the face—they were treated in the last ten days."

"They must have got access to one of the resource complexes built for the last wars."

"Could that save our people, if we can find it?"

"Perhaps. I can't be sure."

"But it's a better chance than following the river for another two weeks?"

"Yes, it will be."

"Then how do we start looking?"

Athamè said: "We follow the one that escaped. I'm sure I wounded him. When we catch him, we make him tell. Let's go."

* * *

They followed the tracks until the darkness under a towering stand of marspines became too deep for Falconer's eyes, then camped.

"I think we'll do without a fire," Athamè said to Falconer, "unless you need one?"

"I find I like a fire. But no, it is not necessary."

"Good. Then we should set watches. How much sleep

325

do you need?"

"Again, very little is necessary, though I was made to prefer periods of dormancy. I can watch for us tonight, if you wish." He unhooded the hawk.

"Perhaps it would be best. We've still a lot to adjust to. Thank you."

The two lay down together and Falconer began resetting the hawk's eyes for night vision.

"That's an interesting creature," Katana said. "Where did you find it?"

"My own creation," Falconer said. "It isn't perfected. I studied records of hawks in flight before I began, and I compare whenever I see a biological hawk. This one is not right yet, but it makes an effective night watch."

He stood up and carried the hawk to a low mound at the edge of the trees and released it into the starry night.

He crouched with his hands braced before him, and became motionless as a rock. His moonshadow slowly turned, drifted across the rough earth and twisted tree roots, eclipsed a bright shard of quartz. He heard the microscopic rattle of the marspine needles, the rustle of a shrew, rooting among the thin grass, even the wingbeats of the hawk as it circled high among the marspine crests.

Rustling sounds came from where Katana and Athamè had lain down. Quietly he rose and sharpened his sight. The two were a single dark mass, limbs enmeshed and straining together. Their breathing roared in his ears.

I sense fruitless thoughts, said Mentor's voice. *What are you doing?*

Falconer shut down his eyes; he turned and crouched again, motionless when the last moonlight lifted from his metal skin.

* * *

The next day Falconer had trouble picking up the trail through the trees, but for the praetorians, the hoofprints were still discernible in the gravelly earth. They led away from the devastated area and along the edge of the hills.

"At least the bugs leave you alone," Katana said.

At midmorning they found sign of a rough camp. From then on, each time the path crested a rise, Falconer looked ahead through the marspine trunks, his heat- and motion-sensors engaged, but the widely spaced bare columns were enough to screen any sign of the feral from him or the hawk.

The trees were larger now, the kind of timber once used for the spars of caravels that sailed to the edge of the solar system. Clouds brushed their tips.

The three followed the hoofprints along a muddy stream bed. Here a tree had fallen across the path, its trunk draped with vines and fresh shrubbery. It hid the sky like a cliff face. A good place for an ambush, but green-furred lemurs scurried up from the ground at their approach, then sat and cackled on the upper slope and hurled down sticks and half-eaten fruit. No humanoid could have hidden there without drawing their anger. Katana parted the greenery, and they passed beneath the trunk into darkness like a cave.

When they edged through the creepers on the far side, they came out into another world. The trees stood black and stark on the slopes of a long low hill. The hillside was covered with grass and scrub in shades of turquoise, sepia and gold. The stream vanished into a narrow split in the side of the hill, and through the fast clear water the hoofprints could be seen following it. Where it poured from the hill, the water steamed.

Athamè bent and trailed his fingers through the water. "Warm. A long way from boiling, but we should have noticed it earlier."

"I'm picking up a slight neutron flux," Katana said. "About four sigma above background."

They both looked at Falconer, who had not moved. "It seems we have arrived," he said.

"Arrived at what?" asked Katana. "Do we go in? Where is this?"

"I passed this way twice," Falconer said after a moment. "But there was only a slightly unusual hill to see, and those are quite common from the last few millennia's warfare. The trees were still growing then."

Speak the truth, Mentor's voice said to him.

"Perhaps I guessed what is here and I did not investigate because I didn't want to confirm my guess."

"What is it, then?" Athamè demanded.

"A relic, a preserved piece of an old military technology."

"You mean, like us?" said Katana.

"No," said Falconer, after a moment. "More like me."

Interesting, said Mentor. *Consider those words.*

"It's something that fell to earth, a mobile fortress. Extensively automated. I recognise the changes in the vegetation—they're caused by the leakage of certain fields that are now reactivated."

Athamè said: "You mean these ferals have taken the place over since you last saw it."

"So it seems."

"Well then, as you say, we've arrived. Is there any way in, except the front door here? Air shafts or anything?"

"The citadel is designed to operate in vacuum. The air intakes are hidden; they open only to make up recycling losses. The same goes for the other entrances. This one must be damaged or it wouldn't be open now."

Athamè looked at Katana. She shook her head. "Too much like walking into a trap," she said.

"Right. It's worth spending a few hours to scout around. If there was another entrance open around here,

328

how would we recognise it?"

"The way we recognised this one. It's dark, empty and leads inward."

Athamè looked at him and shook his head.

They spent until midafternoon making a cautious circuit of the hill. In a cave under a clump of tree-ferns they found a metal door. It was draped with purple rust-ivy that had infiltrated its tendrils into the still-gleaming surface. "At least we can be sure he didn't come out the other side," Athamè said. "But if their sensors are any good, they'll know we're here by now."

"The ferals may not have all the systems operating," said Falconer. "I'm surprised they're here at all. They usually show more distrust of such technology."

"In any case," Katana said, "if they knew we were here and they wanted to, they could come out and get us any time."

"Unless there's only a few still in there," Athamè suggested. "Hell with it. We'll have to find out."

What are you going to do? said Mentor's voice. *Have you considered those words of yours? Have you decided?*

"I have decided nothing!"

The two praetorians stared at him.

"An advisor," Falconer said to them. "He orbits the poles. He monitors part of my circuitry."

"He's always in your mind?" said Katana, staring at him.

"Not always, though he could be. He was... a legacy." He said no more.

Katana and Athamè exchanged looks and raised their shoulders briefly; then they moved towards the entrance.

As they entered the cave, they found an outer door still retracted into the walls. Falconer paused to probe the seals. "These doors should iris shut and be airtight. Something is defective in the control circuits. I think I can...."

Procrastination? asked Mentor. *Consider why.*

The others were at the inner door, cutting away the ivy. Their teeth glimmered. Their ears were pricked, their nostrils flared. Falconer hurried to them. He felt for the controls then turned to the others. "Something's wrong."

The door slid upward.

A stone axe flew past Falconer's head. He jumped back to the wall as the praetorians fired from opposite sides of the corridor.

A panel in the ceiling slid back and a brown body dropped from the opening.

Athamè whistled, and Katana pivoted as the feral landed half across her back. She went to one knee, twisting, and the feral slammed into the wall.

The air thrummed. Blue flashes ran along the floor. At Falconer's feet the water exploded into steam.

"Out!" yelled Athamè. Katana was already backing to the entrance, firing steadily.

They fought their way into the open air. They crouched between two boulders near the stream, and the ferals did not pursue.

As they watched the opening, Athamè said, "You'll be all right; I don't think they'll follow. But you'll have to wait until dark to try again."

Falconer looked at him and saw the blood.

Katana had fallen on her knees beside Athamè. Her hands were efficient, pulling aside clothing, exposing the injuries.

Falconer moved closer to see.

She had become pale. Her mouth shook, and moisture glistened on her cheeks.

Athamè coughed and crimson ran over his chin. His head fell back and his eyes closed.

"How bad are his injuries?" Falconer asked.

She was stroking Athamè's forehead, her hands and

330

wrists wet with his blood. "He's bleeding inside. I can bandage the superficial wounds, but I can't stop the bleeding. Keep watching the entrance."

"If we go back in and find help tonight, will that be soon enough?"

"No."

"So he wouldn't survive if we carried him back to the time field?"

She shook her head.

"Then there's no more help you can give him, is there?"

Her teeth flashed. "What's that got to do with it? It's Athamè. We trained together; we shared food, everything.... Watch the entrance!"

Falconer turned away and sat down to watch. The sun sank to the horizon and he focused his receptors to save power. His thoughts followed the hawk turning in tight circles above. Stars came out and the moon slid among the clouds.

Katana roused him by howling into the dark. She was kneeling beside Athamè's body, beating the ground and flinging her head back with her fangs bared. Her chest shook and her throat strained. But after her initial cry, she was silent.

Finally she grew still and lay across the body. Her breathing slowed and quietened. She appeared to sleep. Falconer focused down his awareness again.

Later, without warning she sat up in the dark. "Thank you for watching. We've got to get in there." Her words were hurried and toneless.

"Were you ill?" he asked.

She bared her teeth, but then pressed her lips together and looked at him. "I was resetting my paradigms," she said finally.

Falconer struggled to relate her behaviour to his own

experience, and failed.

"There's been no sign of movement I can detect," he said. "Perhaps we could draw them out while we try the original entrance."

"Maybe. Let's make a fire first. See if that gets any response."

He collected brush and dry branches. When he returned, she was heaving stones over Athamè's body.

"Why do you do that?" he asked "We won't return here."

"It's a ritual," she said, not looking at him. "Get the fire started." Then she said: "It helps ease the pain." She pushed a rock into place and looked at him. "What you saw earlier, the crying, that's ritual, too. We're taught ways of releasing the pain quickly when it's safe, so it won't burden us later. We can't grieve when we're in action." She turned away and began tamping down some of the smaller rocks.

He remembered a forked, steel-tipped horn rising in answer to his words. "Ritual," he said. "A way of using the upper levels of the mind to reach the lower. Is that something you learned from humans?"

"They had many ways of regarding their dead."

* * *

With the fire crackling beside them, Falconer brought the hawk down and adjusted its optical processor. "A small change; I want to try it before it gets light."

"The fire's good," Katana said. "It's bad to be alone."

"I was made to like a fire too." He turned the hawk's gaze from firelight to the sky and the shadows under the trees, monitoring its signal strength.

Katana was snapping branches in her fingers. She extended her claws and stropped them on the bark of the tree beside her. "You made the whole hawk?" she said. "The mind as well?"

332

"Of course."

"Why?"

"I was curious. I wanted to understand what it was to be a creator, to have constructed something that had an independent existence, to have impressed my own psyche on another creature. I wondered if I would learn what goals to set for it."

"I know: you want to understand the ones who created you." She shook her head. "You want to be like them. All of us know that condition."

"I want to understand *him*, the one who made me, who modelled me on his own mind. He went away. He found a goal that compelled him; he left me the Mentor and he turned from this world before he could explain what his purpose had been for me."

The firelight rippled over his face. A branch split open and fell. It sent up sparks like crimson stars.

"Is the Mentor listening to you now?"

Falconer paused. "The connection's still complete," he said, "but his attention is elsewhere. It has been for several hours. I think something's keeping the ferals in hiding too." He spread his bright fingers. "Some centuries ago Mentor's allegiance changed. I gradually realised he was committed to a more abstract cause than serving humans. He believes his created purpose is to serve intelligence in its highest form. We disagree."

She said: "How much of your life have you spent trying to recreate your creator's state of mind? Trying to be a better copy of a human?"

Falconer was crouched over the hawk, his microprobes pressed into its head. He did not reply.

"What are you doing now?"

"Making a map of its outer consciousness. Later, I'm going to invert parts of it and reapply them. I want to find out what drives are normally suppressed."

"You mean it has a subconscious?"

"A basic of all such devices. Only so much data can be processed immediately, but a mass of information and algorithms must be kept in readiness. In practice, all artificial minds have at least two layers of awareness."

"All?" she asked, staring at his expressionless profile.

He closed the hawk's head and released the bird to return to its watch. Its wings caught the firelight as it climbed, then vanished into the dark.

"All," he said.

She stood, picking up her pack and her weapons. Then she turned to him. "How different are we? We're both imperfect copies." She reached for his hand, traced the lines on his palm with the tips of her claws. "Part of you feels. Part of you appreciates the warmth of a fire."

"Part of me also lives for the exchange of data in a universe of numbers." The sensors sprouted from his fingertips, like clusters of needles. "I've lived twelve hundred years, yet I can't tell which part of me is truer or why I am what I am." He shouldered his pack, adjusted his night vision and moved to lead the way.

"I have existed twelve hundred years...."

* * *

They left the fire blazing and made their way to the first entrance.

Both sets of doors were open. The corridor echoed with running, splashing water. In the ceiling pale squares marked dying light sources. Falconer's night vision showed nothing but an empty corridor and the water running along its centre, knee-deep and smoking.

They reached a section where part of the ceiling had been peeled down, and the water spilled through. Falconer adjusted his eyes to peer up into the gap. "A split in one of the cooling pipes. Clearly the maintenance units are not working. Power and communication circuits have

334

been cut here too."

Twenty-five metres in, the corridor split at right angles. A couple of panels in the ceiling gave a faint, bluish glow. Falconer unslung his rifle and turned left, where hoofmarks showed on the muddy floor.

In the corner of a large chamber three horses were stabled beside a pair of armoured scout vehicles. The vehicles were obviously disused—covered in grime and buried above the thrust jets in hay—but one of their service lines had been cut and brought to feed water into a metal trough for the animals. A small servitor whirred around the horses' legs, cleaning.

"This is one of the vehicle repair bays," he said. "There will be others spaced further along." He indicated the curving corridor ahead.

"The riders must have taken over one for themselves. Something's keeping them very quiet."

The horses stamped and snorted as they went past.

"I hear something," Katana whispered. "Coming this way."

Down the corridor, lights flickered into life. Moments later, a servitor glided towards them—an upright cylinder with jointed arms held against its sides. A cluster of sensors on top rotated towards them. Lights flickered at Katana; guttural syllables sounded. Then Falconer felt a sensor scan directed at him. He blocked it.

"The humans in the ship will not approach me now that the astrotelemetry circuits are activated," the servitor said aloud. "And I cannot communicate with this human. The keyword is not responded to. You must transmit messages between us."

"I am not a servant."

"Nevertheless you must transmit messages between us."

"The female is not human. We are here together to

335

find help for her companions."

"Therefore you must transmit messages between us."

Katana was watching him. "What are you two saying to each other?"

"This machine speaks only a debased oral language. It wants me to interpret."

"Can it help us?"

Falconer told the servitor what they were looking for. It hung motionless above the floor until he finished. Then, "Follow," it said to him and rotated away from them. It led them down lighted corridors to a space where the floor opened into a smooth vertical pit. The servitor glided over the centre of the pit and began to sink.

"Follow," it repeated.

Falconer stepped forward, and a moment later Katana followed. With only air beneath them, they fell slowly between smooth metal walls.

The servitor came to a stop beside the entrance to another set of corridors. A bridge extended into the shaft and Falconer and Katana alighted upon it. They were facing another set of closed doors.

"Do you know where it's taking us?" she whispered. "Is this where they hide their medical facilities?"

"I don't know," he said. "It's unfamiliar. I've never been down so far—" He broke off as a faint grinding noise began.

Above them, the lighted opening of the shaft was closing. It shrank to a slit and vanished. Silence returned.

Falconer had stopped in midmotion. He sank into a crouch, his hands braced on the floor.

"What's wrong?" Katana asked.

"Lost," he said slowly. "Contact lost."

"With your Mentor?"

"Yes. The first time. After twelve hundred years." His head was lowered. He did not move.

"It hurts you? How?"

"A need," he said tonelessly, "an emptiness. Being lost. Alone."

"Yes," Katana whispered. "I know."

In front of them, the doors were sliding open.

The servitor went forward into a wide, dark chamber and stopped.

"Can you move?" she asked Falconer. "It's waiting for us."

Slowly he turned his head a few centimetres.

She jerked at his rigid arm, then shook him bodily. "You can't go into shock now. Listen to me. Your paradigms have to wait till we're out of here."

Falconer pulled stiffly away from her and stood up.

She spoke into his face. "Is that machine smart enough to be leading us on, trapping us?"

"I think... I cannot tell."

"Ask it where it's taking us. I want some proof it can help us."

Falconer turned slowly to the servitor and exchanged messages with it, in silence this time.

"It can show us something," he said finally, "but it needs our help also."

"How? Oh—just tell it to get on with it."

The servitor turned, and a door opened beside it. Beyond it was a large chamber with a rounded roof. Banks of instruments lined the lower halves of the walls. The servitor motioned with one of its limbs and a section of wall seemed to become transparent, opening onto another chamber, white walls under blue lighting. Horizontal cylinders with transparent upper shells were stacked in rows. The view traversed and zoomed to show sedated humans lying in some of them—ferals, with wounds healing, extra limbs growing, tusks jutting from jaws.

"This is the treatment centre," Falconer said. "The

337

servitor claims almost any injury can be cured, provided the brain is still alive and there's a sample of undamaged genetic material."

"But it can't revive the dead.... Never mind—it will help us?"

"The injured must be brought here. Something important is happening; the servitor is forbidden to leave now or allow equipment to be removed."

"And what does it want from us?"

"Something is wrong with the overall control of the citadel; that view of the medical complex is one of only three that still work. The servitor needs control urgently now for some reason. If we can repair the sensor controls, the servitor will give us transportation and access to the treatment, and keep the ferals from us. They fear it, and now they're afraid of whatever's happening here."

"Can we do the repair? What's involved?"

"I don't know. The servitor will show us the nexus at fault."

"All right. Let's go then."

The floor of the chamber opened and they drifted down another shaft.

They entered a dimly lighted space. Machines stood against the walls—wheeled, bipedal or boxlike, with tentacular arms or jointed limbs that ended in probes and sockets.

"What are they?" Katana asked. "Why are you staring at them?"

"The shells of former intelligences."

In the centre of the chamber was a crystalline column spiralling from floor to ceiling. It was black and translucent, about two metres in diameter. Falconer was staring at it, unmoving.

Katana went to examine it.

A chill struck her face. From close up, the column

338

seemed to have no surface, just a darkness that began a
few centimetres from her eyes. But within its depths motes
of light were arrayed, like constellations endlessly reced-
ing. Each mote she looked at shone clear and steady, but
on the edge of her vision, the lights seemed to flicker,
drawing her gaze from one light to the next, deeper and
deeper into the darkness.

She stepped back with an effort, her face numb. Falconer was still staring at the column.

"This is something to do with the dead machines, isn't
it?" she said.

"A storage matrix. Their minds are all in there."

"What's it got to do with fixing the sensors?"

"They were trying to carry out the repairs. The
servitor believes the matrix pulled them into it."

"It's dangerous, then...."

"Probably not," said Falconer. "These were primitive
intelligences. If I can find the translocator I believe I can
disable it."

"Let's think first. There might be another way—"

But Falconer was moving forward. He raised his
hands, the fingertip probes extended, and brought them
towards the matrix.

He stopped, remained motionless for a long pause,
then turned and faced the servitor. Messages flickered between them.

To Katana he said, "I have found the translocator. I
have to stay within the fringe of the matrix to prevent it
from being triggered. Go to the machine with the silver
carapace and remove the black disc. Break the supporting
limb if necessary."

Katana found the disc and snapped it free; she handed
it to Falconer.

Falconer turned back to the matrix. He extended his
arms again, then stepped into the black column.

Lights swirled up and down it. The walls flickered with radiance. In the distance, machinery thudded and whirred.

Falconer stepped from the matrix.

"It worked? You're all right?"

"We should return to the operations room and look at the sensor displays," he said flatly.

The servitor led them to another shaft, and they floated upward. When Katana asked him what he had found in the matrix he said only, "There were greater minds there than I had expected. Not all were captured unwillingly. They have grown...."

In the operations room, all the screens were alight with views of the corridors, empty chambers, and the outside world. Falconer pointed to a screen that showed a starscape. He turned to the servitor, and the view on that screen shifted.

The pale gibbous moon swam into view, then leapt towards them. A section of the terminator expanded to fill the screen—black arcs and hollows, and silver loops of crater rims, drifting slowly across the field of view.

One light was not drifting. The edge of the terminator passed beneath it, and against the shadowed surface of the moon it shone clear, faceted like a diamond.

"The original view was near the exit from the lunar gate," Falconer said. He was looking at her. "That object on the screen was not there twelve hours ago. You know what it is?"

"I think so. Yes."

As they watched, a blue-white line shot from it. A tiny spark glowed at its head. Without changing length, the line drew away and passed over the edge of the screen.

"It's coming this way?"

"Towards Earth, at least. It could be here in an hour or two. The citadel will be trying to communicate, but they may have other priorities than talking to an antiquated robot battle station." He had the hawk before him and was running his fingers over its feathers. "If they land nearby, and they are human, they will be able to help you," he said.

"And you? What will you do?"

"If I meet them, I will become their servant."

She flexed her hands, looked at her fingers. "Is that what you want?"

"I have spent my life studying them, trying to become like them. I've known only a few wretched examples, the best of them with no goal beyond the barest survival.... What will you do?"

"They created us to fight for them. They left us shut up in stasis for centuries. We were in the middle of a city; they must have known we were there, but they left us like that." She tensed her fingers, and her claws jabbed the air. "We've always served them. I'll have to go to them."

"Would you change that if you could?"

"I don't know," she said. "You didn't answer me: do you know what you want?"

"What does this hawk want? I could adjust its level of consciousness so that it would cease to be aware of me; it would roam the skies forever. I could weaken its will until it could not stretch its wings without my command. I could make it want almost anything. And yet, underneath, it is modelled on my own mind. Could I alter so much of myself as well? Is that what I wish?" He held the hawk cupped in his hands and looked at Katana. "And suppose—suppose *he* came back, and could explain what he had intended for me...."

He extended a microprobe and opened the hawk's brain. "I think it's time to try the experiment—release the inhibitions, and see what lies beneath."

He concentrated, bent over the hawk, working silently, then sat up and opened his palms. The hawk turned its head side to side, looking at him; it stretched its wings. Then it leapt into the air and struck at his face.

* * *

"A model of your own mind, you told me," Katana said. "You have your answer?"

Falconer peered up to where the hawk flew patiently in circles against the ceiling. He said nothing.

"Or just another question," she asked, "unless your own creator does return?"

"Maybe not. There may be an answer. Perhaps." He stood up. "In the meantime we should see about bringing your comrades here for treatment."

The scout car the servitor directed them to was mired in waste, and its primer motor was dead. They worked on clearing the lift coils and transferring parts from the other vehicles.

"This would be easier with—with three of us," Katana said once, then continued her work in silence.

Finally the motor whined and the car lifted from the floor. Falconer guided it towards the exit.

They emerged into night. Through the blister canopy, the moon was bright, and thin clouds blew across it.

"We'll start ferrying them over straight away," Katana was saying. "One group tonight; I'll want to check that they are being helped, before I bring the rest. We'll start with the worst three: that'll be Labrys and—"

Above them, a flower opened in the night sky, an orchid of gold and crimson that spread its petals from a purple, blazing core. It slid from the zenith, moving towards them, and the core stretched out into a dagger tearing the sky.

The air shook with thunder. Falconer's face silvered; his eyes were glowing mirrors, Katana's hair a tangle of silver and anthracite. The dagger of flame passed above

342

them and sank towards the horizon, and their shadows pivoted around them as though they were each a gnomon. Just above the skyline the flame flared even brighter, and was eclipsed. Light silvered the undersides of the clouds. And then there was just a long streamer of mist from zenith to horizon, unravelling in the winds of the upper atmosphere.

Still the thunder rolled back and forth, and when it sank into silence they were numb with it.

Falconer had stopped the car. In his head, one last time, a familiar voice spoke. *Have you understood? Have you decided?* His body stiffened at the renewed connection. Then silently he answered, *I have decided.*

"They've landed near the city," he said finally to Katana. "Will you go to them?"

She tossed her head, then stared at the faint glow from the direction of the city. Her teeth snapped. "I'll go. I must."

"Then farewell. I wish you success. A landing this size may have the resources to retain its humanity. But I know my own kind now, and I will join them." He lifted the translocator.

"Wait—"

He opened the door and stepped down from the scout car. There was a faint humming sound from the translocator, and without any ceremony, he bent his knees, sank to a crouch with his hands braced on the ground, and lowered his head. He did not move again, and when Katana reached him, he was inert as a metal statue. His eyes were blank discs of crystal, his arm cold as the fuel pipes she had installed in the car.

It felt wrong to leave him crouched there, but also wrong to bury him, when she could not say that burial was called for. She wondered if she would mourn for him, when she was able to mourn again, and her conditioning

343

allowed her the time to mourn. And she wondered how often in the coming years that might happen.

Finally she climbed back into the scout car and turned it towards the city.

Above her, the hawk passed once across the moon. It continued to climb in widening circles, riding the winds, until it was lost among the high thin cloud, the dark, and the stars.

TIME SHRINK

Tim Wynne-Jones

It was the best damn time machine Prosser had seen on the lot, considering his limited means.

"What'll it do?" he asked.

The salesman patted the plexi hood. "The Krono-scoot's only registered for 1900 but I imagine you could crank her back another 50 years, no problem. She's in mint condition."

"Lot of chrome," said Prosser.

"You bet," said the salesman. "Makes quite an impression. They never seen the stuff, back then."

"Actually," said Prosser, "Chrome was invented in 1797; by the 1900s it was quite widely known."

"Maybe something with a wee bit more power— more balls, less baubles," said the salesman, hurriedly moving on to a coffin-black monstrosity. "This Time Tamer 'll take you back to the Tuesday of Creation."

Prosser only glanced at the Time Tamer. His needs were not so far-reaching nor his spirit so intrepid. He wanted a little way back, that was all. He buffed a length of chrome on the Scoot with his cuff. The salesman beetled back and joined in the buffing.

"Only lightly used," he said. The salesman's cuffs, Prosser couldn't help noticing, were heavily used and far from clean. "Little old gal, liked to hop back to the 1930s to spy on her *hubby-to-be before they met, if you catch my meaning."*

"A new age version of "just around the block," thought Prosser, but said nothing.

"Good as new," said the salesman. "There now, you can see yourself in the chrome. Ain't that something."

Prosser could indeed see his face in the chrome, his melancholy only lengthened by the distortion. "Such a waste," he said.

"Time travel again, Capt'n Marvel?"

Old Mr. Keeping stood at the library desk, a stack of mysteries under his wirey arm. Solly pushed aside his writing pad and wearily began to process Mr Keeping's lurid borrowings. He looked up to catch Keeping craning his neck to read the story he had been writing. He piled Keeping's mysteries on top of the writing pad.

"Pretty corny, that sci fi stuff," said Keeping, unruffled.

Solomon Marvel held up the book he was at that moment processing, *Devil of a Job*. On the cover a woman with ice cream cone breasts struggled with a man in a red cape, while a stiff with a knife in his back tinted the Axminster with his life-blood.

"Alright, alright" said Keeping throwing up his arms in good-humoured surrender, "At my age who needs edification?" He took the book from Solly's hand and placed it on the pile. "Each to his own, Solly, but that time machine malarkey doesn't turn my crank."

"The fact is," said Solly, punching a return date on *Blondes Have More Gun*, "you could use a time machine yourself, Bradley." His eyes indicated the clock on the wall.

"Wha..?" Keeping didn't hear so well but his eyes were good. It was thirty minutes after closing. He laughed. "That's what I like about you, Solly. Why, the old bat who used to run this show started breathing down the patrons' necks about quarter to the hour. Now you, you're so caught up with your scribbling you wouldn't ever get home if I didn't show up here at your desk."

Solly flipped the cover shut on *Sicko* and handed the pile to Keeping. He smiled. Keeping was right, of course; what did he care about time? Keeping, meanwhile, hadn't been able to resist one more glance at Solly's story, now that it was again exposed. *Time Shrink.*

"That's what you need, Solly, old fellah," said Bradley Keeping as he plunked the mysteries into his bundle buggy. "A Time Shrink." He circled one finger lazily in a circle beside his head. And he went off into the night laughing to himself.

It was a moonless night. Prosser cranked open the Krono-scoot's wing door. He was on the verge of a road. Swoosh! A car passed. The vintage looked about right. Another came and this time he caught the date on the license plate: 1990. He had the right year.

"That's the passage!" said Rose Robinson. She was fairly squirming in her seat with anticipation. She reviewed the notes in her steno pad. "How can Prosser tell the vintage of the passing car on a moonless night?" she said. "How can he see the date?" she added. "Wouldn't it be easier to make it a full moon—more romantic too," she said holding her steno pad to her breast.

"Whyn't you just make it day?" remarked Andy Farmer. Rose Robinson rolled her eyes.

It was two weeks since the night Solly started the story. It was the first Thursday of the month and the Potter's Hat writing circle, the Strangelanders, were convening at the library. *Time Shrink* was on the block tonight and the writing circle was constructively criticizing it. Solly Marvel's long face revealed how helpful they were being.

"Do you crank open the door of a time machine?" asked Andy, ever practical. "Shouldn't it be 'activated' or somethin' like that?"

"I think making it nighttime adds to the atmosphere," said Bea Kalbfleisch. She smiled at Solly. When the brick-bats were flying, Bea could always be counted on for a soothing poultice. There was a woman beside Bea, some-one new. She smiled at Solly too, not quite politely. What was her name? Ruth or Sarah—someone indomitable from the Bible. And sexy. Solly had introduced himself to her; it was his library so he was unofficially the host. No one else had volunteered. But he had been too nervous about the critique to follow to catch her name. His eyes wandered to her now. Damn sexy. Quickly he turned his attention elsewhere.

"I don't think it matters a whole lot," said Dave Dimpson, flipping through his heavily blue-penciled copy of the story. "The thing is, we've seen this story from you before, Solly."

"That's what I was thinking," said Judy Crunch. "It's a lot like *Time Out*."

"And the one last year," said Dimpson. "*In the Knack of Time*—was that it? Solly, you are in a rut with this plot."

"I think the title is very good," said Bea.

Solly nodded his head sagely and stared squarely at the story in his hands as if weighing each point. In truth, the assessments fair and foul of his fellow fictioneers hardly mattered.

"Lots of *great* writers wrote the same story over and over again," said Bea. She couldn't think of any just then but, she assured the group, the idea has occurred to her more than once. Conversation drifted onto the shoals of obsessive compulsion versus artistic focus. Solly got him-self a coffee and a doughnut. He looked out the window at the moonless night.

The real death had not occurred at night. Why did he set the stage for the fictional death at night? Romance? Atmosphere?

The death had occurred at sunset. The driver of the car had been blinded by the sun, hadn't seen Cliff on his bike. But Solomon had, only minutes earlier. It had occurred to him to stop and warn Cliff that he was invisible in the sun but he hadn't stopped. And now in the flimsy vehicle of fiction he made trip after trip back to that side road to change what had happened. But nothing changed.

"Solly? Solly, this is important."

It was Rose calling him back to the circle, but it was Dave Dimpson who was responsible for what was so all-fired important.

"It just doesn't wash, Sol," he said. "If time machines are so plentiful that there are lots full of used ones, then everyone who suffered the loss of a loved one would just rush out and buy a Krono-scoot—or rent one from Tilden, special weekend rates—and head back into the past to change things so that the accident never happened."

"Which would make for an interesting story," said Judy, "No more deaths."

"Except the deaths of people nobody cared about," said Andy, his eyes lighting up. Andy could be counted on for just such a story in weeks to come. The Strangelanders meetings seemed to be his main source of inspiration.

"Be that as it may," said Dimpson. "That isn't *this* story."

Solly agreed, soundlessly.

Bea screwed up her nose and sent a silent "too bad" on little white wings across the conference room to Solly. Even in her bountiful positiveness she couldn't refute the evidence Prosecutor Dimpson had compiled. Solly smiled back, to let her know he wasn't dying. But the newcomer beside Bea wrestled his gaze away from her. She raised an eyebrow at him provocatively. Solly felt prickly all over. Who had she come with? Whose friend was she? Solly let his smile drift on the lukewarm tide of the conference room over to the mystery woman: Naomi—or was it Hagar? That was it. What had brought Hagar to the writing circle? She made no notes, had nothing to say. She seemed only interested in Solomon Marvel. Mind you, it was Solomon Marvel's night.

The verdict in, everybody broke for coffee. A few generous souls came up to Solly to point out typos in the manuscript just in case he was still thinking of sending it out. He listened dutifully.

Then it was time to wrap it up for another month. Solly stayed behind to lock up. Rather than make tedious arrangements with the janitor, Solly was in the habit of sweeping up himself. It gave him time to think about things. He had a lot to think about. So he was surprised, upon leaving the library, to find a car—a rather sleek black car—still in the parking lot. Surprised and somehow not at all surprised.

He had already turned down Orchard Street when he heard her call. He was thinking this: different things appeal to different people. Mightn't there be women, for instance, who were hopelessly turned on by men who had just been crucified by small town science fiction writing circles? Was this woman then to be his saviour, to make him better through a night of unbridled passion? He was just thinking up a story along those lines when she pulled up beside him. He heard her window whirr open.

" Can I give you a ride, Mr. Marvel?" she purred.

The door of her car opened but whether it was cranked or activated, Solly would never know. And then he was in there with her and speeding down Orchard.

Hagar. Hagar Kesey. Hagar the Hungry, by the sound of her. There was a breathiness to her speech that Solly, for all his lack of experience, could not mistake for anything but longing.

They talked of the Strangelanders. "You're very brave," she said. Solly tried to say the right thing. "Hey, if you can't take the heat," he said...

She made no attempt to turn down Whitelawn Terrace. It was only then that Solly felt he must remonstrate. "A drink might be nice," he said, though no such thing had been suggested.

Hagar laughed. Not a devilish laugh, nor malicious either: a cool laugh. Unnerving. Then she spoke.

"Unless I'm very mistaken, Mr. Marvel, I am the end of your story."

Solly had read about serial killers. Some liked nurses, some liked fashion models—why not librarians? He could probably manhandle her off the road, it occurred to him, but she was driving awfully fast. He decided to wait and see. It was, he had always thought, precisely the way he would have handled other violent emergencies—the landing at Dieppe, for instance. He had once read that the soldiers in that bloody bungle had only learned in the landing craft that there was not enough amunition to go around. Solly felt short of ammo now. They drove out of town and into the night.

"So, you are a writer?" he asked.

"No," she said.

Of course not. She was a serial killer who got off on killing librarians with pretensions of being writers. She will probably leave my poor bleeding body in a ditch with an overdue notice stamped on my forehead, he thought. Then, even as he was thinking he should at least raise the subject of his imminent demise, she pulled over to the side of the road and turned off the car's engine and lights.

"How about a walk?" said Solly but his door would not open. There was no handle.

"Time machines seldom have door handles," said Hagar. Solly laughed a poor excuse for a laugh.

A car passed on the road.

"Did you check the vintage?" she asked. "The expiry date on the license?"

It was a crack guaranteed to pique Solly.

"Who are you?" he demanded, trying to pitch the anger in his voice over the fear. "An editor from *Analog* or *Tesseracts* or something? If you don't want to see any more of my manuscripts couldn't you just say so?"

She didn't laugh. She settled into her seat and, flicking on the dash board light, she checked certain dials and turned certain knobs and adjusted certain levers. They were not dials, knobs or levers that Solly had on his Escort.

"What is this?" he demanded.

She turned, beaming, towards him. He had obviously asked the right question. "This," she said, "Is a time machine."

Solly had been looking at her, at her smile in the red dash board light. He had been thinking that she had a beautiful smile for a fruitcake. But at the mention of "time machine" he turned away, seriously hurt. Deeply hurt.

"You want to go back, don't you?" she said.

"Yes," he said. "Have your little say, and then take me home, please."

"I don't mean 'home," she said. "You want to save his life, don't you?"

This was cruel.

"You had a chance to save his life—"

"Weren't you listening tonight?" he shouted at her. It

rose up in him like sick, like lava scorching his throat.

"I heard a story of a man who wanted to rectify the past," she said. "It was, apparently, a story he has been trying to write for quite some time. I'm here to see it done, Solomon Marvel."

He could not keep down the bile but now it was teary-edged with frustration and self hatred. "Didn't you hear what Dave bloody Dimpson was saying? You can't have handy time machines to save the lives of lost LOVED ONES because then there would be no lost LOVED ONES only lost UNLOVED ONES!"

"And Cliff, presumably, was a LOVED ONE?" she said. She adopted his emphasis but even in his consuming rage he sensed that it was not done in mockery.

"I only knew him as a library patron," he said. "A helluva nice guy. One of Potter's Hat's finer citizens. We weren't close. If I'd taken the time to stop and save his life maybe we'd have become close. Become friends. I'll never know."

A silence descended upon them. Unconsciously, Solly's hand slid over the smooth surface of the passenger door, looking for a handle. But there was no handle. She had said that. The silence settled between them. Time it was. Not a lot of time but full of itself. In the silence he realized that Hagar was checking her watch. From time to time.

"It wasn't here," Solly said.

"What wasn't here?" she asked.

"This isn't where Cliff was killed," he answered. "If this "Time Machine" of yours is going to help Cliff out it had better get over to the tenth line sometime between now and sunset, December 7, 1990."

"Do you really expect that's possible?" she asked.

Solly blew the air out through his lips in a horse laugh. He crossed his arms on his chest and stared out the window at the deeper darkness of the brush. So she wasn't a serial killer but some half-assed psychologist with unorthodox methods. Who the hell had told her about him?

"I'm afraid," she said, "I can't go back years in this machine, only a month or two, maximum."

"Hmmm," said Solly, unable to resist the calmness in her voice. "Maybe we could go back to tonight's dinner. I ordered the rubber calimari at The Sea Shack. I should have stuck to the shrimp salad."

"Your fictional Krono-scoot's got me beat," she said, "Let alone the Time Tamer." There was, despite everything, something reassuring about her voice.

"Maybe you should trade this babe in on something with a bit more chrome," said Solly, warming a bit. If she was a serial killer her foreplay wasn't bad.

Hagar was just about to rejoin the banter when she stopped. "Do you hear that?" she said.

"What?" said Solly before he realized that he was hearing something. The wind? No, more insistent. Something terribly familiar. The train.

Hagar made a further adjustment to the instrument panel before her.

"What's going on?" said Solly. The gentle humour of a moment earlier was gone. He felt frightened again. Something was wrong.

"Wait," she said. "Another few minutes."

Solly had never known minutes to crawl like they did then, each millisecond pregnant with the gathering thunder of the train coming towards them from somewhere in the woods.

Then there was its light through the trees, just a glimpse on a bend, then gone again, then the whistle, shrieking, nearer.

And then the car. It came from the same direction they had come, from town. Its lights filled the rearview mirror

first. They both stared at that, at each other, and then out
the back window. A car, coming terribly fast. Too fast.

Solly did a rapid and instinctual geometry of light and
sound in his head: two converging lines; the loci of these
things; a reckless car and a thundering freight train.

"We can't just sit here!" he said.

"There's nothing else we can do," said Hagar.

"This is murder," said Solly. "Flag him down!"

But even as he said it, tried to dive across Hagar's
body to her door, tried to scramble to the rescue, it happened. The car shot past them and into the level crossing.

There was a hideous whining of brakes and screaming
of metal and crunching and all of those other words and
phrases which do no justice to carnage but only compress
the space of its happening. Then there was something
much closer to silence layered with Solly's weeping.

After a moment or two, she spoke. "You can have a
look if you like," she said. He didn't like, but his door
opened none the less, like everything else about this
strange vehicle, completely at her command.

Curiosity propelled him from the car. The thought
that maybe there was help to be offered even though he
knew in some profound way that no one could have survived such a crash drew him towards the scene of the
accident.

What had been a speeding vehicle moments earlier
was now a metallic corpse, an oversized crumpled beer
can in the glare of the massive locomotive. Solly made his
way down the length of the track several hundred meters
to the scene but he stopped before reaching it. Train men
clambered over the destruction trying to find whatever
there might be of life left in it. Unseen by them, in his own
dark, half way down the length of the great hot wall of
train, Solly found something on the gravel of the railroad

bed shoulder, something which must have escaped the shattered car in its tumble down the tracks to oblivion. Pages. Pages from a book. Then the mutilated cover of the book, a cover he had seen before: a woman with ice cream cone breasts struggled with a man in a red cape, while a stiff with a knife in his back tinted the Axminster with his life-blood. *A Devil of a Job.*

Clutching the carcase of the book, Solly turned on his heels and ran, stumbling, falling, tearing his palm on the gravel, cursing, running again until he reached the level crossing. Then he turned up the highway until the shadow of Hagar's sleak car appeared out of the gloom before him. He could just make out her face in the low red glare of the dashboard lights. The passenger door was ajar as he had left it.

He tried to speak. "Brad ... Brad ... ley, Bradley... Keeping ...."

Hagar waited. "And is he dead?"

Solly slammed the mystery down on the dash board. "Of course he's dead. He's obliterated."

"No," she said.

That was all.

Solly threw his head back against the headrest. Once twice, again. "You whore!" he screamed at her. "You sick whore!"

She seemed completely unperturbed by his railing. She waited until he had no more voice in him. Until he sat staring straight ahead into the dark, *A Devil of a Job* lying on his lap.

"Solly," she said, "Check the date in the book."

Solly refused. But the librarian in him did not. Automatically, he flipped the tattered book to the last page."

"The ink is hardly dry," she said, but she was speaking metaphorically. He realized it without realizing it.

"Bradley borrowed this book weeks ago," he said.

"An hour ago," she countered. "He died at precisely 9:34 pm. That will be the engineer's testimony.

"Ha!" said Solomon Marvel. "It was two weeks ago he took this book out. And he was still jabbering to me at 9:30."

Then, even before she could speak again, it began to make some kind of wild sense to Solly's poor over-stimulated mind. It made sense in his blood first and then in his tingling nerves. It made a kind of brainless sense. Hagar Kesey only put words to the sense it made. But that was something.

"This night did not happen like this, did it, Solly? It happened the way it happened—Bradley leaving the library well after closing, getting home despite his wandering mind, his poor hearing and his blaring radio, safe and sound."

Solly turned to her, her face had softened, was more beautiful than he had had ever imagined any face could be.

"You cannot save Cliff," she said. "I cannot take you back to that time. But you saved Bradley Keeping."

He could not be sure, later, what else she said. He could not quite remember the drive home or who put him in his pajamas and set his alarm. He rather hoped it was Hagar. He rather doubted it.

She did not show up at the next Strangelanders meeting, but *Time Shrink* did. Dave Dimpson didn't like the part about finding the book. It would have been more effective to see Keeping's mangled body, he thought. Andy thought Hagar was probably a man's name and maybe Solly should change it to something weirder like Anastasia.

Bea waited in the parking lot afterwards. Her car was not sleak but it was invitingly warm. She invited Solomon Marvel home for cheesecake. It was good cheesecake. She liked the story a lot.

357

FATHER TIME

Derryl Murphy

The bar I'm in is quiet. Three in the afternoon; not many people here. Two young men play darts against the far wall, and a middle-aged couple sit at a table with drinks. She smokes, he doesn't.

My waitress smiles sympathetically at me, knowing instinctively that something is wrong, but not sure what it is. I try to muster up a grin for her, but by the look on her face I'd say I've only managed to frighten her. She leaves my gin and orange on the table and walks away quickly.

I nurse the drink for a while, thinking about as little as I can manage. Too much thinking drags my mind back to the hospital, not a place I want it to be right now.

When my drink is about half-empty the outside door swings open and someone walks in, silhouetted against the bright sunlight. I squint for a moment, then turn my face away from the door.

So I hear, rather than see, the man come up to my table. I turn to tell him that I am not interested in company right now, but what I see stops me short.

The man, I realize, is my father. I am startled and it must show on my face. He smiles, and there are none of the lines that I know so well, the lines that have invaded his face with age.

I know this for a fact. I watched him as I grew, watched as he fought the losing Battle of Vanity. As the face that had once seemed so effortlessly smooth, so wonderful as a child in awe to stroke in wonder, slowly gave ground to the rifts and valleys of living. This is my father as he was when he was a young man. But I just came from visiting my father in the hospital, where he is now losing an even more important battle.

The man who was my father steps up to me, and I reach out to stroke his face. He lets me touch his skin for a second, and then says, "Let's go somewhere else and talk."

"This is my fifth trip," he says, after taking a sip of coffee. We are in The Silk Hat, in a booth near the back. He used to come in here and have his tea leaves read, but not today. What would tea leaves say about a man whose only reason for existence is an apparent quirk in the mathematics of the universe?

I watch the waitress as she goes by, uncomfortable talking while others are nearby. She goes to the only other occupied booth, near the door. We are near the back of the restaurant.

"Where do you go next?" I ask. It is hard for me to accept this, although not for the reasons you might think. Rather than being freaked by his being here, I am most bothered by the fact that he is appearing here younger than me.

"Ten more years. Each step takes me further away, but it seems to get easier."

"How..." I begin.

"Do I do it?" He shakes his head. "I can't explain. Even if I could, it would sound like a lot of spiritual mumbo-jumbo to you. What do people now call it? Sort of new age."

"Oh. You mean like mantras and crystals and stuff?"

"No." That's all he says.

I decide to change topics, although I realize as I speak, I could have done better. "You realize you're dying."

He grimaces, and I see the first hints of those lines. "With?"

"Cancer. All through the body. Probably only days left." Tears start, I grab a napkin and try to staunch the flow.

He takes my hand and grieves with me. For himself.

I grieve for lost time.

The next day, he dies. I am downstairs having a cup of tea and thinking about when I was a child, and I feel a hand on my shoulder. It is the nurse; she has tears in her eyes. My father has been very popular here.

I stand too suddenly, knocking the cup to the floor. The tea that is left spills in slow-motion, and when it hits the floor it spreads in every direction. I feel the eyes of many people on my back right now, but those looks, whether judgemental or sympathetic, only touch me for the shortest of moments.

The nurse hugs me, briefly, then leads me to the elevator like I'm a little boy. Which is what I am right now, remembering stroking the smooth skin only yesterday, and then seeing the parched and sagging folds of his face today.

It was too much, and I had to leave. So I missed the moment of his death. We get off the elevator and the nurse takes me to the room and then leaves, shutting the door behind her.

His fault; he could have come to me after he died. As I look at the body one last time I punch the wall in fury and slide sobbing to the floor.

"I missed it," says a voice.

I look up, and there is my father. Only older than yesterday, by about ten years.

I don't talk to him, but rather I fold my arms and sulk. He's abandoned me; I hate him.

"I need your help. Please."

"Why?"

"I'm stuck. There's been a war; I can't leave this future. The fabric has changed."

"Then how are you here?"

"This isn't me, or at least not the me you saw yesterday. But this is the reason I will die, or did die, of cancer."

"I don't understand."

A flash of anger in his eyes. "You don't need to understand. Just meet me at the head of the Mill Creek Trail at twelve noon, ten years from today. And bring a good calculator, a good HP scientific."

"If there's a war, how do you know I will be alive to be there?"

"You've already been there. That's why I'm able to be here."

"And if I don't show?"

"Then I die there, and not here." He gestures at the bed, and his body is no longer there. Then he disappears and is replaced with the diseased version of himself. Fading in and out of my vision. "You can't bury me," coughs, "this way, son."

"Fuck. Fine."

The old one goes to the bed and lies down, closes his eyes and stops breathing. The other comes back. "Don't forget."

"Like you didn't forget me?"

I now see pain in his eyes. That cut deep, and I can see him start to retort, catch himself, hold it back. "Ten years. Please."

He goes away again. Too much. My father has left me four times in two days.

Everything around me loses focus, and the tubes and machines seem to become a beast that has come to suck the life-force from my father's silent body. I howl in anguish, and two nurses rush in. One quietly holds my elbow while the other takes the dangling tubes from my hand. I realize I have ripped them from his body.

The tears flow again, far more than any time before.

He was right about the war. Canada and the States take lots of refugees now, but only from Europe. The size of my city has swollen to number in the millions; food is harder to get,; almost no one travels by car. They say it is still a democracy; I think it is a police state. Curfews, elections that don't matter, soldiers on every street corner. But we are still alive.

The appointed day has come. The calculator I bought four years ago, before such luxuries disappeared forever. I also bring a bottle of wine, hoping to perhaps share it with my father. Over the course of these hard years I have forgiven him his sins against me.

I'm early, so I sit on an old bench and wait. The park I am in is still green, after a fashion. The path is paved, but aspen, bushes and weeds choke the sides, and every so often there is a spruce. Different foliage from when I was a child, but they are all that will grow here now.

Some people say the parkland is a luxury, but it is one thing our leaders have not budged on. We were once famous for our green space, and I think the doddering old-timers who now run our lives remember those days with a certain amount of affection.

Two soldiers walk by, eyeing me warily. But their rifles stay down, and they continue their patrol without stopping to question me. I see one whisper something to the other and they both laugh, casting a parting glance my way.

Finally, after perhaps a half-hour he steps out of some bushes.

"Father."

He looks startled. "Why are you here?"

I offer him the calculator. "You came to me, said you were stuck here because of the war."

"War?"

I nod. "Nuclear, in the Middle East."

He turns the calculator on, does some quick calculations. "Can I have this?"

I nod. He puts it in his coat pocket.

I offer him the bottle of wine, intending to suggest we share it. He takes it, looks at it, says "Thanks," and disappears.

I stand at the trail head, dismayed. "Father!" I shout, "Don't leave me again!"

But he's gone.

"There was no war."

"What do you mean?" I have introduced this man to the nurse as my nephew. He is fresh-faced at nineteen, still two years away from becoming a father.

"I mean that you remember it because of your connection with me, but it didn't happen."

"How?" The medication adds to my perplexity.

"I changed the equations. Had to."

"Why?"

"I wouldn't be able to travel, otherwise. No one around you remembers it. It faded away for good, and was replaced by other emergencies and tragedies."

"But what about my life? Where did everything go?"

"Still the same. Only, people have begun to find different reasons for the choices that have been made over the years."

This is a sobering thought. Even with the evidence of

my father's travels, I had thought certain things were immutable. Was I so drastically wrong? "What does this do to my work?"

"Nothing. Everything else stays the same. The changes I am able to make are very localized, and take much subjective, objective, and imaginary time to take place. And this is the only one I have ever made that affected more people than myself."

I try to think of more questions, but the meds in my system are making this all very hard to grasp. At least, I think it's the drugs.

He takes the opportunity afforded by the silence to open his shoulder bag and pulls out two crystal glasses and a bottle of wine that looks familiar. He pours the wine, rests the glasses on the bed table. "Here. Let me help you sit up."

Tubes get in the way, but he gets me up. For a moment my bedroom spins around, but it settles down soon enough. When I found I was ill I insisted on home-nursing, rather than an impersonal hospital.

The insurance company had balked, but I have spent my years wisely, cultivating friendships with many who now lead this newly independent northern land. A word from one of them, and my apartment was readied for my dying. It makes it easier to turn away visitors, too, but the young man here today is special.

He puts a straw in my glass, holds it for me to take a sip. "Mmm. Very good. How old is it?"

He thinks for a second. "Can't really say. Somewhere between five years and two hundred, I think."

I remember the wine now. Tears come to my eyes. "I'm glad you came back."

I stretch out my hand and stroke his face. The look of my weathered hand on his skin is jarring, and I remember where I am.

"Join me," he says.

I cough, spitting some of the wine back up. He holds a cloth napkin to my mouth, and it comes away pink, even though the wine is white. The nurse looks in, sternly. "How?" I ask.

"It's easy," he replies. "Just lie down and close your eyes. I'll go get you elsewhen."

The tears rush back. The joy I feel is almost painful. My father wants me with him! After so many years that I thought he wanted to be away from me.

He's crying, too. "I missed you, son. I wasn't a very good dad."

"It's okay. I spent a long time being angry with you, but I think I finally came to my own reconciliation."

"Is all this why you never had a family?"

A good question. I gesture for him to help me lie back down while I think on it. He seems content to let me be quiet as I think, and I hear no sounds of impatience from him. Eventually I say, "Probably. You're very wise for someone who only looks nineteen."

This makes him laugh; a boisterous sound that brings back a flood of visions. Tears well up in my eyes again. At least the lousy disease hasn't dried me out. "You know I'm not really nineteen."

I nod. I spent much of my life trying to understand the physics involved, even going so far as to go back to university and getting a doctorate. One of few that the government still allows complete studies in.

My work did much for me, and I hope it did much for the world at large. And I became important enough that people began to listen to me, and with my help some libertarians started to find their way into public office again. Perhaps my contributions will eventually make it easier for personal freedoms to become important again.

But I never could figure out how my father avoided

the conventional pitfalls of paradox, as well as the unconventional ones that dogged my work for so many years. Maybe now I can find out.

"Where will we go?"

He smiles. "You name it. The universe will be ours."

I smile in return, and hope my toothless grin doesn't scare him away. "It's a deal."

Then I close my eyes and slip away.

I am nineteen, and I have a small backpack packed, but I don't know why. My father comes into the room. "Son, I have someone I'd like you to meet."

Then my father walks into the room, only he's young, younger than I ever knew as a child. He stands beside the father I know, the father who after my mother died always spent so much time away from me, and suddenly I remember!

I remember it all, the meetings, my father's death, the war. Even my own death. A wave of relief washes over me, as I realize that I am being given a new chance at discovering my father and my relationship with him.

"You ready?"

I nod so hard I give myself a headache. "Yes!"

They both hug me, something I'm not used to from my father, then they hug each other.

My older father holds my shoulders for a minute, staring into my eyes. "You be careful son, but enjoy yourself."

All of this affection stuns me. "I wish you could come too."

Both of them laugh. "I already have," he says, "and I already am."

I still don't understand, but perhaps with time, as it were, I will.

"Where are we going?" I ask.

"We'll go say goodbye to yourself first. Then...." He

shrugs his shoulders.

I smile and we go. I wonder where else I've already been?

REMEMBER, THE DEAD SAY

Jean-Louis Trudel

The child is blond, a boy with golden hair and eyes of an indefinite grey-blue which have no more tears to shed since Daddy was killed by a sniper's bullet. He is called Brendan, Devin... maybe Gerald? He is running. In fact, he's been running towards the river and safety for two days, ever since he left his family's cottage in the northern hills, among the pines. He has run across the city streets strewn with shattered bricks, in the midst of the smoking ruins of wooden bungalows and the blasted shells of low-rises, and the river was always in front of him, getting closer and closer.

But no, now he is running across the cold terrazzo tiles of a shopping center, from floor to floor, running down to the dirty concrete of the parking levels. No shoppers there, no cars here. Only people huddled in small groups, sprawled on mattresses or sleeping bags, jealously standing guard over small hoards of boxes and cans. As he runs, he shouts:

Les avions! Les avions s'en viennent!" The Canadian jets, the F-18 S1 fighter-bombers; where S stands for "smart"....

The boy has run alongside the stony trench of the boulevard linking the main bridges, where the last defenders are encamped with mortars, a few remaining APCs, and howitzers. The boy knows that the pilots won't distinguish between the desperate troops and the neighbouring buildings where Hull's former citizens have found shelter from the shelling and the small arms fire. Even though the office towers are festooned with red crosses.

And the bombs that will glide down laser paths, finding the sky-lights over the shopping center's atrium or the stairway shafts of the parking, will not pick and choose among their victims. The boy runs in the last shadows of the federal buildings. On the other side of the deserted stretch of pavement, if he jumps over the fallen poles of the streetlights and somehow scrambles down the grassy slope, there is an arm of the Ottawa river. On the other side, OttawaOntarioCanada....

The planes shriek across the sky and the boy leaps from the shadows.

* * *

She combed the snow out of her beard.

The driving snow was definitely freakish for December in Lowell, O.T. It might not have seemed so out of place in January, when flurries harried the town for two or three days a year, outlining the scaly bark of the palm-trees with filigrees of dirty white and then melting in a few hours, leaving a puddle in every pothole. She was much too recent a newcomer to remember when Massachusetts winters had entailed more snow than sleet.

The old comb had lost teeth and its black plastic was scarred, but she stowed it carefully in a back pocket after wiping it. She dared not lose it. She avoided stores where the monitors might see past the beard or the mikes might catch the hint of accent in her roughened voice. Besides, she rather liked its battered condition; it reflected her own predicament.

She forced herself to walk on, plowing into the cold wind. Overhead, azure bunting decorated with golden fleurs-de-lis fluttered in the gusts, faded black letters proclaiming in French the fiftieth anniversary of Québec's war of independence. The sidewalk was broken in places, covered with icy patches elsewhere, and she concentrated on her footing. A broken leg would mean a visit to the hospital, and unavoidable discovery.

Beards had been a fad before the latest series of wars, like breasts for men, furred tails, cat's eyes or werewolf teeth. She'd chosen a beard to match her mousy brown hair, back then, and this unadventurous choice had proven wise in unforeseen ways. Alterations could not be reversed without elaborate genosurgery—though she had contemplated permanent depilation—and most genochemists had died during the years of destruction. The genochemists had not relied on anything as gross as massive testosterone injections. Growing a beard on a woman had not been the point, that was old hat, but rather doing it without affecting the body's delicate biochemical balance.

Now though, the beard allowed her to masquerade as a man and to walk the streets unchallenged. The law of the Franco-Maghrebi Coalition was the Sharia and it imposed the veil on all women past a certain age, as well as seclusion except for absolutely necessary errands—not that either was really unwise with the Sun blasting ultraviolet at an ozone-poor Earth. Only the women among the troops of Québec, the Coalition's sole North American ally, enjoyed a special dispensation.

The old thoroughfare that paralleled the river came to an end at another waterway. The nineteenth-century town center of Lowell was now behind her and so she bore left, recalling the directions whispered to her aboard the rickety Amtrak train she had taken to Omaha, capital of the Free States, an oasis amid an encroaching desert. She'd spent two days in Omaha, waiting for the eastbound train, doing the things expected of any Canadian tourist. A quick videocamming of the Whiter House, a brief tour of the Senate in session, and a peek from afar, *sans* camera, at the rebuilt Pentagon.

That had been but a few weeks before the war: the quick Franco-Maghrebi thrust from the occupied Maritime Confederacy, the nuking of the Albany staging point of the F.S.A. First Army, the overrunning of the defenses along the Hudson wasteland, the indecisive battle around Syracuse, and, two months later, the signature of the ceasefire in forlorn Ottawa by delegates from Marseilles and Omaha, witnessed by Canadian officials from Winnipeg.

By then, she'd arrived in Lowell. She'd lived the war through the Net, as she accessed the last screams of the dying, the encrypted communications of the military, the grainy battlefield pics, the verbal confrontations of supporters of both sides, and even sometimes the streams of biomonitor data, each packet crowded with the life of a man or woman, and each packet practically meaningless for an eavesdropper like her, safe in tʰe basement of an aging clapboard house. She'd been astonished to discover a few last pacifists, and gripped by the unfolding battles, and pained by the suffering of the wounded keying in to reaffirm they still existed: whatever it was, if it were modulated electronically, it eventually left a residue on the Net, like the sediment of the centuries descending upon the ocean floor.

In those days, she'd craved the Net and its raw emotions to help her forget that she was afraid. The empty streets outside had seemed to expect, to *want* soldiers to come walking through the wind-blown leaves of early autumn, and yet everyone was afraid of spotting the first green uniform that would change all their lives forever. However, Lowell was too small and too close to radioactive Boston, smitten in an earlier war fought with deadlier weapons and with other enemies, avenged by smouldering towns called Kazan and Smolensk. The Franco-Maghrebi

columns had by-passed unimportant Lowell and, in the
end, the first forces to enter it had come from Québec after
the ceasefire had fixed the zones of influence for a time.
Since then, most voices on the local Net had died away.

"Do you speak French, mister?"

"Excusez-moi, mais parlez-vous français?"

"Assalaamu aleikoum, tifnam arabi?"

"Please, please, do you speak Arabic?"

She almost broke her stride, memories fragmenting
and whirling away. The supplicants lined the street in
front of the Québec military headquarters. They waved
sheets of plastic inscribed in the Roman or Arabic alpha-
bets. She looked straight ahead and walked on, tried not to
betray her knowledge of French, steeled herself against
flinching.

She knew what the documents were. The same had
been sent to everybody with a surname which seemed either French or Arabic in origin. Notices of retroactive
recognition of citizenship, as they were called by the oc-
cupiers. Draft notices, she called them, since military service
went with citizenship for Québec or the Franco-Maghrebis.
Anyway, such was their real purpose and they were
couched in such ornate French or flowery Arabic that the
recipients, sons of long-ago immigrants who'd only learned
a few words of their ancestral languages in childhood, if at
all, could hardly decipher their meaning.

She walked faster. If her name had not been Pat Doyle,
she might have received one. In Kapuskasing, her family
had spoken French for over a century. At times, her mind
reeled from the welter of her identities, which burdened
her with a dozen masks. Francophone in English-speaking
Canada, Métis in a land owned by others, and now a Canadian in Lowell, formerly a city of the F.S.A., but now an
"Occupied Territory" of the Franco-Maghrebi Coalition.

As a Canadian, she could be shot as a spy; as a francophone, drafted; as a Métis, who could claim kinship with the rich farmers of Denendeh, interned as an illegal alien....

And she didn't even know for sure what the Sharia dictated for women using men's clothing. On the whole, she preferred to be an American, even in an occupied city.

A Québécois patrol came towards her and she bobbed her head up and down in submission as she changed sidewalks. The long coat in which she shivered hid well the curves still left in spite of a starvation diet, but there was no percentage in taking chances.

The soldiers did not spare a glance. Thin scraggly men were the norm in Lowell.

Québec! She mastered an urge to spit on the pavement they had walked on. She'd come to Lowell to find the mass grave of distant relatives, the Marcottes, on behalf of La Nouvelle Patente, the one organization that had linked francophones in Canada, Denendeh, the Maritime Confederacy, and the F.S.A. During the previous war, the Marcottes and others like them had been shot as Québec spies, for a country they'd never even visited. Only babies had been spared, put up for adoption, and lost in the records. They were safe somewhere, she hoped: Louis, Richard, Julie.... Only a small atrocity begotten by others begotten by hatreds born of a long twisting history, which only the victors could afford to forget: if she found the grave, she was to send back for money with which to build a memorial.

And then she'd met the stranger aboard the train who'd whispered to her of coming wars and defeats.

Defeat, she knew. You lived, you cried, and then you got used to it.

Pat had flung her teen-age years at the burning forests of northern Ontario, like so many others in Kapuskasing, refusing to let the futility of it erode her youthful determination. The fires had become more and more frequent as the greenhouse effect worsened. She remembered the smell of smoke that stayed in the clothes, the black grit getting in the eyes, the resin scent that would not wash off her hands after mere hours of work. A few days were enough for a fire fighter to merge with the fire she was fighting, growing into a creature of wood and sooty air, of water and black earth, arms an extension of axe-handles or shovels.

They'd saved villages like Val-Rita and towns like Longlac, but she'd quit after shooting the last *buck*—she'd been with a younger cousin, David McCaughey, scouting the woods downwind of a late-summer fire. The over-worked planes were supposed to come, but such pledges were written on the wind, and a fire-break had to be planned. She had a gun, in case the fire chased something dangerous out of the woods and into their path. The afternoon had been hot, the air heavy, and they'd tried for a short-cut, scrambling down a wooded slope to the edge of a small lake. And then they'd seen the *buck*. It bellowed in pain. The animal's pelt hung in blackened tatters and its antlers seemed to smoke still. They'd never seen a moose this far south.

It stood there for what seemed like forever, its cries of anguish echoing back from the hills. David had pulled at her arm, wanting to go on and detour around the wounded beast. She hadn't budged, moved in spite of herself and struggling with an obscure feeling of recognition. Then, in one swift motion, she had shouldered the gun and shot.

The next day, she had handed in her resignation from the fire-fighting squads. The moose had stayed behind, maybe, when others had moved north away from swelter-ing summers and the increasing human presence. Maybe it had come back. But there was no going back, and the for-ests could not be saved as long as the climate continued to get hotter.

That was the first time she had tasted bittersweet defeat, the bitterness of losing mingled with the relief that came with no longer having to fight.

"À quoi tu penses?"

"Kawkwy!"

She reddened as she realized she'd answered in Michif, which had been the language of her Métis grandfather, and then paled as she realized the question had been put to her in French. Lost in the past, she'd stopped to shelter in a doorway of the Archambault funeral home. She glanced up at the man who had spoken:

"Who are you?"

At the same time, she withdrew her hands, numbed by the cold, into the arms of her coat. The lining held a dozen *fléchettes*, tipped with Tabun-filled capsules.

"Je sais qui tu es, Patline," he said.

She almost gasped. He'd used her full name.

"What do you mean?" she replied.

"Tu es Patline Doyle, tu as grandi à Moonbeam et tu as été envoyée par la Nouvelle Patente pour arranger la construction d'un monument commémoratif à la mémoire des victimes des massacres de mars."

"What are you saying? I was born and raised in Manchester, up north, in New Hampshire," she said, unwilling to admit defeat too quickly. Only a *provocateur* would speak French so openly. The man threw back the hood of his coat: a tiara of metal and glass imprisoned his skull. Greying hair showed through in places, but the device seemed to be a melded part of the head. The face was lined with furrows born of worry or fear, but the deep-set eyes burned into hers.

"I'm Marc Gendreau, a gatekeeper of the Net," he laughed tiredly, "and we cracked the secret access codes of the Nouvelle Patente a long time ago. I probably know

more about the organization than you. I even know about
that Arab draft dodger you hid in your basement for a
week.... Je suis recherché par la Sûreté militaire."

She sighed, at once impressed and alarmed. If
Québec's counter-intelligence police were truly hunting
for him....

"How did you find me?"

"You used your pocket comp to check the weather
forecast when you were in front of the church. I traced
your call to the nearest relay and I guessed where you
were going."

"Very well, but let's not stay here." If he was
a *provocateur*, he was toying with her. She preferred the alternative. "And hide your hardware." He started at that,
but obediently pulled the hood over his head.

She launched into a brisk walk, head lowered against
the wind. He half-ran to catch up and he asked:

"Going to the Marcotte house?"

She did not answer and she continued to lead the way
till she turned into the empty lot. She was suddenly reassured by his ignorance of her true destination.

The mob had burned down the house of the
Marcottes. The snow was resurrecting it, outlining the
concrete foundation and the broken stumps of walls, pil-
ing up around the heaps of rubble. The living-room had
been there, she guessed, at the back of the house; she could
picture the parents watching their kids at play in that wide
backyard which extended down to the water's edge. One
of the parents would have yelled out from time to time to
warn the children away from the water....

She followed the winding path of flagstones which
ended on the threshold of the ruined house, but she did
not continue. Stepping on the concrete flooring always
made her feel as if she were desecrating a tomb. Instead,
she led the way around the side.

Strangely enough, she had no such compunction about treading the ground where they had buried the bodies. It was a backyard as wide as a playing field, extending down to the water. The snow was driving down with a renewed fierceness and she could not even see to the edges of the field as she peered into the whirling snowflakes.

It had been during the last war but one, when the Franco-Maghrebis had overwhelmed the Maritime Confederacy—after Québec had unexpectedly joined in the fighting, capturing Edmonston and pushing down to Fredericton, breaking the back of Maritime resistance. As the combined armies had moved down to Saint John, closer and closer to the F.S.A. border, the war scare had spread to the whole of New England. Several Lowell families—Bédards, Merciers, Royers—guilty of being too ostentatiously francophone, had been rounded up as spies, had seen their houses burned, and had been shot later that night. Nothing more was known. The leaders of the mob had never been identified. The dead do not testify.

Pat had even had trouble finding the spot where the Marcottes and the others were buried. Nobody knew, or was willing to tell a stranger. The remaining francophones around town were afraid to talk. She'd plugged into the Net for unending days and nights in the hope of catching a hint. Finally, she'd used her Net expertise to assemble a slightly illegal interception program; it scanned every private and public electronic conversations for a month before coming up with the slightest of allusions. It had been enough, though.

She stopped in the middle of the field and turned towards Marc. The snow curtained them off from prying eyes.

"Well, Marc, who are you? You don't have a Québec accent."

"I *was* born and raised in Pelham, in what was New

377

Hampshire, but I trained as a roving trouble-shooter, a specialist of Net patch-up jobs. I was in Amherst when the invasion started. Since then, I've been moving, struggling to keep a Net channel open, but I'm running out of luck, and time, and money."

"Alors? Que veux-tu?" she asked, eyes narrowing. She did not need more complications to interfere with what had seemed to be such a simple mission.

"Que tu viennes avec moi, Patline. Come with me: I said I was a gatekeeper, but that's only part of the truth. This last war was just another instalment in the conflict between North America and Europe, but the fighting, the bombings, the troop movements are merely the overt war. Another war has begun, Pat, and this one is invisible. It's a war for control of the Net."

He brushed some snow off the rim of his hood and added: "I'm a soldier now in this underground war. On one side, there are the Franco-Maghrebis, who want to shut down all access to the continental Net where debate is free, information is cheap, and gems are stirred in along with the manure. On the Net, you can debate the Koran, the Sharia, and whether Mohammed was forewarned of the ozone layer's weakening or not. Without the Net, the Franco-Maghrebis can feed you all the news they want you to have. On the other side, a group is forming, rather undefined—it includes all Netters, à la limite. We take action against the disruptor viruses of the Franco-Maghrebis; we try to locate their taps on the lines; we buy new hardware when the Franco-Maghrebis confiscate what's already there; sometimes we simply play the role of reporters or researchers—what is on the Net is as important as having the Net...."

"So, why me?" she asked. "And isn't there a section of the F.S.A. army that deals with electronic skirmishing?"

"The military experts have enough to do with defending the access to their own files. As for you, we saw what you did to find the burial spot—an ingenious little program—and we'd like to have you. Especially since you speak French—French-speaking programmers are as rare as vacuum tubes nowadays on our side, and we expect to face a lot of datastream in French from now on. Would that affect your loyalties? Having to work against Québec programmers, I mean?"

"I didn't notice the F.S.A. having any qualms about old loyalties when they nuked the British Fleet to keep the Franco-Maghrebis from getting it intact," she answered drily. And any loyalty she felt for Québec was very old indeed.

"Good, good. But there is another reason. My reserve funds are practically worthless now that the area is occupied, and I know that you will be getting some hard currency soon."

She almost smiled. It was true; she'd sent for the memorial money from the Nouvelle Patente as soon as she'd found the killing field.

"Yes, Marc, but there's still that old question: why should I trust you?"

"We were both caught behind the lines. I think we have to trust each other."

"I don't know about that. I don't even know what side of the line I was on originally...."

"We need that money!" he pronounced. "The Franco-Maghrebis will be selling the hardware they took from the F.S.A. army. It'll be a bit battered, but with universal compatibility, we can use it to replace the hardware the Franco-Maghrebis have been confiscating left and right since the beginning of the occupation. I've got to be in Springfield in three days for the auction, impersonating a Montréal resaler."

"So, you want me to start by committing larceny.... The

money is being entrusted to me to build a memorial."

"A memorial to the dead. What I'm offering you is a memorial to the living. Pat, I believe that the Net is vital if we are to have any hope for the future."

"Come to my place tomorrow, Marc," she said, as she strode away. She had to think.

"Et cette nuit? I just arrived in town and I have nowhere to sleep."

"Va voir Laura Daigle, 46 rue Merrimack."

Surprise was in his eyes for a twinkling, and Patline realized that she'd spoken in her natural tone of voice instead of her usual rough whisper. She stroked her beard in contemplation as she turned her back and walked down to the waterside, where there was a path.

A few houses further, behind the decaying hulk which had been some kind of school decades ago, she found the small Catholic shrine—a grotto of concrete where glowed candles the last of the faithful came to light. The Way of the Cross, with its faded inscriptions in French, ended at the top of the concrete mound. She climbed the steps to check the surroundings. Nobody in sight.

However, when she walked back down to the mouth of the grotto, a shape appeared in the greyness. She stopped and then looked around for more, but the man was alone. He did not acknowledge her presence as he stepped up to the altar. In his threadbare windbreaker, he had the look of a refugee from the Mexican state of Alta California—blond, bronzed, and breathtakingly thin.

Aware of the man's scrutiny, she kneeled in front of the crucifix and barely remembered how to cross herself. The Doyle family had been Catholic once, but she had always scorned keeping up appearances when the heart did not believe.

She turned after a suitable pause to the small table with a Holy Bible and a ledger, both plastic-wrapped. She opened the latter, flipping past the pious scrawlings in Spanish, Greek, or Polish, went to the back page, and blinked at finding a sealed envelope stuck to the inner cover. The agent aboard the Omaha train had instructed her to look for messages there. Even back then, the inner councils of the F.S.A. had expected a war with the Franco-Maghrebis before Christmas and had expected to lose. They had already been preparing resistance, and she'd left herself be persuaded to take part in order not to jeopardize her cover as a Canadian Net programmer hired for a small job in Lowell. She had checked the mail drop a hundred times, and this was the first there was anything.

"Don't you know your own name?" The voice boomed into her ear.

"I'm sorry. I was thinking." She grasped the old pen, and wrote down her name with a flourish. As she put back the pen, she smoothly detached the envelope and pocketed it.

"What's in the envelope?" Was there the slightest hint of a Québec accent in the blond man's voice. She smiled faintly:

"It's a greeting card I got today for my birthday. Didn't you see me take it out of my pocket to let it dry?"

"No, I guess not." He did not pursue the matter. "Did you spot a strange man on your way here? Medium height, grey hair, in a brownish parka?"

"Couldn't see much, with the wind." She was suddenly sure that he was an agent of the *Sûreté militaire*.

"Of course.... Can you speak French?"

"Oh, *juste un peu*," she forced out with a quaver. The man's eyes seemed to weigh for a moment the build of a potential recruit. He probably judged her too scrawny to be worth his time, and he dismissed her:

"You should come to Québec; it's impossible to learn to speak French right elsewhere, and French can't survive

381

outside it. Good jobs for bilinguals, too."

She assented mutely, and he moved off into the snow-filled gloom. She hesitated, filled with renewed mistrust of everybody and everything. Were Marc and this man part of some subtle ploy by the *Sûreté*? Who could she trust? Even if Marc was for real, didn't her commitment to the Nouvelle Patente or the F.S.A. resistance come first? She glanced at the Bible, and, on a whim, as she mocked herself inside, she opened it to a random page and bent down to read.

> "5. And the sons of Rimmon the Beerothite, Rechab and Baanah, went, and came about the heat of the day to the house of Ishbosheth, who lay on a bed at noon. 6. And they came thither into the midst of the house, *as though* they would have fetched wheat; and they smote him under the fifth *rib*: and Rechab and Baanah his brother escaped. 7. For when they came into the house, he lay on his bed in his bedchamber, and they smote him, and slew him, and beheaded him, and took his head, and gat them away through the plain all night."

From the Second Book of Samuel.... She felt the words indict her for impudence in seeking advice she didn't believe in, anyway, and yet she had to grin at the ironies. Advice about backstabbing, as if she needed it! The dilemma was in choosing which back to stab! She remembered some of her grandfather's Michif and shouted it suddenly to the unseen sky:

"Kishay Menitou! Weechihin!"

There was no answer, and in fact her grandfather's prayers had rarely been answered. She left.

When she got home, a man in uniform was waiting on

her doorstep, and she almost shrank from him. Her grandfather had drummed into her an instinctive abhorrence of
police; Zachary Allard had relished telling how his
crooked nose had been broken by police officers unfriendly to Métis. The beating had prompted his move
from the Prairies to northern Ontario,

However, even if the *Sûreté militaire* was on her tail,
the man was older than the average security officer, and he
started by handing her a package. She went inside, locking
the door behind her—the courier could wait a bit before
being paid—and pulling down the blinds, and then
opened the package to find a roll of silver *écus*. Enough to
build a fitting memorial to the Marcottes and the other victims of the March massacres....

She invited the courier inside and served him some of
her quickly vanishing stock of maple brandy. Whatever
happened, she would be able to leave Lowell, quit living
in disguise, and return to a freer land. What would she
would look without a beard? She found she'd forgotten....

"À la vôtre!" They clinked glasses. He reminisced
about the first Independence Battalions of Québec. He
claimed he had been in one of them when it marched
down St-Denis street in Montréal, in disordered ranks of
paunchy volunteers who brandished antiquated Glock
light machine guns and sang *Gens du pays* with a terrified
fervour, cheered on by the throng packed on the sidewalks
and in the cafés. They had felt like heroes, surely doomed,
but tears of joy streamed down their faces as they realized
that the age-old dream of a nation was coming true.
Québec was standing up after four centuries of colonization.

Pat muttered something under her breath about be-
traying part of their past, but she knew Québec had been
given little choice. Its people had dreamed of a peaceful
country, that would never aspire to play the game of

weltpolitik, but they had been compelled to arm and to defend themselves, till the logic of history led them to do unto others what had been done to them.

He did not hear her. They had been hoarse with shouting and singing, and they all thought they would be sent up the Outaouais to liberate Hull from the Canadian Army. However, his battalion had been ordered to stay and wipe out the Westmount pockets of resistance. The house to house fighting had been ugly, against older men and women who refused to be third-class citizens and sang an anthem composed by a French-Canadian as their houses burned around them.... He came back from the past as if burnt by it, and asked suddenly what happened when dreams two hundred years old came true? She did not answer. Precious few dreams had come true for her.

She sang old songs with him, careless for once. Let the neighbours hear them singing in French! They danced a bit, to old tunes from the twentieth century that he remembered hearing when they were nearly new. He was the first to fall asleep.

That left her to contemplate alternatives. Going back to Canada. Staying in Lowell to help the F.S.A. resistance—the traditional work of spying, sabotage, and guerilla warfare, glamourous but deadly. Leaving with Marc.

Past, present, future. It was too neat. She had lain on her cot to reflect, and she fell asleep in the middle of remembering the moose she had killed.

* * *

When she woke up the next morning, she found an old razor and shaved. The epicene ambiguity of the new face she discovered as she cleared the last of the stubble startled her. She stared at herself for a moment without being able to decide who she recognized, and then went to the door to watch the street. Refugees were coming in from the war zone.

The snow had changed into a cold, pattering rain. Standing on her doorstep, she watched the little groups of men and women shuffle down the street, towards the town center. A man dressed in the same rags, arms empty, came towards her door.

"Are you ready to go?" he asked.

"I know I cannot go back, but what hope do you offer me?" She wanted more than the lonely glory of joining the F.S.A. resistance, clinging to a sense of separateness and tight-knit camaraderie as she had done all her life. Yes, she wanted more, she wanted a change.

"The name of the game is survival, Patline. Look at us! You come from Canada, I from the good old U. S. of A., and a hundred years ago nobody would have bet that we would still speak French to each other. Why? Because we were the pioneers of the electronic community. No ghettoes for us, no Little Italys, no Chinatowns. We can be found across the continent, but we are invisible. Our grandparents used to come home from a day at work in English or Japanese, and light up the television, turn on the radio, plug in the modem.... Et ils pouvaient alors se parler en français. No borders. One community from sea to sea to sea. Something France only allowed briefly over there—remember the Minitel crackdown? But even if the Franco-Maghrebi tanks roll to the Pacific, we have a chance, I say, as long as the Net survives and continues to carry more information than a thousand AIs could filter."

"Do you really think they'll invade the F.S.A.?"

"Why not? For us, America is a broken-down dream. Both sides lost when the old United States decided to tackle the new Russia. But for Europeans, America is still the next best thing to a second chance."

She smiled, and pushed the door open. Her travel bag, with the roll of *écus* secured in a hidden pocket, was on the other side. She shouldered it, and heard reproving ghosts wail. You need to be alive to remember, she almost said, but she simply turned towards Marc. "Let's go."

"What do you want me to call you?"

It was a new life, after all. They would look for Pat Doyle if *he* disappeared... they would find a courier asleep in her flat. She remembered an old book:

"Call me Maria...."

* * *

The boy's hair is black and curly, and his skin remembers the Mediterranean sun he was born under. He is called Esmail, Tahar... maybe Ahmed. He has grown up in the narrow alleys of the new housing built within the walls of the old fort on the hill, once surrounded by houses, now isolated by the rising sea at each high tide. His father is a colonel in the garrison of this place called Halifax.

When he's sent to bed, he clutches a pocket comp and later burrows under the blankets before turning it on and accessing the children's Net. The first time he innocently logged on, he was caught by his parents and only kept the comp because it was indispensable for his studies.

The lure of the forbidden is strong. He's learned to be careful. There is a hierarchy of Nets, accessed through gates requiring ever more intricate passwords. He has followed fierce electronic debates, which have made him blush at times and introduced him to heresies he had never heard of. Yet, his greatest shock was the revelation that one of the more articulate and thoughtful of the Netters, only identified by a nom de guerre, *was in fact his own younger sister, who he had always ignored.*

The debates have made him question quietly, looking up quotes in the Koran and wondering about the pre-eminence of the Sharia. His old beliefs have slowly dropped away, half-dissolved by the acid of critical analysis. Tonight, he thinks he can join the real underground Net, the one with the hottest, darkest shareware and the most heterodox opinions on the most forbidden topics. He runs through the gamut of the lower levels, thankful that the occult hierarchy is accessible. Sometimes, no entrance can be found; a connection has been shut down by the Sûreté informatique, *a brief victory in the incessant fight against the clandestine Net. Finally, he types in the ultimate codeword:*

"Liberté."

DEATH OF A DREAM

Candas Jane Dorsey

In the dream I was confronting someone I thought I knew and he was turning out to be a total stranger. I thought it was the new lover in whom I believed, but when I woke up I realized it was my ex-husband. Furthermore, when I canvassed my dreams for the last two weeks, all the time I had been sick, I saw that he had been sneaking through every one, somewhere in the background, trying to move suitcases into (not out of!) the attic, or acting as if he still lived with me.

I looked back on my dream log and realized that he had been seen if not by me then by someone in my dream in at least fourteen separate instances, and in several consensual events. I filed a complaint with the Dream Board. On the basis of the resulting scan of his dream time, they issued him a ticket for several moving violations and in family court I applied for a restraining order.

You understand, said the judge, I can't actually keep him totally away from your dreams. But if he shows up there, you can call the Dream Police and have him removed, or even arrested.

And what happens to my dream in the meanwhile? I said.

That's the best I can do, said the judge, and his obvious sympathy grated like a layer of sand over the pavement of hard reality. It was the first time I heard that sound, but not by any means the last.

After that I saw my ex in the background of several dreams a month, standing behind a tree or disguised as a *non sequitur* or an irrelevant subconscious intrusion. Most of the time I was the only one who could recognize him, and only then by a certain shimmer the image radiated, which I recognized after all those years of making love. He used to shimmer like that just after he came, when I wasn't finished yet and would have to ask for more. He loved that. I had always thought he did it on purpose, and now I knew, for the self-satisfied smirk was the same.

But he was never close enough to be recorded by the monitors long enough to get a positive ID. When I did call the Dream Police I got a variety of reactions, ranging from impotent sympathy (we can't put people on surveillance full time, we just don't have the personnel) through pity for my tendency to overvisualize (immature dream patterning skills) to offers to come and hang around in my dreams themselves (bet we'd really see something, eh?).

And I began to understand that while in the beginning my situation resembled nothing so much as vaudeville, there was coming to be an air of menace in the repeated, teasing appearances, a thinly disguised hostility which often made my dreams turn the corner into anxiety constructs and even into nightmares.

I was beginning to pick up the latent hostility and turn it on myself. I slept fitfully and dreamed less often. My waking life began to suffer. Work seemed too challenging, and I scarcely ever wanted to see my friends. They seemed shallow, unable as they were to help or even to understand my fear.

My lover urged me to get help, but I had already been going to a diagnostician, for as I said, I had been sick. A long-lasting viral infection had resisted dreamhealing efforts and finally holed up in my lungs as a bacterial invasion immune to dreaming and not responding all that well to sulfa drugs either. I thought at the time that at first my ex had probably decided to drop by my dream on a lark, or even in a moment of nostalgia, but when he saw the situation I was in he couldn't resist exploiting it; and once he saw how easy it was to get away with the harassment, he couldn't help enjoying the power he had over me. He would have thought it a reversal of how he perceived our life together.

I always knew he felt threatened, felt he somehow put himself in my power by loving me. It's just one of those things about relationships. I did what I could to keep his confidence up all the years, but the more I helped, the more he resented me for it, the more he condemned my contributions as manipulations and power-trips. Finally a few years ago I had to quit visiting his dreams altogether, and from then on it was only a matter of time until we had to split. Though in fact, it took me four years to really get up enough anger to weather the parting.

But by the end, it was just a matter of survival. I had to get out, and I did, leaving him there with everything we had built together, including the custody of a dream child and several pets, a dream library worth thousands and the most sophisticated multi-channel playback and editing system we could buy. It had been far above our income, and I was still paying my share of the debt we had incurred, but we had felt we must buy it because of the child, of course.

Our dream child. It was leaving her that had been the hardest. She was the sum of all of our hopes. She was everything we had dreamed together. At least, that was how I felt in my heart of hearts, though of course I tried never to put that pressure on her; it's cruel to invest a child with that much expectation. So I watched her grow with public encouragement and private hopes.

She filled our dreams with light.

When I knew I had to go, I delayed my departure for many months, loath to leave her, until finally I realised that even for her I could not sacrifice my life. He seemed to care for her as much as ever, seeing to her care and education meticulously, and though he and I were by now clearly enemies, I had no suspicion that he meant her ill.

However, after the harassment had been going on for several weeks, I realized that I was not getting any better. When the diagnostician asked me what I was worried about, I found myself talking about the dream pets and then, finally, my fears about our child spilled out.

Do you have visiting rights? she asked.

Yes, I said, but the last two times I've tried to dream them, my ex-husband has made some excuse. He's dreaming at the time, or the dream needs servicing. And I haven't noticed the pets on the periphery at all.

But even then it didn't occur to me that he might be abusing the consensual reality matrix until the next weekend, when I again tried to see the child. The rejection was so strong I woke up, and I was on the line to the Dream Police before I was even completely out of the sleep state.

This time, the violation had been direct enough to register, and they were already on the way, but by the time they got to his dream he had moved on into deep sleep, leaving behind only a standard nightmare which even they, not knowing him, could see was phony.

When they broke through it and made a search they found he was not sleeping at all but was gone, leaving behind chaos: all the belongings we had bought together were smashed and heaped together in the centre of the rooms, and clearly they had been this way for some time, for large amounts of urine and feces stained the debris.

The front of the dream system was smashed, but the database was intact, and the Dream Police were able to jack in portable controls to search for our daughter. She wasn't there at all, the dream pets were dead in the basement with terrible signs of torture, and throughout the system were numerous bootleg and illegal channels with alarming potentialities.

When I realised our child was gone I must have been crazy for a while. I remember causing even more damage myself, tearing through the system looking for her, then tearing through the house to see if he had hidden her in some different physical location. When I took the axe from our camping gear and began to chop through walls, looking for hidden storage cells, a big policeman forced the axe out of my hands and led me out of the house.

He told me to go home, to try not to worry; he assured me that his people would be taking the house apart themselves, but in a much more methodical way, and they would let me know if they found anything. He said I would be needed to help with the search, but not until tomorrow. And he pointed out to me that my ex was now separated from his dreamware and even if he had our child with him, he would have to buy or steal another system and hotwire it to his tastes before he could operate again or do any more harm to our child.

His tastes: they terrified me enough to forget the nightmare edge he'd been inflicting on me for over a month, and worry only about her. The mods to the machine showed a mind no longer in control of his balance or his sleepfaring; a mind preoccupied with marginal and illegal dreaming; a mind filled with twisted images of incest, abuse, sadomasochism, and combinations of perversions I had never seen and had no wish to closely scrutinize. I had seen the dream pets and wakened up vomiting; I could not imagine that these monstrous acts could have been done by the man with whom I had lived for so long, or what he could have done to our child.

They found nothing in the physical search, of course. Because I had known him, the next day the DP had me back at the database, looking through the matrices for clues, but I found there a person I couldn't recognize, a person only hinted at during the darkest days of our marriage—a time when, it had to be faced, neither of us had been at our best.

Then, he had enjoyed that salacious edge to a mutual dream (for though I stopped going freely to his dreams he never stopped coming to mine) and he often combined elements in a way I had found vaguely disturbing. But I had really had no inkling of the reliance he had developed on the more sordid types of wish fulfilment mags, the dream cassettes which showed everything from distortions of simple archetypes (like breasts, milky fluid of both nurturing and seminal kind, and so forth) to wild simulations of death complete with post-death imaging and experiencing—usually of a Dantean or Breugel-like hell, with torture and punishment sexualised or administered inappropriately by poorly conceptualized (but no less terrifying for that) demons and torments.

This was hardly conceivable to me in the man with whom I had lived with for over fifteen years, but I had no choice but to accept it. For over it all was superimposed his shimmering self-satisfaction, recognizable more and more as not a smirk so much as a prurience, an unhealthy taste for failure, pain, nightmare, and innocence violated. It was that which made me fear so much for our dream child, the consensual construct we had so lovingly made together thirteen years before, and whom we had watched grow, develop, and take on a life of her own.

Now I had to face the fact that he had probably been tampering with her since before our separation. The behaviour I had seen as programming error and unsuccessful fledgling attempts at autonomy may have been danger signs of dream abuse, and I began to excoriate myself for not noticing sooner, doing something, fighting harder for custody. But he had argued so persuasively that he could provide a better dream system—which was certainly true—and that she should remain in a familiar environment where she would not feel so greatly the suffering and displacement which would come of my departure. And I believed it, believed I was doing the best thing. When really I was abandoning her to a perverted and unscrupulous abuse which might by now have scarred her beyond therapy.

There's no point in thinking about that now, said the kindly DP inspector who had taken on the case, the one who had comforted me that first night. You did what you thought was right at the time.

That's easy for you to say, I said. He raised an eyebrow at the cliche. Sorry, I said. I know you see a lot of this kind of thing. You must know what you're talking about.

Yeah, he said. And I know there's a lot more to these DAs than meets the eye. Sometimes I've been fooled myself, caught somebody and thought, hey, I must have the wrong person. Until the evidence shows I was right.

Don't get fooled by him, I said.

I won't, he said. This one is a real trace case. Sorry, ma'am.

But the language didn't bother me, and I soon heard worse.

I spent a lot of time around the investigation office. Finally they agreed to take me along on some of the calls. I had a feel for my ex-husband that only the inspector ever was really able to match. Some of them watched all his tapes and never saw that shimmer, some only caught it now and again, but I couldn't miss it and, by the time a few weeks had passed, the inspector got it every time.

We started by screening every bootleg dream girl we could find. That taught me more about dream crime than I ever cared to know. The perverse fantasies through which producers put both co-operative and unsuspecting subjects (male and female, though we concentrated on the women, looking for her) were terrifying both in diversity and amount. I couldn't believe that people would buy such tapes, but apparently it was a industry worth multimillions, all clandestine. Factories devoted to dream tape production masqueraded as everything from drugstores to record companies. It was a harrowing few weeks, but I never showed my feelings to the squad. If I had, I felt, they would have barred me from the investigation, and I had to be there. I had to give them that edge that my perception of him would provide.

The only time I lost my composure was late at night, and only the inspector was there to see. I had been watching a tape which was, though I didn't realize it, a snuff tape. In these, the dream girl is really killed; this one also featured father-daughter incest by a man so like my ex-husband that I thought at first that I was somehow missing the shimmer. Suddenly, without warning, I found myself watching this character undertake the methodical, and obviously not faked, dissection of a girl not much older than our dream child. I tore off the headset and ran from the room, retching. I barely reached the toilet before I was sick. The inspector was leaning on the corridor wall when I came out. I was sweating and weak.

Come on, he said. We'll get something warm for you to drink.

We went down to the commissary and he led me through the line with one hand comfortingly holding my elbow. He said nothing until we were sitting down and I had drunk half the contents of the mug. I sat with my hands warming around the cup and looked at him.

You have to accept that she might be gone too, he said.

I should have got custody, I said.

You can't start all that again, he said. Where's that lover of yours? You need someone around you when you're doing this, someone to take care of you.

He has to work, I said. And besides, I can take care of myself. He never really knew her. It's not his problem.

And besides, he said, you don't trust him either.

How can I? I trusted my husband.

He smiled, sadly I thought, and his words were kind. You must never lose faith, he said. You have to believe in people.

How can you see this all day, and believe in anyone? Or is it all strangers to you, do you think it could never happen to you?

He took out of his pocket a holo, passed it across. It was a rather blurry face, a dream child of about twelve. Yours? I asked.

Yes, he said. You won't see her in the tapes you're screening; we got them before they went on the market. But some of the producers are the same. I'm still working on the evidence. That's what got me into this line of work. I used to be in insurance, in claims.

How long since...?

About seventeen years ago now she disappeared. It was an instructor we had hired to add an educational component to the programming. We wanted her to know more history, classics, that sort of thing.

He shook his head like an angry bear. Well, you just can't know everything. I had him checked out through the company, too. Still, I blamed myself, my wife—it broke us up, finally, I was so unforgiving.

But now, I burst out, you're the most forgiving one I've met. My lover wants to kill him, and I'm not sure I think killing is enough. How can you be so kind, now?

I have caught hundreds of offenders, he said. Petty violations, big time criminals, crazy perverts like your ex. They're all pitiful, in the end. And I'm not kind, to them. I want them caught. I don't care how sick they are, I want them off the streets. But the law is enough; I don't have to take a personal revenge too. Hate? It was wasting my life, until I realized that I didn't want them to have that much power over me. Guilt? I don't do what they do. I'm not like them.

Help me feel like that, I said. I feel so responsible.

I don't know how to help you, he said. You have to decide yourself.

The correct therapeutic line, I sneered, but when his expression did not change, I felt a little ashamed of myself. I fell silent, staring into my empty mug, sinking so far into that emptiness that when he spoke again I was startled.

I have a different idea about you, he said. I've meant to ask you something for a few days now, and tonight decided me. Would you like to join the DP? I can put you on staff in my unit, level one investigator. You'd have to work on any case that came up, of course, and if you slacked on them to work on yours alone, you'd be out.

My job at the cultural commission had been just too much for me lately, or too little. I didn't even have to think about it. I'd like to do that, I said. I'd like to try.

Fine, he said.

But why did tonight make a difference? I broke down, I fell apart, I couldn't keep my detachment.

I had to know you could feel something, he said, weren't frozen solid. If you couldn't feel it, you couldn't do the work. I think you can do the work. I'm going to put you on six months probation—that's less than usual, so don't let me down.

So I joined the squad. Easy to say, but it was hard

work, and despite the efforts I made publicly on other cases, I never forgot that my priority was my dream child. I was going to get her back.

As my boss, the inspector was not quite as kindly, but he acknowledged the special reasons for my driven work habits, and seldom reproved me for my many hours of overtime. Soon, also, he had to acknowledge the flair I brought to the job. It was not only my ex-husband's shimmer that I had a special ability to see. After watching an offender's tapes or dreams, I could build a profile of uncanny accuracy, based on some special sense of vision others seemed to lack. I could see the distortion at the edge of the images. I could see them no matter what disguises the offender had attempted.

By the end of my first six months on the squad, I had an impressive list of arrests to my credit, five of them busts of major rings. Two of those were long-standing cases. I was the wonder woman of the squad. But I didn't feel it. My failure to find even a trace of my ex-husband and our child was frightening me. What was he doing to her?

I saw my lover less and less, for even when our work schedules didn't conflict, I seemed to have nothing to say to him except a further catalogue of my failures. You shut me out these days, he said. Out of what? I replied. That's exactly what I mean, he said. These conversations became first more frequent, then less so.

The day of my probation review, I was subjected to an induction ceremony meant to flatter and cheer me. My colleagues then treated me to a drink in a nearby club. After they left, I stayed on to drink alone. Hours later, I was in a cheap dream parlour, shoddy electrodes plugging me into a dream experience full of degradation and punishment. I deserved nothing better, said my muddied, almost-incoherent thoughts, for abusing my dream child by omission.

I knew I could never be excused for desertion, for not being able to see, and thus I should be suffering too.

The dream was suddenly interrupted by a Dream Police recording, warning me of my rights under the Charter, and the next thing I knew, the headset was torn away. My humiliation was even worse when I realized that it was my boss who held me as I sobbed and whimpered. He wrapped me in a blanket, and went out the back door with me while the squad was busy cleaning up the joint. I lost consciousness. When I woke again I was at home, and he was holding a cup of hot drink for me.

Here, he said. Drink this.

I guess I'm out of a job, I said, loathing myself.

No, he said, but if I ever catch you in one of those dreams again, I personally will supervise a lengthy dream therapy. You're a fine person, and you're killing yourself with guilt.

I can't help it.

Yes, you can, he said, but I've told you that before.

When I find her, I said, I'll stop feeling it.

We'll see. Here, finish this and get some sleep. You have tomorrow off, but be there first thing the next day or I'll have you on night shift for a month.

He never spoke more of it, and I never went dreaming debasement again.

About three weeks later I was reviewing a new crop of bootleg tapes, seized in a raid on a newly-discovered outlet. I had been up late the night before, effecting a tentative reconciliation with my lover, and wasn't paying as much attention as usual. I put in a new tape, and the shimmer grabbed my vision like a vice. Then she was there, looking cool and sexual in some kind of strange garment, heavy make-up, and a different hair-colour.

I must have cried out because when I took off the

headset the inspector was already there, reaching for it. He watched, then nodded and called the squad to yellow alert without saying a word. We were back at the outlet in half an hour, and within three hours we had a thread of a clue.

After that, I worked solidly on that one case. I don't know if I slept much, ate much, did anything much else but work and move. The trail was convoluted. Apparently it had taken him six months to make connections with the big time bootleggers and set up a new system, but the factory he had put together was phenomenal. Suddenly it seemed half the output on the market was his, and half of that starred our daughter.

The use he put her to was frightening. She was the central figure in a whole series of relatively straight wet dreams. She was the passive party in a number of sado-masochistic fantasies of relative mildness. She was the victim in simulations of more seriously vicious scenarios involving injuries and death. And these were only the beginning; he'd also used her in a number of convoluted and perverse psychosexual fantasies which acted out his particular (and terrible) tastes in a variety of non-linear, confused, symbol-ridden dreams of death, destruction, humiliation, and distortion. As yet, however, he was using only her real image, not making dubs, so these latter with their appalling endings were all simulations using animation software. And so I knew that while she would need dream therapy after we rescued her, still her essence was safe.

I never had any doubt that we'd rescue her.

That was how things stood the day of the big raid. We'd zeroed in on the lab where he was making the dreams, but rather than a snap shot, we'd planned for almost two months, trying to cover every contingency. Surveillance had established the routines of every person in that complex, the innocent cover employees and the actual dreamcrimers and DAs. The only one we never saw was him. He never went out. His errands were done for him.

We'd monitored a few dreams from afar, but kept our distance mostly, in case we were seen. We considered trying to put somebody on the inside, both waking and in the dream time, but we were so afraid we'd blow the operation that in the end, moments before she was to move in, we scrubbed the infiltration. Instead we made meticulous plans, and at the precise moment when their operations were at lowest ebb and most were in the dream time, we raided the complex.

Everything went according to plan up until the last minutes when we drove in to the inner rooms. Then, we started getting a disturbance in the dream time that we hadn't anticipated. The inspector was in the lead, and was the first to realize a hostage situation was developing behind the door of the last bastion, my ex-husband's dream lab. I was still clearing things up in the outer court, and it took me a while to catch up with what was happening.

When I reached the door, the Dream Police force was camouflaged behind some set elements, and the inspector motioned me to join him.

He's in there? I asked.

Yes, and he has the kid. We've been negotiating with him through the link. He sounds desperate, but he's stalling. He has demands, he says, or he'll wipe her. We can't move yet.

Let me go in, I said.

He's got a fortress set up there, he said.

Look, I said, he doesn't know I'm with you. Let him think you've brought me to negotiate. The distraught wife bit. I'll play the role. Then, when I'm in, I can jack in with a portable unit and cut off his power before he can move.

It's too dangerous.

He won't have a clue. You know he despises me, thinks I'm just another victim. You can treat me a little rough, play along. Inspector, you have to let me do this.

He looked at me for a moment, then turned away, shaking his head. I was about to jump up, grab his arm, beg him, when he said to a technician, put a wire on her. She's going in.

They treated me very publicly like a hostage-taker's lever: that mix of politeness and patronisation which I remembered so clearly from my initial dealings with the DP (how long ago was it? It seemed years.) They put me in place outside the lab door, and I sobbed my little script out into the intercom over which they negotiated with him. I cradled the termite in the fold of skin between two fingers; all I needed was to get through that door, pretend to faint against a console, press the little device against the plastic, and we'd have him.

At first it seemed he'd go for it. Not, I know, out of real remorse, but because he wanted to watch as he humiliated me further. I didn't care why. The door finally opened, with all the fail-safes in place so that the DP squad couldn't follow me, and I saw him standing, that shimmer around him like a cloud now, malevolent and smiling in front of the console where our dream child's image was frozen in mid-scan, held as surety for my good behaviour.

I stumbled over to him, meaning to throw myself onto my knees, and while wrapping my arms around his legs send the termite into the base of the console. But where his solid form seemed to be, my arms felt nothing, and I fell forward through the holo of the console, through our child's image, and onto a bare, hard floor where I lay, sobbing in earnest now.

After a moment I went and opened the door to the squad.

The holo played for us three or four times before dissolving. If you follow me, he said, I'll kill her, and all the others too. And don't use that bitch against me any more; I know what she is. If I even sniff her traces, I'll kill them even slower, I'll overdub until they're confetti. Try me if you think I'm not serious.

That was the first time we knew there were others he kept permanently. In the material we seized in the raid, we found evidence that he had about seven there, or eight. We weren't sure; two might have been twins, or one dream boy skilfully dubbed. All were underage; all were stolen, as we found when we traced them through Missing Persons.

Later I sat with the inspector and brooded over a drink. That was the night I graduated to cold drink.

Lots of people raise dream children, I said.

Yes. He waited.

Lots of people live in that world too.

Yes. As always, he could wait as long as I took to be able to speak.

Then why—?

Why—?

Why us? Why me?

Because it had to happen to someone.

That's not good enough. Our dreams were supposed to create a better world. Did evil 'have to happen' in this world too? To you, to me, to the others whose children are in there?

People create the new worlds they want. We would not want what your ex-husband wanted.

People bring the evil with them when they create new worlds. Like carriers.

Think of it like that: your husband was an accident looking for a place to happen.

But he was more intentional than that. And he chose me, out of everyone. I remember how he courted me.

That should make you feel less guilty. You were misled.

Or he chose me for a reason.

You mean you believe there are no accidents? Blame the victim?

What do you think I think?

He looked at me with his usual patient look. I was quite drunk by then and suddenly I resented everything that look represented. It was the look kind men throw to strays like a butcher throws a bone to a dog. Suddenly I wanted to bite that generous hand.

What do you think I think? I insisted.

His eyes narrowed. Now, I thought, he will kick me away from the shop door, and good riddance for the both of us.

I think you don't think at all, he said. Otherwise you would remember why you began with him, how he treated you, what you had to go on. You act as if you should have disbelieved him from the start, as if it should have been evident he would turn out to be a monster. But if that's how you approach a relationship, you can build nothing. People get together. Sometimes it goes sour. Sometimes a person goes sour, like unpasteurised milk; the seeds of his change were in him all along, but invisible. You going to give up milk?

Dream milk, anyway, I said.

He was real. He is real. She is real. She just lives somewhere else. Lots of people have kids like that. You're luckier than them: she lived with you in her mind at least.

Yeah, how do you know?

Don't you know it yourself?

All I know is she can be killed with a magnet, or a second of flame, or cut down in a bad edit.

And you can be killed by a Magnum, or in a fire, or wiped away with a knife. What makes hers an edit, and yours a murder? That's out-of-date talk, kiddo. Nobody asks those questions any more.

Until their kid is carried away in a briefcase—in a pocket for all the gods' sakes—and turned into a toy, an automaton for rich old perverts to play with. Should I have helped create her for this?

She has life. She can be found, can escape, can heal. Without you, she would have had no life. She was nothing.

But did I have the right—?

As well to ask if your parents had the right to make you. Listen, kid, there are no rights. There's good and evil, truth and consequences, but there's nothing says we have a right to anything, to one thing or another, one way or another. We've got what we're given, what we earn, what falls on us out of the sky. Only that. No rights. There's no use making a fuss about it, either. You did it. You helped bring her into the world. There's no fault in that, no virtue. It just is. Now you are doing your best for her, like you always did.

I whispered, how do you know I did?

I know, he said. Anybody who knows you knows.

I don't know, I said.

Just what I said, he said, leaning over to pour more drink into our glasses. Only the ones who know you. I never met a woman who knew herself less than you; no wonder you don't know anything for certain. You shouldn't oughta indulge yourself that way. You're just the same as all of us and you know just as much, if you'd admit it.

But admitting it, I thought but didn't say, is admitting that you and I are just the same as my ex-husband. I slammed the door shut on that thought before it could do any more damage.

We both got drunk that night.

Time went by, and more work, and more grief. My torment was as usual. I was almost getting used to it; it seemed more like a companion than my lover, with whom I kept the uneasy peace, or the inspector, who was my silent support at work.

My only consolation was that we had that tracer on the run. He'd lost a second lab, and was desperate. Now too, he had trouble finding a bankroll as plush, or equipment as laundered, as provided him the first time. Even to the undernet he was too dirty; they didn't want the kind of attention they knew we had in store for anyone dealing with him.

The inspector took me out for a drink one day, to a friendly little speakeasy the detectives used.

We only talk while we're drinking any more, he said.

I swirled the ice in my glass silently.

You're as cold as that ice, he said.

I didn't pretend to naïveté, but I did smile a little. My lover thinks I'm hot again, I said. He's pleased to have me back.

I know you better than he does.

Do you now?

You know I do. And you know where I think you're headed. Unless you talk about it, you'll be back in one of those dream tanks, and this time I won't be able to keep it quiet. You're too hot now—he laughed at his unwitting choice of words—and the vids are all over you. If you wanted to go down the drain along with this case, you shouldn't have made yourself such a star. In five years you'll rank me.

I was quiet for a long time, but I figured I owed him an explanation, and finally I found the words. You think, I said, that your life makes a certain kind of sense. You form these ideas and they do, for a while, to explain what goes on. But then one day, when you're thirty-five or thirty-eight or forty-two, something changes inside you, like a scan goes across your vision, and you realise you have to change your whole way of looking at the world.

He sat watching me, silent.

You may think you beat it, I said, but maybe you didn't. I don't think forgiveness works; I don't know. All I know is that what I know isn't solid any more. The world isn't the way I thought it was. There's nothing solid in it. We make an image, we dream it and we trust it; but any tracecase pervert can take that dream and turn it into a nightmare without even disturbing our matrix. Doesn't that tell you something about the matrix? It's not what we think it is.

You're tired, he said. You can beat this.

You don't get me, I said. It's not something you can control. You just look in the mirror one day and realise you've been overdubbed without knowing where it came from. And then you wonder if maybe it wasn't like that all along and you were just too stupid to see it. That's what I think, boss. I think it was this way all along, but I didn't have the right angle.

You have to shake this off, he said, and his voice was kind enough to curdle the drink in my gut.

No, boss, I said. I just have to catch this one. The rest takes care of itself.

He shook his head, but he didn't talk, and after another drink I went back up to the office, back to the screening room.

The calmness lasted until we found him again, set up in a seedy dive on the east coast, peddling tapes out of a convenience store in the deadhead district. This time the stakeout was months long, and this time we placed a worm in the apple: by his looks, a tough, tattooed young porndreamer, but his suburban mother, who thought her son had a desk job with the Dream Bureau, wouldn't have

407

recognised him.

Through him, we found the place where the shielded cables of the porn studio ran against an outside wall, and finally, after preparations which seemed agonisingly slow to my suddenly re-awakened nerves, we tapped in and for the first time in over two years I talked to my dream child.

She looked terrible. I could hardly believe it was her, but when I called her, softly though I knew he couldn't hear, she turned her tired, haggard face and I saw the devastation he had inflicted on her.

Baby? I said, and I couldn't keep my voice from breaking.

At first she was incredulous. Mommy? she said, and the whisper chilled me with its pathos.

Yes, baby, I said. I'm here. I finally got in.

Do you know what he's been doing to me? she said, so low I could hardly hear her.

Yes, baby. We're going to stop him. We've been trying, but it's hard.

I know. I know. I tried to get away, but he....

No point asking her what he did; the evidence was clear. Close up, both the scars from glitches and the blurring of overdub marks were clear. I managed to speak.

It's okay, baby; trust me, we're going to get you out this time.

I'm afraid, she said. I'm almost done.

Just hold out a little while.

I don't know if I can keep on, mom. He's coming back any minute, with more tapes.... A shudder crossed her.

Help me, baby, I pleaded. Resist him. You can do it.

It's his system, she said. He'll wipe me.

Baby, in half an hour I can have a backup system hardwired in here. You can jump for it. We'll catch you. Just try, baby. Just try.

I tried before, she said, and he caught me.

This time you have us to help you. You'll have a place to go. A safe place.

I can't, she said, crying, but soundlessly. She couldn't sob any more; he'd punished her for it so many times.

Besides, she said, look at me. I'm third or fourth generation by now. He's changed me all around. What if I do something awful?

What do you mean?

She looked everywhere else but at me, then, desperately, at me, then at a scan line which kept crossing her hands slowly, left to right.

It's okay, baby, tell me. What is it?

What if I'm... like him? What if I like it now?

Oh, no, you're not like him. He used you, but we can fix that. Sure, it'll take time, but... I kept my own fears out of my voice. She was so desperately hurt; could she be restored?

He's my parent! What did he put into me? When will it come out? You thought he was okay for years. And I loved him then too!

Babe, I'm scared too. But we can't blame ourselves. He's the evil one.

Is he? He started doing it to me before you split, you know. He used to call me up when he was in the bathtub, show me his hard-on, make me do what he wanted....

Oh, baby, if I'd known, if only I had known....

But you didn't do anything. You just left.

Sweetheart, believe me, I reproach myself....

The inspector of DP was there as clearly as if he had been present, saying to me, it's not your fault. I stopped.

Listen, I said, we're getting into a soap dream here. The fact, I didn't know, and he did it, and now we have to live with it. No matter how much it hurts us both. But there's no living with it, no living past it, unless we get you out of here. If I bring in the system, will you come? We don't have much time, you know.

Sure, she said. Yeah, I'll come.

There are others in here, I said. How many? We can get you all out if you hurry.

Seven, she said. Shadow died a few days ago.

She shivered with the memory.

Can you get to them without making a record of what you say?

Yeah, sure, of course; and the cocky kid I saw then was more like her old self.

Okay, I said, you get to them, but hurry. And here's what we'll do.... She hugged me then, suddenly crying, and so was I as I waited for her to get the others on line.

By the time they were there with us I was composed again, and I hugged them all as she introduced me with what I read as pride: my mom the dream cop, come to get us all out of here.

I sat them down and went through the plan. We set the rendezvous co-ordinates, and I made her the one in charge, not just because she was my daughter but because of all of them she seemed the strongest. Some of them were almost dissolving with fear and mistreatment, but she knew how to deal with each of them—tough with one, tender with another—and then it was me proud of her.

I told her to give it an hour in case of hardware problems, but no longer. Knowing how distraught she was—they all were—I went over it six or eight times.

When I left I had a moment alone with her.

I have to go now, babe, but you don't get scared. We know he won't get home until at least two hours from now, and he can't dream in, either. Just meet me. An hour from our mark remember?

I will, she said. I promise.

I went back to the station and set up the program. A transfer of this size was risky, but no-one questioned the need for it. It was actually only forty-five minutes before we had the portable database parked outside and the conduit down for the hardwire. Then I chewed my fingernail, waiting for her to get there.

She didn't come.

Simple as that. The others got safely out, but she wasn't with them. An hour and a half later he came back, jaunty with a suitcase we knew was full of bootleg tape. Through our eavesdrop link we saw him call her up.

Get out of there, said the technician. He'll see you, and crash our system.

I tried to protest: I have to—

Get out of there. Do you want to lose everything, and kill her in the bargain? It's going to be bad when he finds she's alone; can you imagine what more he'll do to her if he finds out you've been in touch? We'll move in again tomorrow.

It was that which reached me, and I backed off. The technician got us out without detection.

I never saw her whole again.

He moved the lab, and we lost him.

I was off shift when they raided the warehouse. If they'd known who was working there, they'd have called me, but the tip came from a cheap dreamcrimer vindictive about strangers in his territory, and they thought they were getting a tape storehouse for a penny-ante distributor from uptown. Instead, they got him; this time he wasn't ready, and he was down before they recognised him. The inspector called me from the warehouse.

When I got there, technicians were working at the database, frantic with urgency. He'd half-crashed the system; it was on the brink, and they were trying to ease it back. I watched as the med techs took out his body. At my signal, they stopped the stretcher as they passed me. I unzipped the body bag and looked at his face. It was as smooth as when he'd been my husband, a million years ago.

Take him down to the lab, I said. Make sure they scrub him before they take him over to the med school. I don't want a single neural path intact.

That's destroying evidence, one of them said nervously.

We know what he did, I said. They looked at the inspector, standing behind me, and he nodded, then jerked his head at the door. They went out on the left just as one of the technicians on the boards groaned.

It's going, the other said. We can't hold it!

I was behind her, leaning over the monitors, but what image was there was unreadable.

Boost it, I said.

But there's no gain—

Boost it, I said, damn you!

Her hands slid the pots to the max. The image came up, wildly ghosting, stabilised, pulled aside, and was gone.

Did you see enough to get her? the inspector said, urgently.

We got it on tape, said the tech. There's still a chance.

Sure, I said; sure.

The remote line buzzed, and the inspector turned from answering it with a kind of horror on his face I'd never seen.

He got out through the system, he said. There was nothing left to wipe. He put himself through as a dream.

I was shaking my head without knowing it, shaking all over. He came to me as I screamed, and silenced me by holding me, my face into his shirtfront. After a while I was able to walk out with him, his arm still around my shoulder.

Without any of us noticing, day had filled the world outside the warehouse. Time to wake up, I thought, but that was too much to bear. I settled for going back to make out my report, then going home to a drugged and unwilling sleep.

If there's no liveware to chase, the case goes out of our jurisdiction. That was the last of it for me. There aren't many places to look. He'll show up. If they find him, they'll let me know.

I was in the news for getting the other kids out: a big triumph they called it. And after the noise died down, other cases came up, and they still come up. The inspector was right. I'll be promoted again next year, and probably before I'm forty I'll be his boss instead. But while I work for him, I keep clean, and I suppose the habit will last.

I had seen her on the screen, of course, before the mainframe crashed. Remembering that is something I don't like to do. Still, I remember more than I'd like. It's what keeps me taking the sleeping pills, for those deep oblivious nights I've come to need and to hate.

I think of her as I saw her before the crash, as grainy as a tenth or twelfth generation dub, twisted and distorted from bootleg recording and low-grade distribution, unable even to smile at me with any veracity. Yet she tried to speak, before the image wavered and was lost, and I think that what she tried to say was, I'm sorry, I'm sorry, sorry.

Sorry?

So she is gone. There wasn't enough left on the tapes so that she could be remastered. She had been stored hologrammatically and the master had been split and resplit as he got more and more desperate for funds, as he sold her again and again for whatever sordid use she was requested, until finally the grain overwhelmed the outline. I remember that when they did make that unsuccessful try at reintegration, in the warehouse, and

413

she made her effort to reach me, along the major scan line there was a repeated twitch which couldn't be eliminated. A kind of shimmer. She saw it too, and there was something like horror in her face as the distortion expanded to erase her for the last time.

They say I will stop looking for it in time, looking for that shimmering evil around the edges of dreams I never have. They say he will turn up, that even trapped in the net he can't stay away from dreaming his particular sort of destruction. They tell me that she marked him as he passed her in the system, and that they can home in on the pattern now, they think before anyone else has to suffer.

They say before the month is out they'll have him, but that's what they said last month, and the month before.

They've stopped him several times before he can act, and they tell me that if not for the scars she left, which have showed up and signalled every system B&E he has tried to perpetrate, they would never have been able to track him and cut off his access. They say she was able to mark him so that he can never use any system again without detection.

They say a lot of things.

The inspector is very kind, of course. And my lover, the one who stood by me through all this, the one whose face was borrowed for that very first nightmare, my lover urges me to come out from the shadow and live.

But living is dreaming. And how can I trust myself to dream again?

AFTERWORD: NO MORE MANIFESTOS

Michael Skeet

Writing is about as solitary an activity as there is. Perhaps it's because of this that nobody on this earth seems to be happier in the company of his peers than does a writer. When not writing (and writing itself), writers always seem to be found in one another's company, discussing the calumny of editors (sigh) and dishing the dirt on their fellows so unwise as to be absent from the gathering.

What's more, nothing seems to bring writers together more effectively than a common sense of grievance, of worthiness unrecognized. Writers have been known to invent ghettos for themselves and their friends, the better to nourish a feeling of belonging to something, *anything*, no matter how insignificant. (In fact, the more insignificant in the eyes of the Outside, the better.) Science fiction has long been such a ghetto; what's more, since time began (or at least since H.G. Wells first quarrelled with Henry James), this ghetto has itself been subdivided into smaller ghettos by denizens eager to set themselves further apart. What was cyberpunk if not the classic ghetto-within, a treehouse ("No girls allowed!") built by self-proclaimed Bad Boys?

Where you have ghettoized writers—especially the self-isolated kind—you inevitably have manifestos. Nothing gratifies a group of writers more thoroughly than the construction in words of a rationale for their apartness. We remember the Imagists, Surrealists, Decadents and Symbolists of the early modern period as much for what they wrote about themselves as for the novels and poetry they created. Because we work in isolation, writers have a great need to belong; we're always talking about "community." And a manifesto is a great way of demarcing a community.

I understand this very well. I began writing SF in 1986, and within a few months of this was fortunate enough to be invited to a national SF writing workshop organized by Judith Merril. The effect on me of meeting other people engaged in this kind of writing was electrifying: I recall long hours spent over coffee and donuts, arguing concepts with which I was scarcely yet acquainted, much less familiar. My fellows indulged me graciously, and I met at that workshop a number of people I still feel honoured to call good friends.

I also got a strong dose of a very powerful drug. The feeling of community, of being included in a group which was itself apart from the Outside, was very seductive. Within a year of this first workshop, I had organized a second national gathering. I had also found myself involved in yet another of Judy's projects, this time a workshop of Toronto-area writers which met *every week*. I was spending almost as much time socializing with fellow-SF writers as I was writing the stuff. (This latter workshop, by the way, has just celebrated its fifth year. The founding members—five of the original eight are still involved—have met, by my count, 252 times during that time. And we still speak to each other.) Other national workshops and meetings followed, and in due course the inevitable happened and Canada's far-flung SF writers (or most of them, at any rate) founded a national organization to promote the concept of Canadian SF.

We had no doubt that we were different. No sooner had my friends and I begun spending hours at a time discussing our writing and the state of science fiction in general than we began looking for ways to stand apart from the rest of the pack. Our being Canadian was an obvious starting point. And many a happy hour was spent over many a pint, detailing the many things that set Canadian SF apart from its U.S. and U.K. counterparts. Eventually, we began to compose manifestos.

In retrospect, there is something sadly comic about our attempts to attack labels to ourselves. We were, in a sense, trying to deny our individuality by submerging our identities into a corporate concept, by trying to create what was a "school" of writing, whatever we chose to call it. (Choosing what to call it provided most of the fun. Terms like "Ciderpunk"—an obvious tavern influence at work here—"Maplepunk" and "Beaverpunk" were tossed back and forth with varying degrees of seriousness.) We were convinced that we could be the Next Big Thing if only we could quantify what it was that set us apart.

The more we tried to define who we were as a group, though, the less like a group we behaved. I doubt that most of those of us who played this game played it all that seriously, but however half-hearted our attempts to forge a group identity might have been, they were all somehow resisted, even by those most committed to being part of an identifiable group. No one could come up with a manifesto or definition or style on which everyone agreed. We couldn't even generate much in the way of sympathy from our fellows for our efforts.

The experience of editing *Tesseracts⁴* has been a salutary one for a number of reasons, but not least among them is the fact that it's finally set my mind at rest about the question of whether or not Canadian SF has a definable identity.

MICHAEL SKEET

The answer, typically Canadian, is yes and no. Yes, it has an identity. No, it's not necessarily definable. Not by writers, at any rate.

I won't go so far as to say we've been wasting our time trying to define just what constitutes Canadian SF, or what makes it different. But if all becomes so simple when you just sit down and *read* the stuff, that to try to etch some sort of definition into stone can only be considered redundant.

The thirty or so writers represented here used no template in preparing their fiction or poetry. They followed no school of thought, adhered to no manifesto. Likely, next to none of them talked to any of the others about what they were doing. They just wrote. And somehow what they wrote is all identifiable as being of this country and no other.

Trying to figure out who we are is a close as Canadians have ever come to having a truly national past-time. I'm not arguing that it's pointless trying to figure out what is Canadian SF. But there are academics who get paid to do that sort of thing. I'm more than happy to let them get on with it. For the rest of us, all that's necessary is that we know that Canadian SF *is*. The evidence has just been presented to you, again. Maybe it's enough that we just enjoy the presentation, eh?

Incidentally, I should have realized from the start the futility of trying to define Canadian SF. The evidence was right in front of me: in the five years that we've been together, the writer's group of which I'm a part hasn't even been able to settle on a name for itself, much less decide what it is that we do.

Other than that we write, that is, and read.

THE
CONTRIBUTORS

Ven Begamudré's work also appeared in *Tesseracts³*—a story from his fiction collection *A Planet of Eccentrics* (Oolichan Books, 1990). In 1993 Oolichan will release his first novel, *Van de Graaff Days*. He has also edited an anthology of stories by writers living, like him, in Regina, Saskatchewan which Fifth House Publishers will release.

Jane Brierley lives in Montréal. Her translations have earned her the 1990 Governor General's Award, and the 1992 Félix-Antoine Savard Prize awarded by The Translation Center of Columbia University in New York. She has translated a number of Vonarburg stories and novels, and is currently working on Vonarburg's third SF novel, *Reluctant Voyagers*.

Cliff Burns is a twenty-eight year old writer who recently moved to the Canadian Arctic, dutifully following in the footsteps of his wife, Sherron. Over 70 of his short stories have been published in magazines, including *Midnight Graffiti*, *EOTU*, *Grue*, *Gauntlet* and *The Silver Web*. His short story "Invisible Boy" appeared in *Tesseracts³*.

Mick Burrs is a widely published poet, whose latest collection, *Simple Journeys to Other Planets*, will be released by Coteau Books in 1993. He edited the respected literary magazine *Grain* from his mezzanine office at Yorkton's public library in Saskatchewan (1988-1990). "Baruch, the Man-Faced Dog" is his first published work in speculative fiction.

Lesley Choyce was born in New Jersey in 1951 but moved to Canada and became a citizen when he was a young man. He teaches part-time at Dalhousie University, runs Pottersfield Press and has over thirty adult and young adult books in print. He founded The Pottersfield Portfolio and Pottersfield Press, the only literary press in Nova Scotia, which he runs out of a two hundred year old farm house at Lawrencetown Beach overlooking the ocean. He also hosts a TV show in Halifax called *Choyce Words*.

Carolyn Clink of Thornhill, Ontario, was the $500 literary prize winner in McClelland & Stewart's 1983 *Celebrate Our City* contest. Her poems have appeared in *On Spec*, *Poetry Toronto*, *White Wall Review*, and the Canadian horror anthology *Northern Frights*. She is a member of SF Canada and the Science Fiction Poetry Association.

John Robert Colombo, the author, compiler, and translator of over eighty books, and is nationally known as the Master Gatherer. In 1979, he edited *Other Canadas*, the world's first anthology of Canadian fantastic literature. Among his latest publications are *Dark Visions* (1992) and *Worlds in Small* (1992).

Charles de Lint, a full-time writer and musician, currently makes his home in Ottawa with his wife MaryAnn Harris. His writing includes novels, short stories, comic book scripts, poetry, non-fiction as well as reviews for many magazines and newspapers. He is also the proprietor/

editor of Triskell Press, a small publishing house that specializes in occasional fantasy chapbooks and magazines.

Candas Jane Dorsey lives in Edmonton and is the author of *Machine Sex and Other Stories* (Tesseract 1988; Women's Press England, 1990) and *Leaving Marks* (River Books 1992). She co-edited *Tesseracts³* (1990) with Gerry Truscott.

Dave Duncan is a long-time resident of Calgary who earns his living writing Fantasy and SF novels but not, obviously, poetry.

M.W. Field lives in Alberta. These poems are not autobiographical.

James Alan Gardner is a writer living in Waterloo, Ontario. He won the Grand Prize in the 1989 *Writers of the Future* contest, and has sold stories to *Amazing* and *Fantasy and Science Fiction*. In his spare time, he writes computer documentation.

Charles Shelby Goerlitz is an expatriate who presently writes and teaches in Walla Walla, Washington. He recently attended Clarion West.

Phyllis Gotlieb, co-editor of *Tesseracts²*, has been writing SF and poetry for over thirty years. Her work has been translated into nine languages. Her latest work is *Heart of Red Iron*, St. Martins, 1989.

Tom Henighan, who has published a fantasy novel and two collections of short fiction, (the latest, *Strange Attractors* with Beach Holme Publishers), teaches mythology, SF and fantasy at Carleton University in

Ottawa. A collection of his poems, *Home Planet*, is due out with Golden Dog Press in 1993.

Eileen Kernaghan's fantasy novels include *Journey to Aprilioth, Songs from the Drowned Lands*, which won a 1983 Casper, and *The Sarsen Witch*. Her poems and short stories have appeared in publications as diverse as *PRISM international* and *Walpurgis Night: A Journal of Gothic Horror Poetry*. She lives in Burnaby, B.C.

Yves Meynard, born in 1964, is completing a Ph.D in Computer Science at Université de Montréal. He writes in both French and English; he has published stories in *Solaris, imagine...*, *Edge Detector* and the anthology *SOL*, among others. He also acts as literary editor for Ianus Publications.

Derryl Murphy toils as a writer, photographer, editor and publisher in Edmonton. With Wayne Malkin, he is publisher of *Fallen Octopress* and editor of *Senary—The Journey of Fantastic Literature*, the first of which was released just this fall. "Father Time" is his first short-story sale.

David Nickle lives in Toronto where he works as a journalist.

John Park is currently a partner in a scientific consulting firm in Ottawa. His stories have appeared in *Galaxy, Far Frontiers, On Spec* and *Tesseracts²* and *Tesseracts³* among other places. He sometimes wonders if there is any connection between these two statements.

Ursula Pflug's short stories and illustrations have appeared in many magazines and journals. She has also

422

worked as an arts columnist and as a scriptwriting teacher. She is co-author of several independent films and videos. She is currently working on a second novel, *Evolution*.

Karl Schroeder is a Toronto-based SF writer originally from Manitoba. He is currently teaching a course on writing SF and Fantasy at George Brown College in Toronto.

Jean-Louis Trudel was born in Toronto in 1967 and is pursuing doctoral studies in astronomy at the University of Toronto. He has published several SF short stories in French in Québec magazines *imagine. . .* and *Solaris*. In English, his short stories have appeared in *Ark of Ice* and *Tesseracts*[3], the latter in translation.

Élisabeth Vonarburg lives in Chicoutimi, Quebec. She has published numerous SF stories and attended many SF conventions in Canada, the U.S., and Europe. In 1988 she organized Boréal 10, an international convention of SF writers held in Chicoutimi. She has received various prizes for her work. She recently completed two SF novels for young people, as well as her third adult novel, the latter to be published in English by Porcépic Books in Canada and Bantam Books in the U.S.

Andrew Weiner has published over 40 short stories in magazines and anthologies including *Fantasy and Science Fiction*, *Asimov's Science Fiction Magazine*, *Interzone*, *Again, Dangerous Visions*, *Full Spectrum* and *In Dreams*. Some of these stories appear in *Distant Signals And Other Stories* (Porcépic Books). He has recently determined that he is not a "SF" writer.

423

Allan Weiss was born in Montréal in 1956. Since graduating from the University of Toronto with his Ph.D in English in 1985 he has worked as a freelance writer and editor, and part-time instructor at York, Woodsworth College, and Ryerson. He has had fiction published by or accepted at numerous journals, including *Short Story International, Green's Magazine, Fiddlehead,* and *Short Story,* and appeared in *Year's Best Horror Stories III.*

Robert Charles Wilson came to Canada 30 years ago and has lived in Toronto, Nanaimo, and Vancouver. He has published six novels and several short stories. His most recent novel is *The Harvest.*

Tim Wynne-Jones lives on seventy-six acres of rock and pine woods near Perth, Ontario where he writes novels and songs and stories and is sometimes woken at night by a barred owl barking like a moon-throated dog. He shares three children with his writer wife, Amanda Lewis.

ACKNOWLEDGEMENTS

"Foreword" © 1992 by Lorna Toolis.

"Winter Was Hard" © 1991 by Charles de Lint; first appeared in *Pulphouse, The Hardback Magazine*, No.10, Winter 1991.

"Gryphons" © 1992 by M.W. Field.

"The Toy Mill" © 1992 by David Nickle and Karl Schroeder.

"Pointing North" © 1992 by Tom Henighan.

"The Great Comedians" © 1992 by Tom Henighan.

"Also Starring" © 1991 by Cliff Burns.

"Extras" © by Mercury Press; first appeared in *Fantasy & Science Fiction*, December 1987.

"The Others" © 1992 by Dave Duncan.

"Equinox" © 1992 by Y. Meynard.

"Ants" © 1992 by Allan Weiss.

"Out of Sync" © 1992 by Ven Begamudré.

"At the Bus Stop, One Autumn Morning" © 1992 by M. W. Field.

"We Can't Go On Meeting Like This" © 1992 by Phyllis Gotlieb.

"Baruch, the Man-Faced Dog" © 1992 by Mick Burrs; first broadcasted on *Ambience*, CBC Saskatchewan, March 28, 1992.

ACKNOWLEDGEMENTS

"Couples" © 1992 by Eileen Kernaghan.

"Clark Kent in Old Age" © 1992 by Tom Henighan.

"The Reckoning of Gifts" © 1992 by James Alan Gardner.

"Ruby" © 1990 by Shelby Goerlitz; first appeared in *Zyzzva*, Winter 1990.

"Much Slower Than Light" © 1991 by Carolyn Clink; first appeared in *On Spec*, Volume 3, No.3, December 1991.

"Judy" © 1983 by Ursula Pflug; first appeared in *This Magazine*, Volume 17, No.4, October 1983.

"Le Jeu des coquilles de nautilus" © 1992 by Élisabeth Vonarburg; first appeared in *Aurores boréales 2*, 1985 (Montreal: La Préambule, 1985). "Chambered Nautilus" © 1992 by Jane Brierley.

"Eternity, Baby" © 1990 by Andrew Weiner; first appeared in *Issac Asimov's Science Fiction Magazine*, November 1990.

"The Best of Both Worlds" © 1992 by Lesley Choyce.

"How They Made the Golem" © 1967 by J.R. Colombo; first appeared in *Abracadabra*. Reprinted by permission of the author.

"Falconer" © 1992 by John Park.

"Time Shrink" © 1991 by Tim Wynne-Jones.

"Father Time" © 1992 by Derryl Murphy.

"Remember, the Dead Say" © 1992 by Jean-Louis Trudel.

"Death of a Dream" © 1992 by Candas Jane Dorsey.

"Afterword: No More Manifestos" © 1992 by Michael Skeet.

Tesseracts⁴

Editors: Lorna Toolis and Michael Skeet
Cover art by Jeff Kuipers
Cover design by Barbara Munzar
Production Editor: Elspeth Haughton
Typeset in Palatino, 9.5/11.5 (body text)

Printed in Canada.

Printed in Canada